The Trail To Titicaca

The Trail To Titicaca

A Journey through South America

Rupert Attlee

Summersdale

First published in Great Britain by Hindon Publishing 1997

This edition published in 1999

Copyright © Rupert Attlee 1999

Maps and sketches copyright © Michael Pask

Summersdale Publishers Ltd
46 West Street
Chichester
West Sussex
PO19 1RP
United Kingdom
www.summersdale.com

Printed and Bound in Great Britain by Cox & Wyman Ltd, Reading

ISBN 1 84024 095 4

To Mike, David, Simon, Jules and India
and to the memory of Sophie

'Create a dream and give it everything you have, you could be
surprised just how much you are capable of achieving.
If you don't have a dream . . . borrow one! Any which way . . .
You must have a dream.'

SARA HENDERSON 'From Strength to Strength'

ON THE TRAIL TO TITICACA

Distance: 6,372 miles
Duration: 320 days
Daily average: 41 miles
Record day: 102 miles
Record speed: 50.1 mph
Highest point: 16,150 feet

Caracas

VENEZUELA

Bogota

COLOMBIA

GUAYANAS

Quito
ECUADOR

PERU

BRASIL

Lima

Lake Titicaca BOLIVIA

Brasilia

La Paz

Santa Cruz

Rio de Janeiro

PARAGUAY

Salta

CHILE

Santiago

Mendoza

Buenos Aires

Montevideo

ARGENTINA

Puerto Montt

Chiloe

Punta Arenas

Tierra del Fuego

Ushuaia

WORLD'S END

CONTENTS

ACKNOWLEDGEMENTS

I acknowledge that this book will not be read for its literary style or the extent or the value of the information it provides. I hope, however, it will be remembered for its truthfulness. It records events that actually happened and all I have done is to embellish them slightly. We are certainly no heroes, just three chaps who believed in what they were doing and it is hoped it will inspire others to do the same.

This expedition is best measured in friends rather than miles. Friends at home and in South America who gave their constant support and encouragement and when the memory of the places start to fade, the kindness of so many people will always be remembered.

On the road we would like to thank: Juan Carlos Faundez and his family who could not have done more to help us; Gerald and Andy Friedli for their warm hospitality; Thomas and Natalie Goodall for helping us through the mussels; the Sotomayor family who had so little but gave so much; Joan and Coco Nauta for taking us in during our hour of need; Efran who taught us Spanish with such patience and restraint; the border guards on the Andean tunnel between Santiago and Mendoza; John Rees in Puerto Montt; Robin Shackel in La Paz; the British Embassies in Santiago and La Paz; and the countless other people who opened their doors and hearts.

At home special thanks are due to the following: Simon Heazell, the 'Fourth Man' of the expedition, who kept the fundraising momentum going while we were away; Lord Oaksey, OBE for putting his reputation on the line by agreeing to be Expedition Patron; our parents for hiding their anxiety and giving their full support; Douglas Osborne, Clare, Susan, Fiona and Philippa at the Leukaemia Research Fund for believing in us; Teresa and Antony Bailey who inspired us to keep going; Michael and Jo Johnson whose encouragement gave us strength; the members of the 'Think Tank' – Helen Pask, Cathy O'Boyle, Jono Nicholls, John Greenan, Edmund Thompson; Susan Hughan for her designs and Simon Barker at Bilko Sportswear for all the tee-shirts; Hallam Murray for his advice and giving us the idea; Charlie Kemmis-Betty and Bombay Sapphire Gin for their generous support; Claire Todd for the vaccinations; Will Patterson for the airline tickets; the children at St George's School, Lambeth for their poems of encouragement; Madison for making such superb bicycles; and Michael Nicholls of Leopard Press for all the expedition printing. Many thanks also goes to the following companies and organisations; Shell, Montgomery Watson, International House, Granville Bank, Cotswold Camping, Lloyds Bank, Cadogan Gardens Hotels, British Telecom, International Management Group, and the Embassies of Chile, Argentina and Bolivia.

In writing this book, I would like to thank: Simon Heazell, Helen Bussell and Julie Attlee for their editing and patient correcting of my interesting spelling; Matthew Hancock who gave his advice as a reader and then sent his fee to the LRF; Susan Brown of Element Books for all her technical advice; and Port Regis for giving me the opportunity to write and all the pupils for their infectious enthusiasm. Thank you also to the authors and publishers who have given their kind permission to be quoted in this book. Every effort has been made to trace copyright owners. If any right has been omitted, the publishers offer their apologies and will rectify this in subsequent editions, following notification.

Without the support and encouragement from all these people, there would have been no journey – just a dream.

FOREWORD

BY DOUGLAS OSBORNE
Executive Director, Leukaemia Research Fund

In the summer of 1993, I received an unusual visit from three young men; Rupert Attlee, David Nicholls and Michael Pask. They had what at the time seemed the crazy idea of cycling 6,500 miles along the spine of the Andes from Tierra del Fuego to Lake Titicaca in order to raise money for the Leukaemia Research Fund. A quick look at the map made me realise that my first thoughts were right on the mark. I told them, tactfully I hope, that there are easier ways of raising money. How about following the footsteps of Ian Botham from John o' Groats to Land's End? Better still cycle it! 'No,' they told me, 'it just had to be South America and the Andes.'

I have become hardened to such proposals. Many 'adventurers' have crossed our threshold over the years seeking charity association to get their expeditions off the ground. This is fine as far as it goes, but at the Leukaemia Research Fund we firmly believe that our involvement must be more than incidental. My mind was soon put at ease on this score because they told me they would fund the whole venture from private means. Even so, I was still concerned. 'How much cycling have you done?' was my next question, expecting a catalogue of journeys and cyclists' tales. 'None,' was the answer and they proudly added, 'we don't even have one bike between us – yet!'

Not a good start you might think, I certainly did! However, it was not long before the infectious enthusiasm and will of these three exceptional young men captured the hearts and minds of me and my colleagues. We soon realised that raising a substantial sum for the Leukaemia Research Fund was just as much part of their vision as the formidable journey itself.

And so this incredible journey got underway. Monthly reports winged their way to us relating extraordinary experiences, saddle sores and great kindness from the people all along the route. Slowly and surely we realised they might even do it. They fought through the winds and deserts of Patagonia. If we needed any more convincing about their commitment, it came with the news that they were turning away offers of lifts and ignored some tunnels through the Andes. Onwards they pedalled towards the darkly shaded topography of Bolivia and here progress slowed dramatically as they climbed . . . and climbed. For months now the word 'Titicaca' had been echoing down the corridors of our office in Great Ormond Street and then suddenly one day on 16 August, 1994, we heard the news that they had made it!

So far this remarkable expedition has raised £43,000 for the Fund. For this, I wish to record our profound thanks to the many friends, relatives and well-wishers who responded so generously to our intrepid travellers. On top of all the money, people in remote parts of South America were reassured to hear that somewhere, someone was addressing leukaemia and its related blood cancers. This message of awareness and reassurance reached a further 10,000 people here in Britain through the post-expedition lecture tour with a highlight evening at the Royal Geographical Society which I was privileged to attend.

This book represents the culmination of an extraordinary adventure and association spanning four years. I am sure you will find it a fascinating and absorbing read. Who knows? – Rupert, David and Mike may yet ride again. Whatever they decide our great thanks and best wishes go with them all the way.

—1—
MUSSEL BOUND

'The more you knew of South America, the more you would understand that anything was possible – anything.'

SIR ARTHUR CONAN DOYLE 'The Lost World'

Before us stood an Argentine gaucho. Shading his weather-beaten face, he wore a black felt hat splattered with blood and coated in dust. Across his broad shoulders hung a red poncho edged with blue tassels. Twice a strong gust of wind caught the red cloth and sent it fluttering like wings. Nestled below his bulging stomach was a thick leather belt, studded with coins and held by a buckle decorated with the emblem of a spread-eagle. To the right protruded the bone handle of a knife – a prized possession in a life of skinning, castrating and, at times, self-defence. Dark pleated trousers covered his bowed legs and disappeared into the black leather of his pointed boots. The only thing missing was his horse.

'Nostros vamos' (we are going) I said, grappling with the unfamiliar Spanish words. *'Gracias por te hospitalidad.'* Pablo Martinez, the gaucho, had been our host at his remote farm on the shores of the

island of Tierra del Fuego, situated at the tip of South America. Huddled around a wood-burning stove and sleeping on a hard dusty floor in a small grain store was where Mike, David and I had spent the first night of our cycling expedition. A journey that we hoped would finally take us some 6,500 miles north to Lake Titicaca in Bolivia. It seemed a distant dream for after only the first day we were stiff, exhausted and somewhat tender in the buttocks region. We were having qualms about facing just another day, let alone many, many months!

The disposal of the bag of rubbish in my hand, stuffed with discarded tins and sea shells from supper and breakfast, was beyond my severely limited Spanish. All I could do was point and Pablo took it with a nod of understanding. I turned to face my bicycle and walked slowly towards it, hoping to delay the agony of straddling the saddle. A hand on my shoulder stopped me.

Pablo was a changed man. The smile had gone and the twinkle in his steel blue eyes had disappeared. Lines of anguish chased across his forehead and his clipped moustache twitched above his trembling lips.

'*Marea Rojo,*' he muttered. '*Marea Rojo!*'

We looked at him with surprise. After hasty consultations using our collectively limited Spanish, we arrived at the literal translation of 'Red Maria!'

'*Marea Rojo,*' he stammered again. He started to pace up and down and with each step the spurs of his boots kicked up plumes of dust. I noticed the calloused fingers of his right hand slowly clenching and releasing as he walked.

'Red Maria' had made Pablo very nervous. Who the hell was she? Could she be a local lusty wench or perhaps more sinister, a notorious brigand or fiery political activist. My mind preferred to conjure up an image of a promiscuous Maria and a faint smile came to my lips. This only increased Pablo's exasperation. With a cry of anguish, he pointed a trembling finger towards the sea. The Beagle channel was certainly in an angry mood. The gusting cold wind had whipped the water up into a frenzy of white crests and was sending waves thundering down on to the frail shingle shore. With Cape Horn just around the corner, I thought it was a day to batten down the hatches rather than attempt such a notorious sailing gauntlet. In the distance I could just pick out the weather-board houses of the Chilean naval outpost of Puerto Williams huddled against a backdrop of snow-capped mountains. So did this 'Red Maria' live in the sea as some mythical mermaid or did she live across the water in Chile? We were confused and Pablo sensed it.

Pablo withdrew his outstretched hand from the direction of the sea. One by one, he gave us a stare of burning intensity. In his eyes, I saw fear and anger and for the first time a chill ran down my spine. He lifted his head to expose his neck. I noticed his Adam's apple was trembling under some wispy strands of black hair. His hand rose again and with a flattened palm, he drew it dramatically across his throat. A hiss escaped his lips. We could not fail to recognise this universal gesture of death.

I had read about the throat-cutting exploits of the Argentine gauchos. I recalled the words of the naturalist W. H. Hudson, *'the people of the plains [the gauchos] had developed an amazing ferocity. They loved to kill a man not with a bullet but they revel in cutting his throat. This method made them know and feel that they were really and truly killing.'* But these were stories of the 1850s, not of the 1990s. Then again, I had heard Patagonia was a place caught in time. Perhaps the graffiti we had seen sprayed on the back of a road sign just outside the nearby town of Ushuaia had been no idle threat.

'Los Malvinas por Argentina. Muerte por los Britanicos!'

(The Falkland Islands for Argentina. Death to the British!)

Pablo, however, did not look the murderous type.

His right hand was moving again. It was dropping slowly and deliberately downwards; dropping all the time towards the handle of the long curved knife. Pablo stretched and flexed his fingers. They lightly brushed the bone handle and seemed to linger. Suddenly they dived for the pocket of his pleated trousers and he produced in his shaking and outstretched hand an empty shell. From its mottled black exterior and smooth mother of pearl inside, we all knew it was a mussel shell.

'*Marea, Marea Rojo,*' Pablo said emphatically.

Mussels mixed with rice and sprinkled with pepper had made up our first breakfast of the expedition. David had found them on the wind-lashed beach while he was answering a call of nature. I remembered we had congratulated ourselves on our self-sufficiency and our ability to live off the land. Now, it appeared commiserations were more in order. But how could mussels be as deadly as Pablo had suggested? Confined to the lavatory for a few days maybe, but surely not fatal! I could not and did not want to believe it.

Pablo beckoned us towards his hut. Dominating the far corner was an old-fashioned radio transmitter. He fiddled with the dial and spoke rapidly into the hand-set, before passing it to Mike. A lady's voice speaking in English crackled across the air-waves:

'Whatever you do, do not eat the mussels! Over.'

'We already have. Over.' Mike replied apologetically.

There was a sharp intake of breath. 'Oh my God, how many?' she said despairingly.

Mike hesitated, calculating in his mind the potentially fatal number, 'About twenty-one, I think we had seven each.'

There was an urgent discussion in the background and then the voice said, 'My father, Tommy Goodall, will be over for you straightaway, but in the meantime, vomit!'

'But why? What is all this panic about?' There was no reply. A hollow hiss echoed down the line.

We had heard of Tommy Goodall. He lived at *Estancia Harberton*, the remote farm founded by the first white settlers on the island of Tierra del Fuego. Tommy, we had been told, was 'a tough nut, probably the toughest to crack in Patagonia'. He was known as a man of few words and little humour, who would run a mile at the mere sight and sound of strangers. But here we were, three strangers and Tommy Goodall was taking the trouble of driving fourteen miles to meet us. All because we had eaten some mussels. Had the world gone stark raving mad or were we the crazy ones? What was lurking in the grey yellow flesh? Who or what was the deadly Red Maria?

'Vomit,' the voice had commanded. Getting rid of the mussels was not as straightforward as eating them. Tentatively, I stuck a finger down my throat, but felt nothing but a tickle. I then tried two, jammed to the back of the throat and pushing down my tongue. I retched and felt my stomach turn over. Bile filled my mouth, but the mussels and rice stubbornly refused to defy gravity. I turned to more unconventional methods. We stood in a circle and took it in turns to stuff one of David's soiled socks from the previous day up our nostrils. I breathed deeply and inhaled. The pungent odour chased up through my nose and filled my mouth. No vomiting, but it certainly made my head spin.

Was this really the end which fate had destined? It was a rather pathetic death devoid of heroism, drama or romance. I would have chosen to have been maimed by a puma, caught in a shoot-out with drug barons, experienced brake failure coming down the Andes or fallen victim to unrequited love rather than this end. Struck down by half a dozen mussels with a dirty sock up my nose. Not a fitting finale to our dream, and all those months of planning and preparation gone to waste. The mussels had absolutely no saving grace – they had not even tasted good!

My thoughts were broken by the screech of brakes announcing the arrival of Tommy Goodall. Tommy clambered out of a rusty white pick-up wearing blue denim dungarees and a brown faded shirt. He was a tall man, with a physique and fitness which belied his 70 years. He sported a full head of hair and a distinguished grey beard. His face had a healthy, ruddy glow and was dominated by dark kindly eyes. As his eyes played over us, a wry smile appeared on his face. I felt sure that he was thinking, 'these damned stupid naive tourists, fancy eating mussels'.

Tommy was not one for formalities.

'Good to see you are still alive!' he said encouragingly. 'Get in the back.'

Our source had been right, he was a man of few words. Quickly and without ceremony the bikes were thrown into the back of the open truck and we clung on for dear life as Tommy drove at break-neck speed down the rutted track to Harberton.

The prospect of impending death affected us in different ways.

DAY 2 HARBERTON 11 A.M.

'I feel I must write now. I am afraid. I wait for changes in my heart-beat, pulse and breathing. My fear is tinged with guilt. Guilt at the stupidity of it all and haunted by the possibility of not saying goodbye to my family and friends. So many people had believed in us and all for what? M is pacing up and down the room – quiet and thoughtful. D is still talking, immersed in a one-way conversation. He has not drawn a breath since getting in the truck. "Be careful of the gears. Make sure they do not bang against the floor! Hold on tight, there's a big pot-hole coming up! What are you writing, Rupes?" I am sorry D, but I really do wish you would be quiet.'

At Harberton we found out the reasons for the panic. Tommy told us that the Beagle Channel was currently experiencing the worst *marea rojo* poisoning the world had ever seen.

There were those two words again!

'Red Tide,' Tommy explained, 'is a red algae floating around in the sea. It infects most of the shellfish. Mussels, as the filters of the sea, are the worst hit and invariably they become deadly as the poison builds up in their tissues. Last year scientists monitored the levels and spread of the poisoning. It varied throughout the Beagle Channel, but the most severe concentration was very close to where you stayed the night. They analysed one mussel from there and found it contained 200,000 rat units of poisoning. The human body can only cope with eighty rat units.'

It was evident, in eating twenty-one mussels, we had been playing a game of Russian roulette.

With a sense of theatre, Tommy presented us with a large red book. It was titled the *Dictionary of Poisons* and he opened it to a two-page spread entitled 'Marea Rojo (Mesodinium Rubrum Dinophysis)'. Directly underneath, jumping out of the page, were the sinister words:

'THERE IS NO KNOWN ANTIDOTE.'

With a sense of foreboding laced with curiosity, I read on.
'The first symptoms are that your lips and tips of your fingers will start to tingle.'

My mind started to play a psychological game that set my imagination running riot. Lips and fingers, which had felt perfectly normal until then, started to itch and throb.
'You will then start to feel light-headed and experience difficulty in breathing.'

I started to feel a tide of delirium wash over me and with it my breathing became intermittent and gasping. Bloody hell, I had it! With intrigued trepidation, I moved on to see what was going to happen next . . .

'In severe cases of poisoning, breathing difficulties will increase, leading to collapse of the lungs and death.'

Was I to be a severe case? I did not want to wait to find out, I needed treatment. I searched for the word.

'The only treatment is to reduce the level of poisoning by vomiting.'

It had been twenty-five precious minutes since our failed attempts. Vomit, I needed to vomit!

Natalie, Tommy's wife, sprang to our aid. She concocted a warm mustard drink laced with salt.

'I have never known it to fail. Make sure you drink it within touching distance of a lavatory,' she advised.

She was right. Within seconds of sipping the cloudy yellow liquid, I was kneeling beside the porcelain bowl. I was not in the mood to be discreet and it was the mere sounds of my outburst which set Mike off with his mustard drink still untouched in the glass. David downed his glass in one and we all waited for the inevitable. To everybody's utter astonishment, David smacked his lips, smiled and then asked for more.

'I do not believe it!' Natalie said shaking her head in incredulity.

'Oh and while you are at it, can I have the recipe?' old iron guts continued.

Quite a crowd had now turned out to witness this bizarre scene. They were *peons* (labourers) and tourist guides from the farm and they all had *marea rojo* stories to share. We were told of a Frenchman who had died only last year. He had been diving off a yacht in the Beagle Channel and he had come up with some mussels. The captain warned him that the mussels could be fatal and he had apparently replied arrogantly,

'What do you mean? I am French, I eat mussels all the time and I will eat them when I wish!'

He defiantly popped one in his mouth and within five minutes he was dead. A young *peon* told us that his uncle had died eating them a few months ago. The trick, he informed us, was to feed a mussel to a cat and if the cat lived then they were safe. This theory explained why we had seen no cats since arriving in Tierra del Fuego. We would remember this suggestion for next time, if there was to be a next time.

While we were vomiting and listening to these encouraging tales, the hospital in Ushuaia had been called. At first, we were informed that a helicopter was being sent to pick us up, but a call ten minutes later told us we would have to make do with a five-hour round trip by ambulance. The helicopter, it transpired, was still in the garage after what had been a four month service.

A dusty off-white ambulance eventually arrived, fortunately before the acute symptoms had taken effect. The men in white coats looked at our tongues and took our blood pressures. They swayed on the side of caution and decided to give each of us a stomach pump. I volunteered to go first to get it over and done with. It was an excruciating experience and even now the thought of it brings tears to my eyes. A tube, the width of my thumb, snaked up my nose, slithered down the roof of my mouth and hit my epiglottis. That was it, I could take no more! As I started clawing frantically at the offending plastic tube, a bright flash dazzled me. It was David.

'What the bloody hell do you think you are doing?' I choked as the plastic became tangled in my left nostril.

'Only taking a shot for posterity,' David replied.

I could have quite easily wrapped that tube around his neck. The doctors discarded the tubes and ordered us to drink the saline solution directly. This time David did not ask for the recipe and promptly vomited.

After only one day of our cycling expedition, we had to bid farewell to the bikes. There just was not room in the ambulance. It was a long, dusty, bumpy trip back to Ushuaia, taking some two and half hours to cover the fifty-three miles. The ambulance only achieved a sense of urgency when we arrived on the paved streets of Ushuaia, where with the siren on, it forced its way through the busy streets.

At the hospital we were all given a thorough check up. The tests were clear, but they wanted to keep us in overnight for observation.

DAY 2 USHUAIA HOSPITAL 11.30 P.M.

'We are in Ward 6. D and M are asleep; D is on his front swallowing his pillow and M is on his back with his mouth wide open catching flies. I cannot sleep, because so many thoughts are racing through my mind. The one question I keep coming back to time and time again is how had we escaped dying in each other's arms in the gaucho's grain store? The odds had certainly been stacked against our survival. It had to be the tiny stream trickling into the sea close to where the mussels lay. The fresh water must have cleansed them and in so doing saved our lives. Life and death in a matter of yards. So much for "living" at one with nature, it had nearly killed us. To complete our journey, we must learn to respect and understand this strange and beautiful land. One thing was for certain, we could not count on being so lucky next time. D whispered "Susan" in his sleep. It was good to know his dreams were untroubled.'

The stream had saved us from the ignominy of the following expedition statistics:

SOUTH AMERICAN TITICACA EXPEDITION
Duration: 36 hours
Distance: 47 miles
Cyclists: Deceased
Bicycles: Deserted
For all you readers, it would have been a very short book indeed . . .

—2—
SANITY IN QUESTION

'The future belongs to those who believe in their dreams'

ELEANOR ROOSEVELT

'You must be mad!'

I had grown used to this statement when the proposed South American Titicaca Expedition cropped up in conversation. When I informed them we would be travelling by bicycle and we had no definite rationale for the venture, I suspected that this opinion was reinforced. I was happy for them to think this. I had a dream and after all, the best journeys are inspired and motivated by dreams.

I had been dreaming for some time. At first I could think of no conceivable way to realise it, but my search ended on a rainy Monday evening at the Royal Geographical Society. It was a venue where I had been many times before to hear the likes of Sir Ranulph Fiennes, Helmut Messner, Doug Scott and Chris Bonington. But, while I was spell-bound by their exploits, I listened with a certain degree of detachment for I knew I could never emulate their levels of expertise or match their endurance. On this particular occasion, as Hallam

Murray talked of his cycling expedition in South America, I crept gradually to the edge of my seat. It dawned on me that I too could achieve a journey of this magnitude. A bicycle in South America was the answer to my 'dream'.

There were, however, three issues that I needed to address. First, I had a good job which I enjoyed. I needed the belief and conviction to jack it all in. Second, I needed to find a bicycle and to see whether I actually enjoyed cycling over a long distance. In the past I had tended to limit myself to ten mile round trips. Third, it was important to know where I was going in such a large continent. From geography lessons at school I had always been fascinated by two places in South America: Patagonia because it seemed to defy description, and Lake Titicaca because of its intriguing name. I tentatively linked the two and the line cut across the three countries of Chile, Argentina and Bolivia.

However, after some two and a half years nothing had changed: I still had the job, I had no bike and the proposed route stayed marked in pencil. I continued to be seduced by a life of travelling around the world looking for land to build golf courses on. It was certainly difficult to contemplate the rigours of life on a bicycle from the sandy beaches of Barbados, the lavender fields of Provence or the euphoric atmosphere of an independent Latvia. But after a three month freezing cold and frustrating assignment near Frankfurt watching the grass grow in winter, I planned my escape. The die was cast – it was now or never!

Even though I was prepared to go alone, I dearly wanted companions to share the experiences and memories. David and I had met in Australia, when we were doing a stint as male models at the Cruising Yacht Club in Sydney. It is a long story involving much changing in and out of a lot of rather cumbersome wet-weather gear. Needless to say, neither of us have ever to my knowledge been asked back on to the catwalk again, but we were, however, offered two sought after positions on a yacht. Fate dictated that we met again in Hong Kong and then finally we ended up sharing a flat in London. David witnessed at first hand my whirlwind spin of trying to get the expedition off the ground and was justifiably shocked by my mental inadequacy towards anything practical or technical. Spurred on by a professional exasperation allied with an adventurous spirit, David, a chartered engineer, finally enquired one morning:

'Where did you say you were going again?'

'Oh, from Tierra del Fuego to Lake Titicaca,' I replied, surprised.

'*Terry*' who and '*titi*' where?' said David, trying to make some sense out of the unfamiliar words. I could sense that the very mention of the word '*titi*' had excited David's interest and curiosity.

'The island of fire in the south, to a sacred lake in Bolivia,' I said, vaguely not wanting to put David off the scent.

'Count me in,' David said casually, as if he was agreeing to a night in a pub, and then he disappeared out of the door.

Mike and I worked together. One evening we went for a beer by the river and I mentioned I was leaving the company.

'Where are you escaping to?' asked Mike, surprised.

'I'm planning to cycle through South America,' I replied casually. Mike was puzzled. 'I never knew that you were into cycling.'

'Well, I'm not, but the idea of cycling is exciting. It promises freedom, challenges and surprises and above all I can ride a bicycle. At least I could the last time I tried. I think that was about eight years ago,' I added, rather falteringly, as I thought back to several wobbly jaunts from the pub at university.

I had become rather used to the comment 'you must be mad!', but instead Mike said, encouragingly, 'You have a head-start on me. The last time I rode a bike was when I was twelve on a paper round.'

Mike was suddenly quiet and his eyes became distant. A minute later he broke the silence with the words, 'I think I will come with you.'

I put this reaction down to the beer, but I was wrong, for the very next day, behind closed doors in the office, we plotted our departure to South America.

The team was in place, and what a team!

David Nicholls – *29, 6 ft tall, thick brown hair, brown eyes, mole on right cheek, protruding ears. Practical, pragmatic, engineer by profession, great at taking things apart but not so good at putting them back together again. Generous, kind, and good in a crisis. Chatty, friendly, could talk the hind legs off a donkey. Opportunity came at a time of disillusionment in his job. More at home on a horse than a bicycle. No Spanish.*

Michael Pask – *27, 6 ft 3 ins tall, curly brown hair, piercing green eyes. Romantic, emotional, artistic, seductive, a lady's man. Weakness for champagne and smoked salmon in the bath. Not inclined towards solving practical and mechanical problems. Vulnerable to illness and injury. Athletic but clumsy. Competitive and ambitious nature. The expedition was a dream come true. Limited bike experience, but likes to wear cycle shorts. No Spanish.*

Rupert Attlee – *30, 5 ft 8 ins tall, stocky build, fair hair, blue eyes, scar down the left side of neck. Romantic and emotional. Weakness for the setting sun, full moon and a bottle of Chateauneuf-du-Pape. Hopeless in mechanical and practical matters. Infectious enthusiasm, restless, impatient and never able to sit still. Driven by ambitious, competitive and egotistical nature. Opinionated on all issues. The expedition was a trip of a lifetime. Limited cycling experience. No Spanish.*

Inevitably, there were concerns about how we were all going to get along. Being friends in the cosy environment of London is a very different matter from being thrown together for twenty-four hours a day over a period of ten months. It was certainly going to be a test of the depths of our friendship. My greatest concern, however, was that Mike and David did not know each other. They had only met on one occasion before, which had left such a lasting impression on each other that they had both forgotten it. With Mike tied up working abroad and David flitting off to Ecuador under the guise of learning some Spanish, it was not until Miami Airport that they met again. It was a meeting between Mike, the romantic, and David, the stoic. When Mike gave David a huge bear hug, two instinctive thoughts flashed into David's mind: when is the next flight back to London, and thank goodness we decided on a second tent. I am glad to say that David chose to proceed.

Concerns of teamship were put on the back burner as we turned our thoughts towards what should be our objectives for the expedition. First of all, we decided that we did not want to embark solely on a trip of self-indulgence. We recognised that the expedition had the potential to be a vehicle for raising money for charity, but we knew this to be no easy option nor a decision to be taken lightly. It required full commitment and in reality entailed even greater planning, organisation and time than setting up the trip itself. For this reason, it was paramount that we chose a charity which we all believed in. I will always be grateful to David and Mike that the Leukaemia Research Fund was chosen in memory of my mother's god-daughter, Sophie, who had died from the disease. None of us could anticipate the inspirational value, fulfilment and sheer pleasure that this purpose would give us in the months and years to come.

Our fund-raising (or fund 'raiding' as one good friend put it!) was governed by two criteria: none of the money raised would go towards the expedition expenses and at all times we would respect the good reputation, public image and resources of the Leukaemia Research

Fund. This philosophy enhanced the expedition's potential to raise money in an ever discriminating and cautious marketplace.

We identified two other factors which we deemed important: recognition and continuity. We approached Lord Oaksey OBE, the distinguished racing commentator, whom David knew from his home village of Oaksey. He kindly agreed to take on the mantle of expedition patron, and his seal of approval was vital not only in giving the expedition recognition, but also in opening many doors of opportunity. Lord Oaksey's description of the expedition as *'three boys driven by an eccentricity that is quintessentially British'* gave us a competitive edge in the search for support.

We needed continuity in the fund-raising, and were concerned it would lose momentum once we left England. We realised that it would not be possible to collect money actually in South America, and as far as leukaemia was concerned we would concentrate solely on raising awareness during our time away. The solution was Simon Heazell, 'the Fourth Man', who operated under the grandiose title of 'Expedition UK Co-ordinator'. Through Simon's energetic and methodical approach, sponsors and friends alike were never given the liberty to forget about us. Now we were four.

We wanted the expedition to be unique and our secondary objective was therefore to cycle every inch of the route using only our own pedal power. We had to take two ferries but these crossings in no way shortened the route. This objective led to many diversions, nights in the middle of nowhere, an international border incident, the refusing of many lifts and running the gauntlet of the Pan American Highway. It became an issue of stubborn insistence even in the most dangerous and testing circumstances.

With fund-raising at the forefront, preparation of equipment and much needed cycle training was neglected. Our limited experience was a concern and thus we resolved to lay the foundations of knowledge by purchasing three bikes. My initial enthusiasm and impatience took me one Saturday morning to a bike shop. I needed advice and approached an assistant:

'I am planning to cycle through South America and need some advice on the most suitable mountain bike,' I announced confidently.

What I thought was a simple request stimulated a barrage of questions:

'How much weight will you be carrying?'

'What percentage of dirt to paved roads will you be on?'

'What gear ratios are you considering and do you have a preference for rapid-fire or thumb shift gears?'

'Do you have a preference for gel or leather?'

I could not understand how such an innocent request had generated such an array of possibilities, all of which were disguised by baffling jargon. I was left gasping for an intelligent response in the wake of this inquisition.

'I think I would prefer leather,' I replied, rather hesitantly, not really knowing what I was committing myself to. I made an extremely feeble excuse and left red-faced.

One of the major advantages about being in a team of three is that democracy can be exercised effectively. Mike and I voted that David was the most suitable person to unravel the terminology and to make an educated decision on the best bikes and components. After much deliberation we chose Madison Ridgeback bikes, with an impressive array of components with interesting accessories: Ritchey, Tange, Shimano, Mavic and Buffo (see equipment list). We were advised to do approximately 1,000 miles to break the bikes in and then to return them for fine-tuning. Even in our state of initial enthusiasm this did seem rather excessive.

As far as our training programme was concerned, we identified two alternatives: to launch into an intensive fitness schedule, or to conserve our energies for the real thing. Having been inundated with stories of the ferocious Patagonian wind, and daunted by the topography of the Andes, we firmly embraced the latter option and the philosophy *the best training is on location*. No amount of training, we were informed, could prepare us for the constant buffeting by the wind in the south. Many times we heard the ominous warning, 'Patagonia without wind is like Hell without Fire.' As for the Andes, they were going to take us to heights way beyond anything Britain or Europe could offer. The challenge of the Andes was exacerbated by the need to travel from south to north in order to miss the winter snows of Tierra del Fuego and the wet season in Bolivia. Not only was this orientation more psychologically demanding, it also entailed starting at sea-level and ending at some 13,200 feet on the shores of the highest navigable lake in the world.

Hence, the bikes remained blue, shiny and pristine and the saddles went unchristened. I still think that Mike took our conservation theory a bit far with his total training of three miles. David and I followed a more balanced programme between training and conservation with fifty and seventy-five miles respectively.

The bikes were not the only unknowns, for South America was an enigma to us all. We looked to media reports for information. Journalists painted a picture of a continent in constant turmoil due to its population of drug barons, terrorists and military dictators. While we wished to reserve judgement, we were constantly faced with questions concerning our precautions against gun toting bandits. In a radio interview with LBC, another threat was entered into the equation when the disc jockey asked,

'What are your chances against the bandits and bears?'

These impressions were also to be found amongst the very young. In a lecture I gave at St George's School in Lambeth, I asked the children what they thought the most important item was to take on an expedition of this kind. A hand shot up in the front row and an eight year old kid replied enthusiastically,

'A gun.'

Against these perceived dangers, however, we decided to adopt the *'no gun, big smile'* philosophy.

In order to ease our path through the potential dangers and bureaucracy, we sought official recognition from the Argentine, Chilean and Bolivian Embassies. They presented us with letters in Spanish, which explained we were on an expedition for charity and requested for any necessary assistance to be given. These letters proved to be invaluable.

Fate, however, does move in mysterious ways. Three days before leaving we received some unsolicited training for these potential hazards. Mike and I were buying the last pieces of equipment. As we left the shop weighted down by our purchases, we sensed something was wrong. An eerie silence reigned over a usually busy Shepherd's Bush Green. We had stepped into the middle of a gun siege. A shooting had taken place in the street and now the gunman was keeping the police at bay by firing randomly from a second storey window. Policemen rushed to our assistance and escorted us down the sight-line of the buildings to my cordoned-off car. As I drove off, I looked forward to escaping in a few days to the peace and tranquillity of what is known as *'the uttermost place on earth'* – the island of Tierra del Fuego.

—3—
WORLD'S END

'South America is a place I love, and I think, if you take it right through from Darien to Fuego, it's the grandest, richest, most wonderful bit of earth upon this planet'

SIR ARTHUR CONAN DOYLE 'The Lost World'

'Como te llamas?' 'Me llamo Michael.'

Mike and I used our time well on the flight. For one hour we grappled with the vagaries of Spanish language and verbs. We became increasingly frustrated as we realised that irregular verbs are more regular than regular verbs. In the interests of our fellow passengers we kept the dictating of these confusing conjugations to a minimum.

My attention turned to my new altimeter watch, given to me as a leaving present. While the watch was light and practical, the instruction manual was the size of *The Encyclopaedia Britannica* and virtually required its own pannier. After forty-five minutes leafing through the manual and pushing buttons I was ready for the ultimate test. I assumed I could check the watch-reading off the data provided by the Captain;

'Good afternoon, ladies and gentlemen, we are currently cruising at an altitude of 33,000 feet.'

At that split second I confidently pressed the relevant button and received a reading of eighty feet below sea level. I decided that in the interest of my peace of mind it was advisable to believe in the Captain's judgement, and I resolved to try out my new watch in less pressurised circumstances.

The ancient Rollei camera that I had acquired in an antique shop was also the focus for the combined technical wizardry of Mike and myself. I had chosen it because it was manual and durable and could withstand extremes of temperature, climate and road conditions. These seemed distant considerations as we grappled to put the film in the camera. The net result of some thirty minutes of fingers and thumbs was an exposed film lying on the floor below my seat. The camera would have to wait for the practical patience of David.

We were to rendezvous with David at Miami Airport, as he had nobly volunteered to go to Ecuador for a month to learn Spanish. This meeting was the first drama. On the flight over, watching and laughing at our antics, was an Argentine pop journalist. Carolina's flowing raven hair, dark liquid eyes and olive skin was quite a distraction and on disembarking we inadvertently followed her through customs into the United States of America. This left David waiting for us in the transit lounge. It took many public address messages before we were united and Mike could give David the infamous bear-hug.

The second drama occurred at Buenos Aires. I had assumed, when booking the flights, that the international and domestic airports would be connected. Not a bit of it! A mere distance of twenty-eight miles and a city of twelve million people separate the two. A gambling man would not have rated our chances of making the two and a half hour connection time. The battered bike boxes appeared on the carousel and, having informed officials of our plight, we were ushered through immigration and customs to a fleet of waiting taxis. The only solution was to lash the three bikes in their boxes to the roof of a taxi. With these perched perilously on top, our leaning bicycle edifice lurched into the erratic traffic of Buenos Aires. After several on-road adjustments we arrived with frayed nerves in the nick of time. It was a small plane for the final leg to Ushuaia and there were strict checks on baggage allowances. A well-placed foot under scales ensured that all our luggage, including the bikes, weighed-in on the total limit of sixty kilos (a miracle with each bike weighing seventeen kilos). The stewardess raised her eyebrows and then tapped the digital display as my foot was steadily going numb under the pressure. She smiled and without fuss she checked us in. I felt a rising excitement as I limped across the tarmac onto the waiting plane.

As we flew southwards to 'el fin del mundo' all that lay below was the flat, arid pampas. Very occasionally a settlement could be seen. Trucks appeared, sending out plumes of dust as they raced along dead straight tracks stretching off into the horizon. We touched down at Trelew situated by the River Chubut. The vestiges of the past are still to be found in this modern industrial city. On the streets the Welsh language can be heard, signs for Welsh tea-houses sway in the wind, and chapels dedicated to the worship of St David break up the monotony of the single storey houses. Looking over the parched windswept landscape prompted the question:

'Why would anyone leave the lush valleys and green hills of Wales to settle in such a place?'

Between 1865 and 1914, the Welsh came to pursue their religious traditions in their own language away from the cultural oppression in Wales and seduced by the promise of exciting economic opportunities. The Chubut valley was not the Utopia they had expected, but the sweet taste of freedom and dogged hard work keeps them here to this day.

It was at Trelew that we first experienced the ferocity and unpredictability of the notorious Patagonian wind. It seemed to whip up from nowhere. As we stepped out of the terminal building, we were greeted by a cacophony of sounds as it whistled around the sheds and set the corrugated iron roofs clanging. We were buffeted by the wind and the dust stung my eyes. A tangled ball of pampas grass brushed across my legs and tumbled at speed across the tarmac runway.

I am not a nervous passenger but the way the plane lurched and shook during the take-off had me clawing at the armrest. Ever southwards we journeyed to the ugly and windswept oil town of Rio Gallegos and it was here that the be-suited and -tied oil executives disembarked. All that was left were fifteen other passengers scattered around the plane. Apart from us, they all resembled last frontier caricatures, with their lined, weather-beaten faces and distant eyes cocooned in layers of clothing. We crossed the grey, white flecked waters of the Magellan Straits, which separate the mainland from Tierra del Fuego. It was then that rivers appeared like meandering silver ribbons draped across the landscape as the early evening sun reflected off their waters. Suddenly, the flat pampas gave way to jagged snow capped peaks, giving us our first view of the mighty Andes. We had chosen these mountains to be our guide and tormentors for the months to follow, and as my mouth dropped open in awe; I began to question our choice of transport. Mike echoed my thoughts,

'I thought you said that Tierra del Fuego was flat!' he said accusingly.

At this moment we all felt relieved that we had prudently conserved our energies rather than over-extending ourselves in training.

As the plane banked to the east, the blue waters of the Beagle Channel appeared and I fancied that I caught a glimpse of the solitary sentinel rock of Cape Horn. Ushuaia emerged huddled in the lee of the snow-capped Martial Mountains, dominated by Monte Olivia and the *Cinco Hermanos* (Five Brothers). So this was the southernmost town in the world and the clear winner in the lowest-latitude competition. Port Elizabeth in South Africa is 33 degrees 58 minutes south; Hobart in Tasmania is 42 degrees 54 minutes; Invercargill in New Zealand is 46 degrees 26 minutes south; and Ushuaia is 54 degrees 48 minutes south, leaving it only 765 miles from Antarctic peninsula. Despite this inhospitable position, the falling sun bathed the buildings and sea in a soft light, giving the setting a beauty that I had not expected. Was this the same town that is described as ugly, bleak and expensive in one guide book?

The plane headed for a thin strip of tarmac jutting out into the sea. We had been warned that on a normal day of strong winds and angry seas, the landing could be frightening. But the gods had been kind in providing a tame wind and calm sea to welcome us. As we touched down we were reminded of our luck when we glimpsed the mutilated wreck of a plane peeping out of the water.

On stepping on to the tarmac, the first thing we did was to shed layers of clothes. We had come prepared for sub-zero temperatures, but were instead greeted to a warm evening. Wishing to conserve our energy further we hitched a lift with Dario, a tourist guide, across the narrow peninsular into town. To thank him we offered to buy him a drink later.

'That would be great,' he replied 'Eleven o'clock at the Bar Esquina.'

This was our first introduction to Latin American time and what better time to start than within hours of alighting from a twenty-seven hour flight.

Ushuaia (population 40,000) was not how I had expected it to be. Instead of a sleepy, remote outpost, we found a young, noisy and vibrant town. The population has increased by nearly six times in the last fifteen years, drawn by tax incentives and employment in the tourist industry, sawmills, fishing and electronics. The strange variety of the architecture reflects this growth. The early wooden houses, clad in corrugated iron, have a stark Russian flavour. Many were built by prisoners from the in famous local jail (1906-1940) and are marked by the decorative cornices in the gingerbread style. With more people than homes, these have been joined by a chaotic jigsaw of uninspiring modern concrete structures, imported Swedish prefabs and hundreds of small, new, wooden shanties. Land is at a premium, hemmed in by mountains and sea, forcing houses to sprawl up the steep slopes.

As part of the government incentives, vehicles are offered at half price. The result is traffic mayhem and the noise of screeching brakes, revving engines and shrill horns resounding through the streets of Ushuaia, day and night. It must be a cure for the all-pervading boredom to drive your quad bike or four-wheel drive at break-neck speed, time and time again down the high street, showering pedestrians with dust, ice and grit.

'This is relatively civilised,' Dario observed. 'Imagine what it was like two weeks ago when the seasonal traffic regulations changed. You see in the summer, vehicles on the flatter roads running parallel to the waterfront have priority. But in the winter, it is switched because of the steep icy gradients. Believe me, it is chaos every year.'

I had expected that in the world's southernmost town, there would be a sparse number and variety of shops, dominated by those catering for the necessities of life. I had hardly thought that perfume, designer clothes and hi-tech stereo systems were crucial for survival, but it was these products which dominated the high street windows and the conversations of the inhabitants. I overheard several snippets:

'I am going to buy a new stereo system. Not one of those ghettoblasters; a proper set-up with speakers round the walls.'

'Have you tried that Chanel number yet?'

'My wife prefers Calvin Klein.'

The array of shops made a mockery of all our last minute purchases back in England.

Ushuaia is also the home of a large naval base. Its presence is explained by the fact that Chile, Argentina's traditional adversary, lies just ten miles to the south and west. More recently, however, the town was in the front-line during the Falklands War. I walked down to the jetty where, in April 1982, the *General Belgrano* had set sail on its final voyage. There was a hand-beaten copper plaque in memory of those who had died – a poignant and simple reminder of the tragedy of life so pointlessly lost.

The next day Dario invited us for *maté* (an Argentine tea pronounced 'ma-tay'). It was here that we met Sabrina. I remember thinking that if all the girls we met were like her we would have to be extremely self-disciplined if we were going to reach the shores of Lake Titicaca. Together they initiated us into the rites of this traditional drink. It is a home-grown tea, and its infusion is sucked through a silver straw from a gourd which is refilled again and again as it passes from mouth to mouth. It is like the ceremony of the Indian peace pipe, without the hallucinogenic effects. It does, however, become somewhat of an addiction as Sabrina explained:

'My *maté* is my soulmate, a companion when I'm alone, a comforter when I'm troubled, and a devoted nurse when I'm sick.'

It is, indeed, a common sight in Argentina to see the people fondly cradling a thermos and a gourd.

With the *maté* still coursing through our veins, we prepared to leave the following day. We planned to go on a two-day training run to *Estancia* Harberton. We would then return to Ushuaia for a Hallowe'en party on Friday night. It was a vicious circle of packing and unpacking as we fought a losing battle to squash everything in. Amongst the essentials were three chosen luxuries. David had a pair of brogues ('*you can judge a man by his shoes*'), Mike some blue jeans ('*they make me feel relaxed and normal*') and for myself I had a fishing rod ('*to catch supper and get out of setting up camp*'). Eventually, we admitted defeat and left a suitcase of equipment behind at the hotel to be retrieved on our return. Thus with the bikes three-quarters laden, we were ready to go.

I would like to relate that we all jumped on our bikes and, without drawing a breath, sped up the hillside out of Ushuaia, stopping only for lunch at the top of the pass. In reality our progress was far from smooth. Mike was having problems with his pedals, which were, despite his best efforts, continually jamming against his panniers. It did not require Sherlock Holmes to detect that the panniers had been put on the wrong way round. I, on the other hand, was not confident enough to climb on the bike in its present position on a steep incline with the dark waters of the Beagle Channel glistening uninvitingly at the bottom. I gingerly pushed the bike down the hill and lost it as the momentum increased and my feet slipped and slid on the icy surface. From the sanctuary of a level stretch and in a respectful lull in the traffic, I pedalled the first wobbly yards of the expedition.

I marvelled at the efficiency and professionalism of my bicycle. Here I was overloaded, unfit and tentative and my bicycle, without fuss or ceremony, was propelling me through the streets. It was at this moment that a bond started to develop between us. We were kindred spirits with a common goal and a need for each other if we were to succeed. I realised I could no longer refer to 'my bicycle' in such an impersonal and detached way and thus, in the waters of the Beagle Channel, my bike was christened '*Arriba!*' (the Spanish exclamation for 'go on up'). In this touching ceremony, Mike named his bike '*Shadowfax*' after the swift and steely white horse in the *The Lord of the Rings* and David chose '*Woop-Woop*', the Australian Aboriginal term for the middle of the back of beyond. We certainly must have looked quite a sight as we stood tyre and ankle deep in the icy waters, and while locals stopped to witness this bizarre ritual, we heard for the first time the words 'gringos locos' (mad foreigners).

At the water's edge we also filled a test tube, for we had the romantic notion of mixing the waters of the Beagle Channel with those of Lake Titicaca. Our farewell to Ushuaia was restrained, because we knew we would be returning in a couple of days and, more immediately, the Martial Mountains loomed ominously overhead. Arriba was not living up to her name as we set a snail's pace up the hill. At the top we collapsed in an exhausted heap beside a stunning waterfall framed by snow-capped mountains. With a sense of achievement, we tucked into a hearty lunch. We were all fairly quiet and thoughtful over lunch as it finally sunk in that after months of preparation we were on the road. With full stomachs we were left to bathe in our own thoughts as we took a siesta.

DAY 1 ON THE ROAD TO HARBERTON 2.15 P.M.

'We are on the road at last after months of preparation. I feel free and exhilarated. It is now just us, our bikes, the road and months of adventure. The scenery is breathtaking. There could be no place more beautiful than this for our first lunch. A shadow crosses the page. It is a condor circling some fifty feet above – white collar and black plumage silhouetted against the snowy mountains, the tips of its wings like an outstretched hand. So majestic, graceful and effortless. It is the first condor I have ever seen and one I will never forget. It seems to symbolise my new found freedom. I was that condor;

"As I stared into the sky
I joined the condor up on high."

One thing was for sure, there was no place on earth I would rather be, and in M and D, I could have no better companions.'

An hour later, we set off through a landscape that was reminiscent of *The Lord of the Rings*. We rode in the shadow of the jagged white peaks which represented the very start of the mighty Andean range. Roaring streams cut a path through the mountains for the narrow gravel road to follow. Beside us lay thick impenetrable deciduous forest (high beech) which rose steeply to the tree-line. At times, this scenery disappeared as we were enveloped in a cloud of dust from gear-crunching trucks. When we turned off the main road the Alpine landscape soon changed as we reached the coastal plain, where low scrubby beech woods gave way to bush land and putrid swamps. It was now late afternoon and we were still thirty miles away from Harberton – it had become a race against time. With a chill in the air and the light fading, we knew it was a race we were destined to lose and we must look for alternative shelter and water. Eventually the road brought us down to the shores of the Beagle Channel. Not far away we spied a twinkling beacon of light radiating from a small homestead.

We discussed strategy, agreeing as a matter of courtesy that we would ask for permission to camp on their land. We did, however, harbour reservations about how warmly we would be received at the tiny outpost. In Ushuaia, we had seen the memorial to the *General Belgrano*, been confronted with a huge sign declaring *'Los Malvinas por Argentinas'* and witnessed several pieces of graffiti promising terminal consequences for those of British descent. While signing the hotel register in Ushuaia, the proprietor had asked,

'How long do you think it will be before your *mujer de hierro* (Iron Lady) and government sees reason over the Falkland Islands?'

We could not answer him.

With some trepidation, we drew up into the yard of the farm. A door creaked open off to our left and a stocky figure was silhouetted against the light. My voice trembled as I explained that we had run out of daylight, and requested water and permission to camp on his land. The gaucho shook his head and smiled and then showed us to a small grain store. He returned with a broom and firewood.

'*Buenos noches*' (good night) he wished us.

We could hardly summon the energy to cook and eat supper, and with the last mouthful, we collapsed around the stove. I awoke to find David fumbling with his thermal long johns.

'I'm as stiff as a board. Just off for a pee. I won't be a tick.'

RETURN TO THE SADDLE

'If at first you don't succeed, try, try, try again.'

ANON.

Our story spread fast. Ushuaia, in its remoteness, embraces gossip like a small village. For the locals, it was news indeed that for the first time in four years, three people, and crazy tourists at that, had survived eating mussels. The remaining cats in the town breathed a huge sigh of relief for many of them had virtually exhausted their share of lives.

We first got an inkling that we were the subject of gossip in the town when David went down to the coastguard to request a lift by boat back to Harberton and our bikes. The coastguard was most concerned, and enquired,

'But where are your two friends?'

'In the hotel,' David said puzzled.

'So they are alive then. How are you all feeling?' he asked.

'Fine, but how did you know?' David replied.

'We all heard the radio call from Harberton to the hospital. You have all had a very lucky escape,' said the coastguard, echoing the words we had heard many times over in the hospital.

At the same time, I was receiving a similar reception from the Navy, who had also heard about us on the radio. Even though both authorities showed a great interest and concern, neither was able to help us with a lift back to Harberton. Our story did not escape the media either, for the next day we were featured on the front page of the local newspaper and interviewed for the radio. The theme of the reporting was 'how could these crazy tourists have been so ignorant and silly'. It was one of our objectives to receive media coverage along the route, but this inadvertent publicity stunt was not quite what we had in mind.

That night we went out to drown our embarrassment. It was our first Saturday night in Latin America. We started at a Chinese restaurant where you had to carve your way through the monosodium glutamate and everything tasted the same. It was then off to the Bar Esquina where Dario introduced us to a friend of his, Carlos. He ran a trading company and offered to take us on the following day's boat to Puerto Williams and drop us within eighteen miles of Harberton. We jumped at the chance, even though it meant a five o'clock start the next morning.

We then went to the 'Hallowe'en Disco', arriving there at what we thought to be an appropriate time of two o'clock. The place was empty – it was either too early or out of favour. As I stood propping up the bar, I decided it must be the latter. The disco was a dive. Suggestive tacky posters lined the walls, which were already dripping with condensation. A musty damp odour mingled with the smell of stale cigarette ash. Soon these were joined by the reek of cheap perfume and after shave. People were starting to arrive. The men, dressed in black and covered in tattoos, stood around conspiratorially, sucking away at cigarettes and talking through pursed lips. The ladies were a motley crew hitting their late twenties, and trying to cling to the last vestiges of youth by wearing clothes two sizes too small. We were out of our depth and at four o'clock we left. Outside there was a queue of similar clones pushing to get in. We made a couple of mental notes – never arrive before three o'clock and never go there again!

We packed our one suitcase, three rucksacks and a few plastic bags and walked down to the docks for our lift on a fairly ancient catamaran. It had been painted in green and white stripes, but the sea and weather had taken its toll. I stared back over the foaming wake and witnessed Ushuaia bathed in the soft blue light of dawn. I hoped we would not be back for some time. On board we met one of the crew, Fernando. On hearing that we were British, he proceeded to chant the only three words he knew in English, 'Fuckie, fuckie, Maggie Thatcher.'

'Many of my friends died in the Falklands War', Fernando explained in Spanish. 'They were seventeen years old and just out of school. They were no match for your professional soldiers. It was like sending lambs to the slaughter!'

We felt distinctly uncomfortable and in an attempt to change the subject we started showing Fernando pictures from home. It worked, for within minutes he had opened a bottle of sweet sherry and fallen head over heels in love with Mike's sister. Now Fernando chose to use his one English verb on a woman other than Maggie.

We were dropped off at the tiny police outpost of Puerto Almanaz. An arch of two white whale bones marked the entrance. The bones and the buildings were dwarfed by two large artillery guns that were pointing directly at Puerto Williams in Chile, situated some ten miles away across the channel. Tension still exists between Chile and Argentina over disputed borders and islands in this region. It was only in 1978 that both sides came close to confrontation during 'the six day crisis'. War had looked likely until, at the eleventh hour, Pope John Paul II intervened and offered himself as a mediator.

Unfortunately, it remains a fragile peace because of the high stakes represented by the potential mineral wealth of the Antarctic. This line of defence was held by two rather bored policemen, who were kind enough to give us breakfast, but were unable to help us with a lift to Harberton.

Harberton was eighteen miles away. It promised to be quite a struggle with one large suitcase and our individual rucksacks and plastic bags. We were not alone because we had attracted a posse of three dogs: two German shepherds and a small cross between a poodle and a terrier. We and our entourage passed Pablo's place at Puerto Brown, but unfortunately there was nobody at home. We left a bottle of whisky on the doorstep as a thank you and to let him know that we had survived. We walked on until we found a grassy knoll overlooking the Beagle Channel, where we could rest and have lunch. We had not managed to shake the little mongrel off our tail. It was now some five miles from the police outpost and we thought that he would never find his way back again. David volunteered to run the little chap back, while Mike and I fell asleep under the midday sun.

On David's return, we reluctantly left this idyllic spot and staggered on. The scenery was breathtaking in its sheer variety. At one point we climbed up on to a rock outcrop close to the road. Below lay a scene that could have graced the sets of the film *Out of Africa*. The ground dropped away dramatically to a plain of brown grassland gently rippling in the light breeze and stretching out into the distance against a backdrop of snow-capped mountains. A silted river meandered gently across the plain and glistened in the sunshine. When I turned the picture changed. Gone was the tranquillity and blue skies of an African rift valley, to be dramatically replaced by the moody waters, cloud streaked sky and jagged shoreline of the Beagle Channel. These white flecked waters were framed by a desolate moorland, which appeared to have given up its struggle against the elements and reminded me of the bleakness of Bodmin Moor.

We descended into a valley and a wood of miniature beech trees. It looked as if a Japanese bonsai tree enthusiast had been let loose in the wood, but we were to find that these trees are a common sight in Patagonia. Their size (an average height of about twenty feet) is indeed nature's answer to the climatic extremes and the constant wind. As we walked through this rustling avenue, David fell in love with these trees and started to harbour dreams of growing them in his garden at home. 'Every time I look at them I will be reminded of Patagonia,' he mused. It is an indication of the sheer force and romance of the scenery that the usually unemotional David was falling under its spell. We left the shelter of the wood and witnessed the fate of the trees on the fringes. They were all nearly bent double, with branches stretching out as if in a plea for help towards the east. These trees were the victims of constant torture by the ferocious west wind.

We then walked into a landscape dominated by lakes. From afar they looked beautiful and inviting, but as we got nearer their colour changed to a peaty brown and a putrid smell hit our nostrils. Dead trees stretched upwards from their murky depths. These tangled fingers created abstract reflections in the water.

At last, after some five hours, we turned a corner and there lay Harberton, glistening in the afternoon sun. A trail of black smoke rose up from one of the chimneys and I could hear the cries of geese from one of the nearby islands. I imagined that little had changed from the days of Lucas Bridges, as described in 'Uttermost Place on Earth' many years before.

'Our new home,' he wrote, *'received the benefit of the summer sun till well on in the afternoon. Then the sheltering hill at the back cast its heavy shadows over the place and the hills and woods across the harbour would stand out with marvellous clearness as daylight faded. This was*

the hour when father and mother, arm in arm, would take their evening stroll, until the dusk crept over the land and the air grew chilly. Then it was that the reflection of the hills on the calm, darkening water made a picture of peace beyond my power to describe.'

We staggered in and Tommy came out to greet us, pleased to see us alive and healthy. Tommy could sense our exhaustion and kindly showed us to an outbuilding of bunk beds and invited us to dinner. We knew Tommy's aversion to tourists, so this was a kindly gesture. I recalled a conversation in John Pilkington's book, *An Englishman in Patagonia*. The author was talking to Tommy's mother, Clarita.

'So you camped at Harberton,' she said with an amused smile. *'You must have made a good impression. Tommy usually sends people packing after the guided tour.'*

Before dinner, Tommy proudly showed us his coin and note collection, which covered numerous countries and included some coins dating back a hundred years. We were able to add a £5 note and £1 and 20 pence coin to the collection and in return Tommy gave us each a silver dollar.

'For better luck,' he said with a wry smile. This silver dollar still hangs, along with a silver horseshoe and a sixpence, from the toggles of my water-proof jacket.

We were joined for dinner by Estella and Regina, two lively tourist guides from Buenos Aires. Tommy told us of the dilemma he faced at Harberton. He could no longer run the *estancia* on an economic basis with sheep alone. In the last ten years, he had seen the price of wool drop from £1.40 a kilo to 45 pence a kilo. It meant that once he had paid the shearers £2,850 he only had £2,850 left, which was very little to live on. He had turned to cattle, for which the ground was far from ideal and then, most reluctantly, to tourism.

'I do not want tourists swarming around the farm,' he declared. 'But tourism has become our lifeline for survival.'

'I have, by and large, managed to stay immune to tourism,' Tommy continued defiantly, 'by running like hell at the merest sight or sound of them. I leave all the entertaining to my wife, Natalie. She was in an American tour party visiting the farm when we first met. She fell in love with the place and me, so she stayed. I suppose Natalie is the one good thing that has come out of tourism. I tell you that once the wool price rises again, I will shut this place down to tourists and return to the peace and tranquillity of the old days.'

Tommy went on tell us what it was like running one of the most remote farms in the world.

'It is like being a captain of a ship,' he explained. 'In a severe winter we can be cut off for months from the outside world, so we need to be self-sufficient in everything from medical supplies to food and fuels. I also need to be everything to all men: manager, priest and doctor. It is a life full of surprises. I remember one evening we were in the sitting room and there was a knock on the door. I opened the door to four bedraggled and shivering strangers, two men and two women. Their yacht had gone down near Cape Horn. Their life-raft had been swept by the currents into the Beagle Channel. They had then walked for two days guided by the smoke and light of Harberton. I looked after them until the ambulance arrived, two were very badly burnt as they had failed to remove their petrol saturated clothes.'

Tommy continued, 'Harberton is my home and I could not imagine living anywhere else. My family has always been accepted here, for over a hundred years, first by the Indians and then the Argentines. The Falklands War was only a minor hiccup. I was expecting more trouble, but all that happened was a little sheep rustling and a few suppliers refusing our orders.'

We retired to the sitting room after dinner for whisky and Venezuelan soap operas. Tommy does not drink, but he is a serious fan of the soaps. They were of the most elementary quality with the cameras miraculously ghosting through walls while following the action from room to room. They did, however, follow the Latin American recipe for success: unrequited love, infidelity and male chauvinism. I was easily distracted and my eyes roamed around the room. I thought we could be in any Victorian living room with its heavily draped sofa and armchairs, gilt clock on the mantelpiece and leather-bound books lining the walls. The television and the large radio were the only indications of a more modern age. There was, however, one more clue: a paper mobile hanging from the centre of the ceiling. It was from a Kellog's 'Fruit Loops' cereal packet.

Before retiring to an early bed, I went to ask Estella and Regina up to our quarters for some maté. I stopped dead in my tracks when I heard a rhythmical chanting coming from their room. I thought that they were at prayer and decided to leave them in peace. Next day, they told me that they had been reciting and practising their lines in preparation for the arrival of a large tour group the following day.

I had a sleepless night, kept awake by the cold. I was concerned. If I was having problems here, how was I going to cope with the more severe temperatures on the Bolivian altiplano? At first light, I headed for the outside bathroom, hardly relishing the thought of washing in the cold water. With bleary eyes I opened the door and was enveloped in white confetti. The cold during the night was explained – the fields and buildings now lay under a blanket of snow. It seemed hard to believe that only the day before we had fallen asleep in the warmth of the sun. I remembered what Tommy had said the previous night,

'If you do not like the weather, wait a minute.'

In the morning we were guided around the farm by Regina. She showed us how the farm was totally self-sufficient. There was the generator, the Australian water tank, the food store, the carpentry hut, the sheep shearing sheds, the vegetable patch and the herb garden. The garden was a sea of colour, with flowering lupins, roses, pansies and white jasmine. It certainly would have put many a garden in England to shame and I marvelled at how such colour and growth was achieved in these southerly climes.

We were invited to a lunch of a delicious vegetable soup followed by lentils. In the afternoon we reluctantly prepared to leave for we knew we must take to the road. We hoped that this time we would stay on, and with, our bikes for slightly longer than thirty-six hours.

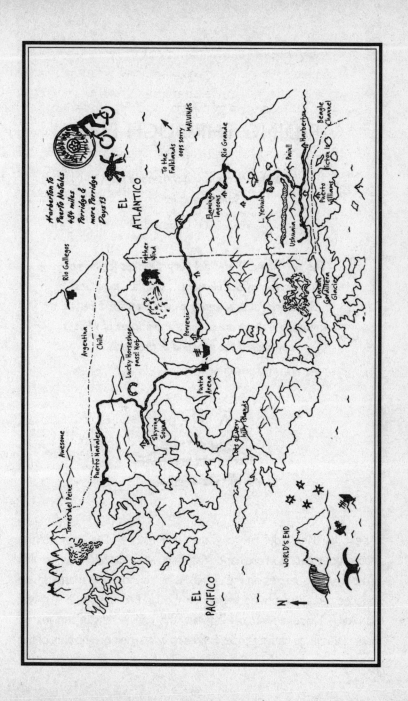

—5—
RIDING THROUGH FIRE

'Some say the world will end in fire
Some say in ice.'

ROBERT FROST 'Fire and Ice'

'The very name, Tierra del Fuego, evokes feelings of
distance, fear of the elements, isolation, loneliness.
Shrieking gales, towering waves, snow and ice,
desolation – these are some of the images of what is
considered the very end of the world.'

RAE NATALIE P. GOODALL 'Insight Guides Argentina'

Ahead lay Tierra del Fuego – the Land of Fire. The origin of the name goes back to Ferdinand Magellan, who in 1520 was the first European to set eyes on the island. As he rounded the mainland, he noticed a curious phenomenon on the land to the south – it was smoking. Unbeknown to Magellan, the native Yahgan Indians on seeing this huge native canoe, lit fires to warn their neighbours of this sinister arrival. He christened it 'land of smoke' but the Spanish king, Charles V, thought 'land of fire' might be more poetic. The fires and smoke died out and the Indians became extinct, but the name survived.

Since Magellan, Tierra del Fuego has had a history as turbulent and wretched as its weather. For centuries, the island was dreaded by sailors for its ferocious storms and freezing rains and Cape Horn became known as a nautical version of hell. According to Charles Darwin, the Fuegian Indians, who had been living in the far south for tens of thousands of years, reflected the state of the weather.

'I never saw such miserable creatures,' Darwin wrote in *Voyage of the Beagle*; *'stunted in their growth, their hideous faces daubed with white paint and quite naked . . . Their red skins filthy and greasy, their voices discordant, their gesticulation violent and without any dignity. Viewing such men, one can hardly make oneself believe that they are fellow creatures placed in the same world . . . What a scale of improvements is comprehended between the faculties of the Fuegian savage and a Sir Isaac Newton!'*

The 19,000 square miles island, an area larger than Switzerland, remains sparsely populated and large tracts will always defy habitation. The island is now shared by Chile (to the west and south) and Argentina (to the north and east). Shared is perhaps the wrong word, because the two countries have been divided for over one hundred years over the border issue. It was Queen Victoria who when officiating in one of the numerous border disputes, ignored natural phenomenon and drew the straight line that marks the border today. As recently as 1978, the two countries nearly came to blows and this inherent animosity was the main reason Chile supported the British during the Falklands War.

Tierra del Fuego had already given us a hard time, tempting us with mussels at our very first breakfast. We did not expect things to get any easier during the next five hundred miles to the port of Porvenir and the ferry to the mainland. From the aeroplane we had seen what we had to cross – first a snow-capped mountain range which then gave way to flat windswept plains. Our greatest concern was how, in our untrained condition, we were going to cope with the legendary wind and the corrugated dirt roads. They were unknown quantities as well as the three of us on bikes.

We lasted forty-five minutes. Aching muscles took their toll and a patch of lush open grass nestling in the arc of a river proved to be too tempting. It was our first camp-site of the expedition. We had two tents: a Bullfrog and a Tadpole. I wished the manufacturers had chosen more stylish and inviting names for what were to be our sleeping quarters for some ten months. I could imagine a future amorous encounter ending with the words; 'Would you like to come back to my Bullfrog' or 'Come back and I will show you my Tadpole.' With Bullie, sitting back on its haunches and mouth gaping wide open, and Taddie standing in child-like imitation, our thoughts turned to cooking.

The meal we had to celebrate our first night under the stars was rather simple – sardines in tomato sauce mixed with rice. I was surprised just how delicious it all tasted for as a rule I loathe the taste and sight of tinned sardines. It must have been the euphoria of the occasion and intoxication of the fresh air, as I am convinced that caviar, followed by filet mignon and bottle of Chateauneuf-du-Pape would not have tasted any better.

Well-stuffed and with the delicate taste of the sardines still playing on my lips, I lay back to appreciate the stars. There were, however, none to be seen. 'Why, oh why,' I thought, 'on this of all nights.' As if in answer a large white flake landed on my nose, followed closely by two on each cheek and then one smack in the eye. Within seconds I was covered in white polka dots. After this initial flurry, the flakes soon developed into snow balls, which cascaded rather than floated down from on high. We packed hastily and dodged these missiles while we stumbled back to the sanctuary of our tents. Unfortunately, Bullie and Taddie were having a hard time as their poles strained to resist the weight of the smothering snow. We swept the snow off, forcing a passage to Bully's gaping mouth and all clambered in. We must have looked like three dead dogs as we lay on our backs with stiff arms and legs holding the straining poles and walls in place. Thankfully, it stopped snowing as quickly as it started. 'Welcome to life in the outdoors,' I thought, as I drifted off dreaming of bicycle snow-ploughs.

I awoke early. Miraculously the snow had disappeared and the skies were clear. What a perfect day for cycling, I mused, and then went promptly back to sleep again. Much later, David and I immersed ourselves in the icy waters of the river to clear our bleary heads. It was a time of agonising numbness, beating of chests, fanatical singing and shrivelling manhood. Mike watched with a quizzical air. It took us three hours to pack up and for our circulation to return. A time we would have to improve on, or we could be destined never to leave the shores of Tierra del Fuego. Thankfully, the 'summer' days were long in this southerly region – four o'clock sunrise and ten thirty sunset.

Our objective that day was named after a fig roll biscuit sitting on top of the Andean range – *Paso* Garibaldi. We knew that this pass represented our first cycling challenge of the expedition. Intent on reserving our limited energies, we cruised for the twenty miles of undulating wooded track until we turned a corner and saw a sight more daunting than any of us had expected. Two thousand feet above lay a neat linear cut in the jagged mountain skyline. From here a dirt track unfurled and meandered down the steep slopes to our feet. Our reaction was to sit down with our backs to the mountain and to cook up a late lunch. The congealed asparagus soup certainly settled the butterflies in our stomachs but did nothing to whet our appetite for the climb ahead. We did however have a serious chocolate fix, which was the start of a short, slippery slide to addiction.

As we set off with heads bowed, I realised that competitive spirit was going to be an important driving force. So far on the trip none of us had admitted defeat on any of the hills we had faced. I knew that I for one did not want to be first to get off and walk. I was confident and set off at a steady pace, leaving Mike and David in my wake. The slope was endless and every turn held a false hope of the summit. My spirit was willing, but physically I was starting to flag and my legs were failing to respond. It felt at first as though hands were clawing at my panniers, pulling *Arriba* downwards, and then the mud of the road took on the adhesive properties of super-glue. I turned to see the demoralising sight of Mike and David catching me at every turn and this spurred me to one last effort. I vainly hoped the summit would come down and meet us. They passed me and I was left to come to a trembling halt and to nurse my bruised pride. It did not matter that Mike collapsed exhausted some twenty yards ahead, I had been the first to throw in the towel. It was this competitive nature between us which was often to push us beyond our physical capabilities in the times to come.

Another collapse and one chocolate break later, we did eventually make it to the top. As the sun was setting and snow was again starting to fall, our celebrations were cut short. We sped and froze our way down the other side and at last saw the sign we craved 'Hotel Petrel.' Our hearts sank when, having travelled some two miles off the road in the gathering darkness, the wooden lodge appeared to be closed. Eventually a bleary-eyed proprietor opened the door and took pity on our three trembling and exhausted figures. The therapeutic combination of a hot bath, open fire, barbecued fish and crisp linen sheets will always be a wonderful memory.

The next day, we left the mountains behind and reached gently undulating grassy plains. The landscape was bathed in unusual tranquillity as only the most gentle of breezes played across the grassland. Where was the ferocious wind that had shaped the bushes and flattened the trees? I knew we were living on borrowed time and this thought pushed us on for two days. When the wind eventually did arrive it came from behind and we were swept at a delirious speed down the road. Unfortunately the ruts and corrugations should not have been taken at such a pace and within the hour we had the first casualty of the expedition when a bolt sheered on the front pannier rack of *Woop-Woop*. We carried hundreds of nuts and bolts, but as fate would have it (or was it bad planning?) nothing fitted.

We limped into a nearby *estancia* to see if we could find a replacement. A strange looking man came out to meet us, bristling with hostility. He wore the dress of a gaucho, with tanned leather breeches and pointed steel-capped boots. His weather-beaten and furrowed face was dominated by his eyes, which shone like dark coals. I will, however, remember him most for his ears. They resembled hanging baskets planted with black, curly weed. I thought he must be going through the metamorphosis of a werewolf. Remembering a full moon was imminent, we made our apologies and beat a hasty retreat. Behind us we heard a tirade of excited grunts. None of us looked back.

David managed to nurse *Woop-Woop* and the crippled pannier rack to a roadside campground. Being Sunday, there were a number of young people around playing football and having a barbecue. The smell of the chicken dampened our enthusiasm for our meagre rations of tinned tomatoes and rice. They must have sensed our longing for within minutes we were sitting with them, sharing the limbs of chicken and cans of beer. I was soon engaged in a puzzling conversation:

'Oh, so you are the three crazy English guys on bicycles. We have heard all about you,' Roberto said.

'What have you heard?' I asked defensively.

'Oh, that you are mad enough to eat mussels from the Beagle Channel. Your fame has preceded you.' He took off his white canvas hat and passed it over. 'Will you please autograph it?'

This was fame indeed!

DAY 12 ON THE ROAD TO RIO GRANDE 8 A.M.

'Last night, I dreamt I was fighting the wind and the sea from the helm of a yacht. My eyes were stinging from the salt water as I tried to pick a path through the crashing, white-crested waves. The night was full of the roar of breakers intermingled with the high-pitched scream of the wind in the rigging and the rhythmic clamour of beating canvas. I awoke with a start. A screeching wind had burst through the tent door sending rain and flapping nylon across my face. The infamous Patagonian wind had now bared its teeth with a vengeance. Amidst this cacophony, I turned to find David sleeping like a baby with rivulets of water running down his nose and across his cheek. I struggled to zip up the bulging door, while David lay blissfully unaware.'

We had expected a gentle two and half hours riding to cover the twenty miles to the town of Rio Grande. In this time, however, we had achieved a meagre eleven miles and were holed up in a ramshackle farmstead sheltering from a violent hailstorm. It was important for us to reach the town by nightfall, because we were down to our last grains of rice and were suffering from the withdrawal symptoms of no chocolate for some two days. We dragged ourselves back onto the bikes and with heads bowed set off into the teeth of the wind.

DAY 12 HELPLESSLY CLOSE TO RIO GRANDE 3 P.M.

'The wind is driving us mad. We had been warned, but up until now I had not realised the havoc and frustration the wind can cause. It is tormenting us and we are helpless to resist. We have just spent an hour climbing a fairly innocuous looking hill – exhausting work, sapping every ounce of energy. Rio Grande is in sight, but the downhill is no easier – forced to use first gear and achieving a heady pace of three miles an hour. If we do not pedal, we would be swept back over the top. It is all so demoralising! Trying to streamline, but we have different rhythms and speed. I hate the concentration it requires and having D and M breathing down my neck. Too annoyed to write more . . . I just wish the wind would bloody go away!'

3.30p.m.

'Another 500 yards and I'm just picking Arriba out of a ditch. A gust hit us side-on and sent us reeling off the road. The air is thick with expletives. The nightmare continues . . .'

4.05 p.m.

'I am shaking all over. A truck has just thundered past. It nearly sucked Arriba and me under its wheels. I had to fight for control and so nearly lost it.'

Exhausted we crept into Rio Grande (population 60,000) some four hours behind schedule. Situated on the South Atlantic and sprawling across the coastal plain, the *rio* (river) and the town were anything but *grande*. The river was muddy and silted and the town was ugly and soulless. Row upon row of stilted barrack-like houses, built in haste to cater for a tripling of population in the last fifteen years, gave the town the character of an army camp. Some lay half finished, others uncared for and many decorated in graffiti – symbols of failed industries and subsequent unemployment.

Rio Grande's past is dominated by sheep, an abattoir and a giant *frigorifico* (freezing plant). The Freezer was still in operation, as a mere shadow of its former days, to the south-east of the town. In the 1920s, during the season between 3,000 and 5,000 sheep were being slaughtered daily. The sheer scale of the killing left its mark on the men working there. A. F. Tshiffley, a visitor to the town in 1938, reported,

'The few men who do the actual killing are so fond of taking life that on Sundays . . . armed with their knives, they set out to a land point near the settlement, and they pass the Sabbath competing as to who can cut the throats of the greatest number of harmless seals. Having enjoyed the slaughter, they leave the dead animals to be eaten by the birds, and home, happy and satisfied, ready for another week's throat-cutting of sheep.'

The macabre history and the onslaught of unemployment was reflected in the faces and behaviour of the people. While we cycled in, we were greeted by sullen blank expressions, crossed by people shuffling in haste with heads bowed and watched by shady characters standing on street corners. We felt intimidated and headed for the sanctuary of a crowded bar. It had a staggering and slurring clientele. We were fortunate to be approached by the only sober person in the place.

'You cannot blame them,' explained Augustus, reading our thoughts. 'Alcohol is their only escape!

'In the seventies, people in their droves were attracted to the town by government incentives and the promise of employment. But now, with the slump in the wool and meat price, the depletion of the oil reserves and the decline of the *frigorifico*, they have been left to fight a daily battle against the wind, dust and boredom. They are trapped here, jobless and without the means of returning north.'

'How come you have kept your sanity?' I asked.

'My dreams are my escape. I was left some land by my uncle and one day I dream of building the southernmost golf course in the world,' Augustus replied.

I could not help but to be sceptical as I thought about who would come to play on this golf course. Certainly not this crowd in the bar, and the few tourists we had met so far had been laden with thermals rather than golf clubs.

As if reading my thoughts, Augustus continued, 'The salmon fishing around here is regarded as some of the best in the world and this already attracts many rich Americans. If I were to build a golf course and a luxury hotel, more would follow.' I had images of 'The Gleneagles of Tierra del Fuego' and I had to admit it had quite a marketing ring.

As we left Augustus shouted out, 'Remember bring your golf clubs next time.'

We were only too pleased to leave Rio Grande the next day. We were bound for Estancia Maria Beherty, which had been part of the estate of Don Jose Menendez, the most famous of all the Patagonian sheep entrepreneurs. This property was managed in the late eighteenth century by a Scotsman, Alexander Maclennan. His victims, the indigenous Ona Indians, gave him a somewhat different name, 'The Red Pig', on account of his ruthless nature and his face made ruddy by constant boozing. He hunted the Indians and lured them into traps by offering food. Maclennan regarded them as 'pests' and 'thieves', while the nomadic Onas saw the sheep as the easy and satisfying prey and the fences as unacceptable encroachments across their traditional lands. The Onas resisted and the white men punished them for their defiance.

Bruce Chatwin wrote,

The Whites came with a new guanaco, sheep and barbed wire. At first the Indians enjoyed the taste of roast lamb, but soon learned to fear the bigger, brown guanaco and its rider that spat invisible death.'

Maclennan did not escape retribution. According to local gossip, he became so haunted by the killings and maddened by alcohol, he ended his days naked, on all fours, eating grass and bellowing like a bull.

One could only sense the past splendour of Maria Beherty. In its day, the farm had supported nearly two hundred *peons* (labourers), fifteen thousand head of sheep and the world's largest sheep-shearing shed. Now it reminded me of a set for a second-rate Hollywood cowboy movie, with its one dusty street, paint peeling off buildings and faded, creaking signs. They suggested a past community: kitchen, library, chapel, office, carpentry and dormitories but several had been left to the ravages of dust, cobwebs and the biting wind. The smell of mutton fat, however, drifting from the *peon's* kitchen hinted at life within.

At supper we shared a table with the nine remaining *peons*. Inevitably, mutton was on the menu – a line of chops stretching across a large metal tray. They produced their knives to hack off the chops and using their hands they attacked the meat.

'It is not always mutton,' one *peon* explained. 'You are unlucky you weren't here two days ago. Then we were given a dish of stewed testicles and penises. Bulls, they were – the very finest quality. Ever so tasty, but perhaps a little salty. Talking of these things, we will be castrating a horse before breakfast tomorrow morning. You are welcome to come and watch.'

For the first time on the expedition we were off as the sun rose. We headed for the vertical borderline which divided Tierra del Fuego between Argentina and Chile. The invisible border followed no river or mountain range but was merely the arbitrating straight line drawn by Queen Victoria at the end of the last century.

The border was unremarkable: a collection of sheds set at either end of an eight mile windswept stretch of no-man's land. No noticeable change in landscape, language, people and no relenting of the wind or the poor condition of the roads. Prices, however, dropped dramatically in the space of a few miles. We had been on the verge of bankruptcy in Argentina on account of the austerity budget which had brought the peso in line with the US dollar. In Ushuaia and Rio Grande, prices had been on a par with London and our budgets had been blown within a matter of hours. Now, in Chile, we could have three beef burgers for the price of one in Argentina. Our bank managers back in England could now breathe a collective sigh of relief.

At the Chilean control, David was involved in an incident which confirmed what Mike and I had suspected for some time. David had not, by any stretch of the imagination, learned any Spanish while he was in Ecuador. When he went off to the toilet, he realised that he had left his helmet at the border post. At first he was unable to make the guard understand what he had come back for, until he used the toilet roll as a prop. He slowly wound the white paper around his head in an imitation of his helmet. The guard took this display to mean that David had hit head and perhaps this would explain his extraordinary gringo behaviour. The first aid box was produced, which prompted shakes and nods from either side. David went searching for another prop, and in the kitchen he found a colander which he put on his head. The guard finally clicked and David returned triumphantly with his white helmet.

It was exhilarating being in Chile for the first time and we made good progress. That is, until four o'clock. We had all decided at the beginning of the expedition to observe the ritual of tea wherever possible. Thus we pulled off the side of the road and, with hail splashing in our cups, we sipped tea and ate chocolate biscuits. I looked up the road and saw two strange forms gradually appearing out of the plumes of dust sent up by a passing lorry. As if in a developing photograph, two cyclists emerged. They looked exhausted and we called out to invite them over to tea. Carole and Dougie readily accepted our offer and within minutes were hungrily devouring the tea and biscuits. It transpired they had only left London eight days before, and had for the last four days endured a baptism of fire on the road from Punta Arenas. The wind, ruts and dust had taken their toll and their morale was now at its lowest ebb because they had run out of food. We were pleased to give them the welcoming news that the border and provisions lay only two hours away.

We set off again into the gathering wind and yet another hailstorm. Our hearts were not in it, and before very long we were looking for a place to stay the night. We spied a small homestead just off the road. The door was slowly opened by a tall, bearded farmer in dungarees, while a young lady peered shyly from the shadows. We asked if we could camp in their field, but were instead ushered to a small room with bunk beds. They introduced themselves as Felix 'like the cat', Margarita 'like the drink' and their five year old daughter, Roxanne. 'Like the song,' I said, but this was greeted with blank stares.

Over supper of soup, lamb chops, pizza and rice pudding washed down with red wine, we were engaged in conversation on the subject most immediate to Chilean hearts: the political debate between Salvador Allende, the ousted head of the Left-Wing Coalition in 1973 and General Pinochet, the leader of the coup and military dictatorship.

'Salvador Allende was our champion: the Champion of the *Peons*. He gave us land and hope,' Felix declared. 'Pinochet and the United States killed that hope along with many innocent people. I remember my maths teacher failed to turn up one day. I heard later that he had been taken in the middle of the night. I never saw or heard of him again.'

I thought of the difference in our lives. We were both thirty and had been at school at the same time. While I had been concerned with making the athletics team and the level of my pocket money, Felix had had to contend with teachers who were 'disappeared'.

Refreshed, we set off the following day into punishing headwinds. Even though our map showed what seemed to be settlements along the way, Felix informed us that they were simply deserted corrugated iron sheds. The next town was the ferry port of Porvenir, which lay about eighty miles away. Two days, we calculated and then a wild Saturday night in Punta Arenas on the other side of the Magellan Straits.

DAY 16 ROAD TO PORVENIR 7 P.M.

'It has been two days of hell. Only managed a mere thirty-eight miles. Our progress has been all the more demoralising by the featureless landscape – no trees, hills, streams or animals. Nothing but brown, patchy spruce grass and the angry sea. The horizon knows no limits. Today we saw a lone distant tree and set our hearts on reaching it by tea. We have now stopped for the day and the tree appears no closer. We must aim for more realistic goals tomorrow – perhaps every four hundred yards. Alarms set for 4 a.m., to try and beat the wind.'

DAY 17 STILL ON THE ROAD TO PORVENIR 10 A.M.

'Awoke at four o'clock and the wind was worse. Pointless to venture out so we slept on. We have struggled on for two hours and are now collapsed behind a gorse bush. Food is the only thing keeping us going, but we are now out of porridge, chocolate, sugar and low on rice and water. It is a dilemma – should we ration ourselves and jeopardise our strength, or keep eating and pray the wind relents. We voted for the latter option.'

Needless to say, the wind kept blowing and we ran out of food and water.

We had one hope – Felix's brother, Victor. He lived at an *estancia* some thirty-five miles before Porvenir. The sun was setting as we scoured the barren landscape for any sign of human habitation – a house, a light, a track. Finally, in the gathering dusk, I spotted a faded sign: 'Estancia Eliena'. Our minds were made up when David started describing an Eliena he once knew: beautiful, blonde hair, blue eyes . . .! With high expectations, we rode up the narrow grassy track and arrived at an immaculate farm tucked in the fold of the hills. For two days we had heard nothing but the constant roar of the wind and now from the house our ears were filled with the sweet music of Vivaldi's *Four Seasons*. Victor was a lover of classical music, I thought, as I knocked on the door.

The gentleman who appeared bore no resemblance to Felix and 'no' he did not know any Victor. He wore a tweed jacket with matching waistcoat and bottle-green cords. A gold watch chain hung from his waistcoat pocket. His dress and the music were all such a far cry from the dust and rigours of the road. Not for the first time, we incited pity and we were shown to a small sheep-shearer's hut.

'Do you need any food?' he asked.

Embarrassed that we had run out, and not wanting to abuse his hospitality, we replied, 'Some bread would be great, thank you'.

He could, however, sense the torment of our self-restraint and said, 'Are you sure you do not want some jam, sweet corn, eggs and steak?' We could not resist, and an array of goodies were presented to us. The two foot slab of meat was certainly quite a test for our Swiss Army knives, stove and small cooking pots, but driven by a ravenous hunger, our powers of improvisation had the meal cooked in two hours.

We had a ferry to catch and at five o'clock the next morning three alarms went off simultaneously. After the initial din, we were left in an unusual peace. Could it be that the wind had finally died, or was it an illusion created by our sheltered location? Buoyed with optimism, we headed for the road to find with relief only the most gentle of breezes. The ferry was now in our grasp – a mere thirty-eight miles in eight hours. Just when it appeared nothing would stop us, Mike had the first puncture of the expedition. It was not so much the time it took to fix, but the psychological damage of knowing our kevlar tyres and latex puncture-resistant inner tubes were not impregnable. These were the tyres that had been sold to us under the slogan, *'made of the same material as bullet-proof vests'*. Perhaps, they would have been effective against gun-slinging bandits, but they were certainly no match for a rusty six inch nail. It took Mike quite a time to re-discover his confidence and to strike up a rhythm again.

DAY 18 NEARING PORVENIR, AT LAST! 11.30 A.M.
'Tiredness and exhaustion has brought friction. D and I have just had an argument and we are not talking. Started when D questioned my motivation behind the expedition, declaring I was driven by ego rather than charity. It hit a raw nerve! Yes, the expedition had been born out of egotistical reasons, but once the commitment to leukaemia had been established the two had become inter-linked. It made me question myself and I hated it! I said many stupid things in the heat of the moment.'

Our simmering tempers drove us at speed into Porvenir and left Mike some way behind, wondering where our sudden spurt of energy had come from. Even the trials and tribulations of the past four days could not transform the town into a beautiful and welcoming place or give credibility to its chosen name – Porvenir, which means *'future'*. We could see no future in the deserted streets and the pre-World War One corrugated iron buildings. *Our* future lay in the ferry to Punta Arenas. With no people around, we looked for a sign giving directions. The sign we did find betrayed the origins of the town but not the way to the ferry – it read: Yugoslavia 18,662 kms (11,600 miles). Porvenir is a Yugoslav enclave. Unrest at home for over a hundred years had sent Yugoslavs searching for freedom, peace and economic opportunities throughout the world. Many arrived in Punta Arenas and then travelled across the water to Tierra del Fuego. Here they were safe from intrusion, but it was not the kind of place many people would choose to spend their 'future'.

I approached a shadow in a doorway and asked the time and the direction for the ferry. I had discovered a philosopher in logic:

'The ferry and the weather have their own time. If it does not leave to day, it will leave tomorrow. If it does not leave tomorrow, it will leave . . .,' he continued. I left, but he had not finished: 'If it does not leave this week . . .'

A week in Porvenir was a sobering thought. A second, maybe third, fourth and fifth opinion was needed. We were given a confusing array of replies: not on Sundays, noon today, four o'clock today and 'buy me a drink and I will tell you'. The only definitive option, it seemed, was to ask the captain of the ferry;

'I will leave when the crew is sober,' came the encouraging reply.

DAY 18 ON A BOAT TO THE MAINLAND 3.30 P.M.
'D and I have made our peace. I am sad to be leaving Tierra del Fuego. Such a wild, mysterious and beautiful island. It was the place where we had first pedalled, where I had seen my first condor and where we had defied death. I would always remember it.'

Perhaps too we would not be forgotten on the island. Some Spanish girls on the ferry related a story they had been told by their guides. It involved three English guys, who were on life-support machines after eating mussels . . .!

—6—
ALLURE OF TORRES

*'Torres del Paine is the sort of park that changes
its visitors . . .'*

South America's National Parks

'Come in my beauties, you are welcome in my house,' purred Dinka,
our amorous Yugoslav landlady in Punta Arenas.

She was in her fifties. Her face was plastered with make-up –
powdered, rouged cheeks, pouting lips of crimson, finely pencilled
eyebrows and a painted beauty spot. You could see the dark roots of
her dyed blonde hair as it was swept up and stacked on the top of
her head. She wore a bright, floral dress which stretched over the
impressive contours of her body. Above all, I will always remember
Dinka for her astonishing cleavage – a plunging valley between twin
Andean peaks.

Dinka had the overwhelming urge during our stay to mother us.
Being the shortest and cutest, I was the one who received the full
force of her motherly and, at times, amorous intentions. Even the
most brief absence would spark a tirade of endearments and the
most passionate of embraces. I remember sneaking in the back door

to try and avoid a confrontation. I stealthily tip-toed through the house and as I reached for the door to our room and safety, the scent of perfume made my fingers tremble on the lock. Fatally, I turned and saw Dinka, resplendent amongst the tassels and fur of her pink dressing gown, advancing down the corridor. With a deep sigh, I succumbed to her embrace.

On another day I returned to hear Dinka sobbing uncontrollably in her bedroom. She sat on the edge of the bed with her head buried in her hands. A newspaper lay open at an account and pictures of the latest atrocities in Yugoslavia. Dinka raised a mascara-streaked face and sobbed, 'My country, a country I have never seen, but of which I am always proud, is tearing itself apart. I do not know where I belong any more.'

Dinka became particularly emotional when we left. It was a full two hours of tears, embraces and photos. I will never forget the sight of Dinka, straddling and suffocating poor *Arriba*. She wore my white cycling helmet perched precariously on top of her bun and sported my wrap-around shades. The final embrace, however, was like a dream. I took a deep breath as my head was pulled into the soft, enveloping floral folds. At first, I felt alarmed but very soon became relaxed as I was serenaded by the soft beat of her heart amongst the overwhelming peace. I was released back into the world feeling faint and dizzy. In a trance, I weaved my way off down the dusty street.

Dinka's direct approach differed from the traditional courtship ritual practised in Punta Arenas. When a girl likes the look of a boy, she will, with the help of her friends, launch into an intensive stalking and spying mission. Her objective is to gain an insight into his habits, beliefs and friends and, most importantly, to find out if he is seeing another woman. These investigations can last as long as four months before the girl is ready to make a formal approach. Unfortunately, our nomadic existence did not allow us to stay long enough to become the targets of such attention. Secretly we were quite relieved, because we had reservations about our credentials to pass a test of such scrutiny.

Punta Arenas (population 113,500) has an almost Dickensian character, with rusting corrugated iron buildings intermingled with grandiose mansions from the turn of the century. The class divisions of old were still apparent; there were elegant parlours and clubs where aperitifs were sipped with aristocratic grace, alongside seedy wooden bars full of sailors, naval recruits and a ubiquitous collection of weary old men, huddled over glasses of *pisco* (local white spirit) and whisky.

The golden era of the city was at the end of the nineteenth century. The industrial age in Europe and North America created a boom in sea trade and Punta Arenas, as the port-of-call for all ships going around the Horn and the World, became one of the busiest ports on earth. All this ended with the completion of the Panama Canal, which made the trip around the Horn no longer necessary. The city remains the hub of oil and gas exploration in Antarctica, fishing and naval activity in the Magallanes and it is the established launching post for expeditions to the ice-cap.

We all dearly wanted to go Antarctica and we tried to hitch a lift there by plane. We had met the support crew of an expedition to commemorate the first crossing of the continent by husky dogs. I remember Alfredo the pilot. He was bursting with pride, because he had been chosen to be the first Chilean to land on the ice-cap. A two week delay in the delivery of supplies meant we were destined to miss the opportunity. It was fate. Some three weeks later we learned the plane had crashed while attempting to land. Alfredo was seriously injured and the husky dogs had run off into the snow never to be seen again.

On the way out of the city, we cycled via the Plaza de Armas, the main square. Here stood a bronze statue to Ferdinand Magellan, looking proudly over the heroic figures of various local Indians. In turn, we touched the shiny toe of his right boot, for legend says it brings fortune to all travellers. We hoped it would bring good luck during our journey up to Puerto Natales, where we were due to meet up with friends from England to explore the Torres del Paine National Park. This ninety mile leg could take us anything from two to six days. Everything hinged on the state of the wind, and the law of averages suggested we were in for a rough ride. We had already decided to prolong the potential agony by taking a hundred mile detour to the beautifully named *Estancia* Skyring.

Skyring was owned by friends of the family, and we had kindly been invited to stay for the weekend. It was not long, however, before we were questioning the wisdom of this decision, when the wind rose and confronted us head-on. The single track road clung to the jagged shoreline of Skyring Sound. In places it came so close to the sea that waves lapped at our tyres and the salt water spray stung our faces. Away from the sea moorland stretched upwards to the craggy white peaks. Sheep grazed in amongst the dead gnarled carcasses of the trees that littered the landscape. Fire and exploitation over a period of a hundred years had killed them, but the extreme cold had preserved them from rotting. Some pockets of pine and occasionally a solitary tree stood bowed but defiant against the harsh wind and weather. Very few people lived on this weather-beaten coast.

David was having problems with his knees, which even under heavy strapping were causing him to grimace in pain as he pushed downwards on the pedals. Mike and I would cycle just ahead to try and shield David from the full force of the wind. It was, however, slow progress, which became even more pedestrian when Mike lost a filling while chewing an Olde English Toffee.

David suddenly forgot about the pain in his knees. Since the expedition had started, he had been dying to use the self-sufficiency dental kit which we had tucked away amongst our medical supplies. He had already read the instructions on administering fillings and had practised the procedure in front of a mirror in Tierra del Fuego. Within seconds, David's hands were in white gloves and he stood poised with file and cement. If I had been in Mike's position, I would not have been very keen either. It was not that we did not think David's intentions were entirely honourable, we simply questioned the delicacy of his fingers. Not wanting to upset David, Mike came up with a diplomatic solution:

'If I allow you to operate on my tooth, you must permit me to take a scalpel to your knee. Is it a deal?'

David quickly took the white gloves off.

It was getting late and we were expected at *Estancia* Skyring. I left David and Mike on the road and cycled down to a nearby farm to let Skyring know of our position by radio. I was welcomed by a farmer with blond hair, blue eyes and a clipped moustache. Any doubts I had of his German origins disappeared when I saw pictures of the Fatherland lining the walls. I had arrived in time for tea and the table was laid with cakes and biscuits. They must have noticed the longing with which I regarded the chocolate cake because they invited me to sit down. Reluctantly, I explained I had to catch up with the others and could I please quickly use their radio. Franz's wife asked how many we were and driven by greed I replied, 'Six' but immediately revised this to, 'Three hungry boys'. When I eventually caught up with David and Mike, I triumphantly produced the food package: it contained six sandwiches, six slices of cake and some pain-killers for David's knees.

In the gathering dusk, we arrived exhausted at *Estancia* Skyring and we were greeted by Gerald Friedli and his wife, Andy. Having dusted ourselves off and changed, we joined them for a pre-dinner drink. We were introduced to *pisco* sour for the first time. *Pisco* is a white spirit which, when mixed with egg white and lemon juice, is both delicious and refreshing. The Chileans drink it to distraction. The glasses were quickly downed and Mike eagerly asked for some more:

'*Esta possible por autre pequena pico sour,*' he said.

This attempt to speak Spanish was greeted by peels of laughter from Andy and Gerald. When Gerald recovered, he translated for our benefit:

'Mike, you have just asked if it is possible to have another small sour willy.'

DAY 24 ESTANCIA SKYRING 9.00 A.M.

'I awoke to the scent of flowers, birdsong and clear blue skies. I heard the distant rumble of the waves on the shingle beach of the Sound. I walked into the garden: roses and pansies were sparkling in the early morning dew. A light breeze carried the scent of pine.'

Estancia Skyring had not always been a place of such peace and tranquillity. 'The Old Man', Gerald's father, recounted the hidden history. He had arrived here in the 1950s in search of land and riches. He had staked out a claim of approximately 22,000 hectares comprising of moorland ideal for grazing sheep and also areas of forest. The Old Man had personally supervised the building of the thirty mile access road.

'In 1970,' he explained, 'I lost everything. I lost my farm to the Communists. I could not understand why or how they could, in one day, take away something I had worked for all my life. I created Skyring with my own bare hands; I bought the land, built the farm and laid the road. I remember the Communist bully boys arriving from Punta Arenas and taking the place over. I should have left with Gerald and Andy, but could not bear to leave. I watched helplessly as my farm deteriorated in front of my eyes: sheep were left unsheared, carcasses rotted in the slaughter-house and pigs roamed in the kitchen garden. By the time General Pinochet came to power, it was all too late. My farm was a shadow of its former self.'

Gerald also remembered these times. 'One minute the children were playing happily in the sunshine and the next minute the Communists arrived. We could not allow them to play outside anymore, because we feared for their safety. One day I was returning from town and there was a drunken man on a horse blocking the road. I hooted my horn and the horse reared up, throwing the man to the ground. He threatened to kill me and my family. I rushed home and stood on watch with a loaded gun for two days. He did not come. This was no place to bring up children and we went to Argentina for sixteen years. At the time, I vowed never to return.

'Now we have other problems. The fall of the wool price and pumas. Last year, pumas killed some three hundred sheep. It was not for survival, but for sport or to teach their young cubs how to hunt. The sheep lie dead in the fields, untouched apart from their ripped throats. Legally, we are helpless to stop this wanton killing because they are on the protected list. There are professional hunters however, who charge us $2,000 (£1,140) per puma.

'Judging from your performance just now you would pose more of a threat to the sheep population than the pumas,' Gerald joked. He had a point. In the last three weeks, eating had become an obsession, as our muscles cried out for strength and our bodies for energy. We had just achieved a prestigious feat at the *asado* (barbecue) where a lamb had been sacrificed in our honour. For two hours we had eaten and now nothing remained but a pile of bones. Thankfully, Maria the maid relished the challenge and threw down the gauntlet; 'I bet you I can produce more food than you can eat!'

'You're on,' we replied.

Maria won with a spicy beef curry the next day. As a rule, cycling and curries just do not mix.

It was Maria and her family who took us fishing on Saturday evening. They took us to a spot where a fast-flowing river met the turbulent salt water of the Sound. I was armed with my telescopic rod and assortment of feathers and spinners. In contrast, the locals had battered processed pea cans. I watched with a confident and cocky air as they unravelled the knotted nylon and rusty spinners and with a lasso technique threw their lines into the river. They looked on with fascination as I pulled the rod out to its full length, threaded the smooth nylon through the seven eyelets and deftly tied a carefully chosen spinner. I released the catch on the reel. In one smooth movement I curved the rod backwards and flicked my wrists. It was a beautiful cast. The spinner glimmered in the moonlight as it looped upwards. I had not allowed, however, for the strong wind. It cleared the far river bank and landed in an adjacent field.

'So you *are* out to catch some sheep,' laughed Maria.

The final score was four salmon to the tin cans and a big round zero to my telescopic rod.

We had to exercise a lot of self-discipline to leave Skyring. The blow was softened, however, by a strong following wind. It was while we were racing at high speed that *Arriba* became a victim of my superstitious nature. I think I inherited it from my mother. I will never walk under a ladder, will always touch wood and will never tempt fate. I had taken on the expedition an array of lucky trinkets: a silver sixpence, a silver horseshoe and a Saint Christopher. I also treasured the silver dollar given to us by Tommy Goodall. When I saw an aluminium horseshoe lying in the road, I just had to stop. I slammed on the brakes and in doing so took Mike and *Shadowfax* by surprise. They came careering into the back of *Arriba* and we all collapsed into an unsightly heap in what was our first accident of the expedition.

'Some lucky horseshoe,' said Mike sarcastically.

I carried that horseshoe all the way to Lake Titicaca.

Soon after the collision we met Lionel and Lois. They had met in Auckland Airport: Lionel from France cycling around the world, and Lois from New Zealand escaping a marriage proposal. On the plane to Buenos Aires they had decided to cycle together. Before setting off, the experienced Lionel went through Lois' panniers and found thirteen pairs of knickers. 'What are you doing with these? You only need two. Throw the rest away,' he ordered. It was the start of a beautiful relationship; they were now very much in love.

We could all sympathise with Lois, not because we each carried thirteen pairs of boxer shorts, but in comparison to Lionel we were embarrassingly decadent. He did not have a stove, but preferred to use candles for his coffee in the morning and existed on cold food. Carrots and bananas seemed to be his favourites of the moment. He carried a total of nine items of clothing while we each weighed in at about forty items each. We did not allow Lionel anywhere near our panniers, but I would dearly liked to have seen his face as we pulled out the brogues, jeans, cassette recorder, bottle of wine for the evening meal and, of course, the horseshoe.

In the evening David was struggling with his diary. He was talking incessantly and seeking distractions while Mike and I wrote down the day's events from our own individual perspectives. During the day, David had attempted to use a Dictaphone to record his thoughts. This enterprising ploy had, however, ended in failure because the strong wind had drowned out all his choice comments.

DAY 26 DAVID'S DIARY - DIARY HASSLES

'2nd Nov - 32 miles; paved road; very strong headwind; max speed 12mph; Av speed 5 mph (I should re-calibrate speedo to km/hr then figures won't be quite so depressing!); 9.5 hrs cycling (incl. breaks); stopped 60 miles S of PN.

How do R&M enjoy writing their diaries? Just cycled all day into the wind (surprise, surprise) and now in the late light of the evening - tent up and fed, they quietly relax by writing today's entries into their diaries. M's diary is all neat in a hard backed A5 note book and is full of poems, descriptions of colourful landscapes and arty maps, while R's is rough, dog-eared foolscap with dramatised events hastily scribbled down. I find their discipline and obvious enjoyment rather impressive. Much as I try to keep this diary up to date I still find it tedious to write and boring to read. They are beginning to give me a guilt complex - been looking for an excuse not to write tonight - even the washing-up is preferable!'

We were all heading for the town of Puerto Natales some sixty miles away. After a hard morning battling the wind, we left Lionel and Lois to go on while we stopped for some lunch. Mike and I made the fatal mistake of eating too much and by the time we were back on the bikes our minds were dominated by thoughts of a siesta. David, on the other hand, was raring to go and was insistent on making it to Puerto Natales by nightfall. We had a plan! It was just a matter of time before David stopped for a call of nature. Mike and I sped ahead and on finding a grassy bank fell asleep before he reached us. It was a sleep democracy and David was forced to join us. Even with the luxury of the siesta, we made it to Puerto Natales as darkness fell. In our elation we arrived singing the Simon and Garfunkel song, 'Cecilia, you're breaking my heart.' We had a good reason: we planned to stay at a hostel called Casa Cecilia.

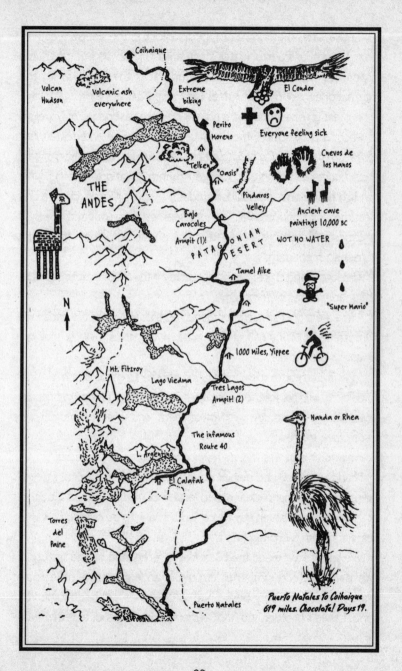

Coihaique

Volcan Hudson

Volcanic ash everywhere

Extreme biking

El Condor

Perito Moreno

Everyone feeling sick

Telken

"Oasis"

Chevos de los Manos

THE ANDES

Pindaros Velley

Ancient cave paintings 10,000 BC

Bajo Carocoles

Armpit (1)!

PATAGONIAN DESERT

WOT NO WATER

N

Tamel Aike

"Super Mario"

1000 miles, Yippee

Mt. Fitzroy

Lago Viedma

Tres Lagos

Armpit! (2)

Nanda or Rhea

The infamous Route 40

L. Argentino

El Calafak

Torres del Paine

Puerto Natales

Puerto Natales to Coihaique
619 miles. Chocolate! Days 19.

Cecilia is not the only reason people flock to the sleepy, weather-board town of Puerto Natales, situated on the shores of *Ultima Esperanza Sound* (Last Hope Sound). It is the gateway to the internationally renowned Torres del Paine National Park.

'It is not a mere park, but a park of parks, a destination of travellers to whom a park is more than a place in which to be entertained, but rather an experience to be integrated into one's life. It is the sort of park that changes its visitors . . .' (South America's National Parks).

High praise and expectations indeed – could it really change and become a part of one's life? The idea seemed ridiculous and it reeked of tourism hyperbole. I arrived at the entrance to the Park with a hardened scepticism.

The loving and child-like translation from the Chilean Tourist Board softened my negative thoughts:

'Here there are divers environments represented, with flora and fauna characteristics of the Magallanes zone, and that as a whole they are unique in the world.

We invited you to know, to enjoy its beautiful landscapes and specially to enjoy its wildlife, for that wake up in you your love for them, because when we love somebody, we protect them, and when we protect, we insure their existence.

Help us to that this love be multiply and would be perpetual.'

I had always relished being in love. Until now I had not considered falling for a national park and a collection of wildlife. Could it be that at the end of our seven day trek, I would have to be dragged away in tears and with a broken heart?

We spent a week off the bikes being serenaded by the beauty of the park and walking the '*circuito*', an eighty-five mile loop encompassing the very best it had to offer. We had been joined by Jono, David's brother and Nick, a friend from England, together with several people we had met at Casa Cecilia: Felicity from Australia, Kate from England and Charles, Elkie and Chris from Belgium.

Our team was first drawn to the 'Towers of Paine', which give the park its name. As we approached we saw that they were mere stumps, swathed in swirling grey clouds. We could only guess at their height and shape – a guess the inclement weather forces many a visitor to make.

DAY 32 TORRES DEL PAINE 4.30 P.M.

'The clouds were not there to keep the towers secret. They were nature's form of gift-wrapping. Suddenly, the clouds unfurled and parted to reveal three majestic granite monoliths reaching for the sky. The sun hit the sheer grey faces, turning them a splendid pink. They glowed and seem to melt the encroaching cloud. No one spoke or moved – this was a memory we would treasure forever.'

The towers, while being stunning and beautiful, were too strange and mysterious to inspire love.

On the second day, we reached the plains. Herds of guanacos glided with grace and dignity among the grasses of the rippling golden plains. Their necks and legs were the colour of sunshine on sand, while their bodies were covered in a fine fleece the shade of biscuit brown. With white-tipped ears pricked and necks extended, they watched our progress inquisitively through their enormous brown liquid eyes. Occasionally, they blinked and fluttered their long curled eye lashes seductively. I did not, however, fall in love. Their supercilious expression and legendary spitting habits left me cold and explained why the water-canons used on protesters during the Pinochet dictatorship were nick-named, 'guanacos'.

The mottled grey rheas – South America's answer to the African ostrich – were, in contrast, noisy and skittish. One minute they would be strutting sedately with chests puffed out, the next they were squawking and fleeing in a rolling run resembling the gait of a professional American footballer. As John Pilkington said of the rhea, *'it's a cowardly bird, and if Patagonia had more sand I'm sure the rhea would spend much of its time with its head in it.'* The rheas were too flighty to be trusted with love.

We left the grasslands and started to climb.

DAY 34 MIKE'S DIARY – PASO JOHN GARDNER 12.30 P.M.

'We climbed through the emerald green beech forest along the side of the fast-moving Rio de los Perros. The trees became thinner and we were faced with a grey wall of scree leading up to Paso John Gardner. I at once set about the ascent, anxious to reach the pass and catch a few minutes alone. Nothing which had gone before prepared me for the view from the top. It was without doubt the most beautiful I have ever seen; it sent a tingle down my spine and made the small hairs on my neck stand on end. Below, resembling an expanse of cloud lay Glacier Grey, glistening white in the pale sunlight. I marvelled at the strength and the size of this wall of ice. A condor glided just above my head, close enough for our eyes to meet. I felt for that fleeting moment that we were kindred spirits. Yes, this was what life was all about and yes, I was indeed very happy.'

We found Mike bewitched at the top. It must surely be one of the finest views in South America. Below and beyond, Glacier Grey swept down the valley from the north-west. It was a contorted tongue of ice unfurling and rasping its way through the mountains. Defying its name, it was white, highlighted by areas of dazzling steely-blue. I followed its course right from the forked tip to where it disappeared into the sky, high up on the icecap. It did indeed have its origins in another world. It was too alien for love.

The path down off the pass and along the side of the glacier was hazardous. It was riddled with landslides, collapsed bridges and fallen tree trunks. While I cursed my every fall, I realised that out here, away from the roads and hotels, Torres del Paine would always remain one of the most untouched wildernesses on earth. No amount of money or engineering expertise could ever tame the combination of the fierce weather and harsh, inaccessible terrain. In the last four days, we had only seen eight other people. We felt an overwhelming sense of freedom and honour to have this paradise of nature all to ourselves. There were risks – we had all signed a form at the entrance declaring that our death was our responsibility. Within three weeks of our trek, three people had been killed in separate accidents and two others were missing.

On my part, I escaped with only losing my sight. It happened as I was walking slowly across a narrow log bridging a fast-flowing stream. In either hand, I clutched a long pole to give me confidence and balance. For the mosquitoes lurking in the eddies of water, I was a proverbial sitting duck and they knew it! They ambushed me halfway across, attacking my arms, legs and face. I had a dilemma: resist and risk falling, or be bitten. With gritted teeth, I opted for the latter. I saw him coming, body stretched, wings rigid and probius aimed for my right eye. I blinked too late and he scored a direct hit. Blood was not his prize, but instead a gas-permeable contact lens. He was not a short-sighted mosquito, because he chose to discard it in the stream after only ten yards. My lens is now buried somewhere in Glacier Grey.

With or without a contact lens, my thoughts and dreams were still haunted by the mysterious Towers. To this day, I cannot explain my actions and feelings.

DAY 37 CAMP BRITANICO 4.45 P.M.

'*We could see the peaks of the towers rising above the ridge. I felt lured and compelled by them! D and I climbed and became separated from the others. The higher we climbed, the greater the excitement as the towers rose before us. Ice and scree littered our path. The weather was closing in. Only twenty minutes to the top. After forty minutes we were still climbing, held by an irresistible force. Did this explain the mystery of 'Picnic at Hanging Rock'? I heard D's distant voice echoing around the rocks, "We must, we must go down! Go down." No, they are so tantalisingly close. We could not give up – a few more minutes and we would be able to touch them. I felt D's hand on mine, dragging me downwards. The spell was broken. At the time, I thought I would never forgive him. By the time we stumbled back into the camp, we had been away for three hours. The others were relieved and angry, and on the verge of calling in the mountain rescue.*'

It was only on the sixth night that I wished I was somewhere else. We were camped by the sapphire waters of Lake Pehoe – we had only a bag of rice, no wood for a fire and little shelter from the biting cold wind blowing off Glacier Grey. Previously, we had found campsites nestling amongst the beech forests or a *refugio* (a wooden and corrugated iron shelter). A typical night had been to eat to distraction and then recount stories around the fire, before retiring to bed. Now, we could but dream! We taunted ourselves with the thought of luxuries we left at home – Theakston beer, taramasalata, Haagen-Daaz ice-cream and a hot bath. A young Racquel Welch also slipped into the conversation and was voted the most desirable person with whom to share a sleeping bag.

Relief came from two unlikely sources – horse dung and a bottle of mayonnaise. I stepped in the dung while I went off on a call of nature and after my initial annoyance, I thought, why not burn it? If you ignored the fruity smell, it made an excellent fire of glowing blue flames and emitted sufficient heat to keep us warm. The bottle of mayonnaise was found hiding at the bottom of David's rucksack. When mixed with the rice, our meagre rations were transformed into a gastronomic delight. There is nothing like a combination of dung and mayonnaise to lift the spirits.

In all, we spent seven days trekking in the park. I will always treasure the memory of the majestic towers, the dazzling blue of the ice-caves, the vivid sapphire waters of Lake Pehoe, the emerald green of the beech forests and the sheer power and mystery of Glacier Grey. I would also remember the grace and the heraldic poise of the guanacos and the squawking rolling run of the rheas. Together, they had weaved a wonderful web of memories, but not love. Perhaps I was too English and too reserved to lose my heart to nature and wildlife? I had, however, succumbed to a more conventional love. I had fallen in love with Felicity. We had walked, talked, shared rucksacks, split a chocolate bar, saved each other from falling and ultimately shared a tent. It all seemed as natural as the setting. On the last day, we picked the red berries of the box-leafed calafate bush. The berries are thought to be the elixir of Patagonia – one taste will compel you to return. We kissed through blood red lips and dearly hoped so.

—7—
MONSTERS
AND GLACIERS

*"'Please can I have the piece of brontosaurus." Never in my
life have I wanted anything as I wanted that piece of skin'*

BRUCE CHATWIN 'In Patagonia'

*'The ice was here, the ice was there
The ice was all around:
It cracked and growled, and roared and howled
Like noises in a swound!'*

COLERIDGE 'The Rime of the Ancient Mariner'

Ahead lay the plains and deserts of Patagonia. For years, its very
name had inspired me to seek out the mysteries it held. Now, at last,
its secrets lay before us . . .

Patagonia is a land of legendary monsters. The strangest of these
were the giant glyptodons and ground sloths. The glyptodons roamed
and grazed over the empty plains. They were heavily armoured –
bodies cased in rigid shells nine foot long, heads protected by bony
shields and tails covered with knobs and spines. Against what unknown

threat did they need such protection? It was not, however, to ward off the attentions of the giant ground sloths. They were herbivores and fuelled their huge bulk, the size of an elephant, by eating vast quantities of foliage, bugs and insects. They must have resembled King Kong, as they rose up on their hind legs to a height of ten feet to claw down the branches of trees and pick off food with their curled upper lips. These monsters were marooned in time and were still roaming the Patagonian wilderness when man arrived.

The Patagonian man mirrored the giant beasts of the plains. Ferdinand Magellan, while sheltering from a storm during his round-the-world voyage in 1520, noticed a gigantic figure on the beach. The man wore only a guanaco skin and rough hide moccasins, and was dancing, leaping and singing in the most strange way. Antonia Pigafetta, Magellan's chronicler, was impressed by this Tehuelche Indian. *'So tall was this man,'* he wrote, *'that we came up to the level of his waist-belt. He was well enough made, and had a broad face, painted red, with yellow circles round his eyes, and two heart-shaped spots on his cheeks.'* Magellan, however, was more staggered by the size of this Indian's feet. *'Ha, Patagon!'* (Wow, Bigfeet!) he exclaimed and the land became known as Patagonia – 'The Land of the Bigfeet'.

With the arrival of the Europeans, the Tehuelche Indians slowly became extinct, but their legendary feet achieved immortality as well as one of the beasts of the plain. Milodons, a species of giant sloth, were thought still to be around at the turn of the century. In 1895, a German sea captain, Hermann Eberhardt, while exploring a cave on the shores of the Last Hope Sound, discovered a strange four foot stretch of red-haired scaly skin, embedded in the powdered rock. A year later, a Swedish explorer found a huge eye socket, a claw and a putrefying heap of bones. Meanwhile, Listai, an Argentine scientist, announced the scaly skin was so fresh that the beast had only recently died and a surviving example could not be far away. This verdict attracted much interest, and in 1900 the *Daily Express* sent the zoologist Hesketh Prichard to find a living specimen. Despite reports from *estancias* of 'positive' sightings of the huge hairy beasts and hearing many Indian tales, no example was ever found and little more than piles of sloth dung were unearthed in the cave. Years later, radio-carbon dating on the remains revealed the futility of the quest, by showing that the skin was about 10,000 years old. Despite the failure, Prichard's book on the expedition gave Arthur Conan Doyle the idea for *The Lost World*. This cave had also provided the focal point for Bruce Chatwin's classic travel book, *In Patagonia*.

We wanted to see the Milodon cave for ourselves. We had fondly imagined it would mean an arduous journey along narrow, twisting paths and much searching amongst the limestone cliffs to reach the cave on the shores of Last Hope Sound. We were disappointed. A road now takes air-conditioned buses there from Puerto Natales. Many other things had changed. Chatwin had either been exaggerating or the cave had shrunk – instead of a gaping mouth some 400 feet wide, it now appeared a somewhat modest 150 feet across. Neither could we find a piece of 'coarse reddish hair' embedded in the cave wall or a pungent pile of sloth dung. In their place, we discovered swept concrete paths, a ten foot fibre-glass model of one of the past inhabitants, graffiti on the salt-encrusted walls and a group of clicking and whooping Japanese tourists. The cave of myths and legends had been destroyed – no Milodons or Tehuelche Indians would ever be coming back, only streams of tourists.

We set off northwards to the Chilean/Argentine border. For the time being our days in Chile were over because from here the thin country tapered off into an impenetrable land riddled with fjords, islands and glaciers. The only way north was to the east of the Andes, far removed from the cool sea breezes, swirling mists and leaden skies we had become accustomed to. It meant cycling in Argentina through the fierce arid wastes of the Patagonian desert.

We planned to take a sixty mile short cut across the border and the Andes to the town of Calafate, situated on the edge of the desert and close to the Perito Moreno glacier. We had been given special permission to cycle through the closed *Paso* Zapata; obtained from the Argentine Consulate with help from the British Consul in Punta Arenas, John Rees. This route would save us a vital ninety miles.

On arriving at the Chilean border post, we explained our plan and showed the letter of authorisation. *El Capitan* of the border control became most animated and distressed.

'There is no way I will allow you to attempt it. It is too dangerous. The road has been mined and the bridges blown, during our last confrontation with Argentina. I already have three Swiss climbers up there, who have now been missing for three weeks.'

'But what about the letter of approval? The Argentines seem to think the road is safe,' I pointed out.

'What do they know? Dressed in suits and stuck in their cosy, heated offices in Punta Arenas. They do not know and have probably never seen these mountains. It is the weather that makes them dangerous! Believe me, if it snows you will be stranded up there for weeks, with no one to help you. I do not want your blood on my hands!' *El Capitan* declared with an air of finality.

To be told we should not go was a numbing anticlimax. We had been looking forward to, and were prepared for, cycling through snow, crossing an abandoned border post and wading through icy waters with the bikes on our shoulders.

'What the hell, let's do it anyway!' was our initial thought. 'After all, we could always turn back if the going became impossible. Then at least we could say we had tried.'

The memory of the mussels undermined these thoughts. Caution now crept into our discussions.

DAY 44 AT THE CHILEAN BORDER

'We were vulnerable in this strange land. There were so many things out there which we did not understand and were beyond our control. If we ignored El Capitan, we would be endangering ourselves and the lives of those who came to save us. We would just have to live without knowing what would have happened up at Paso Zapata.'

We may have saved ourselves from the pass, but not from a malicious elastic bungee which held a tent and sleeping bag to the rack. In no-man's-land, still within sight of the border, such a strap got caught in David's spokes. It did not look immediately serious until we noticed that part of the broken bungee had become imbedded in the chamber holding the axle bearings. Our worse fears were confirmed when, instead of spinning freely, the wheel soon came to a grinding halt. We returned to the border post for the delicate operation of removing the bearings and cleaning the chamber of all fragments of elastic. It took hours and in that time we attracted quite a crowd of people – mainly tourists waiting for their passports to be stamped. A group of Germans came over to us clicked their tongues and shook their heads in unison.

'It is not good. Das ist kaputt,' one of them said helpfully.

'Ja, Ja,' replied a chorus of voices.

Just the sort of encouragement we needed. They were wrong: with the help of the mechanical skills of El Capitan, we were on the road again within two hours.

Our relief was short-lived. The skies suddenly darkened and we were caught in a violent hailstorm. The icy stones stung my face and pelted my bare arms and legs. They fell with such velocity that they sounded like a machine gun going off as they crashed into the road and ricocheted in all directions. I jumped off *Arriba* and knelt down in a crouch position with my head buried between my knees. While I held this undignified pose for some ten minutes, two thoughts came to my mind: thank goodness the Germans had not seen us like this, and what would this storm have been like in the mountains?

To make up the time and miles we had lost, we cycled until 10.30 p.m. In the dusk, we set up camp. We were intent on becoming acclimatised to life with one tent, for *Taddie* was on the short list to be chucked before attempting the desert. We had tried three in a tent before. It had proved to be a long ordeal. I had awoken to find Mike breathing in my ear and subconsciously stroking my hair. David had complained of constant snoring interspersed with bouts of flatulence. Mike had dreamt he was a tube of toothpaste as he lay squeezed in the middle. It was an experience we did not relish repeating.

We drew lots and, having lost I ended up under the stars. Cocooned and naked within my sleeping bag and silk in-liner, I felt warm and secure. Sleep came easily. Shooting stars raced across the sky, a cool breeze caressed my face and I was lulled by the mating calls of Patagonian hares. I awoke at first light. The sun rose slowly over the horizon and bathed the undulating plains in a rosy hue. In the light, the dew glistened like sparkling jewels and flames seemed to leap from the tips of the yellow spruce grass. I rolled over and heard a cracking noise. I moved again and the same sound followed. I looked down my sleeping bag. It was not bright pink anymore but white with encrusted ice.

A bone of contention so far in the expedition had been our ability to get up and off early in the mornings. I hated to lie in with a day's cycling in front of us, while Mike and David positively relished the opportunity. I found it the more frustrating because the mornings tended to be blessed with a gentle breeze. The Patagonian wind was a late riser and tended, as a rule, to blow through at about eleven o'clock, just as we would be setting off. I know that I drove Mike and David to distraction with my constant nagging and endless attempts at trying to get them out of bed. In the past, I had dismantled the tent, thrown cold water over their faces and with more subtlety offered them a strong cup of coffee at six o'clock.

DAY 45 DAVID'S DIARY - IRRITATING R

'R is on an all time high now that we are on the road - endless amounts of energy that is not being sapped by cycling. He has so much excess energy that he is irritating me. Have nicknamed the "terrier" for his incessant yapping and snapping at our heels. I am glad that he is irritating M too. This calms an underlying fear I have of the IMG boys making an unspoken pact (marketing versus engineering!) and always forming the majority. There is an up-side to R's high though - instead of his usual noise (read pestering) in the morning he brought M and me some 'strong' coffee in bed. Playing up to R's ever eagerness to get underway M & I managed to snatch a further half hour snooze while the coffee cooled!'

These methods had only succeeded in strengthening their resolve. A new tactic was needed.

In a moment of inspiration I positioned the cassette player just out of reach of the tent and turned on Tina Turner at full blast. They had to get out of bed to switch it off.

Thanks to Tina Turner we were on the road early. We expected *Ruta Quarenta* (Route 40) to be bad, but it came as a surprise that it was nothing more than a farm track. It was quiet though and guanacos, rheas, foxes and Patagonian hares watched us from amongst the rocks and spruce grass. It was not long before David got the call of nature induced by porridge – a daily occurrence brought on by several undulating hours in the saddle. It was not the ideal place – no bushes or trees to be seen on the flat terrain, but it was not the time for prudish hesitation. The plume of dust advancing quickly from behind us went unnoticed. David was concentrating and distracted. The wind muffled the sound of the engine until it was too late. The audience was captive and wide-eyed. Certainly, the sisters of the Francesian Order had never seen a sight quite like it.

'That is Patagonia for you!' I imagined the driver announcing.

David blushed with all four cheeks.

We headed for El Cerrito – a place marked in big letters and bold type on our map. We thought we would have lunch here before the long run into the town of Calafate. We arrived at the junction where Cerrito was situated. There was nothing apart from the decayed evidence of a building not much larger than a garden shed. It offered no shelter from the weather. We were forced to run the gauntlet of isolated squalls. They came sweeping in from the snow-capped Andes to the west, bringing buffeting winds and drenching downpours. They approached in waves. We searched for gaps within these leaden curtains, often having to pedal like mad or slow down. We tried to grab some lunch, but a squall developed from nowhere soaking us and blowing the sandwiches from our hands. Wet and exhausted, we arrived in the glacier town of Calafate as darkness fell.

We wondered why we had bothered! Calafate, owing to its proximity to the famous Perito Moreno glacier, is a victim of tourism and commercialism. The sight of numerous gringos walking aimlessly amongst the gauche Swiss chocolate shops, French patisseries and mock cowboy restaurants was all too much. We had to fight the urge to cycle back out again into the primitive untouched plains of Patagonia. The lure of the glacier, however, kept us there.

It would have taken three days to cycle to and from the glacier. To save time and to keep on schedule for the town of Coihaique by

Christmas, we swallowed deeply and took the tourist bus. It was a sobering experience. On entering the bus we relinquished our freedom and became anonymous items on a production line designed to make money. The commentary was dictatorial and patronising.

'Lavatory stop, the last for one hour. You have ten minutes. Do not be late!' 'Do try some *mate*, the traditional drink of the Argentine. Only one dollar a sip.' 'Time to get off the bus and pay for entrance to the park.'

I looked out the dusty window to seek some relief. It only increased my claustrophobia. My senses were all immune to the surroundings beyond the window. My eyes never had the time to focus and appreciate the beauty of the landscape. I had to rely on a couple behind me:

'Look, honey, there's a dead sheep by the side of the road.' 'Hey doll, see that there rock, it looks like an elephant.'

Their accents mingled with the deep drone of the engine and my sense of smell did not escape the stench of petrol. I recalled the words of the travel writer, Eric Newby: *'If there is any way of seeing less of a country than from a motor-car, I have yet to find it.'* I longed for *Arriba* . . .

'We are stopping for lunch. You have exactly one hour.' Now was my chance to escape! I asked Georgina, our glamorous tour guide and the one beautiful sight to remain unblemished by the couple's commentary, how far it was to the glacier. Eight miles was a small price to pay for freedom and I decided to walk it.

DAY 46 PERITO MORENO GLACIER

'The glacier is truly spectacular and majestic. A white gleaming tongue uncoiling down from a distant mouth high up on the ice cap. Rasping at the mountainous shores and licking at the waters of Lago Argentino. Its tip is alive and moving. With a resounding roar, vast chunks of ice are disgorged

*into the water, sending waves crashing against the rocks. Oh, the power
and beauty of nature.'*

The *Perito Moreno* glacier, standing at one hundred and sixty-five feet
high and two miles across, remains defiant and invincible to the
scourge of global warming. It is one of the few glaciers in the world
that is growing. In an approximate four year cycle, it advances to
meet a spit of land, thus cutting off a portion of the lake. The water in
the separated part begins to rise, and the pressure builds until, finally,
the water breaks through the icy dam to rejoin the rest of the lake.
The collapse is breathtaking and the roar of crashing ice, we were
told, could be heard in Calafate some fifty miles away. It was now
mid-cycle and we certainly were not going to wait two years.

I had lost track of time and committed the terrible crime of returning
late to the bus. I was reprimanded and greeted by much clicking of
tongues. Mike and David had not been so distracted by the beauty
of the glacier and had indulged in the pleasures of chatting up Georgina.
An hour of British charm and humour had initiated the response, 'I
am sorry, I prefer tall blond Germans'. More racism was to follow.
We passed an *estancia* which had been the home of a British family.
We were told they hunted Indians and claimed bounty on their ears.
We were singled out for looks of severe disapproval. I could not wait
to get off the bus.

We just had to leave the following day and we set about the
preparations. Mike and I went off to buy provisions for the desert,
while David went off to report to the army that we had made it
safely across the mountains – a condition of the approval from the
Argentine Consulate. We thought it was a formality, but instead we
were ordered to present ourselves and our passports to the
Commandant the next day. We wondered why.

'Please sit down,' the Commandant greeted us. He was an ugly, bullish man, with sagging jowls and a protruding belly. An oily sheen covered his puckered skin. His dark hair was heavily greased and he constantly fingered the tips of an overbearing handle-bar moustache. Judging from the decor around the room, he was a vain man. A flattering portrait dominated one wall and a full length mirror sat opposite his desk. Some medals were displayed in a glass case.

'Hello David, it is a pleasure to see you again. You sit here,' he smiled, indicating a chair in touching distance from his desk.

He did not seem at all interested in our passports. He ignored Mike and me, and turned all his attention to David. He was flirting.

'Come on, let's have an arm wrestle,' he urged. 'I will show you my strength.' He won, but not without many beads of sweat appearing on his greasy forehead.

'I will show you my medals,' he continued.

It was all very nauseating but thankfully David was not impressed!

BLAZING SADDLES

*'In calling up images of the past, I find the plains of
Patagonia frequently pass across my eyes; yet these
plains are pronounced by all to be useless. They can be
described only by negative characters; without
habitation, without water, without trees, without
mountains, they support merely a few dwarf plants.
Why, then, and the case is not peculiar to myself, have
these arid wastes taken so firm a hold on my memory?'*

CHARLES DARWIN 'Voyage of the Beagle'

'From Calafate, the cycling becomes a veritable nightmare,' Hallam
Murray had warned. 'Route 40 takes you north some four hundred
miles through one of the most inhospitable places on earth – the
desert of Patagonia. Mile upon mile of little water, sparse population,
ferocious wind compounded by appalling road conditions. My advice
would be not to take it! I, for one, nearly lost it out there.'

This was the 'mouth-watering' prospect we faced for the two
weeks leading up to Christmas. No parties, carol singing or last-

minute shopping for us, just a desert to pedal through. It promised to be a Christmas to remember . . .

The police in Calafate echoed this warning and fuelled our fears.

'Where can we expect to get water out there?' I had asked.

'That is an easy question. You can't,' the policeman replied, shaking his head. 'I would not attempt it by car let alone by bicycle. You are *muy muy loco* (stark raving mad).'

He told us, therefore, nothing we had not heard before.

If ever there was a time to be ruthless with our baggage, this was it! We needed to create room for extra food and water if we were to attempt the desert and survive. Some pieces of equipment we had considered to be necessities on leaving England were either sold or sent up to Santiago. First to go was *Taddie* the tent – a difficult and an emotional decision for David, in particular, as it had been his saving thought during the embrace at Miami Airport. The second stove was sold and used film, surplus tools, spare batteries and some fifty nuts and bolts were all boxed up and sent.

Our medical kit was a prestigious size. Felicity of Torres del Paine fame, was a pharmacist by trade and she helped in cutting it down by half.

'You are a bunch of hypochondriac junkies,' Felicity observed with some justification. 'One hypodermic syringe, not fifteen, and chuck these four different tubes of mosquito repellent. This dental kit has to go, it's a gimmick!' Mike and I smiled and breathed a sigh of relief. I was particularly chuffed as I had surreptitiously slipped two tapes into the box – Mike's *Tubular Bells* and David's *Elton John Collection*. It would mean uninterrupted Tina Turner and Ennio Morricone for the road ahead.

We calculated it was just over five hundred miles to Coihaique, our Christmas destination. We had twelve days which meant averaging forty-one miles per day. On paper it seemed an easy prospect, but pedalling fully loaded bikes through clogging sand in the searing heat, we knew it was going to be difficult. We had identified three staging posts where we could find food and water: Tres Lagos (98 miles), Bajo Caracoles (320 miles) and Perito Moreno (400 miles). With trepidation, we set off into the desert. We carried five day's worth of food, consisting of a mixture of pasta, rice, tuna, pate, porridge, biscuits, packet soup and chocolate – hardly a gastronomic combination but it should get us to Tres Lagos. We risked seven litres of water per bike: a bare minimum for cooking and quenching thirst in the searing temperatures. With all this new weight, the bikes felt sluggish and cumbersome.

DAY 47 ENTERING THE DESERT 3.00 P.M.

'It is a wilderness. A parched and barren land devoid of life and colour stretched out before us. Already, I am finding the monotony and emptiness oppressive. Only an occasional scrub bush, tuft of grass, turn in the road or an outcrop of rock, to break up the boredom. I feel an overwhelming urge to cycle faster and leave it all behind. Sand dunes spill onto the road, pulling at the tyres and dragging the bikes down. How the hell am I going to survive four hundred miles of this without being driven mad? The sun beat down relentlessly and there was no avoiding it, in this undulating landscape of sand, rocks and spruce grass. I had never seen so many shades of brown.'
I escaped into day dreams.

DAY 48 DAY DREAMING 5.00 P.M.

'Today I dreamt I scored a century for England. Coming in at four wickets down and two hundred and fifty runs needed for victory to decide the Test Series against Australia. Logic dictated caution, but I set about taking apart the Aussie attack. I relived every shot – a sweeping on-drive, a scything hook and a six straight over the bowler's head. The match-winning innings lasted four hours.

In the afternoon, I was playing in the F.A. Cup Final for Southampton against Manchester United. After thirty minutes, we were two goals down and the situation looked hopeless. We conceded a penalty. If it went in, it had to be all over! It was brilliantly saved. It was the inspiration we needed and we came storming back in the second half. Two goals and we were level. The last five minutes saw both sides going all out for a winner. I took the ball thirty yards out, jinxed past two players and hit a swerving shot into the top left hand corner. The crowd went wild. I saw my grandfather with tears running down his face in the front row.'

With the cheering still ringing in my ears, Mike cycled into a flock of rheas. There were fifteen of them grazing peacefully by the side of the road when he came storming around the corner. Immediate panic ensued and instead of swerving into the scrub, they set off at full pelt down the road with Mike in their wake. They lowered their necks as they ran and their gangling legs flew all over the place as they gathered speed. Mike clocked them at twenty-eight miles an hour on his speedometer. After about a mile, one of them had a bright idea and left the road. The others followed, bouncing off into the distance.

The rheas left us at Estancia Lucia – a splash of life and colour hidden in the folds of the brown landscape. We were shown through a wicket gate flanked by white and pink roses into a field surrounded by poplars. To our surprise, there was another tent, from which protruded two enormous feet. They belonged to Michel, a Frenchman walking all the way from Bolivia to Ushuaia. I was intrigued; perhaps we had met someone crazier than ourselves.

'But, why do you do it?' I asked.

'I love it,' Michel replied. 'It is only when I am walking that I have time to think and experience true peace.' There was no questioning the sanity of the answer.

To ward off the monotony, I had also taken up song-writing and singing. It passed the time and gave me a rhythm to drive my aching limbs. Mike and David tended to keep out of earshot.

DAY 49 SONG WRITING 12.30 P.M.
'I stole the tune and some words from Andrew Lloyd Webber's musical,
Evita.

> *We won't cry for you, Patagonia.*
> *The truth is we cannot leave you.*
> *Stranded in your desert,*
> *A mad existence,*
> *We keep on cycling,*
> *You keep your distance.*
> *And as for thirst*
> *And as for wind.*
> *I cannot explain why I feel*
> *That I need to forgive you after all you have done.*
> *hum . . . hum*
> *Chorus.'*

'What a bloody racket!' Mike protested, having cycled up within range, 'Can we please listen to the peace and calm of the desert.' It was quite obvious that Mike was no connoisseur of music.

Inspired by singing, some fifty miles had disappeared by lunch time – a record-breaking performance. We had also achieved the milestone of 1,000 miles and we had indulged in a ceremony of building a pile of stones to mark this bicycling feat. It was, however, getting hotter and by now the temperature had soared into the nineties. We sought some respite and tried to rig up a plastic sheet across the bikes for shade. It was unsuccessful for the gusting wind kept ripping it away. We were left to sweat into our rice and tuna.

Our water was low, having lost three litres when I dropped my bike through exhaustion and we now had to ration ourselves to one mouthful every half an hour. It did nothing to quench our burning thirst. Much to my disappointment, I could no longer sing for my mouth was so dry.

'Thank goodness for that!' David declared, without compassion.

After such a good morning, everything now seemed to turn against us. Water was not the only problem. David's in-growing toe nail came back to torment him, and each time he pushed down his right foot, he winced in agony. A puncture then stopped us. Usually it would take us some ten minutes to fix, but with valves, rubber and pump slipping across our sweaty fingers, and trying to focus through salty tears, we were there for over half an hour. I tried to escape into day dreams and song again, but the heat and thirst were too intense. The final straw came when a gusting wind started to blow against us. Dust swirled around our heads and stung our eyes. Our legs and eyes cried out for us to stop, but the fear of our water situation forced us on.

We so nearly missed it in the blinding dust; a faded wooden sign announcing '*Estancia Angostura – 4 kms*'. Fate led us to the home of Mario and Patricia. Nearby a natural spring bubbled out of the earth, spreading life and colour, and allowing ten cattle, three horses and twenty-one sheep to survive.

'Call me *Super Mario*,' he greeted us modestly. Even the wilds of Patagonia, it seemed, were not immune to the scourge of computer games. He did, however, look like the character with his natty moustache, roly-poly figure and large sash belt. On seeing our state of exhaustion, they would not allow us to camp, but insisted on making up three beds in the house. We were invited to a dinner of Patagonia hare washed down with a gallon of water and a bottle of wine. In those moments we forgot the torment of the road.

It was easy to appreciate, but difficult to understand the overwhelming warmth of the hospitality. Was it because we were linked by a common spirit? The same spirit which brought Mario and Patricia from the suburbs of Buenos Aires to eke out a living in the desert had taken us to South America by bicycle. We could both understand the hardship and the tenacity needed to survive in this harsh environment. There was, thus, a mutual bond and respect between us.

It was blowing a gale the next day, and took us an hour to struggle back to the road. Here the wind was gusting in from the side, making cycling extremely difficult. To keep our sanity we devised a challenging game – 'see how long you can stay on your bike' with the prize, a curry and a pint in the next town. We all started salivating at the thought of this fantasy. With determination etched on our faces, we would line up and totter off in unison. Often a gust would take us all out simultaneously, making it a dead heat at only ten yards. Then Mike went an unbelievable three hundred yards without falling off.

The game became boring after this freak performance. We decided to sit it out and save our legs from any more bruising and our bikes from further damage. But where? There were no trees, no rocks, not even a solitary bush. David spotted a culvert under the road. At a squeeze it fitted all three of us and had the added luxury of a soft, sandy floor. The bikes were propped up at either end to stop the worst of the wind. It was in this Hilton Culvert that we spent six hours of the Sunday before Christmas. Our thoughts and conversation were of our friends and families back at home. Perhaps they were slowly waking up from the excesses of a Christmas party the night before, or just about to tuck in to a Sunday roast. Here we were huddled up in a sandy drainage tunnel, eating pasta, reciting the Colombian author Gabriel García Márquez, and dividing the last pieces of chocolate.

This was one of our biggest nightmares, running out of chocolate. It had become an obsession – it was our heaven, our energy, our will to go on. So many times in the last few days, Mike and I had succumbed to this craving for chocolate. David had been much more sensible.

DAY 50 DAVID'S DIARY - EMERGENCY RATIONS FOR PUDDING

'I don't believe it - they have done it again! When will they ever learn? Running out of food on the first day which meant we nearly killed ourselves with the romantic notion of living off the land - should have been a warning to keep high energy food in reserve. M's mischievous "go on just a little bit" (more than R could resist) meant that last night the flapjacks got served up as pud. And now tonight against all my arguments to the contrary we had Kendal Mint Cake and the last bar of chocolate for dessert. No shops for days - so I wonder what they will devour for tomorrow's pud - rhea droppings?'

'We must save it,' David advised. 'Now, after supper, we do not really need it, but on the road in the blasting wind, we will be crying out for it!'

He had been right, of course, but we really did not have the will to resist. Yes, we had felt guilty and decadent, but the sensation had been simply overwhelming. Now, like a ritual, we each popped one last piece into our mouths. I started to suck it and then moved it around with my tongue to make it last. It tasted wonderful and soon the temptation became too much. I chewed it with urgency. At least now, with the chocolate gone, we would be free from the torment.

Eventually, the wind allowed us to leave the culvert and we struggled five miles to the next farm, named optimistically *Estancia Verde* (Green Farm). Ahead lay a testing gauntlet – a forty-four mile stretch of road heading straight into the prevailing westerly wind. It could take us anything between five hours to three days. Strategically placed halfway along this stretch lay Tamel Aike. Those students of Bartholomew blow-up globes will know this place. It is marked in the same way as Birmingham, Lyon or Milan, but Tamel Aike, we had been warned, was in reality a police station. This place was our goal.

To outsmart the wind we left as the sun rose. The wind had not woken up yet and we managed to snatch twenty miles. Tamel Aike lay tantalisingly close, when the wind came out of nowhere. It was like crashing into an invisible wall. I remember seeing *Shadowfax* rearing up on her back wheel like a horse and twisting in the air before galloping off in the direction we had just come. Mike fought with the brakes and the handlebars and could only bring *Shadowfax* to a halt some hundred yards down the road. David and I threw ourselves and *Arriba* and *Woop-Woop* to the ground. The final two miles was a struggle. It was difficult to get a firm grip on the pebbled road and often our feet would slide backwards as we attempted to push the bikes on. Flying sand stung our faces and small stones pecked at our ankles. I wrapped a tee-shirt around my head and pretended I was Lawrence of Arabia and *Arriba* was my camel. Anything to take my mind off the pain, exhaustion and the little white outpost, which seemed to get no closer. Without chocolate, it took us some two hours.

Tamel Aike was how it had been described – it was certainly no Birmingham. It had a population of six: the two policemen, Roberto and Luigi; Roberto's wife, Angelique; their eight month old daughter, Francesca, and two rough, dusty dogs. To this day, I do not know why a police station is located there. After all who do they police, the odd guanacos or rhea? Perhaps it was a ploy by the authorities so that they could keep their policemen in check: 'Look if you step out of line again, you will be posted to Tamel Aike'. Despite their career prospects, they were a happy bunch. When we arrived they were in tears and bent double with laughter. It was not every day, they explained, that they saw three crazy *gringos* battling against a dust storm gusting to some ninety miles an hour. They kept themselves amused in different ways. Roberto would spend his time pruning his hair in the mirror and polishing his knee-length cowboy boots. Luigi played a lot with Francesca and went off shooting black swans. Angelique prepared and cooked food. Francesca ate, gurgled and banged her little fists on the table. The two dogs passed every waking minute fighting, which accounted for their patchy coats.

During our visit, Tamel Aike achieved another claim to fame. It became the most remote hairdressers in the world. Both David and I had become fed up with the wind constantly blowing our hair into our eyes. Roberto had been a hairdresser before becoming a policeman, which explained the amount of time he spent in front of the mirror. He volunteered to cut our hair. I think his previous clients must have come from inside a prison, because we came out looking like two convicts.

The next day the wind had died down sufficiently for us to leave.

DAY 52 ON THE ROAD TO BAJO CARACOLES 1.00 P.M.
'I feel knackered. What makes it worse is that M and D seem to be cycling so effortlessly, leaving me trailing in their wake. God, it bugs me! I hate to follow and I refuse to let them know I am suffering. I would see them waiting and as I draw closer, I would take a deep breath, smile and start singing without a care in the world.'

'Are you feeling all right?' Mike asked.

'Why? Yes, of course,' I replied nonchalantly. 'I have just been chasing a few rheas.'

I do not think they believed me.

It was our competitive nature which drove us on. We all relished being in front, but hated being left behind. Each of us had different paces. I was a moody cyclist. Sometimes there would be no stopping me, but invariably I was distracted and dreaming, and thus left trailing. I also had the disadvantage of short, bandy legs. Mike, on the other hand, could call upon his long legs on the pedals. When fit, he was fast and strong, but he tended to be particularly vulnerable to injury and illness. David was by far the steadiest, often monitoring and controlling his pace based on the weather and road conditions. He did, however, stop often to change his clothing and adjust his cycle shorts. There were only a few occasions when we were all cycling at the same pace.

Despite my tired state, we rode for thirteen hours and exceeded all expectations with a record eighty-one miles. On arrival in Bajo Caracoles, I collapsed off *Arriba* and had to be helped to the doors of the hostel. Over the last ten miles, I had been thinking of and glamorising this place, our final destination – a sanctuary of piping hot water, a bubbling jacuzzi, ice cold beers, a juicy T-bone and a delegation of Swedish masseuses. Bajo Caracoles is, in reality, a godforsaken hole of dilapidated sheds, dominated by a stark concrete building resembling a prison. This was the hostel. The jailer or proprietor had the air of someone who had suffered a terrible bereavement.

He was also a man of a few grunts and a nervous twitch which moved his head from side to side.

'Do you have any beers? (shake), Chocolate? (shake), Hot water? (nod), Jacuzzi? (eh . . .), Beds? (nod), Steak? (shake), Food? (nod). What's on the menu?' Mike asked.

'Mutton or corned beef with rice,' came the grudging reply.

We could hardly wait and we dashed off to change for dinner, buoyed by the thought of hot water. There may well have been hot water, but without a tap it was difficult to release it.

'Oh, the last guests a week ago must have nicked it!' The proprietor smiled maliciously.

The next morning, the stringy tough mutton we had eaten the previous evening hit me with a vengeance.

DAY 53 DELIRIOUS ON THE ROAD 2.30 P.M.

'I awoke dizzy and nauseous. It had to be that tough old mutton of the previous evening. The last thing I felt like doing was to go cycling, but we had to get out of this armpit of a place. It is too hot on the road. I feel detached from reality. M and D's voices seem to fade in and out. I was floating in an ethereal haze unable to focus on anything but the overwhelming desire to curl up and sleep. I do not even care about the road to Paso Roballos. I keep drifting in and out of consciousness and, at one point, I find myself lying in the dust. I did not know how I had got there. I need to get out of the heat and this desert. We stop for lunch; the mere mention of food makes my stomach turn. I crave shade, but it is too windy to put up the tent. Instead I crawl under a cattle grid. I sleep fitfully and dream of a helicopter air-lifting me out of the desert to a hospital bed with cool linen sheets.'

I awoke with a start. Was that the hum of helicopter blades? No, it was the whistling of the wind through the bars of the cattle grid.

The bout of food poisoning could not have happened at a worse time. Ever since Hallam Murray had waxed so lyrically about *Paso Roballos* some six months before, I had set my heart on attempting it. He was not alone, for Bruce Chatwin had been enchanted and so overawed by the beauty of the Pass, he had gone as far to suggest it was the site of the legendary 'City of the Caesars'. *'Another El Dorado hidden in the Southern Andes,'* he wrote in *In Patagonia*. *'A mountain fortress, situated below a volcano, perched above a beautiful lake. The buildings were dressed of stone, the doors studded with jewels; the ploughshares were of silver, and the furniture of the humblest dwelling of silver and gold. There was no sickness; old people died as if sleep had come upon them.'*

DAY 53 4.30 P.M.

'Feeling more in this world. Now the memory of missing Paso Roballos is haunting me. My illness had robbed us of the opportunity. Just so close, yet so far! Perhaps it was Fate, but this thought made me feel no better. The Pass was not the only casualty of the mutton, for it now looked as if we would be celebrating Christmas in the middle of nowhere.'

I cannot remember how I or we got to the small farm, *Casa Piedra*. Apparently I collapsed off *Arriba*, was stripped and put into my sleeping bag. I awoke some sixteen hours later feeling better, but by now David had succumbed to the dreaded poisoning. The lady of the farm, dressed in bulging lycra cycle shorts, was kind to us and brought us eggs, bread, milk and a local remedy made out of herbs. On leaving, she and her children rushed out and gave us each a slice of Christmas cake; *'Feliz Navidad* (Happy Christmas),' they waved. Now only four days to go.

Progress was slow as both David and I felt weak. A car hooted and pulled up. We were taken by surprise. It was only the thirteenth car we had seen in eight days. A cheery voice said in English,

'God you look awful! Could you do with a lift?'

Before either David or I could speak, Mike recited the well rehearsed lines: 'Thanks for the offer, but we are cycling for charity and we are committed to pedalling every kilometre.'

'Well, you are going to be no use to anybody if you kill yourselves out here,' the lady pointed out, sounding somewhat like my mother.

'Listen, our farm is some twenty kilometres up the road, you are invited to stay the night.' Three hours later when we got to the turn-off to the farm, we could not resist the temptation.

A local spring had created an oasis of beauty and colour in the desert. *Estancia* Telken stood amongst fields of swaying grassland and was bathed in the light of the late afternoon sun. The house was white with a poppy-red roof and was surrounded by manicured green lawns, lupins and roses.

This scene hid many years of despair.

'I remember waking up and looking out of the window,' Joan explained over dinner. 'The air was choked and the ground was covered with black ash. It was a terrible sight. It was as if it was the end of the world. I went outside and the ash came up to my knees. I could hear the mournful bleating of our sheep and lambs. We lost a third of our flock through suffocation and starvation and virtually a whole generation of lambs. This was our version of *The Silence of the Lambs*. Some two months later we were still wearing gas masks and protective clothing when we were outside. We would stick our names on the masks so we could recognise each other in town. I always remember the joy of seeing the yellow flower of a dandelion pushing up through the ash some three years later. It signified hope. It has been eleven years now since Volcano Hudson erupted some four hundred kilometres away.

'We have one thing to thank Volcano Hudson for. It forced us to open the farm up to tourism and we have met so many wonderful people over the years,' said Joan philosophically. I do not think her husband, Coco, shared her enthusiasm. He was a quiet, tall man of Dutch descent, who had listened to the conversation over dinner with a bemused detachment. His reticence might have something to do with another guest, the loud and arrogant Juan. He had opened the conversation by boasting, 'I have never done anything for charity and I do not intend to start now.' He was in his fifties. He embodied the Buenos Aires tennis club mentality; he was in love with himself, Argentina and the idea of a superior race. It seemed his wife, Cordelia, came a distant fourth. Now also in her fifties she still kept the poise, charm and beauty, which had made her the belle of the debutante balls in Buenos Aires. I had to bite back the question; why on earth did you marry Juan?

Over breakfast the next morning the conversation turned to the late Bruce Chatwin.

'His book certainly put Patagonia on the map,' Joan explained, 'but in his attempt to make everything stranger and larger than life, many stories were contrived. He hurt a lot of people by writing things which were very unfair and, in certain cases, untrue. We can be a strange bunch but he made us look ridiculous. We are a proud people; I see myself as Patagonian before Argentinian. I will never have that book in my house.'

I gently slipped a tee-shirt over the book's green cover in my bag.

We had to leave because Christmas was only three days away. Coco had shown us on the map a path through the Andes to a border post which had only just opened again after fifteen years. This route promised to save us some time. These are the instructions he wrote down:

'At border post take only the road with white pebbles. Go through three gates and then turn sharp right. Follow the river and after four more gates, you are in Chile.'

'Surely they will be able to show us the way at the border post,' I reasoned.

'It will be closed at Christmas and they are more than likely to be drunk or sleeping,' Coco said. 'The road is so bad only four-wheel drives can get through, so they certainly will not be expecting you.'

A stiff breeze was blowing in our faces when we reached the road. It was not easy going and David was lagging behind because he still had not fully recovered. Mike and I had been waiting some time, when David cycled up and announced,

'I am glad the wind is up because it is keeping me cool.'

David was always a great one for tempting fate. Six days before he had boasted to have cycled one thousand miles without a puncture. Within five miles, he was out with his glue and patches. It was he who had said how lucky we had been with our health. Within hours we had eaten the mutton. His last comment was like a red rag to a bull, and sure enough within minutes we were trapped in gale force winds.

We struggled eventually into the town of Perito Moreno. For many it represents the end of the desert. From here a paved road leads west to the frontier town of Los Antiguos and east to the Atlantic coast some two hundred miles away. We planned to keep heading north for a further sixty miles. Then we would reach the Andes and leave the desert behind. Before this, though, we needed a drink. The bar we chose, like so many in Patagonia, was packed. Here we met Mario, a five foot nothing Italian. He was a travelling salesman selling, amongst other things, ice-cream. He fancied himself as a gigolo and he came with the obligatory medallion entangled amongst the sprouting curly hairs on his chest. Without prompting he told us his life history.

'People call me *Super Mario*,' he said, proudly fingering his medallion.

Not another one, I thought, Patagonia seemed plagued with them!

'I came over from Italy ten years ago. I believed this was a land of opportunities. And what a land and what opportunities!' he declared, beating his chest. 'I am now on my third wife and I am having an affair with a leggy twenty-five year old. She's absolutely beautiful. Look, if you stay around, I could fix you up. If you know what I mean?' He nudged Mike and then launched into a tirade of grunts and suggestive pelvic thrusts.

'Not bad for a forty year old. Don't you think?'

He was making us feel jealous. We resisted the temptation and moved on.

DAY 55 NORTH OF PERITO MORENO 6.00 P.M.

'The desert remains and the road is absolutely appalling. At times, it is ankle-deep in volcanic ash. The bikes sink and then slide to a halt. It takes all our strength and energy to push them through. When free from ash, the road is severely rutted. It requires great concentration to steer along these narrow avenues of loose pebbles. The bloody wind (surprise, surprise) is still against us. I hate to admit this, but if a car came along now, I would take it! I would not care about the direction, just anything to be free from this road. Busting our guts to achieve four miles an hour – it seems so pointless!'

A car did come. The driver stopped and asked if we needed help. We looked at each other – not with defiance, but willing and daring one another to say, 'Yes!' Silence reigned, as stubborn pride and egos fought a battle against aching limbs.

'Well?' asked the driver.

'No, thanks,' we replied, without conviction.

Frustrated, we pulled off the road and headed for a cluster of poplar trees – a sure sign of water and habitation. We were greeted by an ancient gaucho, dressed in baggy, stained trousers, a thick, woollen shirt and black, leather boots. He had blackened teeth, and as he spoke a tattered cigar hung precariously and miraculously from his lips. He invited us in to his candle-lit home and offered us the leftovers of his supper of mutton and bread. We could not resist, and after eating he showed us to the sheep-shearing shed. We quickly made beds out of the discarded fleeces, and collapsed. While drifting off to sleep, I really did wish I would wake up somewhere else.

Christmas, now just two days away, would wait for no man, so the alarms went off at four o'clock in the morning. Even this thought could not prise us out of bed and it was not until nine o'clock that we could face the road again. The fateful mutton chose this moment to strike Mike. He turned green and vomited. For ten miles he valiantly fought bouts of nausea and dizziness before collapsing.

DAY 56 HIGHWAY TO HELL 12.30 P.M.

'Mike is vomiting by the side of the road with his head planted between his knees. There are traces of blood. I am scared and worried. Why the hell are we torturing ourselves like this all for the sake of Christmas? We took a big decision – we would defiantly take the next car and get Mike to the nearest estancia.'

Fate dictated that *'the'* car never came and after some three hours Mike had nothing left to vomit, so we struggled on. Fifteen miles and four hours later, a car did come. It was travelling in the wrong direction and we could not face retracing all those hard-fought miles. The driver, however, had some good news: there was an *estancia ingles* (English farm) a mere four miles away.

The English connection went back three generations to a Scottish grandfather, who had left behind the wet slates and shipyards of Glasgow for the boundless horizons of Patagonia. His motivation had been different from the Italian *Super Mario*. He had come for the 'opportunity' of making a fortune out of sheep farming.

'The government was giving away the land,' Judith, our hostess, explained. 'All my grandfather had to do was to stake out his claim and build a road in. It was no mean feat – it took him some four years to get the farm established. He then returned to Scotland for three weeks and came back married to my grandmother.'

I was impressed. 'That must have taken some doing,' I said, as I imagined him rushing around Glasgow with a marriage proposal and two return tickets to Patagonia.

'Not really, dear, he had always been the apple of her eye,' Judith replied.

They gave us a little cottage, a slab of lamb and a sprig of mint. David and I nursed Mike. Our methods were rather unconventional – we fed him chunks of lamb and read him *Love in the Time of Cholera* by Gabriel Garcia Marquez. Amazingly it worked, for on the morning of Christmas Eve, he awoke, not cured, but free from nausea.

DAY 57 MIKE'S DIARY – A CHRISTMAS EVE TO REMEMBER

'I was better, but still feeling jaded. I should not have been on a bicycle, let alone on Christmas Eve of all days. But we had set our hearts on Christmas in Chile and to Chile we must go. Chile and Coihaique seemed a million miles away across the Andes. I felt we were three Davids (instead of the usual one) against this mighty Goliath. On reaching the mountains, the harsh north-westerly wind, which had been the bane of our lives for the last three days, abated. With the wind went my sickness, and I became high on the cool rich aroma of a breeze borne from a valley cloaked in all the colours of spring. The world awoke anew.'

Coco had been right about the road. After so many years of closure and neglect, it resembled little more than a farm track, with grass growing up the middle and many cavernous potholes to negotiate. As we climbed, the air grew cooler and the landscape became greener. At first, there were only isolated pockets of green defying the dry, sandy soil, but gradually a carpet of grass, flowers and bushes unfurled before our wheels. We blinked as our eyes grew accustomed to the new colours and we took deep breaths of the heavily scented air. The dust and heat of the desert now became a distant memory.

After three hours climbing, we arrived at the top of the Andean pass (7,400 feet).

MY DIARY ON THE ANDES 6.00 P.M.

'Behind us lay the barren desert of Patagonia and ahead Chile was regaled in the rich shades of luxuriant growth. We were standing on the fulcrum between green and brown, life and death, at the very point where the clouds sweeping in from the Pacific Ocean hit the Andes and venture no further. A crystal blue lake lay huddled in the mountain folds to catch the last of the precious rain drops. On the shore, a flock of flamingos stood basking in the late afternoon sun and two condors glided across the azure sky on the dying thermals of the day. A tall, iron cross afforded a rippling reflection in the water. It was Christmas Eve and we prayed.'

The border guards were surprised and drunk. Drinks were obligatory and the stamping of our passports laborious. It appeared that neither country would take responsibility for the track through no-man's-land. It simply disappeared into a field of cattle.

'Through three gates and turn sharp right to the river,' Coco had instructed. We found and followed the river over four more gates. So this was Chile, and at this point we could see the lights of the town of Balmaceda in the gathering darkness.

MIKE'S DIARY

'The town was silent. One would never have guessed it was Christmas Eve had it not been for the flickering fairy lights strung across the plastic trees in the windows of the corrugated iron houses. We stopped at the small, white-washed church and stepped into a children's nativity service. The church was simple in decoration with wooden pews and a plain altar table. Centre

stage was Joseph in jeans and a young Mary dressed in a floral skirt and matching blouse. The three kings were distinguished by their brightly coloured bobble hats while the shepherds sported woollen hats without the bobbles. The children sang familiar tunes in Spanish, accompanied by the soft strumming of a flamenco guitar. I sat at the back of the church, exhausted. The scene and the music were soothing and mesmerising. The locals were bemused by our presence, but at the end inhibitions were swept away when they came to hug us and wish us a Happy Christmas. Even Joseph came to greet us and it was with his help we found a room to lay our weary heads.'

Santa even delivered to the wilds of Patagonia, for a stocking lay hanging at the foot of my bed. It was packed with the source of our addiction – chocolate. Home was also not far away. A public phone sat in the house just around the corner. Getting through to England was easy in comparison to the ordeal of waking the telephone operator at ten o'clock on a Christmas morning. Eventually the door was answered by a bleary-eyed young lady, dressed only in a pink dressing gown lined with fur.

'Please excuse my attire,' Christina apologised, blushing to the colour of the gown. 'Too much pisco, I am afraid. I will never touch the stuff ever again!' Fortunately, despite her hangover, Christina was able to put us in touch with our parents.

We did not leave for the final forty miles to Coihaique until after the Queen's speech.

'My husband and I would like to wish you a very happy Christmas,' crackled from our short-wave radio and then followed an accompanied rendition of 'God Save the Queen'. The inhabitants of Balmaceda had not seen or heard anything like it, neither had the local dogs, who started to let out an almighty howl. This was not good for Christina's hangover, so in her interests we decided to leave on the final leg.

Travelling on the road was bedlam, even after we were out of earshot of Balmaceda. Drivers hooted their horns and shouted *'Feliz Navidad'*. Unfortunately, most of them had yet to throw off the effects of the piso, which made their driving dangerous and erratic. Often we would find ourselves helped into bushes and ditches by their inebriated but well-meaning behaviour. We came up behind a swaying horseman. He was fighting sleep – his chin kept dropping on to his chest and then with a start he would jerk his neck back up again. Finally, his head lurched forward and, as if in slow motion, he slipped sideways off the horse into the gutter. We passed him snoring happily in the dust, while his mount continued on oblivious.

DAY 58 CHRISTMAS IN COIHAIQUE

'At seven-fifteen, we arrived in Coihaique. As we passed the sign, we punched the air in joy and let out a resounding "YES!" This was our moment of triumph against all the odds. I was overwhelmed with relief and sense of achievement and I could not stop the tears as I embraced M and D. I knew now survival and success did not depend on physical strength alone, but more on an overwhelming conviction. A conviction we all shared and which would take us all to the very end. We were now a team that needed and existed for each other. Memories of the dust, ash, heat, mutton and wind are melting away and, yes, I could understand what Charles Darwin had been alluding to. Patagonia, in giving us such a special Christmas; would always have a hold on us, shine bright in our memory and be dear to us.'

—9—
CARRETERA AUSTRAL

'Pinochet's dream road, the little travelled Carretera Austral, took up the baton at Puerto Montt and went south.'

SARA WHEELER 'Travels in a Thin Country'

Coihaique (pronounced koy-aye-ke) is so named from the Indian language. 'Coy' is the Mapuche Indian word for tree, while 'haique' is the local Huiliche term for place. There are now few Indians in the streets and not many trees either. The great beech forests which used to surround the town disappeared during the wave of settlement which followed the Chilean colonisation law of 1937. Not so much a law but a licence to environmental devastation! Without machinery or sufficient manpower, the forests were simply set alight. The fires would rage for days feeding on and eating up vast tracts of land, many of which were destined never to be treaded by sheep or cattle. The evidence remains for all to see. The short summers have left gnarled, rotting tree-trunks strewn and littered across the hillsides.

Coihaique (population 40,000) has not only lost its Indians and trees but also, in 1988, its isolation and pioneering status ended.

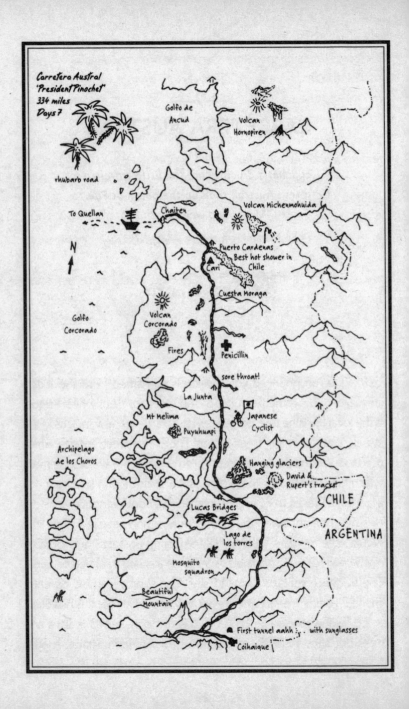

This was when a road, the Carretera Austral Longitudinal, was completed. It opened up 550 miles of previously impenetrable territory to the south of the city of Puerto Montt and thus linked Coihaique to the outside world. There were still relics of the pioneering past – squat weather-board houses and wooden rails to tether horses outside some of the shops, but now supermarkets, concrete buildings and even ice-cream parlours dominated the town centre.

The road's purpose was not only economic, for it also had a strategic military importance, which explains why General Pinochet was so adamant to have it built. The Carretera Austral assured control and encouraged settlement and thus secured the remote Aisen region against foreign invasion from the traditional adversary, Argentina. It was this road which was to take us some 300 miles north to the port of Chaiten.

'It will be a great change from the desert,' Luigi, the owner of our *hospedaje* (hostel), told us. 'There is certainly no lack of water. Rain, rain and more rain is what you are letting yourselves in for. Everyday without fail! I think you should know, you will be cycling through one of the wettest places on earth. Ask the locals along the way. They will tell you it rains 366 days of the year.' So this was what life was like in the rain shadow of the Andes.

The Carretera Austral would have to wait. We had to recover from the trials and tribulations of *Ruta Quarenta* (Route 40). It was time to treat ourselves and indulge in our luxuries. I went off fishing on the *Rio Simpson*, while David and Mike strutted around town in their brogues and jeans. It was beautiful down by the river and just the therapy I needed. I spent hours staring into a deep eddying pool as the trout rose to the early evening flies which were tickling the water with their wings. They viewed my imitation English mayfly with a mixture of curiosity and contempt and it was left to Carlos, a veteran fisherman of the river, to teach me the idiosyncrasies of the Patagonian trout.

'You will need some of this to fish here,' Carlos explained. He reached for his inner pocket and instead of producing some tried and tested bait, he brought out a plastic flask full of brandy. In fact, he did more drinking than fishing, preferring to wallow in the memories of past catches.

'When I was younger I used to pick trout out of the river with my bare hands. I then moved to luring salmon. Bigger and more intelligent. I caught a monster salmon at this very spot.' Carlos spread his arms expansively to indicate a size close to three feet. 'She put up quite a struggle. I eventually landed after playing her for over an hour.'

'Well, I nearly caught a sheep once,' I replied. 'It was this long and this wide.'

While I was catching trout, David and Mike caught giardia. This nasty bug floats around in untreated water and, when swallowed, takes up residence in the stomach and proceeds to manufacture a foul-smelling wind. I watched their bellies swell and grow to the size of footballs. A girl on the till at the ice-cream parlour even congratulated Mike and David on their pregnancies. The wind was always looking to escape. It was wise to keep well clear while giardia had a hold and that was why I took to sleeping down by the river. Night after night the stars and the sound of the water serenaded me to sleep. I did not feel alone. A blue kingfisher sat perched above me in the willow tree and an otter had its home in the river bank across the water.

We met several interesting characters during our stay in Coihaique. Most memorable were Jenny and her bicycle, Rocky. She was an imposing, talkative and independent Australian girl, who was on her way down from Alaska to Ushuaia.

'I have not always been alone,' Jenny told us, much to our surprise. 'I started with a friend from Oz. We had a bit of a baptism of fire up in Alaska. One night, a man burst into our tent brandishing a gun. He led us away to a house and kept us under lock and key. He threatened to rape us and kill us. He even requested a ransom from the Australian authorities for our release.'

'How did you escape?' I asked.

'I talked him out of it,' Jenny replied. Certainly, if anybody could achieve this feat, Jenny could. The kidnapper simply did not stand a chance!

'My friend and I parted company in Guatemala,' Jenny continued, without drawing a breath. 'She met a man and I left them to get married.'

'Who do you talk to now?' I enquired, intrigued.

'To Rocky, of course,' Jenny replied. 'I positively love him. I am never happier than when I am riding him. Do you know, when I start cycling in the morning, I never feel like stopping.'

What an enigma – I simply could not relate to this at all! As soon as I started, I would be thinking about the next resting place. I obviously had a long way to go before becoming a cycling groupie.

We also met Mick, a metal polisher from Canterbury. He was festooned with tattoos. The letters LOVE spread across his knuckles and there were scissor marks around his neck with the instruction 'cut here'. He would snigger nervously after every pause of his incessant, but entertaining banter.

'I like Cant'bury. It's a nice place. It has culture and is dead historical. Do you know it has a real fine cathedral,' Mick paused to snigger. 'I keep out of trouble by polishing metal. I have a BSA motorbike all shiny and polished mounted on the wall in my living room. It looks dead good,' more sniggering.

As well as history and the joys of metal polishing, he was also into marriage guidance. 'I have a Peruvian wife. Look, fellows, I would recommend you go to Peru to look for a wife. They are dark and beautiful and even if you have an argument the tea is still on the table. She is brave too. I came back one evening and she was pulling a tooth out with a pair of pliers. I never thought I could be faithful to one woman, but we have been married for two years now without a thought of a bit on the side.'

He was not however with his wife now, but with a friend from England. We never met him, he seemed to spend his time permanently in bed.

'We have a problem,' Mick explained. 'We bought crates and crates of beer for the five day boat trip down from Puerto Montt. The weather was so bad we did not even feel like touching the stuff, and instead we spent the time vomiting over the side. John has only two days left in Chile and he is intent on finishing the beer. As a result, he spends his time either in bed or on the toilet.'

New Year's Eve was so nearly an anticlimax. It started well with the multi-national group staying at our hostel celebrating different New Years as midnight chimed around the world. First, it was Australia, then Israel, Belgium and Britain. I remember standing with glasses raised as the twelve chimes of Big Ben sounded on the BBC World Service. We were, however, holding back for a wild and crazy Chilean New Year. At eleven-thirty we left on a short walk to the central plaza to mingle with the throngs of excited and fire-cracking Chileans. We thought it was strange the streets were deserted, but assumed that people had left early to stake out some space. An eerie quiet hung over the plaza. We were alone save for a bored and hopeful candy-floss salesman. He was surprised to see us; Chileans, he told us, celebrate their New Year behind closed doors with their family.

We were running out of time. Laden with booze we scoured the streets looking for some sign of life. We heard music and voices. With three minutes to go we invited ourselves to a family *asado* (barbecue) party. They made us feel very welcome and we saw the New Year in to the sound of champagne corks and kissing. The Fernandez family must have been good practising Catholics. Grandparents, mums and dads, brothers and sisters, cousins and in-laws queued in an endless line to greet us with a hug and a double kiss. We were then dragged on to the grass dance floor by the three sisters. Uncle Pepe strummed at his *charango* (a small stringed instrument made with an armadillo hide), brother Oscar pounded away at the *bombo* (an Andean drum) and cousin Victor played the harmonica. The rest of the family formed a ring around us. They were laughing, clapping and stomping their feet with great gusto. We were dancing, rather attempting to dance, the traditional Chilean jig called the *cueca* (pronounced like the 'quaker' in porridge oats). It is a courting dance. First we were told to advance towards our partners in a seductive fashion. In turn they kept their distance, setting up the pattern of pursuer and pursued.

'Pretend you are an amorous rooster stalking a shy, flirtatious hen,' my partner instructed. I blew out my chest, flapped my wings and strutted off in hot pursuit. The clapping grew faster and louder and I was given a handkerchief to twirl around in the air. Just as the jig was reaching its pulsating *finale*, David started to crow. David and I failed to catch our partners, who disappeared into the crowd, but Mike ended up still clutching his handkerchief, and holding the younger sister captive. We put this feat down to Mike's years of experience with the Kettering Morris Dancing Troupe.

We put away our handkerchiefs as the sun rose on the New Year. We planned to go to Villa Castillo, a mountain in the shape of a castle. It would have taken us days to cycle, so we decided to hitchhike. New Year's Day was not a good time to choose. There was little on the road and those vehicles that were tended to be driven by victims of the excesses of the night before. So it was that we found ourselves in the back of a truck with a bunch of swaying and leering drunks. They were on a mission to push a neighbour's jeep out of a ditch. We jolted to a halt beside the stricken vehicle and slowly, with unsteady step, the work party disembarked. They took up pushing positions. By the time it had taken to say, 'uno . . . dos . . . tres . . . EMPUGE (push)!' half of them had fallen asleep.

We left them snoring and draped over wheels and looked for alternative 'moving' transport. There was nothing. The only beings active on this sultry day were the flies. I have found flies an enigma ever since getting a puncture in the Australian Outback. We were in the middle of nowhere. Before you could say 'jack,' we were ambushed by squadrons of flies crawling and buzzing through our hair and across our eyes. How did they know we were going to stop at this spot? Had they been waiting all their lives for this very moment or did they have their own inaudible bush telegraph which called them from all the mounds of dung in the area? The flies in Chile had the same patience or homing device, but they were different in other respects. They were bigger and more ferocious. These horseflies had quite a kick. It was kill or be bitten. Piles of corpses rose at our feet, but still wave upon wave flew in to meet their death. David started counting and claimed he was killing forty-eight flies every fifteen minutes. We were stranded there for four hours, which meant a total death toll of over 2,000 flies. Eventually a car did come. Enough was enough; we hitched back to Coihaique and away from Villa Castillo.

Some 300 miles of rain and the Carretera Austral lay ahead of us. We planned to take a week to reach the port of Chaiten and then immediately take a ferry to the island of Chiloe. The ferry left at ten o'clock in the morning on the eighth day and if we missed it, it would mean four days stranded in Chaiten. This was not to be recommended.

'There is nothing to keep you in the port for more than a day, apart from a frequently delayed ferry,' one guide book warned.

We foresaw no problems because much to our surprise and delight, Jenny had told us it was paved all the way. In anticipation, David cleverly switched to slick tyres, while Mike and I, through laziness compounded by a lack of practical skill, stayed on our fat, knobbly tyres.

It was a beautiful road. The white foaming waters of the *Rio Simpson* rushed below us, and the wooded valley walls rose steeply on either side. A colourful array of wild spring flowers – six-foot lupins, marguerite daisies, fine-petalled poppies and giant rhubarb lined our path and scented the air. Humming birds danced amongst the wild red fuchsia and a Chilean southern-ringed kingfisher swooped down to pluck a small trout out of the water.

There were many tunnels carved into the steep sides of the valley. We were descending at speed in our wrap-around shades when we entered a particularly innocuous looking one. Immediately we were plunged into total darkness. Brakes screeched, my bike wavered as I fought to whip off my glasses and the tunnel echoed with the sound of unrepeatable expletives.

David was the first to spot a pinprick of light.

'Bear left, bear left!' he shouted.

I realised this was sound advice when my right shoulder brushed against the wall of the tunnel. We were soon in for another shock. Two miles on the Carretera Austral branched off to the right and turned into rutted, dusty dirt road.

'Where is the paved road?' we asked a young girl on a horse.

'The paved road goes only to the port of Puerto Aisen,' she replied. 'The Carreterra Austral is just like this from now on.'

It was then that we remembered Jenny had taken the ferry down this particular section. It did, however, have its funny side for Mike and I. In the space of only five miles, Mister 'Slick Tyres' David got two punctures. We just had to laugh.

The road was playing havoc with Mike's buttocks. They were both tender and sore and he was forced to cycle with his bottom high in the air. Any amount of talcum powder and extra cushioning stuffed down his cycle shorts were failing to solve the problem. Drivers and riders slowed to wonder at his extraordinary style and shape.

'You should become a jockey. Here have a go on my horse,' one passing rider offered.

Mike nursed his buttocks along to the shores of *Lagos de los Torres*.

DAY 68 LAKE OF THE TOWERS 7.30P.M.
'A place of breathtaking beauty. The surrounding trees and white mountain peaks are mirrored in the still waters. Flies skim across the water teasing the trout below. All is quiet except for the sound of birdsong and the occasional splash of a rising trout.'

I then heard a distant hum. The beauty was masked forever by an invasion of mosquitoes. They were everywhere; crawling into our ears, floating in our soup and buzzing in our hair. They must have had probes of steel for they seemed capable of biting through our fleeces, shoes and boxer shorts. We bathed in the repellent 'Jungle Juice'. Instead of repelling, it seemed to send the mosquitoes into a frenzy of excitement and they started to bite with renewed rigour. We dived for our sleeping bags and wrapped our heads in towels. Still they came, sneaking through cracks and crannies, driven by the aroma of blood and 'Jungle Juice'. Sleep was impossible. Just when I thought I had expelled or killed the last survivor, a distant buzz began again. The 'zzzzZZZZZ' became louder and then fluctuated as the mosquito pilot circled to identify a worthy artery. Then silence; I knew it was on me, about to raise its probe and lance a vessel. But where, oh where . . .? I thought as I finally drifted off to sleep, defeated and itching.

I awoke to the most unusual sight. Mike was up making breakfast and the sun was still low in the sky. Judging by his colourful language, it was evident the mosquitoes were to blame. They had succeeded where Tina Turner and Elton John had failed. Insects were not only keeping us awake, they had also become an integral part of our diet on the Carretera Austral. I had swallowed so many insects, I had become able to tell their identity from their taste. A horsefly had a lingering kick, a mosquito had bite, a greenfly was good on salad, a butterfly played on the tongue and beetles were crunchy. I remember cycling downhill at some twenty-five miles an hour, when a beetle flying at ten miles an hour thwacked into the back of my throat at a combined velocity of thirty-five m.p.h. It left quite a bruise.

Flying insects were not the only hazards of the road. David was looking pregnant again with a fresh bout of giardia. Giardia and cycling is a lethal cocktail; this disease produces wind, and cycling increases your propensity to expel it. In the afternoon, a breeze had freshened and we were forced to streamline. I had the misfortune to be positioned behind David. I was enveloped in a bubble of toxic air. I spluttered and choked. While I fought back the tears, I lost control and careered into a hedge. It was a long time before I cycled behind David again.

After the previous night at the lake, we were intent on staying at a place free from mosquitoes. It was getting late and the sun was setting as light mist rose above the dense green canopy around us. We stopped to camp on a grassy verge and were almost immediately swarmed by mosquitoes. It was impossible to unpack as we danced, slapped and swore. We decided to keep moving. By this time it was dark. We did not know where we were going, but anything had to be better than being bitten alive again. A dog barked and David saw a faint light twinkling amidst the dense forest. We cycled down a narrow rutted track to find a tiny log cabin. A woodcutter lived there with his family and in response to our request for permission to camp, he invited us in.

The cabin consisted of two rooms (measuring 22 by 16 feet) and was shared by five members of the Sotomayor family. One room was for living, cooking and eating and a smaller room was reserved for sleeping. A wood-burning stove was in one corner, providing both a source of heat as well as a place to cook. Fish and lumps of meat hung from wires above the stove, filling the air with a pungent smell. A single oil lamp threw shadows across the room, and above the rough, wooden table, a white candle burned. It cast a flicking light over a small shrine to the Virgin Mary.

'Do use the stove for cooking. You can get water from the stream outside,' Antonio Sotomayor instructed.

Conversation was difficult; our Spanish was still poor and the family was shy of the three gringos who had come in from the dark.

'*Nostros sumos Ingles* (we are English),' David volunteered, in an attempt to break the silence.

They smiled with incomprehension. '*Que es Ingles* (what is English)?' came the reply.

DAY 69 LOG CABIN 9.00 P.M.
'*The younger son has just swept the dirt floor under the table for us to sleep on. Their hospitality knows no bounds. I am frustrated. All we can say is "Gracias, Gracias" but even if we were to say it one hundred times, it is not enough to express our gratitude. There is just so much I want to say and explain to them.*'

The next day Mike's problem with his buttocks had moved to his throat. At first, I put it down to the flies, but when he started to cough up blood we realised it was more serious. Mike became convinced it was tonsillitis and David and I nursed him along for the next two days until we reached a tiny country hospital. It was run by a young female doctor, who asked Mike to drop his trousers and injected the contents of a syringe into his bottom. To this day, we do not know what it was. 'Something local,' was the only clue she gave us, but it did the trick because Mike was back on the road within hours.

The bikes were starting to suffer as well. David broke his chain. To Mike and I, this was a disaster. David did not seem unduly worried and calmly knelt down to fix it. All I had to do was to periodically fan him to keep the flies off. I must have looked like a sultan's lackey as I stood waving a tee-shirt over David's kneeling form. *Arriba* and I were also in the wars. She got a blow-out coming down a hill. I lost control and was thrown into a bed of stones and thorns. I was left with cuts and bruises. There was, however, a hanging glacier nearby. My limited medical knowledge told me that ice was good for bruises. I decided I would climb up and rest my leg on the ice. I followed a path up the hill marked with splashes of red paint. I was surprised when the markings and the path disappeared. I searched around looking for an alternative route and found only a discarded paint pot and brush. I returned with a swollen leg and opted for a milky blue glacier lake instead.

Even though the Carreterra Austral cuts through wild dense forests, we found we were never alone. There were often woodcutters' cabins nestling in amongst the trees, while on the road itself there were few cars, but many riders and cyclists. We differed from the other cyclists in three crucial respects: we were travelling north, there were three of us, and we had cycled *Ruta Cuarenta*. These differences dominated the conversations we had with them.

'How can you cycle as a three?' they asked. 'You must argue all the time. I could only travel alone.' With most of them you could see why!

'You must be crazy to be cycling north. It is psychologically demoralising,' they declared. They certainly had a point for both the wind and gradients were against us.

'I cannot believe you cycled Ruta Cuarenta. Isn't it 500 miles of desert with no water?' they enquired. We told them it was not a route to attempt on your own.

We found it reassuring rather than disturbing to be different.

As well as cyclists, we met several eccentric hitch-hikers. One day, we saw a canoe propped up by the side of the road. We stopped and it was not long before a man came out of the undergrowth buttoning his flies. Franz was from Switzerland and he was hitching from river to river with his canoe. So far his longest wait for a lift had been fifteen minutes. On another occasion, I heard a strange sound. It was unlike any bird, human or machine I had ever heard before, but somehow it seemed familiar. I could not understand why the aboriginals of Australia suddenly flashed into my mind. We turned the corner and cross-legged on the side of the road sat a girl playing the didgeridoo. Lucy was from a hippie commune in Australia and she was travelling around with her eight year old son, Nathan.

Amongst all our troubles fighting tonsillitis, giardia, mosquitoes and bruises, we were fortunate enough to experience no rain. This was why we were able to make it to Chaiten by ten o'clock on the eighth day. It was, however, all in vain. In Coihaique, we had misread the ferry timetable, confusing *Samedi* (Saturday) for *Dimanche* (Sunday). The ferry had left the day before and so we had three days to kill in

Chaiten. We nearly died of boredom, but it did give us the chance to reflect on the Carretera Austral.

DAY 73 CHAITEN

'It has to be one of the most beautiful roads in the world. Name me a road where you can cycle high on the sweet scent of spring flowers, through avenues of giant rhubarb, past hanging glaciers, across azure rivers and alongside sheltered bays rippling from dolphins. Show me a road where hospitality is a virtue and people with so little are prepared to give so much.'

—10—
MYSTICAL ISLE

*'The island of Chiloe is celebrated for its black storms
and black soil, its thickets of fuchsia and bamboo, its
Jesuit churches and the golden hands of its woodcarvers.'*

BRUCE CHATWIN 'What Am I Doing Here'

Chiloe, the second largest island in Latin America (155 miles long and 31 miles across), is no ordinary archipelago. According to Mapuche Indian legend, it was created not by a geographical phenomenon but as a result of a fight between two serpents, *Cai Cai* and *Tren Tren*. The Mapuche recall that Cai Cai, the evil one, rose in rage from the sea and flooded the earth. Cai Cai then moved to assault Tren Tren's rocky fortress high in the mountain peaks. Tren Tren, however, cannot be woken from a deep sleep.

'Meanwhile Cai Cai had almost reached Tren Tren's cave, swimming on the turbulent waters. Her friends, the pillanes of Thunder, Fire and Wind, helped her by piling up the clouds so it would rain, thunder and flash lightning.'

Still Tren Tren did not awake. At last she was aroused by the laughter of a little girl, who was dancing with her reflection in the sleeping

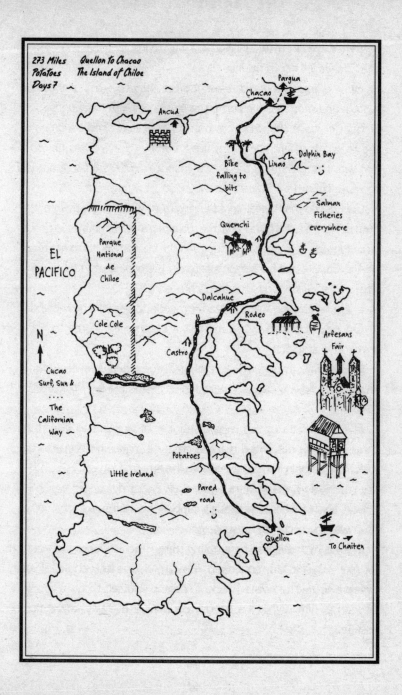

273 Miles   Quellon to Chacao
Potatoes   The Island of Chiloe
Days 7

Pargua

Chacao

Ancud

Bike
falling to
bits

Linao   Dolphin Bay

Salman
Fisheries
everywhere

Quemchi

EL
PACIFICO

Parque
National
de
Chiloe

Dalcahue

Rodeo

Cole Cole

Arfesans
Fair

N

Castro

Cucao
Surf, Sun &
....
The
Californian
Way

Potatoes

Little Ireland

Pared
road

Quellon   To Chaiten

serpent's eye. Tren Tren giggled in a way so insulting that Cai Cai and the Pillanes fell down the hill.

'But the amusement didn't last: Cai Cai charged again, all the more furious, and shattered the earth, sowing the sea with the islands . . .

Cai Cai made the water climb ever higher and almost submerged the mountain where her enemy lived; but Tren Tren arched her back and with the strength of the twelve guanacos in her stomach, pushed the cave ceiling upward and the mountain grew toward the sky.

Cai Cai and the Pillanes kept bringing more water and Tren Tren kept pushing her cave roof higher until the mountain reached above the clouds, close to the sun, where the Pillanes and the evil serpent could not reach it. And Cai Cai and her servants fell from the peak itself into the abyss where they lay stunned for a thousand years.'

In the legend the waters steadily recede to reveal a new island.

Once Chiloe rose out of the sea, it became the home to many mythical characters.

'As you walk through the forests of Chiloe, keep an eye out for *El Trauco*,' an old lady had whispered to us beside the ferry ticket office in Chaiten.

El Trauco, it transpired, was a seducer of virgins. No taller than three feet, this deformed manlike creature makes his home in the fork of a tree or in a small cave within the emerald forests. His clothes are made of vegetable fibre and he always carries a staff which he knocks against trees and uses to support his stump-like legs. What then was the secret of his success?

'It is his hypnotic and penetrating stare which seduces the young women,' the old lady continued. 'Be careful; one look could kill you or leave you with a twisted neck. To defend yourself, throw a handful of sand at him. While he is busy counting the grains, make your escape!'

We discovered that *El Trauco* also serves a social purpose. Belief in his existence provides an acceptable explanation of teenage pregnancies and has even been used to cover up incest that could have an explosive effect on the close-knit island communities.

El Trauco was not the only magical being roaming the forests and seas of Chiloe. The *Pincoya,* a blonde and beautiful mermaid, slips out of the surf at sunrise and dances on the shore. The *Caleuche,* a ghost ship, sails along the coast, with its crew of wizards and cargo of tragic guests caught in an eternal party. Then there is also, hidden among the clouds and volcano peaks, another *Lost City of the Caesars*, a place of great riches and infinite pleasures where no one is born or dies. With all these mysteries and figures of fantasy, we could not miss Chiloe. Indeed, we felt compelled by an irresistible force to cycle through this land of magic, legend and dreams.

On the ferry, I flicked through the official tourist brochure for Chiloe. It, too, hinted at a place divorced from reality. The English translation commanded visitors, such as ourselves, to engage in the following activities:

'You have to travel along its wet roads . . . (we could hardly wait!); lie on the sands of its islands . . . (that sounded more fun); admire the curious vegetation; try to embrace the sea, that can be ferocious or calm . . . (we could give it a go); contemplate the beautiful depth of the lakes; defy the pure sun and the windy storm.'

We were also ordered to meet the local people.

'One has to go to the harbour and have a rich dialogue with the locals, who with their families have sailed for days. Meet the "chilote peasant" that works with the spade, axe and scythe to clear the land. Enjoy the opportunity to be invited into the warm kitchen, where the family gathers and shares its most intimate solidarity and tenderness; listen to the rain while slowly and quietly, legends and myths come forth.

These things are not meant to be read about, you live them when you are in Chiloe.'

We landed at the fishing village of Quellon, with feelings of high expectation. We were not to be disappointed. We had cycled a mere ten miles through the gently undulating green fields enclosed by tight hedges, when we heard some strange noises. There was a tirade of grunts and groans coming from the hill just above us. We turned the corner and saw a figure four and a half feet tall, with stumpy legs pumping in a frenzy. It had to be *El Trauco*! I averted my eyes for fear of catching his gaze and sprouting a hump or a twisted neck. While my eyes were turned, I heard a cry of exasperation and the sound of metal hitting the ground. I could not resist the temptation to snatch a glance. It was not after all *El Trauco*, but Reinhardt from Germany standing in a pool of sweat with his bicycle lying twisted at his feet. He was indeed short and broad, and his stumpy legs were encased in cycle shorts, which must have been prised on with the help of a shoehorn. He was not, by any stretch of the imagination, a seducer of virgins.

'I hate that bike. I hate cycling,' Reinhardt screamed and then took a kick at his unfortunate bicycle. 'The gears are *kaputt*.'

'Oh, we are sorry,' David sympathised.

'*Ruta Cuarenta* is to blame,' he grunted. 'The heat . . . thirst . . . mirages . . . wind . . . dust . . . ruts . . . emptiness . . . boredom . . . Never again!'

The desert had evidently left its mental scars on Reinhardt. He would never forget it, but for very different reasons to those expounded by Charles Darwin and W. H. Hudson.

We left him still groaning by the side of the road and headed for Cucao, a village of weather-board huts situated by the crashing surf of the Pacific Ocean. It was a wild and primitive place, where the people fish, farm, pan for gold and do without most things, such as electricity and running water. For one day in Cucao we swapped saddles, from bikes to horses. I was given a docile clod-hopper with a droopy head and weighted eyelids. Nothing could wake him up, so I asked for a replacement. I wish I had correctly interpreted the smile that suddenly came over the farmer's face. I was presented with a horse, which looked more like a mule.

'He is fast and has spirit,' said Pedro, the beaming farmer. What he neglected to tell me was that this horse was possessed by the devil.

To get to the beach we had to cross a pedestrian suspension bridge over the river. It was made up of twisted steel cables and intermittent wooden planks. While we stepped gingerly across this creaking and swaying structure, *El Diablo* (the Devil), the name I christened him, sank his teeth into the rump of Mike's mount. This provocation was followed by a hefty kick, which sent El Diablo rearing up in agony. I was so nearly dumped into the river.

After surviving the bridge, I looked at my watch. Nine forty-five, it read, which meant fifteen minutes to go till the reputed assault by horseflies.

'Hold your horses at exactly ten o'clock. This is when the horseflies come out to play. The horses hate them, especially that one,' Pedro had warned, pointing at my mount. I started to question, with relief, the punctuality of these flies when, with one minute to go, there was no hint or whisper of them. On the dot of ten, they flew in out of nowhere, just as we set foot on the beach.

DAY 77 HORSE RIDING

'I had just mastered El Diablo. At last in control and relaxed. Then the horseflies hit. They swarmed in his eyes and stung his rump. He shook his head frantically and swished his tail. The flies continued their assault. El Diablo was sent over the brink and with it went my authority. He broke into a reckless gallop without rhythm, direction or control. In contrast, D and M

on their horses maintained a sedate amble, while I raced and bounced back and forth. The harder I pulled on the reins the faster he seemed to go. Many times my feet jumped out of the carved wooden stirrups and I was forced to lean forward and cling on to the mane. He would then jerk his head downwards to try and break my grip. Suddenly El Diablo stopped. I breathed a sigh of relief and relaxed.

It was all a clever ploy. As I loosened the reins, his ears pricked up and his eyes bulged with excitement. Slowly he turned towards the Pacific Ocean and then accelerated towards the crashing surf. He didn't even break his stride as he plunged in and the water rose quickly to my knees. A wave caught El Diablo full in the face and its force sent me reeling into the sea. The weight of my clothes dragged me down and I had to kick hard to reach the surface. I spluttered out a tirade of expletives as he turned and with head held high returned to the beach. Is this what the tourist brochure had meant about "embracing" the sea?'

When a big wave threw me floundering on to the shore, I had the indignity of hearing peals of laughter from Mike and David. When David finally managed to wipe away the tears, he set off after El Diablo. I could see their heads bobbing up and down amongst the sand dunes as he steadily closed the gap. It was an heroic performance and David, with justification, indulged in an orgy of self-congratulation.

By now El Diablo was smug and subdued. It was mission accomplished and I for one was not going to rush back into his saddle. David gave me his horse and with bruised pride and soaking clothes, we moved gingerly down the beach. We rode for five miles before leaving the sea for the mist shrouded hills. We climbed through dense bamboo forest, along a narrow, twisting path with high moss-covered sides. We rose above the clammy sea mist and the territory of the horseflies and at last I was able to enjoy the ride – earthy smells, the colours of the barberry and the cries of invisible forest birds. It was a

Where did the road go? Saipina, Bolivia

Arriba and a new found friend, Abra Pampa, Argentina

Down and out on the Bolivian altiplano – 14,500 feet

Miners underground in the Cerro Rico, Potosi, with the pagan 'tio', which is believed to ward off evil spirits and ensure safety. The 'tio' is given gifts of coca leaves, alcohol and cigarettes

Motorway service station Bolivian style. Taking lunch between the cities of Sucre and Potosi

Endless road in the deserts of Patagonia

Impromptu disco in a classroom at Tambo village school

Some like it hot! On the way to Santa Cruz, Bolivia

Red ribboned llamas carrying salt bricks to market from the lake of Urunyi, Bolivia

beautiful ride, but ten hours was too long for our buttocks, especially as the saddles were a shabby combination of metal, leather and wood and covered with odd scraps of sheepskin. By the end, I had developed bruises in places I did not think possible.

Riding and cycling do not go together. It was positively painful on the bike the next day and it was with a sigh of relief that we arrived in Castro, the capital of Chiloe. The town is dominated by its double-spired cathedral. It has the shape of a wedding cake and is dressed in blue and pink corrugated iron. It may be bizarre on the outside, but the interior was standard European Gothic, but fashioned entirely of wood. It is hard to believe this building has survived many earthquakes.

The cathedral was not the only unusual building in Castro. Many houses are built on stilts over the river. In the Far East, this type of housing is popular to escape the heat of the jungle, but in the wet and foggy Chiloe, the reasons were different. The owners avoid the expense and formality of having to buy land so they simply pay a small concession to the state. The houses are also flexible; when an occupant becomes bored with their particular stretch of river, they up sticks and tow their home to another location. It gives a new meaning to 'moving house'.

Many things in Chiloe are unique, and the food is no exception. We had been forbidden to leave the island before we had tried a 'curanto', a traditional Chilote dish. It was invented by fishermen who sailed off to remote places. They took with them supplies which would last for many weeks – dried vegetables, smoked sausage and potato dumplings. They would liven up this food by mixing it with shellfish such as mussels, sea urchins, barnacles and squid, wrapping them all in a giant rhubarb leaf. It would then be buried between heated stones under a fire and in this way it would keep warm for a day or more. Even though a cooking pot has now replaced the leaves, the result is unbelievably delicious and a match for the most ravenous appetites. It was not, however, for the squeamish – often an unidentifiable tentacled finger or a dark yellow tongue floated to the surface.

The next day we headed for the Sunday market at Dalcahue some twenty miles away. I had enjoyed little sleep and was hungover after a night at a Castro disco. I felt terrible. After only two miles my stomach was churning and my head was spinning. I searched for distractions to take my mind off my aching body and pounding head. I concentrated on remembering the names of the Uruguayan girls we had danced with at the disco and where I had put their telephone numbers. I also recalled a conversation I had with a drunken Chilote at the bar.

'Do you know who our capital is named after?' he asked.

'I have no idea,' I replied.

'After Fidel Castro, the President of Cuba. Not many people know that he was born here.'

Even pondering this bizarre statement could not clear my head. I gave up and took a lift, while Mike and David bravely cycled on.

In Dalcahue, it was the day of the annual rodeo, the most popular sport in Chile. It is an indication of how seriously they took the event that the only sober people in the town were the riders and the judges. We gathered around a tight wooden ring. Sixteen pairs of riders sat decked in striped woollen ponchos, knee-length black boots and glistening spurs. Their gaucho hats were held across their chests as they remembered a colleague who had lost his life in last year's event. The crowd showed their respect by holding a minute's silence.

The national anthem was sung and the rodeo was ready to begin. A pair of riders came into the ring to cheers and foot-stamping from the crowd. The noise reached a crescendo when the bull entered. He stood blinking and bemused and he visibly flinched at all the shouting. The white, blue and red lines painted around the wall of the ring are not for decoration. The aim of the game was to guide the bull at speed around the wall and then, at a specified point, turn the horses into the side of the bull, forcing him up the wall. The higher the bull rose, the greater the score – to hit the white line was five points, the blue was three, the red was one. Every 'white hit' was greeted to a standing ovation and followed by a Mexican wave. The bull would then be turned and guided to another specified 'target' area. The riders repeated this routine three times.

The rodeo was won by a father and son act, with a solid eleven points of one white and two blue 'hits'. Their surnames of Messner and Aryan looks hinted at their German origins. They had won for their disciplined performance against more flamboyant but fallible Latin contestants. They did not even display a hint of a smile as they rode up to collect the silver salver. The dark Chilean riders in second place embraced each other and spilt tears of joy and disappointment.

Dancing followed the rodeo. The *cueca* was led by an old-timer, whose energy and rhythm belied his ninety years. It appeared his zest for life was not confined to the dance-floor, for his partner was half his age. Girls swarmed to the sides of the heroes of the ring and these hens did not require much chasing from the roosters. It was not so much a courting dance, but a preliminary mating ritual. The evening spun into a faint memory.

I felt simply awful the next day, the price of two nights of excessive drinking and dancing. We could not leave, however, until I had retraced my tracks to where I had taken a lift the previous day, thus maintaining our objective of cycling every inch of our route. I returned from the twenty mile detour feeling distinctly fragile. In contrast, Mike and David were rested and keen.

We decided to take the coastal route rather than riding directly northwards on the paved road. It was little more than a track, which not only hugged the coast, but also clung to every contour. We realised, as we meandered up and then down, why Chiloe is considered one of the wettest islands in the world – it is simply riddled with streams and rivers cutting their way to the ocean. The rain that everybody had warned us about finally hit. It was torrential, and soon our path was transformed into a sea of mud, which sucked and held our wheels. We arrived at a tiny village and looked for shelter from the storm. Many curtains twitched, but no one came to the door. Who could blame them? We must have looked like three drowned *gringo* rats.

We cycled on, and as night fell we found ourselves in the sleepy seaside village of Linao, which consisted of fifteen weather-board houses. Curtains continued to twitch but doors remained firmly closed. We heard a call and turned to see the hunch-back figure of an old lady. She was beckoning to us with one hand, while she lent on her stick and craned her neck upwards. She led us into her house. The ceiling was so low that even I had to stoop and Mike was virtually bent double. Maria, our hostess, had lived here all her seventy-four years and it appeared her posture had evolved to fit her home.

Maria muttered something. We assumed it was an invitation to sit down. It was not, for she started to shake her head violently. Mike thought he might have sat on the cat and stood up quickly hitting his head on the ceiling. She tried again, but we failed to catch it. She started tugging at her clothing and very slowly said,

'Take your clothes off!'

In failing to understand her we were not being bashful. It is just difficult to comprehend Spanish spoken through toothless gums.

Our dripping clothes were hung above the wood-burning stove in the kitchen and Maria set about cooking us a meal. It was evident she was in a hurry.

'I must cook and we must eat quickly. The wrestling starts in less than an hour,' she surprisingly said.

'Wrestling, what wrestling?' we asked.

'All the way from America. Hulk Hogan is on tonight. He is my favourite!'

The allotted time came. She drew up a chair within feet of the television and turned it on. She peered through straining eyes and gradually leaned closer until her nose was virtually pressed up against the screen. Her head and tongue followed every movement of her hero, Hulk Hogan. Her muffled cheers kept us awake until well into the night.

Maria stood bleary eyed at her gate and kissed us goodbye. We thanked her and headed for the ferry to the mainland and the city of Puerto Montt. This city represented to us the end and start of many things.

DAY 83 PUERTO MONTT

'After three months and two thousand miles, it was time to say goodbye to Patagonia. With it went the wind, glaciers, rheas, guanacos, desolate plains, the overwhelming hospitality and pioneering spirit of the people.

"Civilised Chile begins at Puerto Montt," the Chilean Consulate in London had told me. Despite the warning the city came as a shock. It was as if we had suddenly cycled out of a primeval land and society into the twentieth century. Here marked the start of the Pan American Highway, Coca-Cola billboards and Kentucky Fried Chicken restaurants. I for one was not ready and craved to retreat back in time!'

—11—
VINO AND VOLCANOES

'The Lake District symbolises everything healthy, unspoiled, and pure in Chile.'

Advertising slogan for the Region.

'The deep coal mines are in Lota: it's a cold seaport.'

PABLO NERUDA 'Canto General'

We were on the brink of a land of volcanoes, lakes and vineyards. Together they stretched 1,000 miles north, all the way to the capital of Santiago. It also was a region of cities, traffic, tourism, industry and coal mines.

Chile is the home to 2,085 volcanoes. Fifty-five are still active and the majority of these are to be found in the Andes to the north of Puerto Montt. These volcanoes form part of the Pacific Rim of Fire which stretches from Alaska down through California and Central America to western South America, and reappears on the opposite side of the Pacific Ocean in New Zealand, the western Pacific islands, Japan, and the Kamchatka Peninsula of USSR. Chile's volcanoes are particularly dangerous because many have perpetual snow covering

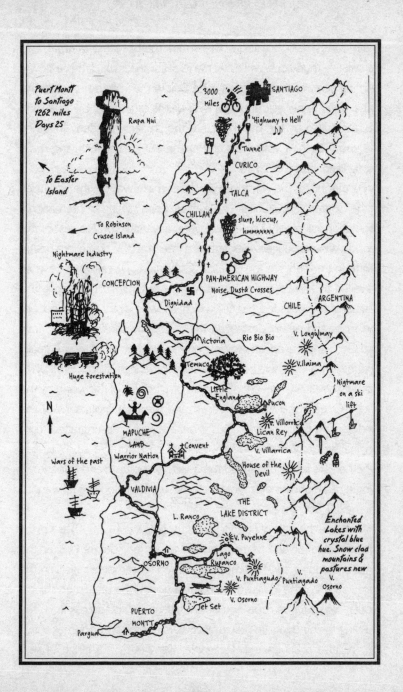

their cones. On eruption, the snow melts, causing rapid and devastating mudslides, while the lava itself advances much more slowly burning away everything in its path. Below the volcanoes nestle the lakes. They are of glacial origin, their basins carved out by advancing ice, then filled by the melting ice as the glaciers receded. Together the snow-capped volcanoes and shimmering lakes form the most recognised image of Chile.

Further north the volcanoes and lakes make way for the vineyards of the Central Valley. Chilean wines have been gaining an international reputation for quality. Chile has a great advantage on the rest of the world's wine producers – its vines are free from the phylloxera beetle blight. In the 1850s, Don Silvester Ochagavia, a wealthy landowner travelled to France and returned with vine cuttings just before the plague of the dreaded beetle, which chewed away at the roots of the vines and nearly destroyed the wine industries in France, Italy and Germany. European growers only saved their vines by eventually grafting onto tougher, beetle-resistant American stock. Phylloxera has yet to reach Chile, cut off as it is from the rest of the world by the Pacific Ocean, the Atacama desert and the high mountains of the Andes. The Chilean vines thus grow naturally and ungrafted from original stock. We planned to conduct an extensive study to see whether this factor enhanced the quality of the taste and bouquet. It would be an understatement to say that we were looking forward to the next 1,000 miles.

We used the port of Puerto Montt (population 112,000) as a place of acclimatisation and preparation. It was not long before I kicked the urge of stepping back in time, and started to immerse myself in the temptations of the 'civilised' world. In amongst the unpainted shingle fronts, high pitched roofs and quaint balconies, and across from the bustling fishing boats lie restaurants, bars, discos and cinemas. After our relative abstinence in Patagonia, we went on a binge of self-indulgence. Our self-restraint was not helped by staying at a *hospedaje* (hostel) owned by Efran and Pearla. They were a fun-loving couple, who embraced the excesses of life with a vengeance and had banned the word 'no' from their home. Pearla took great relish in preparing meals of a legendary size, while Efran had a habit of proposing a toast between each mouthful. At one end Pearla would be ladling out food, saying,

'You must have more fish! More soup? More tomatoes? More ice-cream, you cannot say no.'

At the other end, Efran would rise and announce,

'To the Knights of the Round Table' (his name for us), 'To Maggie Thatcher and the Falkland Islands,' 'To unrequited love.'

These meals tended to last about three hours and they would always be followed by dancing the *cueca* with unsteady steps and much dropping of the handkerchiefs.

With the benefit of hindsight, perhaps this was not the best time to take Spanish lessons. Efran was our long-suffering teacher and I will always remember his baritone voice booming out in exasperation,

'Muy flojo y muy borracho, pero buenos caballeros' (Very lazy and very drunk, but good fellows). By any stretch of the imagination, we were not natural born linguists.

In only a week, we became rotund and unfit. We had to leave before we succumbed further. While we cycled out of Puerto Montt, I could imagine *Arriba* straining under my new weight and thinking, 'Goodness gracious, what has he been up to?' Thankfully, the next town of Puerto Varas, the gateway to the Lake District, was not far away. We rested here the next day, with the lame excuse that we did not believe in cycling on Sundays. In reality, we had the shakes after cycling only twenty miles the previous day.

I do not know whether it was newly acquired weight which loosened *Arriba*'s bottom bracket and caused her pedals to start wobbling. As fate would have it, we had sent the relevant tool up to Santiago in our clear out at Puerto Natales. I was fearful of damaging the pedals by cycling on, so I had no other option but to turn back. David and Mike decided to go on and wait for me at the settlement of Petrohue. It was an emotional moment for it was the first time in the expedition we had spent any time apart.

Back in Puerto Varas, I was directed down a back street to the door of a bicycle mechanic. His appearance was far from reassuring; he was in his seventies, his hands trembled and he peered at me through thick lenses, which distorted his eyes. He said it would be no problem and I noticed with some relief the Shimano sticker in the dusty window (the pedals were made by them). I am not a mechanic, but I was surprised when he took out a hammer and chisel and tried to prise one of the pedals off. I threw myself over *Arriba* to bring an end to his manic hammering. Poor *Arriba* still bears to this day the scars of 'the bicycle butcherer of Puerto Varas.'

Arriba was fixed in the sane and calm environment of a shop in Puerto Montt. I was asked about the origins of the scars and as I explained there were knowing glances all around. With firm pedals, I cycled through the pouring rain in pursuit of Mike and David. I found them holed up in the school on the misty and rain-drenched shores of Lago Todos los Santos (the Lake of All Saints). It is reputed to be one of the most beautiful lakes in Chile, because of its emerald waters and its position below the perfect white cone of the Osorno Volcano. When we were there it was miserable, the waters were grey and the volcano was shrouded in mist. We did, however, celebrate reaching the 2,000 miles with smoked salmon we had bought in the fish market of Puerto Montt.

I was getting excited, because we were edging ever closer to Lago Rupanco. Three years before, I had been involved in a golf project, which was to be located on its shores. I never thought I would see or experience the snow-capped volcanoes, the crystal waters and the deep evergreen forests, which I had written about in such glowing terms in the project prospectus. Now, we were within fifteen miles of the lake and the site we had called 'Bahia Encanto' (the enchanted bay).

I was so carried away I did not notice what must have been quite a rattle in my handlebars. We came to a sweeping left-hand corner. I eased my hands round; the handlebars moved easily, but the wheel did not. I never made the turn and instead careered straight into the hedge opposite. It was blackthorn and it took days to remove all the thorns.

The accident was the reason we did not make it to the Enchanted Bay until nightfall. I found it difficult to orientate myself from the photographs I had seen some three years before, but eventually we did make it to a farmhouse that looked familiar. In the darkness, I knocked tentatively on the door. We heard steps and voices inside and it was only when I knocked for a second time that an attractive lady in her forties appeared. Behind her stood three kids peering curiously at the three strangers covered in dust, sweat and thorns.

'I am sorry I thought you were the cows,' she said with surprise and relief. 'They kept us awake all last night with their banging and mooing.' Thankfully, it was the right house.

We were permitted to camp on what I remembered to be the eighteenth green. The course had yet to be started and was still in the hands of the planners and bankers in Santiago. When I awoke in the morning I was glad of the continued delay, for we were allowed to lie in peace without being peppered by golf balls and interrupted by shouts of 'Fore'. That is until the three children arrived and dragged us out of bed for a game of football on the beach. England lost to Chile, six goals to seven.

Unknowingly, we had arrived into the high society of Chile. We found that Lago Rupanco was their exclusive playground during the summer months. Carolina, the mother of the children, turned out to be the sister of the Chancellor of the Exchequer and she introduced us to an assortment of prominent politicians, architects, businessmen and artists. They all seemed to have one thing in common: they had at one time met Margaret Thatcher. I found it hard to understand the enthusiasm and pride with which they described the meeting. For two days, we were the underdressed novelties at drinks parties and dinners.

In the golf project prospectus, I had waxed lyrical about the ski resort of Antillanca, which lay in the shadow of the alluringly named Volcano Casablanca. I had to go there, and David and Mike reasoned it would be excellent training for the mountains of Bolivia. It was a tough climb and when we finally reached the top, we vowed to return to our initial philosophy of energy conservation rather than training. For other reasons it was worth it. The early morning view from the summit was breathtaking. Some thirty lakes and lagoons sparkled in the sunlight and the slopes around them were coloured pink with fuschias. Of the five snow-capped volcanoes, which pierced the blue sky, the perfect cone of Osorno was the most striking. Sara Wheeler is not exaggerating in her book, *Travels in a Thin Country*, when she writes, '*it is to volcanoes what Krug is to champagne; it is the Taj Mahal of the natural world.*'

It was all downhill to the city named after the volcano and with darkness approaching we found ourselves by chance at the door of Bernardo and his wife. They had just finished their *asado* (barbecue) house in the garden and we were honoured to be given the opportunity to christen it. Bernardo was an outcast of the 1960s. In the cellar he had a shrine dedicated to the memory of James Dean and every day we would light a candle to his hero. In the garage he had a polished white Buick. His wife felt she was a widow to James Dean and the Buick.

It was here in the garden that David had an unfortunate incident with his cycling helmet. He and I experienced a simultaneous call of nature – a result of trying to keep pace with Bernardo as he knocked back the pisco. In 'mid-pee' in the dark, I noticed a curious phenomenon: while I made the sound of water on grass, David made the shrill splattering noise of water on plastic. There had to be an explanation. As if in answer the moon appeared through the clouds and the light glistened on the newly baptised cycling helmet, which David had dropped while unpacking. He never wore that helmet again.

With two helmets and the sound of Bernardo singing the songs of Jimi Hendrix, we rode for the city of Valdivia nearly a hundred miles away. On the road, Mike and I had some problems through overindulgence. We had called into Osorno for money and almost inevitably ended up staying for lunch. Mike decided to venture off the menu with a mind-boggling combination of avocado, fried egg and chips. The mix of the rough road and this food bumping around on the wall of his stomach, made him feel nauseous. I was not a victim of food, but of drink – not alcoholic, but of the gaseous variety. It was hot cycling and I contracted a raging thirst. At a roadside stall I downed two litres of fizzy lemon. The build up of wind was so great that I could not resume a sitting position for some thirty miles. How we achieved ninety-three miles that day I will never know.

Valdivia is a historic city. The port was founded by the colonist Pedro de Valdivia in the sixteenth century. He fortified the city's position building a series of forts along the estuary, guarding against attack from the sea. These forts failed to protect either Valdivia himself or his city. On Christmas Day, 1553, Valdivia was captured by Mapuche Indians, tied to a tree and then, as the legend goes, was forced to drink molten gold. The city itself fell in 1882 during the War of Independence to the dashing young Scot, Lord Thomas Cochrane, who was fighting for the Chilean revolutionaries.

The principal fort at Niebla now lies in ruins. I was just reading about the audacious exploits of Lord Cochrane, when a tee-shirt caught my eye. It was one of our expedition tee-shirts, which had been specially printed and sold to raise money. How had this blond-haired chap got hold of one of these unique shirts? Had he stolen it from our hotel room? Had it been copied and pirated internationally?

'My mother gave it me for Christmas,' he replied in surprise.

'How did she get hold of one?'

'Her husband and my step-father is Lord Oaksey. I believe he is the patron or something. I think he said it was in aid of three eccentric guys cycling up the Andes. How did you get yours?'

'I am one of those eccentric guys,' I replied.

David knew that Mark Crocker was somewhere in South America, but it was a complete fluke he was here at this time and he was wearing one of the expedition tee-shirts. He was working as a canoe instructor in the rich resort town of Pucon.

'You must come and stay. It is a great town full of life and parties,' Mark said.

A detour of 130 miles seemed a small price to pay for a stay in one of the most famous playgrounds in Chile. We accepted.

While on our way to Pucon, nightfall took us by surprise. We were in the middle of nowhere, apart from a large rambling house hiding behind a row of poplars about half a mile off the road. We decided to chance it and cycled along a grassy track until we got to an imposing gate. A small hand bell hung down on a frayed piece of rope. Mike shook it. After about two minutes a nun arrived and peered at us with some trepidation from the other side. We explained we were three weary travellers, looking for a roof for the night.

There was a shrill shout from behind her and without another word she scuttled off. Mother Superior appeared from the shadows of the doorway.

She was a tall, proud lady with a presence and voice that made you want to obey her. She ordered us to follow and we walked meekly down a corridor of creaking wooden floorboards. The air was rich with the smell of polish and my mind filled with memories of my prep school. She led us into a room with four wrought iron beds.

'You will be wanting some food?' she asked. We nodded.

She left, shutting the heavy oak door behind her. We heard the clanking of a key and then the thud of a bolt being drawn across. We were locked in a nunnery! Thirty minutes later we heard footsteps, and a small hatch in the door slid open. A hand appeared bearing a large plate of food. Three plates later and the hatch was closed again. As the door was not opened until six thirty the next morning, we were thankful for the toilet pans that had been thoughtfully left under our beds. We discussed the reason behind the lock-in and concluded that Mother Superior had feared our intentions on her nuns rather than, as David suggested, the other way round.

David's hormones were indeed high. It had all started when he met Carolina at the Lake of All Saints. On the rain-drenched shores, David had realised she was the girl of his dreams and he was counting the days and hours until they met again. There was a chance she could still be at Lican Ray, a lake-side resort a mere fifty miles away. For Mike and I that day, David was just a trail of dust disappearing off into the horizon. In Lican Ray, we found holidaymakers crawling like locusts over the streets, beaches and campgrounds, but, much to David's distress, no Carolina. It really was like trying to find a needle in a haystack. In David's eyes the solution was easy: we should cycle to her home town of Concepcion. After all, it was only three hundred and fifty miles away.

We put these plans on ice and cycled to Pucon to visit Mark. The town is dominated by the active Villarrica Volcano. Its presence is not just physical, for the locals believe that the mood of the volcano affects their lives and minds. While we were there, the volcano was going through a particularly volatile period, issuing plumes of smoke and visibly melting the snow around its cone. Down in the town it was a turbulent time for marriages and relationships. I remember sitting in a bar with Jimi, a friend of Mark's. He was being philosophical about his girlfriend's latest affair.

'She is always like this when the volcano is active. She just cannot control herself. I know we will be back together again when the smoke dies down.'

'What happens if it doesn't?' I asked.

'I will go up there with a bucket of water.'

'And if it erupts?'

'We will meet in heaven,' Jimi replied.

We felt compelled to take a closer look at this physical and mental force. We hired a guide, crampons, boots and ice axes and took a ski-lift up to the snowline. The guide had instructed us at some length on how to use the equipment, but had failed to tell us about the idiosyncrasies of the lift.

DAY 110 VILLARRICA VOLCANO

'Mike and I were travelling together in a two-man chair. When we reached the wooden platform at the top, we raised the bar and lifted ourselves out of the chair. At this point the chair seemed to speed up and started hitting us in the backs of our legs. We ran and the chair chased. In heavy boots we were no match for the renegade chair. Finally, I executed a incisive side-step out of its path. I turned to see Mike had not been so lucky. The chair

caught him in the back of the knees and hurtled him, to my horror, directly at me. Mike careered into me and I was catapulted head-first over the back of the platform. I landed in a bed of cables, wood and dirt some twelve feet below. I got away with a couple of bruises, but I shuddered to think of the damage the ice axe would have caused if I had landed on my back.'

After this, the ascent to the sulphurous and molten crater of Villarrica was easy.

Just when we were ready to leave Pucon, two incidents delayed us. First, we were persuaded to don lifejackets and to take to the river. There was no idle meandering, for the *Rio Pucon* was in an angry and turbulent mood. We were guided down by a lunatic Peruvian helmsman, who took great relish in hearing us scream. The shakes subsided after twenty-four hours and then we prepared to leave.

'You can't go now,' Mark announced. 'Tonight is the Miss Chile pageant at the hotel.'

We stayed and had absolutely no regrets.

After the pageant, the affairs of the heart won the day over reason. We collectively decided to go to Concepcion, so that David could see Carolina. The road took us through the centre of Chile's main forestry area. When the road was paved it was pleasant enough to be passed by convoys of freshly-cut, sweet-smelling pine. But invariably the road was dirt, and we would be smothered by a blanket of dust from each thundering truck. It made cycling dangerous as we coughed and peered through the thick haze. Even though the trucks had their lights on, visibility was down to a mere twenty feet. It was hard to believe the sun was shining overhead.

With relief we left the pine forests and rode into one of the poorest areas in Chile. It was all a far cry from the richness and purity of the lakes. The towns of Lota and Coronel have been thrown into depression by the decline of the coal industry. In Lota, Pablo Neruda had *'never seen mankind more abused'*. He continued to write in *Canto General*:

> *'Man's life is dark*
> *as coal: tattered night,*
> *miserable bread, harsh day.'*

With the poverty, however, came an overwhelming friendliness. Children shouted and waved at us while they played on the top of the slag heaps lining the road. When we stopped they slid down on their bottoms and shook our hands and asked us a barrage of questions: 'where are you from?' 'do you like Chile?' 'do you want a piece of coal to remember us by?' Passing truck drivers clapped their hands at our progress and one even stopped to hand us down three masks for our choking mouths. The most stirring image was that of a young boy standing by the road. His face was caked in coal dust and his clothes were in tatters. As we passed he smiled, put his thumb up and wished us 'good luck'.

Concepcion, even though it only has 265,400 inhabitants, is the second largest city in Chile. It was again founded by Pedro de Valdivia back in 1550, but today it is a modern city with little remaining testimony of the past. The address for Carolina was Avenida O'Higgins 54. On this wide, tree-lined street, number fifty-four turned out to be a forty storey block of flats. She lived with her family on the thirty-third floor and the lift was broken. We carried the bikes up the stairs and tied them to the balcony of their tiny flat. Directly below lay the cathedral and I remembered a story Efran had told us in Puerto Montt. It was about a man called Sebastian Acevedo who set fire to himself in the doorway of this cathedral in 1983. It was in protest of the repeated torture by the authorities of his twenty-two year old son and twenty-one year old daughter, who it was claimed had been distributing anti-government propaganda. Acevedo had written pleading for them to stop and he had warned them of what he would do if they did not. They didn't, so he walked to the cathedral, doused himself in petrol, lit a match and incinerated himself. According to Efran a wooden cross was raised in his memory and the military authorities sawed it off at the base.

So far on the expedition, I have painted a picture of complete harmony between us. This was largely true, apart from trivial disagreements about the washing up, Tina Turner and the therapeutic qualities of my singing. It was in Concepcion that we had our first major argument. It stemmed from two hearts being in different places. David's heart was now with Carolina, while my heart remained focused on our spiritual halfway point of Santiago and my parent's arrival in six days time. I am an idealist and was adamant, after all that we had been through, that we cycled the next 350 miles together into Santiago. David, on the other hand, saw his short-term future in Concepcion.

We had reached a stale-mate.

It was broken by Mike's decision to press on with me, combined with an article in the local newspaper. We had been called many things on the expedition so far: 'lazy and drunk,' 'crazy gringos' and 'the Knights of the Round Table,' but never until now, 'The Three Musketeers.' The article started:

'The old legend of the three musketeers is alive today . . .'

Underneath was a photo of our three smiling faces with the caption: *'all for one and one for all'.* David softened, and *The Three Musketeers* cycled as one out of Concepcion bound for Santiago.

We were faced with covering approximately 350 miles in six days to get to Santiago. We could not keep my parents waiting, so we would have to be disciplined in our cycling, but worse still rise early every morning. The race was on! We did, however, get distracted in the district of Parral, which is famous for its German communes. These communes had been set up after the Second World War by Germans fleeing retribution. Chile was a particularly popular destination, because it was the only South American country not to declare war on Germany. We had heard rumours that Nazi ideals and the Aryan race were still practised behind their high barbed-wire fences.

When we saw a ten foot high poster featuring a blond-haired and blue-eyed boy pointing the way to the 'Colonia Dignidad', we felt compelled to investigate. Dignity Colony is the most infamous of all the German communes in Chile. It was founded in 1960 by Paul Schaefer. Schaefer was a medical orderly in Hitler's army, became pastor of his own Lutheran sect in the Bonn area in the Fifties and then fled to Chile while on bail after being charged with sexually abusing children at a youth centre. Since its inception, Colonia Dignidad, has been the centre of allegations and controversy. Schaefer is accused of heading 'a state within a state', which allegedly practises child abuse, kidnapping (including the snatching of children from Germany), arms trafficking, Nazi genetics and also of collaborating with Pinochet's military regime of the Seventies and Eighties. The Commune is said to have provided a rent-a-torture chamber service, within which political opponents received electric shock treatment to the music of Wagner and Mozart. German-speaking doctors reportedly administered drugs to the torture victims.

We rode four miles down the pot-holed gravel road to the Commune with open minds. A bold message slung across the top of the gates, declared 'We seek Acceptance and Understanding'. Once inside we saw nothing sinister – no underground chambers, no bruised or frightened children and no arm caches. It was a scene of a hard working, three hundred strong, community. We caught a glimpse inside the single storey white housing. The accommodation was functional and spartan; no pictures or carpets adorned the walls or floors but there were what appeared to be bibles beside each iron bed. In the fields of maize and potatoes, women tilled the ground with hoes, dressed in calf-length frocks and black tights. We were invited to the Commune kitchen and were given pork and sauerkraut. The language, food and the fair looks of the inhabitants were all a far cry from the Chile we knew to be outside.

Colonia Dignidad presented nothing but the image of a working, self-sufficient, commune. If this is simply what it is; why did we see and experience a high level of paranoia? Was it really necessary to have a fifteen foot barbed-wire fence around the perimeter? Why did they forbid the use of cameras inside the compound? Why were we frisked at the entrance, even though we were wearing only cycle shorts and tee-shirts? Why were we escorted the whole way round? We left with the feeling that Paul Schaefer and *Colonia Dignidad* did indeed have something to hide.

We left the cloistered environment of *Dignidad* for the 'free for all' of the Pan-American Highway. We had met many fellow cyclists who had taken a lift on this three hundred mile stretch to Santiago. It was with justification; it was a biking hell. The two lane road was narrow and extremely busy. There was not enough room for two trucks and a bicycle to pass at the same time. Many times we were forced off the road onto the kerb by the fierce hooting of a horn and the manic screeching of brakes. We passed many victims of the road: dead dogs, frogs, snakes and cats. There was even a sign which declared there had been thirty-three deaths on the road this year. It was only the end of February!

The road was lined with vineyards. We had cycled many days and miles to reach this region and we were not going to leave without having a tasting session. After all, we had to make a judgement on the qualities of phylloxera-free vines. The manager was as pleased to see us as we were to view row upon row of wine bottles.

'Welcome to the Vineyard of *Miguel Torres*, the exporter of more bottles on a pro rata basis than any other Chilean producer,' he declared grandly.

'Good, we have obviously come to the right place. We were feeling . . .,' David said, before being cut-off.

'Miguel Torres was established in 1978 when the family came over from Catalonia. We were the innovators of the Chilean wine industry and first to introduce temperature-controlled fermentation. Many foreign investors followed our lead and now even Baron Eric de Rothschild has his share in the Chilean grape,' he continued.

'That is all very interesting, but we are feeling quite thirsty,' Mike pleaded.

'The Chileans do not know much about wine. They do not appreciate a good wine. If it is cheap and in a carton, they will buy it,' he said.

I could sympathise with the Chileans. I thought back to the wine we had drunk in the last couple of months and yes, it had been cheap and in a carton. I was not going to admit it and instead I made an appeal to the manager's vanity and love of his wine.

'We are greatly looking forward to the soft and lingering taste of a Miguel Torres Chablis,' I hinted.

'Wonderful.' He clapped his hands. 'It is great to meet people who love and appreciate wine. The government likes us because of the foreign currency we bring in through exports. The Pinochet regime was a particular supporter of ours. I remember in October 1991, after a freak frost hit the Maipo valley, Pinochet offered the army helicopters and they duly took off over the vineyards creating a wind to thaw the frost,' the manager said, and at last started to pour four glasses of wine.

'*Salud!*' (Cheers) and we raised our glasses. We gulped the wine down, completely oblivious to the delicate scent and flavour of almonds.

It was the manager's day, for a coachload of wine tourists from France arrived. This was not their first port of call, and as we left they broke into an unruly chorus, '*It's a long way to Titicaca, it's a long way to go*'. They were right, we did have a long way to go. At this present moment, however, we were not worried about the distance to Titicaca, but concerned with the width of the road to the next town, Curico.

Curico is the old-fashioned and provincial capital of the Chilean wine industry. Apart from wine, it is famous for its central plaza, Plaza des Armas. In amongst some sixty palm trees, there were lovely fountains, delicate sculptures of nymphs and black-necked swans, a monument to the Mapuche warrior, Lautaro, carved from the trunk of an ancient beech tree and a cast-iron elevated bandstand. I sat and read to the sound of running water. Suddenly, the tranquillity was shattered by a wailing and the clapping of hands. The local gospel choir had arrived to rehearse for the following day's concert. Wine, reading and gospel do not go well together, so I left.

We were now within one hundred and fifty miles of Santiago, which was just as well for my parents were due to arrive in two day's time. I simply could not wait to see them. We needed, however, to put in a big day, so that I could avoid cycling straight to the airport. We were committed, and we took only the briefest of pitstops as we pushed to break the hundred mile barrier. At ninety-three miles, we reached an obstacle, a tunnel through a ridge of hills. We had heard much about tunnels in Chile; they tended to be narrow, dark and thick with carbon-monoxide. In a nutshell, they were to be avoided at all costs. For the sake of establishing a new daily record, we decided to risk it, but not before putting on lights and wrapping tee-shirts around our heads and mouths. We need not have bothered – the tunnel was only one hundred and fifty yards long and we sailed through it without drawing breath.

We stumbled off our bikes having clocked up one hundred and two miles. The town of Paine had no hotel or campground. We had spied a firestation on the way in and we tried our luck there. The men in blue were only too pleased to help and they allowed us to camp in their back garden. I went off to buy a celebratory carton of wine. On my way back I heard a siren and to my surprise a police car veered across my path and stopped just ahead of me. Two policemen slowly clambered out and walked towards me.

'Are you cycling with another person?' one of the policemen asked.

'Yes,' I replied, puzzled.

'Do you speak English?'

'Yes.'

'We have your friend. Follow us.'

I had only left Mike and David some ten minutes ago. What could they have done in such a short time? Maybe set off a fire alarm, released an extinguisher or played around with one of the hoses. But why did the police have only one of them? The policemen returned to their car, hooted to catch my attention and drove off. On arriving at the station, I was shown into a stark room. The walls were discoloured and the reek of cigarette smoke hung in the air. The only decoration was a picture of Pinochet on the opposite wall. At a simple wooden table in the middle, sat a rather forlorn looking chap. We stared blankly at each other.

'Aren't you going to embrace,' a policeman said encouragingly.

'Why? I have never seen this fellow before in my life,' I replied.

'But I thought you said you were not travelling alone.'

'Yes, with two friends, but he is not one of them!'

Patrick, an American tourist, had lost his friend while cycling along the Pan-American Highway. Apparently, the friend had vanished into thin air. It had been six hours now and Patrick was becoming increasingly worried about his friend's safety. I invited him to come and stay with us at the firestation and promised to help him search in the morning.

We were dreading the last leg into Santiago. It promised to be hot, busy and judging from what people had told us, on bicycles we were likely to choke to death. We had heard the smog is so bad that cars are restricted by their licence plates as to when they are permitted into the city. Ahead the snow-capped Andes appeared to be floating on a brown haze, which masked traffic-ridden streets and over half of the country's manufacturing industry. After a while, the Andes disappeared and the sun was eclipsed by a brown shadow.

We had still found no trace of Patrick's friend. No one at a roadside cafe, toll booth or road works could remember seeing a lone cyclist the previous evening. Patrick had one hope left. His friend might have decided to wait for him in the main plaza of Santiago. He was there, and initial accusations of 'how could you have been so stupid' were soon followed by tears of relief. We were left to celebrate with beer and ice-cream. We had made it with twenty-four hours to spare before my parents arrived, but more importantly, we had completed the first three thousand miles of the expedition *together*.

—12—
SADDLE FREE

'Nobody has ever worked harder at inactivity, with such force of character, with such unremitting attention to detail, with such conscientious devotion to the task.'

WALTER LIPPMANN 'Man of Destiny'

The capital city of Santiago (population 4 million) is the fifth largest in Latin America. It nestles below the snow-capped Andes, which form a magnificent backdrop when rain and smog permits. While it is a big city, it has a provincial atmosphere. High-rise buildings and bustling narrow streets are confined to the centre and then after only a few blocks; leafy avenues, residential suburbs, fashionable shopping malls and low commercial buildings predominate. In the streets, we witnessed economic extremes, the contrast between sophistication and underdevelopment. Outside banks, financial services and telecommunications companies, which are the most up-to-date in Latin America, the poor were hawking cheap Taiwanese trinkets and selling grimy candy. Aggressive yuppies in designer suits, the legacy of General Pinochet's capitalist policies, weaved their way amongst shoe-shine boys and car minders.

We stayed the first two nights with Audrey, who we had met three months before in Torres del Paine. We were looking forward to sleeping on crisp cotton sheets and soft mattresses, and with a roof over our heads. When it came to it, we could not sleep. In the morning, Audrey found us all in the garden snuggled up in our sleeping bags and let us know in no uncertain terms that she thought we were completely bananas.

We then moved to the *barrio alto* (posh) suburb of Los Condes, an area of well-tended green lawns and leafy streets. We were the guests of the Faundez family. I had met Juan Carlos Faundez through an old school friend before we left England. It had only been for twenty minutes, but in that time Juan Carlos had offered to be our drop-off point for equipment and in effect 'Our Man in Santiago'. He had already proved indispensable by sending down to us such things as a chain rivet remover and bottom bracket sprocket, after the problem I had had near Puerto Montt.

Even though we were living in the lap of luxury we found it difficult to shake off the habits of the road. We continued to sleep under the stars, to eat porridge in the mornings and to cycle daily around the streets relishing the sensation of riding without panniers. Juan Carlos and his parents looked on with amusement and put our behaviour down to being too long in Patagonia. 'That region is so wild, it sends everybody who goes there a little crazy,' Juan Carlos' father declared one day.

The Faundez family helped us not to lose sight of one of the principal objectives of the expedition – leukaemia. They were a family of doctors and were able to arrange a visit to a children's leukaemia clinic in the Roberto Rio hospital. It was moving for us to meet the children and I remember two in particular: Pia and Jonathen. Both had acute symptoms, but they did not let the pain of their treatment show as they smiled at us with brave and innocent eyes. Mike wrote a poem about Pia.

Ode to Pia
In your dancing eyes I see
Such strength and innocent bravery
They ask me with their piercing stare
'Why me' you know this is not fair
I shed a tear as answers I do not possess
And all I offer is a moving caress.
Perhaps you know not how strong you are
Or what lies ahead on this journey far
Down a painful and exhausting road
That some demon with rotting seeds has sowed
At times it may be difficult to cope
But never forget the chant of hope.

Soon after visiting Pia and Jonathen, we heard some wonderful news from England. I had been introduced to Anthony while taking Spanish lessons at International House. He was the son of Teresa Bailey, one of the Directors, and at the age of six, he was going through painful treatment to combat leukaemia. He had invited us to his school in Lambeth to give a talk about the expedition and since then he and his class had been sending us letters of encouragement. Anthony, we heard, had been diagnosed clear of leukaemia. It was an emotional moment and one that I will never forget. We had Anthony, together with Pia and Jonathen, to thank for giving us an overwhelming sense of purpose.

Promoting awareness of leukaemia was also an important part of our objective. With the assistance of the British Embassy, we reached a wide audience by appearing in the well-respected 'Courier' newspaper and on a zany open-air music show aimed at teenagers.

I remember arriving at the park for the filming, and the place was swarming with young girls. Our arrival seemed to set them screaming and instead of rushing away, which was the response we had come to expect, they ran towards us. We basked in this attention, until they stampeded over us as if we were not there. Unbeknown to us, a jeep had drawn up behind us and four members of a Chilean rock band had clambered out on to the tarmac. We were not allowed to forget our appearance on this programme. At a lecture we presented to the British school, The Grange, the audience hummed the theme music to the show as we walked in.

We decided to leave Santiago for a while with my parents. According to what a drunk man had once said to the author, Isla Navarino, we still had one more geographical phenomenon to see in Chile.

'When God created the world he had a handful of everything left – mountains, deserts, lakes, glaciers – and he put it all in his pocket. But there was a hole in this pocket you see, and as God walked across heaven it all trickled out, and the long trail it made on earth was Chile.'

Our planned cycling route was not through the Atacama desert in the north of Chile, so we decided to take my parents there.

We hired a jeep and packed light for the trip. I chucked out my father's waterproof jacket, with the words, 'You won't be needing this. We are going to the driest desert in the world.'

When we saw San Pedro, however, it lay under dark and threatening clouds. Within minutes we witnessed a dramatic thunderstorm over the Volcano Licancabur. Children rushed out on to the streets and stood with arms outstretched, gazing bemusedly up into the heavens. For those who were under seven years old, it was the first time they had seen or felt rain. My father got very wet in his tee-shirt and I was not allowed to forget it!

The locals, of course, could explain the rain – it had nothing to do with meteorology, but rather, as is often the case in Chile, volcanic activity. Under the shade of the pimento trees of the plaza, a drunk called Miguel was my tutor:

'*Volcan Licancabur* is in a volatile mood. The rain is to put out its fires,' he explained. 'By the way, do you want to know where the most romantic place in San Pedro is?' I was not sure that I wanted to know, perhaps it was on top of the volcano.

'It is the cemetery,' he whispered. This would certainly explain why it looked more like a fairground, with garish accoutrements and lurid wreaths.

The modern world, like the rain, had passed San Pedro (population 1,600) by. Electricity came from a generator, which was switched on half an hour before sunset and then it was up to the whim of the operator. He was a bit of a TV addict so if there was a good film on, it was more than likely the lights would stay on beyond the normal deadline of 11.00 p.m. One night the electricity was on all night, because the poor chap had fallen asleep while watching the movie, *Rocky 2*. Who could blame him! Water, like the electricity, was intermittent, but that was probably just as well because it was heavily laced with arsenic owing to the acidity of the soil. The houses were primitive: squat and white-washed and constructed from baked mud mixed with straw. They had not been built for the rain, and after the downpour the whole village appeared to be mourning as brown tears streamed down the white-washed walls. The church, the subject of so many picture postcards, had become a brown shadow of its former self.

In our dreamy little hostel on the main square, we did not escape the rain. We awoke early one morning to find our wooden beds, which were draped with llama skins, floating in a sea of mud. With only the lights of candles, we had to pick our way through puddles.

We had awoken before dawn as we were off to the El Tatio geyser field, which at 14,500 feet is considered to be the highest in the world and is best viewed at first light. After two hours of climbing in the jeep the sky began to lighten. It is impossible to sleep through the colours and beauty of an Andean dawn. Snow lay frozen over the pampas grass giving the effect of white coral and in the distance a volcano was smoking, silhouetted against a silver blue sky. Llamas stood watching us with a supercilious air, a family of rheas danced through the white coral and a troop of seven baby partridges played excitedly in the snow, while their emerald mother looked on with a bemused expression.

The geysers lay shrouded in a condensed fog. The sun could not penetrate this secret world alive with the sounds of gurgling and croaking and ghostly shadows floating in and out. It was freezing cold, while under our feet stirred the simmering heat of volcanic activity. I attempted to harness this energy by lowering three eggs into the shallows of a geyser. It will not rank as the best breakfast I have ever cooked – the eggs tasted of sulphur and I singed the front of my hair giving me the style of a punk rocker. Even my mother could not look me straight in the face. Evidently I should have taken the hint from a rusty relic of previous attempts at harnessing the potential electrical energy of the geysers. It stood now, like a forlorn, squat piece of sculpture to failure. Needless to say, I still managed to trip up on the thing and fell flat on my face. All was forgotten, however, when the sun finally burnt through the fog and unveiled the stunning beauty of forty white fumaroles spiralling up into the blue sky.

In the Oxford English Dictionary, a desert is described as *'a place marked by dull monotony, a depopulated region'*. The Atacama desert does not fit this description. It was full of surprises and life within its dunes, plains and mountains. There were hidden lakes shimmering with pink flamingos and concealed green ravines alive with the sound of bird song and perfumed by citrus groves. In the tiny villages, children walked to school in immaculate white uniforms to sit behind their cactus wood desks. We also found salt lakes evaporating in the sun to create spectacular formations and moonscapes sparkling with giant crystals of gypsum. We did not see, however, Indian 'mummies' lying in the shifting sand.

Mummification, the art of preserving dead bodies in a cocoon of textiles, was very much part of Inca culture. Many mummies have been found beside sacrificial platforms and had given their lives to appease their gods of land, sky and underworld. There were several in the museum in San Pedro. Appropriately they were all Indian women, so we saw no 'daddies' who had been transformed into 'mummies.' However, the most famous of these, a young girl of the age of nine, had only become a 'mummy' at her death many years before the Spanish Conquest. She had kept her looks, for at the grand old age of four hundred and seventy-five, her long black hair and endearing smile had won her the title of Miss Chile.

Amongst the beauty and history of the desert lay a sinister catalogue of mineral exploitation. We had seen many ghost towns on the way up from Santiago. These had grown and flourished on the back of nitrate which was vital for explosives and fertilisers. The discovery of synthetic saltpetre during the First World War, made these mining communities obsolete overnight. Pablo Neruda wrote in memory of these miners:

> 'Beneath the nitrate and thorns,
> I found a drop of my people's blood,
> and each drop burned like fire.'

We visited the deserted town of Chacabuco, whose ruins for some perverse reason had been designated a national monument. A nitrate community of some two thousand people was now reduced to a series of crumbling mud walls, a cracked basketball pitch, a twisted goal post and a tattered hymn book lying on the floor of the roofless church. In the cemetery, colourful paper garlands hung from the wooden crosses on the nameless graves.

The exploitation of some minerals has survived today. At Chuquicamata near Calama lies a colossal copper mine, the largest open-pit mine in the world and reputedly the greatest pollution factory in the Southern Hemisphere. (Brazil claims the mine has damaged the Amazon rainforest, which lies thousands of miles away.) After such an introduction, Chuquicamata did not disappoint. From miles away, we could see thick clouds of smoke erupting into the sky and the towering slag heaps of waste rock. Below us a small stream meandered, glowing yellow and blue. In the dormitory town for the mine, a yellow sheen seemed to hang over the joyless, empty streets, which were lined with identical barrack-like houses marked with numbers and not names.

At the mine itself convoys of massive trucks were spiralling their way down the terraces to the bottom of the two thousand foot hole. The wheels alone are thirteen feet in diameter and the drivers are perched a further seven feet above them. Regular vehicles, with long poles and bright flags to announce their presence, dashed around watering the roads to ease the wear on the huge tyres, which cost £6,000 each. At the bottom the ore was loaded and it took some thirty minutes for the trucks to crawl their way back to the top. Despite the fact that copper only represented 1.6% of these loads, Chuquicamata is responsible for a third of Chile's 1.6 million metric tons of fine copper. With copper still bringing in 40% of the country's foreign exchange, it is fair to say that Chuquicamata has a cornerstone role in the national economy.

This may well be the reason why the government, despite promises to address environmental issues after the military regime, have brought in very little anti-pollution measures. They fear such measures will limit copper production at Chuquicamata. The miners are left to combat the effects of sulphurous gases and arsenic poisoning, and one report has identified a link between leukaemia and working down the mine. A miner told us a tragic, but not unfunny tale. Four years before, a retired worker and his wife travelled to Spain on holiday. He was unexpectedly taken ill and died. His wife was arrested on suspicion of poisoning him when the forensic specialist found high levels of arsenic in his blood.

Despite all the dangers, Chuquicamata was continuing to expand its quest for more copper. We saw plans for building a second, even bigger, hole. It would be some time before Chuqui camata would go the same way of the nitrate communities. In the meantime, I said a silent prayer for the miners working on the contaminated ore, their families living in the yellow streets and the Amazon rainforest. We returned quickly to Santiago.

It was time to say goodbye to my parents. I was keen to know whether they considered five months on a bicycle had changed me. I was expecting a profound statement along the lines of 'you seem to have found yourself' or 'you appear fulfilled in your sense of purpose'. My parents did not allude to such qualities, but observed:

'Darling, you eat even more than you used to and your level of maturity now seems to be that of a ten year old.'

Five months in the company of Mike and David could explain that!

We had originally planned to leave Santiago four days after my parents' departure. However, not for the first time, affairs of the heart triumphed over our best intentions. We were distracted and tempted by Alexandra, Cecilia and Nicole. Mike had met Alexandra in the Atacama and David and I had danced with Cecilia and Nicole at the disco in Castro, Chiloe. The only trouble was while Alex lived in Santiago, Cecilia and Nicole were in Uruguay. It was not until one week later that David and I returned on a plane from Montevideo, the capital of Uruguay.

During our exploits of lust and love, we had often heard the golden and compelling lines of the Chilean poet, Pablo Neruda. We found his poems sent the girls trembling to their knees. After all, who could resist the words, *'Quiero hacer contigo lo que la primavera hace con los cerezos'*, which in sanitised translation means, 'I want to do with you what spring does to the cherry trees'. To Cecilia, Neruda was 'the institution and embodiment of love'.

We could not leave Santiago without visiting his former home at Isla Negra, which had become a shrine for lovers from around the world. As Jacobo Timerman, the Argentine writer, once proclaimed:

'His words and his rhythms will forever be the only expression that we Latin Americans have when our heart overflows with love for another human or with love of the universe.'

The romantics say that Neruda, ever the Communist, died there of a broken heart in 1973 brought on by General Pinochet coming to power. It is certainly a moving notion, but the coroner's report did not declare a broken heart, but cancer of the prostate.

The house was built on an outcrop of rock, overlooking the Pacific Ocean. The views and garden were beautiful. *'In Isla Negra everything flowers,'* Neruda wrote in *Passions and Impressions*. *'Tiny yellow flowers linger all winter, turning blue and later burgundy in spring. The sea flowers all year round. Its rose is white. Its petals are salt stars.'* Inside the house was a revelation. It was truly the house of a poet; a collection of beautiful things chosen and arranged with feeling and sensitivity. The dining room, with its mahogany table and high-backed chairs, looked over the sea at the front and the garden and pine trees at the back. To enhance the colours, blue glass lined the window to the water and green glass reflected the shades of the garden. The sitting room was dominated by figureheads, which had graced the bows of ships from around the world. I fell for the nymph with glass eyes, Maria Celest. She had the habit of weeping in the winter, when the warm air from the fire condensed on her eyes and sent tears streaming down her cheeks. Five writing desks lay under different windows, each affording a different view, mood and inspiration. Unfortunately, there were no cherry trees and it was autumn, so I never did find out what spring does to the cherry trees. After this pilgrimage of love, we were at last ready to leave for the Andes and Argentina.

—13—
SHADOW OF ACONCAGUA

'I live not in myself, but I become
Portion of that around me; and to me,
High mountains are a feeling, but the hum
Of human cities torture.'

LORD BYRON 'Childe Harold's Pilgrimage'

The ominous shadow of the Andes lay ahead. High up in the clouds at nearly 14,000 feet and 100 miles ahead lay the *Paso de Christo Redentor* (Pass of Christ the Redeemer), which would take us into Argentina. There was a lower route, but the tunnel was considered to be too dangerous for cyclists. The mere thought of crossing the Andes filled us with dread, particularly as the thirty-one days off the bikes had reeked havoc with our waistlines, fitness and resolve. We had indeed become soft. After only three miles cycling out of Santiago, it started to rain. David took on the role of a rather officious cricket umpire and declared that cycling should be stopped until the rain relented. When it did, he argued the light was not sufficient for us to see the fast-moving traffic. Whereas before such comments would be treated with derision, this time we all agreed without a second thought.

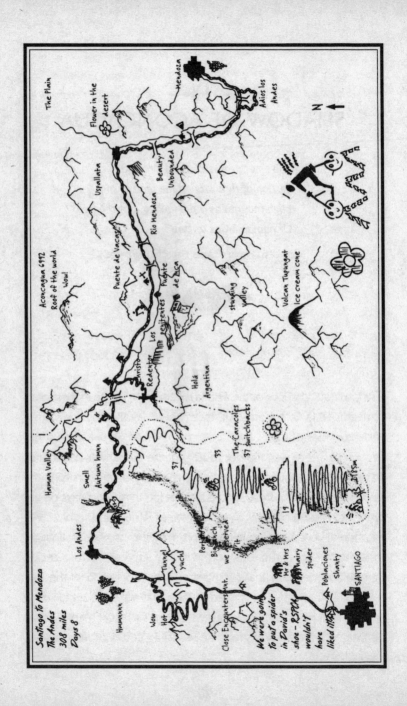

The skies had cleared the next day and we left the smog and traffic of Santiago for the vineyards of the Maipo valley. It was good to be on the road again. In the city, we had missed the moon and stars, the vagaries of nomadic life and the daily catalogue of surprises. On the city streets, you are unlikely to come face to face with a tarantula spider. Now in the foothills of the Andes, I saw him walking across the road and I had to swerve to miss him. As we eyed each other, his long black fingers gently stroked down his bristles, like a cat with its whiskers. He was the first to break the stare, when he turned and headed with stealth and purpose to the other side of the tarmac. Some distressed croaks coming from the verge revealed his target. A frog lay injured in the grass. It tried to back away as the tarantula approached, but with one broken leg succeeded only in moving in circles. When he struck, the frog leapt in the air and performed a frenzied dance, before collapsing. This then was the Italian *tarantella* folk dance, after which the spider was named. It reminded me more of David's performances on the disco floor.

We were close to one of the infamous Andean tunnels. Many times we had been warned against them.

'They are choked with fumes, narrow and poorly-lit,' Australian Jenny had told us way back in Patagonia. 'Two French guys nearly died in one when they were overcome by carbon monoxide poisoning. You either take a lift or go over the top. If I were you I would take the lift, for it will cost you days rather than hours to go over.' To fulfil our objective of cycling every yard – it was the top or nothing!

It was late afternoon by the time we reached the tunnel and it was so tempting to say, 'What the hell!' Not only did it cut out the snow-covered ridge above us, but it would take us to the next town of Los Andes by supper. We did, however, decide to check the tunnel out to see if cycling was possible. There was no better way to do this than from the back of an open top pick-up. Within seconds of entering the tunnel Mike and I were spluttering and when our eyes adjusted to the gloom, the damp walls were so close we could touch them. This was no place for three self-respecting cyclists. Instead of Los Andes, that night we camped beside a water-hole and shared boiled mutton with two gauchos while we prepared to go over the top.

It was a hot and twisting climb. A farmer in a tractor stopped.

'Do you know about the tunnel?' he enquired.

'Yes,' we said with a smile.

'Have a beer, you crazy gringos.' It seemed to simmer and then evaporate on our tongues.

It took three hours to the top and on the other side the road brought us down to the tunnel again. It was only two miles long and would have taken us minutes to cycle. Going over the top had been thirty miles and it had cost us a day. Jenny had been right, but there was nothing like feeling virtuous.

Aconcagua, which at over 21,000 feet is the highest mountain in the Southern Hemisphere, now stood between us and Argentina. We spent a whole day climbing, before collapsing, exhausted, at an out of season ski hut. It was owned by a fat and jolly chap called Fernando. When he heard of our mission, he offered his services as a fund-raiser.

'I have a great idea,' Fernando said. 'I could go to Buckingham Palace (his 'b' sounded suspiciously like an 'f'), take my clothes off and dance around until people pay me to stop.' He lifted his tee-shirt to reveal a bulging belly. 'I think even Queen Elizabeth would give a donation.' Yes, I thought, as in horror I imagined a naked Fernando, that is not beyond the realms of possibility!

Fernando did try some fund-raising closer to home. A lorry drew up and a wizened old driver jumped out. You could read his life story of toil and hardship from the wrinkles on his face. Against our better judgement, Fernando asked him for a donation to leukaemia. The old man sighed, 'Alas I cannot, I have no money,' he apologised. 'For eighteen years, I and my fellow workers have suffered at the hands of Pinochet and his military henchmen. We worked harder and harder for less and less money. Ask me in fifteen years time, and I may be able to give you some money then.' Fernando was not to be outdone, he wrote a letter to the government and the peoples of the world. It read:

'Look into your hearts and stop corruption, wanton spending and petty selfishness. Think of others and set up a culture for giving. We can then start to save lives rather than taking them. I implore you to help and support these boys, Rupert, Mike and David, in their crusade for leukaemia and the curing of children and adults from around the world.'

As he wrote, tears ran down his cheeks and dropped on to the page, causing the ink to run. He sealed the missive in an envelope along with a white feather for luck and peace. It was only the other day that this same white feather had fallen out of my diary. It reminded me of a scene from the film, *Forrest Gump*.

As a tearful Fernando disappeared from view, we caught our first glimpse of the *'Caracoles,'* a wall of rock and shale surmounted by a twisting road of thirty-seven switchbacks. It is the twists and turns that have given the road its nickname, for *Caracoles* means snail in English. For us it was doubly apt, because our cycling was at a pace befitting a snail. In a fit of madness, I decided I was going to cycle the whole way without stopping. It became an obsession of pride and I was reduced to tears of pain at the thirtieth turn and beyond. Without the hoots of encouragement from the lorry drivers, I do not think I would have been able to have made it.

At the top was the ski resort of Portillo. In season, it was the playground of the rich and famous, but out of season, it was drab, seedy and cold. The 'luxurious' Hotel Portillo, festooned in blue and yellow paint, was a blot on the landscape against the steel grey lake and shale foothills. The outdoor swimming pool surrounded by a wet, wooden terrace, was green with algae. The hotel looked very different in its brochure; the blue and yellow looked a picture against the snow-clad mountains and the crystal blue waters of the lake, and on the terrace, children played in the clear blue waters of the heated pool, while adults sipped *vin chaud* and tucked into *rostis* behind polarised sunglasses. The interior looked and smelt like a government-run Russian hotel, and I was surprised to find that a 'five-star' hotel deemed it necessary to put padlocks on its toilet rolls.

It was another hour to the international tunnel between Chile and Argentina. We were prepared to go over the top, but there were rumours that the track to the summit had been heavily mined. We felt sure we could squeeze the bicycles between the craters. We enquired about the possibilities at the border post.

'Is it possible to cycle through the tunnel?' Mike asked.

'No, it is too dangerous,' the border guard replied, in no uncertain terms.

'Then, we will go over the top.'

'No, it is not possible,' the guard replied. 'The path has been swept away and blocked by landslides. It also snowed last night, so if you make it to the top, which I doubt you will, you will be up to your chests in the stuff. Your only option is to hitch a lift through the tunnel.'

This presented a dilemma. We were halfway through the expedition and the last thing that we wanted to do was to break our route for the sake of a three-mile long tunnel. I remembered the disused railway line that we had followed up the valley. I had thought how sad it was this feat of engineering and human endeavour, which had cost the lives of hundreds of brave men, now lay rusting on crumbling embankments and under collapsed wooden tunnels. I wondered whether one of the tunnels had survived and could it by any chance be the one which had taken the railway into Argentina. The guard shook his head.

'We mined it to stop the Argentines marching through during the hostilities of 1984,' he replied. 'I simply do not understand. The solution is easy, just hitch a lift through. Around here is no place for heroics!'

We explained our objective and to our surprise, he understood:

'So what you are saying is that by taking a lift, you will be breaking your promise to your sponsors and to the leukaemia charity,' he became thoughtful and finally he said, 'I have a plan.'

The plan, he explained, was to close the international tunnel to traffic for one hour. This would give enough time for the fumes to die down. He would then escort us through the tunnel in his car, to give us light and to help us if we got into difficulties. We could not thank him enough.

In preparation, we wrapped tee-shirts around our heads, leaving only a slit for our eyes. We did breathing exercises to test our lung control, and we calculated that for three miles cycling at an average speed of fifteen m.p.h; we would need approximately sixty breaths. By now the traffic was piling up. The guard explained the situation and the drivers were not in the least annoyed at the delay, but instead were openly encouraging. Three young guys in a flash red sports car dedicated a song to us. It was 'Every Breath You Take' by the rock band, Police.

We cycled into the dark mouth of the tunnel, to the muffled cheers from behind. Instead of pacing ourselves and preserving our lungs, we cycled like crazy beings and our breathing quickly became ragged as the excitement and the overwhelming need to get to the other end got the better of us. After what seemed like miles, our legs started to tire and I started to choke on the heavy air. I felt my speed drop dramatically. Just when we most needed it, a pinprick of light appeared in the distance and I felt a fresh breeze on my face. Within a minute, we cycled, blinking and gasping, out into Argentina. We thanked our escort.

'I am honoured that I could have been of service,' the guard said and as he drove back through the tunnel, I thought with regret that we did not even know his name. But perhaps this was just as well, because for us he had put his job on the line.

The Argentinian guards were laughing.

'You looked like startled rabbits in there,' they said, pointing to a series of television monitors showing the interior of the tunnel. As it was close to nightfall we asked if we could stay the night.

'I would not advise it,' one of the guards warned. 'I have no problems myself, but the road workers in those huts over there, if they hear you are British, might want to come and slit your throats. Many people in Argentina have yet to forget the Falklands War.' We took the hint and we cycled to the village of Las Cuevas, only two miles down the hill.

Here we found a policeman, who was young enough for the Falklands War not to have influenced his judgement. He kindly gave us our own private police cottage, on the promise we would give some money to paint it. Around the fire, with a snowstorm blowing outside, I wrote down my feelings towards Chile.

DAY 160 GOODBYE TO CHILE

As we left its borders for the last time, what were our lasting impressions of Chile and Chileans? In assessing any country, I often think of a picture; it is the places and the scenery which provide the black and white outline but it is the people who give it colour and depth.

Chile and the Chileans create a vibrant and beautiful painting. Many places I will remember: the towering granite peaks of Torres del Paine, the dripping rainforest of the Carretera Austral, the mythical atmosphere on the island of Chiloe, the snow-capped volcanoes of the Lakes, the shifting sands of the Atacama and the cave of the Mylodons. However, the sheer warmth and the friendliness of the people, I will never forget! They could not have done more to help and support us.

As well as friendship, the Chileans have several other endearing and memorable characteristics: an obsession with love, an overwhelming need to gossip and a highly sentimental and superstitious nature. The basis of these rather unique traits is a pervading sense of isolation. For centuries, in geographical terms, Chile has been one of the most isolated countries on earth; cut off from the world by high mountains, dry deserts in the north, the Pacific Ocean on the west and Antarctica and the Straits of Magellan in the south. In the 1960s and early '70s, with the advent of world-wide communications, Chile developed a place and acceptance in the shrinking global village. However, when General Pinochet came to power in 1973, the doors were again closed on them and the feelings of isolation returned. Chileans, as they had done before, found escape in a world of love, intrigue, gossip and superstition.

In the 1990s, these characteristics live on . . .

Love rules their lives. Love is not just smooching with a loved one under the moonlight or seducing a partner during the 'Cueca' dance, it is also a passionate obsession for their country. The Chileans constantly need reassurance of what a wonderful place they live in. The question we were most often asked was, "Don't you just love our country?" and followed closely by: "Have you ever seen anywhere more beautiful?" "Don't you think Pablo Neruda is one of the world's greatest poets?" and "Isabel Allende has to be one of the best living female writers!"

A girls' public school would have nothing on the Chileans in terms of an ability to gossip. A small village mentality sweeps across the country and encompasses all generations. Even though we were total strangers and knew nothing or little of the people involved, we were often made privy to intimate scars received allegedly in a torture chamber, the nocturnal indiscretions of the local mayor and a neighbour who was in league with the devil. Gossip and intrigue reached their peak during the first rounds of the World Cup of 1990. Chile's national team walked out in the middle of the qualifying game against Brazil after their goalkeeper 'El Condor' Rojas collapsed with a gash to his head. The team believed Rojas had been hit by a Brazilian fan with a 'bengala' (a kind of firework). However, Rojas confessed soon afterwards that the wound was self-inflicted. The idea was to stop the game because with Brazil 2-0 up, he considered Chile had no chance of winning. Subsequently, a ban was imposed not only for the 1990 World Cup but also on participating in the United States in 1994. Far from being reviled by the Chilean people, they were heralded as heroes of the scandal-mill. This indeed was a piece of gossip which could run for years and years in the bars across the country. We had even been victims of Chilean gossip when, on the ferry to Punta Arenas, we were innocently informed that we were still seriously ill in a hospital in Ushuaia.

A sentimental and superstitious nature was also to be found lurking within many Chileans. They thrived on believing in the 'malo de ojo' (evil eye), 'El Trauco' (the seducer of Virgins), the ghost ship 'El Caleuche,' the existence of the City of the Caesars and the emotional power of the volcanoes. We had witnessed the way the press covered our progress and had been flattered by the symbolism that the journalists created. "The old legend of the three musketeers is alive today . . ." was how the media in Concepcion chose to interpret our expedition.

In the 1990s, as Chile emerges out of the shadow of the Pinochet regime, the Chileans might appear outwardly to have changed, but underneath, the deep-seated obsessions with friendship, love, gossip and superstitions will remain for generations. After all, it is these characteristics which create such a vibrant painting and makes the Chileans one of the most intriguing and attractive people in the world.

No discussion on Chile would be complete without addressing a debate which still dominates the lives of all Chileans – Allende versus Pinochet.

Chileans have a habit of only seeing issues in black and white and failing to recognise there might be some shade of grey in the middle. Thus they were either for or against one or the other. On our part we were evenly split: David for Pinochet, I for Allende and Mike providing the shade of grey in the middle. David argued that Pinochet had been a 'good' dictator in bringing political as well as economic stability to Chile. I disagreed and said that Allende should have been given a chance, free from the spoiling tactics of the Right, whose opposition had been supported and financed by the Americans. I believed Chile would be in a better position without Pinochet. Mike argued that Allende had led Chile into a disastrous economic situation, but the cost of torture and killing during the Pinochet regime could never be justified by recovery and stability.

My view was largely based on gut feeling. The last words of Allende are the most moving I have ever read. They come from a man genuinely in love with his country and its people, indeed a love he felt was his duty after being democratically elected. On September 11th, 1973, as the guns and tanks of the military advanced towards the Presidential Palace, Allende said goodbye to the Chilean people:

"Other men will survive this bitter and grey moment . . . sooner than you think avenues shall be opened up down which freemen shall march towards a better society . . . These are my last words. I am convinced that my sacrifice shall not be in vain. I am convinced that at least it shall serve as a moral judgement on the felony, cowardice and treason that lay waste to our land."

If Pinochet had believed in Chile and its people, why did he wait for sixteen years before submitting, and even then with much reluctance, to democratic vote in 1989? It was because he did not trust the people to vote for him. He was right, for in 1989 he lost to the opposition leader, Patricio Aylwin. This debate went on well into the night fuelled by two cartons of red wine.'

The next day, we decided to ignore the tempting sight of the road snaking downwards into Argentina and to pursue our original ambition of reaching the *Paso de Christo Redentor*, which marked the border between the two countries. Argentina had more confidence in its military might than Chile. Whereas Chile had mined their road to the pass, Argentina had consciously kept their side open. After all, it was good for tourism. Our policeman friend, however, said, in no uncertain terms, we should not attempt it because there was too much snow. To reassure him, we told him we would put spikes on our tyres.

'Oh, that is all right then,' he replied with a puzzled look.

We had three thousand feet to climb along a twisting dirt track which, as we rose steadily, became lost under snow and ice. We met a Japanese cyclist who nodded and grunted aggressively at our questions and said,

'I no speak English. I no speak Espanol. I Japanese.'

It was good of him to let us know. We bowed goodbye and around the next corner, we found a casualty of the road, a white Mercedes perched precariously on the edge. A family stood distraught beside their car. The driver and the father, an Evangelical minister by profession, was leading them in prayer, *'Please God deliver our car from this mountainside'*. They opened their eyes and saw us. They assumed, much to our embarrassment, that God had sent us and we were greeted to hugs and 'Alleluias.' To their disappointment, we did not use a miracle, but brute strength as we bumped and lifted the car away from the edge. They thanked the Lord and departed.

The views at the top were magnificent and it felt as if we were on top of the world at 13,800 feet. The *Christo* stood fifty feet tall and with arms outstretched, as if blessing the lands of Chile and Argentina. A plaque announced that the statue had been erected in 1904 to celebrate King Edward VII's decision in yet another boundary dispute of 1902. Around the statue, there were many discarded buildings surrounded by shattered glass and crumbling bricks. It must have been a particularly inhospitable posting in the times before a tunnel was built. To the north lay Aconcagua, the king of all the Andean mountains. We also took a series of publicity shots for our principal sponsor, Bombay Sapphire Gin, showing the three of us in our Bombay caps with the bikes heroically slung over our shoulders. We took one shot of the three caps lying in the snow with Aconcagua in the background. We were not offended when this photo was chosen for the company Christmas card.

When we set off from the *Christo* back into Argentina, we knew it was the start of some two hundred miles downhill. It promised to be a routine of waking up, jumping on the bikes, steering and braking occasionally, and stepping off in the evening. Landscape is so much more inspiring and appealing when you are freewheeling. Whereas the long climb in Chile had been memorable for its monochrome and monotonous scenery, in Argentina we cycled at a delirious speed with the wind coursing through our hair, down a valley alive with colour and beauty.

The white Rio Mendoza roared and cascaded below us, awash with melted snow from Aconcagua. On either side rippling pinnacled rocks rose steeply. In the light of the setting sun they glowed a deep rustic red, while the snow above glistened. The rocks were sculptured by the wind and rain and I thought I saw a church perched up high on the snowline with a procession of cowled monks climbing upwards. Such was the delirium of speed on a road which clung tenaciously to every fold and contour of the cliff face. We were by no means the first people to journey through this valley. Hundreds of years ago the Incas had forged a route along the river, assisted by one of the little known wonders of South America, the Bridge of the Incas, an ancient natural crossing formed from the minerals deposited by the hot springs. More recently a certain Alberto Martinez had careered off the road in his truck. A rustic wooden cross daubed with white paint, a knot of twisted metal, a set of black tyre marks and a sea of green shattered glass now marked the spot. A truck stopped behind us and emptied some more bottles on to the pile. We asked the driver why he did this.

'It is a tradition amongst truckers and is a sign of respect. Poor Alberto, he had only been driving this road for a week. Previously he had been on the straight and flat roads of the Pampas.'

Suddenly we left the mountains. The road flattened out, the temperature rose and we found ourselves in a desert of blooming cacti. Just below lay the irrigated oasis of Mendoza, the capital of the Argentine wine industry. This was without doubt a place to indulge and enjoy. Our time in this city was thus lost in a sea of oblivion as we experienced at first hand why Argentina is the fifth largest wine producer in the world.

—14—
OASIS HOPPING

'What pleasure does it give to be rid of one thorn out of many?'

HORACE

Mendoza (population 600,000) is a city steeped in history. It was founded by Pedro de Castillo in 1561, as a staging post for the major route across the Andes to Santiago. For three hundred years, its cultural and economic ties were with Chile rather than Argentina, but this isolation ended with the arrival of the transcontinental railway from the east. Most of Mendoza's history has been destroyed by earthquakes, which periodically rack the region. In 1861, an earthquake killed 10,000 people and razed the city to the ground. More recently, in 1985, 40,000 were left homeless, but fortunately there were few deaths. Thus, to the eye, Mendoza is a modern city of low colonial style buildings, tree-lined avenues and well-kept gardens and parks. It is a city in which to relax, drink wine, relive crossing the Andes and forget about the surrounding desert.

Mendoza is an irrigated oasis. Ahead of us lay over a thousand miles of desert stretching all the way north to the city of Salta. The

route, however, was dotted with oasis towns and villages. They promised to be our saving graces between sweltering and thirsty desert stretches. We had only cycled fifteen miles out of Mendoza, when we realised the effectiveness of the city's irrigation system. The poplars shading the road and the green fields on either side abruptly ended. In their place, a dull barren landscape populated with sentinel saguaro cacti appeared. It suddenly became hot and sticky and it was not long before we were looking for a place to stay. We spied a humble homestead beside the road. The family was poor and shy, but they welcomed us and showed us to a solitary thorn tree amongst the brown, parched earth. Pedro, their eleven year old son, was sent for a broom to sweep away the thorns. As we settled down to cook, we noticed three children staring at us from behind a small mud wall. We called to them and they rushed off screeching back into the house. It was not long before they were behind the wall again, and with growing confidence they were soon to join us around the stove. I still carried some animal holograms I had brought over from England for just such an occasion. I gave them an elephant, giraffe and lion to share amongst themselves and they sat fascinated by these three-dimensional animals flickering before their eyes. Their parents called and before returning they hugged us and wished us goodnight.

In the morning, I awoke to the sweet sound of singing. Pedro was milking one of the goats.

'I always milk the goats,' he explained, 'because they love my singing so much they yield more milk. If my brother, Miguel, was to do it they would dry up. He *was* all right until his voice broke about a year ago. Miguel has moved on to the cows, while my little sister sings to the hens to encourage them to lay eggs.'

I have never regarded animals as music lovers before, but I suppose the singing enabled them to escape the realities of the hot and harsh environment.

Back on the road between Mendoza and San Juan, we were stopped by a blue BMW. We were asked the usual question, 'Where are you from?'

'Ah . . . you are British,' the driver said with interest. 'I have nothing but respect for the British. I was in Mussolini's army and on being captured I spent three years in a British prisoner-of-war camp. You treated us well and fairly. It was where I learnt to cook and I now make pasta in San Juan. They call me Bruno the Pasta Maker. By the way, where are you heading?'

'San Juan,' we replied.

'Excellent, then you can be my guest at my shop. I would be honoured and it will be a way of saying thank you for my treatment during the war.'

We promised.

We still had seventy miles to travel along a road which had now become littered with temptation. The reclamation of the desert had started again. The combination of water and heat has created a belt rich in vineyards. Row upon row of vines stretched out on either side as far as our eyes could see. It is so famous that there is an Argentine expression, *'to be between San Juan and Mendoza'*, which means having drunk too much. We ended up overdosing on melons, corned beef and *dulce con leche* (sweetened, boiled condensed milk) to concentrate our minds on the road.

San Juan (population 122,000) is not only the city where Juan Peron first came to national prominence while raising funds for the devastated town after the earthquake of 1944, but it is also the capital of cycling in Argentina. It was indeed wonderful cycling along the flat, straight, tree-lined streets without a cloud in the sky or a hint of wind. On entering the city, we were greeted to hoots of encouragement and at every corner we were stopped and asked what gear ratios we used and whether we thought Shimano components were overrated. We found Bruno and he greeted us with the hugs of a long lost friend. He plied us with aluminium cartons brimming with pasta:

'This will build up your energy and muscles,' he said.

He was not alone in his generosity. With our bikes as our passports, we were given bananas, mandarins and apples from a market stall, an expensive Blackburn pump, a basket of provisions from a supermarket and a round of beers at a bar. In return all that they asked was to cycle once around the block on our bicycles. The inhabitants of San Juan simply loved cycling and their infectious enthusiasm made us feel humble.

For the first stage of the route north, there were two options. There was the shorter way of 100 miles via San Jose de Jachal or a longer alternative through San Agustin del Valle Fertil. We had learnt that short cuts can be deceptive. We decided to consult the local police. He did not mince his words.

'Do not go via San Jose!' a policeman explained. 'You could die out there. No water or villages for kilometres and a road covered by shifting sand. You must go through San Agustin. This road will take you past the shrine to the *Difunta Correa*. It is not to be missed, especially as you are travellers on a dangerous mission. If you leave her a present she will protect you.'

The legend behind the *Difunta Correa* is of a young lady who was found dead of thirst in the desert with a child still alive and suckling at her breast. She became an unofficial saint and the place where she died has become the centre of an industry selling bare-breasted statues and pictures and a depository of personal items left in tribute. It was a bizarre collection of gifts: a room of wedding dresses, a cast of a broken arm, a pair of silver stilettos, an electric guitar, a blown gasket, a policeman's detective school diploma and a packet of condoms. We were not there during Holy Week, but if we had been we might have found 100,000 pilgrims, with some crawling the final mile on their backs. We left a bicycle tyre to ward off punctures and a rather historic picture of the complete Royal Family.

Perhaps I should also have bought a bare-breasted statue, because the very next day, now deep in cacti country, cacti of all shapes and sizes – rounded pin cushions, fifteen foot tridents and swaying tentacles – scattered threatening thorns across our path. Progress was intermittent as we received eleven punctures between us. As I was bent over yet another puncture, I was nudged in the back of the legs. I swore and turned to tell Mike or David I was not in the mood for games. I was in for a surprise; the culprit was a baby donkey. She seemed to be looking for affection, for as she stared up with big sad eyes, she nuzzled her nose against my chest. I did not feel like playing and returned to the tyre. I heard a plaintive whine but chose to ignore it. When I was at last on the road again, I turned and saw her with her head bowed and back turned. Just over the rise of the hill, I swerved to avoid a dark, rounded object. It was the dead mother of the baby donkey. I felt pangs of guilt and cycled back. I could hardly fit her into one of the panniers, so I decided to wait for a truck to pass. We sat in each other's company for one hour before Mike and David returned worried I was in trouble. For a further hour, we all comforted our distressed orphan, before a kindly truck driver agreed to take her away.

The next day the wind was fierce and dead against us. It was tough going, and we were forced to slip stream. The paved road was heavily scarred with potholes and littered with cactus thorns. Visibility was poor for the following riders, so the leader had to shout instructions; 'pothole right', 'potholes left and right', 'dirt road', 'rocks' and 'thorns left'. David was leading when I heard the shout of 'snake!' It was too late and I could not avoid cycling over a three foot long snake. To my horror, in its death throes it lunged up and sunk its fangs into my back tyre. At least the snake could say it went out with a final hiss!

We arrived exhausted in the town of San Agustin. We were greeted by a bunch of children, who escorted us to a friendly hostel. One of the kids, Frederico, came up and whispered in my ear,

'Where are you heading?'

'*Valle de la Luna* (Valley of the Moon),' I replied.

This prompted a sharp intake of breath. 'It is very dangerous out there,' Frederico warned. 'It is full of lions, crocodiles and serpents. My father went there once, but he vowed never to return! If you have to go, you must take a guide.'

I thought he must be joking and said as much. He was shocked that I did not believe him.

Sitting on the toilet that evening, I was thinking about what Frederico had said, when I heard a throaty bellow. I felt sure it was not one of my own bowel movements. It came again. I was now certain, because never in my life had I made a noise like that and I hope I never will. I looked around but saw nothing. There was another bellow, followed by the sound of splashing. It was coming from directly below me. I looked down and saw a pair of big bulbous eyes staring up at me. It was an enormous toad. The urge to 'go' now left me!

The next day, we held an impromptu farewell party. The kids of the village turned up, bringing gifts of honey and *maté* pots. Frederico sidled up and pressed a small, hand-made wooden knife into my hand.

'Good luck,' he whispered. 'Here is my address, let me know if you survive.'

It was Sunday, so before leaving we decided to buy some treats. At the local butcher, we purchased onions, ox liver and two cartons of red wine for the evening meal. The anticipation of this culinary delight meant it was a particularly mouth-watering ride.

It was not until well after sunset that we arrived at the national park of 'Valle de la Luna'. It was not dark, for the moon was as bright as I could ever remember. For two hours, we had been chasing our shadows along the road and marvelling at the beauty of the landscape bathed in the blue light. An oil lamp burned in the ranger's cottage and we knocked on the door to ask for a place to stay, armed with a carton of wine as a gentle persuasion. Three glasses later he said we could stay in the Dinosaur Museum.

In the museum, we met a fellow cyclist, Stefan from Germany. He had become obsessed by us. For the entire five months of his travels, ever since leaving Ushuaia, he had heard nothing but stories about us.

'Everywhere I stopped I had to listen to talk about the three British cyclists. I heard how you ate the mussels, how wonderful you are to be raising money for leukaemia, how you never start cycling before midday and how you are carrying so much weight and luxuries,' he recounted. 'Now that I have passed you, you will only hear about me!'

We lived up to one part of our reputation, by taking the ox liver and wine from our panniers and starting to cook.

'I do not believe it, all you are missing is a white tablecloth,' Stefan observed. We asked him if he wanted some, but he declined and tucked into an Argentine equivalent of a pot noodle. The atmosphere and our appetites were shattered by Stefan tuning in to a 'crucial' football match featuring his favourite team, Frankfurt AFC. We were treated to a chorus of cheers, grunts and groans. Unfortunately, Frankfurt lost and we were forced to listen to a damning post-mortem on the referee. I left him for the more stimulating company of the dinosaurs. I imagined them thinking, 'Thank goodness we are extinct. We have escaped the tedium of a life dominated by football!'

I was rudely awoken by an arresting noise and sight. It was Stefan singing 'Kommen Eleen' by Dexy's Midnight Runners, clad only in a pair of clinging red lycra tights. It was so awful, I wished I was having a nightmare, but I realised it was not to be when I curled up in agony after Stefan dropped a pannier on top of me. He said 'Shit!' and carried on packing. It was not the last time he uttered this word, for in the process of preparing to leave I heard it at least twenty-three times. Until I met Stefan I thought we must have the world's worst record for getting away in the mornings. Our problem was we found it difficult to get out of bed, but once up we would expect to be away in one and a half hours. It took Stefan three hours. He would pack a pannier, say 'shit' and start to unpack it. He had four panniers, so he did this four times. He then decided he wanted some breakfast, which entailed a noisy vocal search through his bags again. I stopped wondering why he travelled alone – no one in their right mind could cope with his singing, red ballet tights, swearing, packing and passion for Frankfurt AFC.

The *Valle de la Luna* is so called because it resembles the surface of the moon – full of craters and covered in white silt. It is a large natural depression, which was once, in prehistoric times, an immense lake. It is Argentina's answer to Jurassic Park for around its shores, in the Triassic period, dinosaurs and flora thrived. As a result of constant erosion the earth on which they lived and roamed has now risen to the surface. It has become an open-cast mine of dinosaur skeletons such as the six-foot long *Dicinodonte* and other fossilised animals. We were shown around by a real-life Indiana Jones, Professor Rodiguez, who had a white Stetson, a monocle and a stick to support his limp. He would poke around with his stick and within minutes announce 'dinosaur bone'. To our uneducated eye, it just looked like any other white rock.

'Philistines!' he shouted.

There was one phenomenon in the valley even he could not explain. It was the origin of the fifty round stone bowling balls lying in a shallow dip. All around you could see other balls emerging from the sand and rock, waiting to be released by erosion from the wind and rain.

'How these balls are formed in such perfect circular shapes remains one of the mysteries of the planet,' the Professor declared. 'Here is my address; if you come up with any bright ideas, please let me know.'

Erosion by the wind and rain had also unveiled and shaped many stunning rock formations. We saw a submarine floating above the desert, a lion leaping from the rocks, an eagle perched ready for the kill, a dragon breathing fire and a sphinx sitting back on its haunches. So it was from the rocks where young Frederico had got all his stories of lions and reptiles. We lost track of time and it was only as the sun fell that we started back to our dinosaur sanctuary.

DAY 176 VALLEY OF THE MOON 8.30 P.M.

'I have just witnessed the most dramatic transformation from day into night. Behind us as we cycled the sun was a flaming ball of orange, sending streaks of red and yellow into the sky and turning the desert sand the colour of crimson. Ahead the silver moon rose suddenly over the hills, illuminating the sky and land with a blue light. I became convinced I was not alone on Arriba, for my lengthening shadow in front had now been joined by a shadow bringing up the rear. It is an eerie feeling having two shadows. Above and below, the sun and moon fought a battle of domination; skies of silver blue and flaming red clashed. I knew the victor, but it did not stop me standing in awe and amazement. The sun was heroic in defeat, for as it sank below the horizon,

it let out a green flash and launched a burning comet of red which lit up the whole sky. Only then did the red tide retreat before the advancing silver blue. So this was the legendary green flash, which is said to bring good luck and fortune to all who see it.'

That night, in the company of dinosaurs and free from Germanic dirges, I dreamt of green flashes and riches.

Within minutes of hitting the road the next day, I thought we had been transported back to the times of Moses and the Egyptians. The only difference was it was not a plague of locusts, but grasshoppers. They were everywhere: entangled in our hair, kicking in our ears, crunching under our tyres, pinging off our spokes and trying to land on our eyelashes. The sun was eclipsed by their jumping bodies and the air was alive with a hypnotic, rhythmical hum. We were driven to distraction as we fought to carve a way through this shifting sea of long-legged, bulbous-eyed beings. They left as suddenly as they had arrived and we watched with relief while the dark cloud swept across the desert towards the waiting sphinx.

At least for a while they took our attention away from the burning north wind – the *Zonda*, which swept down from the northern deserts. Not only was it dead against us, but it sucked the moisture from our throats and parched our skin. I reached for a water bottle to quench my raging thirst, but the water evaporated on my tongue before reaching the sides of my cracked mouth. If you turn on a hairdryer to maximum heat and velocity and hold it to your face for five hours, then you will start to realise what it was like on the road that day. Mike put two tea bags in his water bottle and then cycled for ten minutes to bring the water to the boil. It was not a great success, because the tea tasted as though it was laced with molten plastic.

We were absolutely exhausted by the time we arrived at *Puerta de Talampaya* Provincial Park. While we struggled around the last corner before the ranger's hut, Mike declared;

'I do not have the strength to meet Stefan again!'

Mike's prayer was not answered for as we pulled up, out shot Stefan's leering face.

'Shit, what kept you? You must have been indulging in a lie in again!' he commented.

'What kept us was the bloody grasshoppers and the *Zonda*!' Mike said, while managing to squeeze in an audible 'you fool' under his breath.

'You should have come with me yesterday then, it was a real breeze,' Stefan smiled. The sixty-one miles had only taken him four hours, while we had struggled to do the distance in less than eight.

Thankfully, there were other gringos crowded into the ranger's hut. Petra and Thomas, a German couple on a massive 1,000 cc BMW motorbike, remembered seeing us before. On our part, all we could recall was the throbbing sound of an engine.

'You were the guys crashed out on the side of the road between San Sebastian and Porvenir in Tierra del Fuego. I remember you were tucked in behind a gorse bush. We thought you were dead, until one of you raised an arm to acknowledge our presence. We decided against stopping because we did not want to disturb your beauty sleep,' Thomas said.

'Sleeping again. They are always sleeping!' Stefan chipped in.

In contrast to Thomas and Petra, the other German couple in the hut were travelling around in a dusty red Citroen 2CV. Thomas and Cordelia had driven this car along the same route that we had followed in Chile. Apparently, the 2CV had not even suffered a hiccup and it sailed across the bumps and corrugations of the dirt roads. Much to Stefan's annoyance they had heard about us in Patagonia through

Joan and Coco at *Estancia Telken*. It was great to chat about experiences and to share stories of adventure and fortunately their company diluted the presence of Stefan to a tolerable level. The night passed with only one incident. While we slept, a discriminating skunk took a shine to Stefan's hair. We awoke to a barrage of expletives and shoes flying around the room. This time we did not mind – it was amusing rather than annoying.

They all left the next day: Stefan parted swearing about the batteries in his Walkman; Thomas and Petra's BMW purred into life: and the 2CV coughed, spluttered and then disappeared in a cloud of smoke. We hired a four-wheel drive and a guide to take us into the park. The impressive red sandstone gorge at Talampaya, with cliffs towering to nearly 500 feet, was once the home of pre-Hispanic man. On the rocks and in the caves they painted and engraved objects, animals and incidents of their time. Some have even been dated back to 6,000 years ago. The story painted by the drawings was that llamas, cows and pumas roamed the earth, fish were abundant in the desert and condors had to compete in the skies with comets, UFOs and Martians. More recent petroglyths showed the Spanish arriving on animals the Indians had never seen before, horses. The Indians thought man and horse were attached at the hip and this characteristic propelled the Spanish to the status of gods and eased the way for conquest.

We drove through a red walled gorge and suddenly we emerged into an open expanse of desert littered with massive rock formations, which dwarfed the jeep. It was like a scene out of Alice in Wonderland, for these towering rocks were in the shape of mythological objects and living beings. In the distance we could see a fairy castle perched at the top of a sheer rock face, just ahead the three Magi appeared on camels, to the side a monk was kneeling in prayer, and standing guard over the canyon was an Indian with a prominent nose. There were, however, other formations that brought the beholder back to earth. One rock, with its straight sides and narrow neck, looked like a massive Coca-Cola bottle, and another bore a striking resemblance to Deputy Dawg, the cartoon cowboy sheriff. Martians, fairy castles and Coke bottles, it was all too much, so we returned in the jeep to the ranger's hut.

We were bound for Famatina. She was large, tall and positively dripping in jewellery. It is indeed her riches that have made her the source of legends and the focus of attention for hundreds of years. Famatina is a snow-capped solitary mountain, standing completely out of place in the middle of the desert. There are many stories as to how she got there, but I took to the theory that she was a meteorite, which had dropped from the heavens. The Incas were the first to find her hidden riches of gold and onyx and they built a road specially to transport the wealth back to Peru. When the Spanish arrived, the legend goes, the Indians buried thirteen guanaco necks stuffed with gold somewhere in the mountain. Despite numerous explorations, the necks have never been found. I remembered the green flash I had seen at the Valley of the Moon and decided it must be worth a look. After all, in a bar in *Villa Union* we had met the man who knew the mountain better than any other living person, an Indian named Leonardo.

Leonardo was now in his seventies and he was head over heels in love with Famatina.

'When I was young I was obsessed with finding the thirteen guanaco necks,' Leonardo told us. 'For years I scoured all the known Indian settlements, crawling through their underground maze of tunnels and levering up their great ceremonial stones. I found nothing but odd bits of jewellery and fragments of pottery. I now look back and I am glad that I never found them. I have no doubt they exist, but they belong to Famatina and I could never rob her of them. Famatina is my friend.'

He reminded me of an opal miner I had met in Lightning Ridge in Australia. He had invited me to lunch in his humble two-roomed hut, which stood within spitting distance of his claim. Now in his eighties, he had been mining for opals for some fifty years, and judging from the squalor of his home, he had been fairly unsuccessful.

'No, I have been one of the lucky ones. Look, I will show you a secret,' he whispered.

He opened a drawer in the old wooden dresser and took out a screw of newspaper. He pulled at the paper and revealed five of the most magnificent black opals I had ever seen. Then out came a small box, inside which was a large polished opal. I held it up to the light and when I saw the red flecks shining from within the stone, I realised this was the most valuable object I was ever likely to hold in my hand. The miner sensed my disbelief.

'I found that stone some twenty years ago,' he recalled. 'It was funny, I had been looking for the 'big one' all my life and when I found it I could not bring myself to part with it. I take it out every day and the sight of it fills me with pride and fulfilment. Something that money could never buy.' It was evident that Leonardo had reached this same level of happiness and contentment.

We went climbing up Famatina with Leonardo. He put us to shame. For all his seventy years, he had the agility and stamina of a mountain goat and within minutes he left us trailing in his wake. We stumbled along a narrow path up a steep gorge and became lost in the early morning mist. It was soon burnt away by the sun to reveal a collection of deserted stone conical huts. The village had once been the home of a thousand Indians. Each hut was connected by a maze of underground tunnels and we crawled and explored through them as Leonardo had done in his youth. Like him we found only fragments of ceramics, but no guanaco necks. He pointed out the stone carving which had started the legend. It showed the Spanish arriving on horses surrounded by thirteen neckless guanacos. There were no clues, so after another hour of fruitless searching, we returned down the mountain. Famatina could keep her secret.

After Famatina, we headed for another lady, *Cuesta de Miranda*. This was the tortuous and colourful pass across the mountain to the town of Chilecito. It was on the long hot climb that David declared he would no longer be writing a diary. Since we had started the expedition, David had been struggling to keep it up to date and had tried many different methods to maintain his motivation. He had tried blank and lined paper, A4 and A5 booklets, a Dictaphone and was just coming out of a phase of coloured paper. The writing was on the wall the previous evening, when David had asked me at ten minute intervals about what had happened in days going back some three months. With the announcement, he volunteered to edit Mike's and my diaries. I thought of all the stationers in Argentina, who would now have to declare bankruptcy, because David had given up on his diary.

On the other side of Miranda and Famatina, we eventually reached Chilecito (population 20,000). It was a quiet and sleepy town famous for its wine, olives, walnuts and old chapel of *Los Sarmientos* dating back to 1764. We were greeted by a large sign declaring '*Los Malvinas por Argentinas*' and then by an American basketball player. Chilecito had a basketball team which competed in the National League and Winston, a 6 foot 7 giant, was their only foreign player. He was bored out of his mind.

'All the girls want to do here is talk. It is very frustrating,' Winston mourned. 'You will notice that they will never look you in the eye. It is the way they keep their purity.' I did not know about purity, but despite craning my neck, I was having problems making eye contact.

It was Saturday and we decided on a night on the town, despite Winston's warning. At midnight we found ourselves in the Forum disco. Collectively our Spanish had by now reached a reasonable level of comprehension, but despite this we could not make head or tail of the announcements on the tannoy. They had something to do with the word 'espuma' and time. All we knew was that it was creating great excitement. Soon it came down to the 'espuma' countdown and still we were none the wiser. People started to clear the dance floor and crowd up on to the tiered seating. The tannoy announced 'cinco, cuatro, tres, dos, uno . . .' (5,4,3,2,1 . . .) and large pipes were dropped down from the ceiling. Foam gushed out and spread across the disco floor. We were caught in the flow and it was not long before the foam was rising over our shoulders and we were wet to the skin. It served to loosen the inhibitions and after all, it was not possible to talk under the foam! I gather that 'foam discos' have really caught on in North America.

The next day, we met two girls whom we had discovered under the foam, Veronica and Alexandra. We made up for lost time by talking and, as is often the case in Argentina, the conversation soon turned to the Falkland Islands. For the first time I started to understand the Argentine love affair with these islands. The girls were in their late teens and they spoke of Los Malvinas with a moving passion and love.

'Please tell me something,' Veronica asked. 'Why is Britain so interested in some islands which are so distant from them? It is like Argentina laying claim to Ireland. We love them and we want back what are rightfully ours!' They had a point, I could hardly imagine a teenager in Britain talking with such feeling about the Falkland Islands. Alexandra wrote a note in my diary:

'Do not forget us or Los Malvinas.'

After a day of rest, we set off refreshed but not before doing some exercises. We always limbered up to shake out any stiffness and to get the muscles working. We were rolling our necks and shaking out our shoulders, when out of nowhere a mirror image appeared from behind a bank opposite – a group of children imitating our every move. For some fifteen minutes we held an impromptu aerobics class of star jumps, press ups, squat thrusts and cycle kicks. We left the laughing kids for the hot, straight and fly-infested road. To avoid the flies, there was an optimum speed of about twenty miles an hour, but anything below that would allow them to crawl across your eyes and through your hair. Unfortunately, Mike's knees were still playing him up ever since the strain of the ascent over *Cuesta de Miranda*. He was unable to cycle fast enough and was thus being driven to distraction by the flies. David and I waited for him by sprinting up and down the road at a steady twenty miles an hour. It was in amongst the flies that we celebrated 4,000 miles of the expedition.

That night we pulled into the police station at Pituil in a quest for somewhere to stay the night. The three policemen manning the station were all in tears. It came as quite a surprise because this was not a reaction we were used to; laughter yes, but never crying. Amidst their sobbing one of them pointed to the television. On the screen flashed a slow-motion shot of a blue and white Williams car flying in the air. It was with these policemen we witnessed the death of Ayrton Senna.

'He was in the same mould as our great motor-racing champion, Fangio,' one of the policemen said. 'Even though Senna was Brazilian, we regarded him as one of us.'

In Latin America, everybody remembers where they were and what they were doing when they heard that Senna had been killed.

We were far away from home but we were heading for *Londres* (London). The town has the distinction of being named in honour of the marriage of Mary Tudor and Philip II of Spain in 1558 and it even has a copy of the marriage certificate to prove it. At nightfall we were in the middle of nowhere and still some thirty miles from Londres. I felt emotionally inclined to head on and Mike, ever the romantic, agreed. David was all for stopping, a decision partly influenced by the fact that Mike was almost blind in darkness. Ever since Mendoza, when he had sat on his spectacles, Mike's only option was to wear his prescription sunglasses. Not only did they give him the look of an ageing rock star, but they rendered him hopeless at night cycling. Despite this handicap we cycled on, with me guiding Mike from the front and David shepherding him from the rear. Suddenly a large black object loomed up before me and I slammed on my brakes. It was too late, I went skidding into the side of the soft underbelly of a black bull. Mike and David fortunately were alerted by my muffled cry and the bull's shocked bellow. I contemplated my good fortune; if the bull had been facing forwards I could have been impaled on his horns and if I had crashed into the bull's rear, I could have ended up covered in excrement.

The gauntlet to Londres had yet to be run and the night still held another surprise. Before we left on the expedition we had received many warnings, from Hallam Murray in particular, about dogs. Many dogs in Latin America were rabid and they had a taste for cyclists. Mike and David had bamboo sticks for waving and a cache of pebbles to throw at any predacious dogs. For my part, I did not trust my dexterity on *Arriba*, so I went armed with the Spanish word, *'basta!'* (that's enough). We were passing a collection of huts, when the dog population got wind of our presence and there was an almighty barking uproar. Suddenly, our wheels and feet were surrounded by snapping jaws gleaming in our torch lights. This is when we learnt the cover of darkness brings out the aggressive and courageous nature of dogs, helped by the fact that they cannot see the sticks and stones.

We cycled frantically through these baying hounds, but I was not fast enough to stop one of them sinking his teeth into my back pannier. He clung on tenaciously, as I swerved around the road to try and shake him off. Thankfully dogs are territorial and once this invisible line was reached, he dropped off and the pursuing pack stopped. It was a false respite, for it only meant we were handed over to another even fitter, leaner and hungrier pack. We arrived in Londres with nerves in tatters.

The population of some 3,000 people, living within the mud bricked walls and along the dirt streets, were fascinated to see pictures of the other London. They were particularly taken with the bright, flashing lights of Piccadilly. We were treated like royalty: the town put us up at the local police station, an entourage of people would follow our every move and we were given gifts of walnuts, walnuts and more walnuts. The experience was even sweeter for David. Not for the first time, he fell in love. I will always remember the image of him waiting for Maria under a street lamp in the plaza while reading the poems of Pablo Neruda. It was a cameo straight out of *Love in the Time of Cholera* by Gabriel Garcia Marquez, particularly when she failed to turn up. In a small way we were able to repay the hospitality with the help of Alderman Christopher Walford, the Lord Mayor of London. At our request, he wrote personally to the Mayor of Londres.

'On behalf of the Corporation and citizens of The City of London I send our sincere appreciation to you and the citizens of the town of Londres for the hospitality extended to the three members of the recent British cycling expedition to South America to raise money for the Leukaemia Research Fund.'

By all accounts it is now framed beside the marriage certificate for Mary and Philip.

When we knew there was no room left for the walnuts in our panniers, we left. We did not get very far before we were stopped by a man with a microphone. He was the disc jockey from the local radio station and he was desperate for stories, which probably explained why he was talking to us. Previously, we had only agreed to TV interviews because we could cover our faltering Spanish by dramatic gesticulations and demonstrations on our bikes. The radio medium, however, was without props and quite intimidating, especially when you are out of breath having climbed a steep hill. The Argentine media differed in their line of questioning from their Chilean counterparts. They were more interested in leukaemia and the chances of a cure, while in Chile, leukaemia was a secondary issue to how much we loved their country and how friendly the people had been.

It was slow progress, for a further two miles down the road we stopped for a drink of water outside the 'General Belgrano School'. The children ended their games and gathered along the wall to ask us a whole barrage of questions. Within minutes we had been invited into the school to give a lecture to over two hundred children on our expedition. They were fascinated by our travels, but could not comprehend one underlying issue. As one young boy put it,

'I do not understand why you are on bicycles. Surely it would be much more fun by bus or in a car.'

During the next four days we had to admit he had a point. Not for the first or the last time we decided to take a short cut. It seemed such a good idea at the time; a road going due north, saving some one hundred and fifty miles. Given this situation, it was easy to ignore the possible condition of the road. For the record, the road going from Belen to San Jose Norte was absolute hell.

DAY 182 THE ROAD TO SAN JOSE IN THE HEAT OF THE DAY
'It is difficult to know whether it is quicker and easier to push or ride the bikes. Either way it is tortuous and the sand on the road is like cycling

through thick, sticky treacle. This morning we cycled and pushed for four hours through the searing heat (must be in the nineties) and only achieved seven miles. It is all very demoralising. I am sure I can see snow on the mountains and all I can think about is rolling in it. M and D say it is a mirage. Nothing seems to grow out here, apart from cacti and chillies. Chillies seem to be the only food for sale; they are the very last thing I feel like eating. Things are getting so bad that Mike and I have started to eat toothpaste. Anything to quench the thirst. David reckons the heat has got to our heads. I think he might be right!'

Our spirits were not lifted by the prospect of lunch. All we had left in our panniers was a packet of instant mashed potato. It gave my parched mouth and aching stomach no satisfaction. When the times were hard, we sought escape by reverting back to childhood ways.

MIKE'S DIARY – THE POTATO FIGHT AT THE OK CORRAL
'The road was hot and dusty and the mashed potato was disgusting. We were resting in the shade of a deserted and crumbling mud hut and I stared over the shimmering parched landscape. As I shook the dust from my shorts and wiped the sweat from my eyes, the echoing chords from the film, The Good, the Bad and the Ugly entered my mind. I looked with disinterest at the insipid pile of mash heaped on my spoon and rose slowly. David had his head bowed while with care he picked out the remaining pieces of tomato buried in the mash, when I shot him full in the face. As the mash slid slowly off his forehead and got caught in his eyelashes, the shock froze him for a second. I turned quickly at the sound of Rupert laughing, bent back my spoon and launched a sticky missile on to his chin. The mashed potato gunfight had begun. We circled, eyes narrowed and darting from one to another, with spoons at the ready. Potato balls hissed through the air and landed with a resounding splat. I was hit in the eye and then right in the belly-button. I was running out of ammunition and was forced to recycle

mash by spooning it off my body. A final barrage left us peppered with potato, convulsing in laughter and still somewhat hungry.'

At San Jose Norte paved roads started again, bringing to an end the sandy and corrugated hundred and ten mile nightmare. We hoped it would now be plain sailing all the way to the wine oasis of Cafayate, some forty miles down the road. As usual the wind had other ideas and came sweeping into our faces. I was finding it hard going, and to take my mind off the pain I started to dream of when I was a helmsman on the South China Sea Yachting Race. I was miles away and so, it appeared, were Mike and David. For the last thirty minutes I had lost visual contact with them. This was unusual for as a rule we tended to keep in sight of each other or at least wait at intervals of fifteen minutes. I assumed they had pressed on, anxious to reach Cafayate by nightfall, particularly as Mike was in his ageing rock star sunglasses. I decided to opt for plan B, which if we were ever split up we would meet in the plaza of the next town. I was therefore surprised when there was no sign of Mike or David in the plaza.

I started to ask around. We had found people in South America were so willing to please, they would often give you the answer you most wanted to hear, irrespective of whether or not it was true. Quite often we would ask about the road ahead:

'Do not worry, there are only a few hills. It is mostly flat though and you will find nearly all paved,' came the answer. We would cycle off with renewed vigour and enthusiasm, but after three hours of constant climbing along a rutted sandy track, we would start to wonder what the hell they were talking about.

Many times we had asked how far it was to the next town:

'It is just around the corner, you will be there by lunchtime.' Often we would be lucky if we made it there by nightfall.

Thus when I asked:

'Have you seen two gringos on bicycles?' Everybody confirmed a sighting. The only problem was that Mike and David seemed to be in many different places at once: in the campsite, drinking in the *Bar Esquina*, checking into the *Hotel Confort*, and most intriguing of all, disappearing into *Juanita's Massage Parlour*. I had to admire their energy and stamina in what had been less than an hour. I had no joy in all these places. I decided to be more discriminating in my questioning.

'Were the cyclists you saw wearing black shorts and blue and white tee-shirts?'

'Oh yes, I am positive,' came the reply.

This type of question was another fatal mistake in South America. People did not want to upset you or cause you distress, so they tended to answer 'yes' to everything. Many times we had fallen into the trap of asking,

'Is this the road to the Post Office?' We would receive an affirmative answer only to find some half an hour later we had been sent in totally the wrong direction.

I decided to seek some sanity in the Police station. I asked whether two cyclists had been in.

'Yes,' the policeman replied. I breathed a huge sigh of relief. 'But that was a few months back,' he continued. Eventually, we did meet up, without the assistance of the citizens of Cafayate. The story was that David had suffered three punctures and I must have cycled past them while dreaming of the South China Sea Race.

—15—
HIGH ROAD TO SALTA

'In trouble to be troubled
Is to have your trouble doubled'

DANIEL DEFOE 'The Further Adventures of Robinson Crusoe'

We had a dilemma. There were two options: one; to continue due north along the paved road to the city of Salta, a guaranteed two days cycling, or two; to go on the much longer and challenging dirt road via Cachi, which could take anything up to a week. On paper it appears an easy decision, but that would be to ignore the underlying issues at play. The paved road would help to ease the perennial problem of Mike's knees and would quickly end what had been a gruelling three weeks in the desert. The dirt road, on the other hand, had its attractions. For one thing it was part of cycling folklore in South America:

'Whatever you do, do not miss it! It is beautiful, challenging and an experience you will remember for the rest of your lives,' several cyclists had told us.

We subjected many innocent people to our deliberations. We went to the police again. They understandably recommended the paved road as there was less chance of getting ourselves lost. The girl at the tourist office and the man at the ironmongers did not escape our quest for advice, nor did a generous Belgian couple, who took us out for a meal as a gesture of their support for our expedition. In the end, emotive reasoning eclipsed practical considerations. For my part, I was still haunted by the memory of missing out on Paso Rabolles in Patagonia and remembered Hallam Murray's only other 'must do' experience was this very road via Cachi into Salta. I could not ignore his advice again. David declared any easy option was a soft option and was of the opinion we would always regret not taking the more testing road. With David and I in agreement, Mike was helpless to resist. Not for one moment did we consider Mike's aching knees or our mental exhaustion!

It must have been difficult for Mike for we started on the paved road to Salta, in order to see the spectacular *Quebrada de Cafayate* (Ravine of Cafayate). The *Rio Guachipas* has cut like a scythe through the red sandstone and together with the wind and rain has created a fascinating collection of rock formations resplendent in differing shades of red. Guarding the ravine is a sandstone 'castle', high up on the cliff was a gash called 'The Throat of the Devil' and across the top was a line of twelve sharp peaks, named 'The Devil's Teeth', but they were more like a cock's comb. Below a 180 foot tall rock named *'El Obelisco'* sat a distraught young boy, Ramon. He explained he had borrowed *el patron* (the landlord's) bike without asking and now he was in real trouble because he had a puncture and had no way of getting home. His inner tube looked like a patchwork quilt, but we had been given a can of 'Big Shot', a solidifying liquid foam suitable for any tyres from tractors to bicycles. It did the trick and we escorted him back to his *patron's* place. After Ramon had crept the bike back into the garage, with relief he asked us over for some tea to celebrate.

We had reached a sign reading 'Salta – 140 kms,' when we branched off to embark on our two hundred and thirty mile detour. At a small roadside cafe we met Evan, a French cyclist. He was looking pale and I asked him if he was feeling all right.

'I would not advise eating here,' he replied. 'I have just bitten into a piece of cake and ended up with a maggot wiggling on my tongue. I got charged $3.50 (£2.00) for the privilege.'

This prompted David to tell a joke. It is true to say that he was not famous for his tact or subtlety. Mike and I feared the worse.

'What is worse than finding a maggot in your cake?' Blank stares all around before David said, 'Half a maggot!' Understandably Evan quickly made his excuses and left.

He did not, however, get away that easily for in the evening we found ourselves at the same campsite. We shared stories and talked of the people we had met. We came to admire Evan, because he had cycled for a whole week with Stefan, the obnoxious German.

'It was terrible. He never stopped swearing and talking about himself, and one night I was subjected to listening to a Frankfurt AFC match,' Evan told us. 'He was really rough on his bike, forever crunching the gears and riding too fast over bumps. I nicknamed him *Senor Malo* (Mr. Bad).'

'We christened him Gollum, after the loathsome character in *The Lord of the Rings*,' Mike replied.

We hoped Stefan's ears were burning, because now he had his wish: we were hearing and talking about him.

'The people in Argentina have been so friendly and hospitable,' Evan continued. 'A French friend of mine had his bicycle stolen in Alta Gracia. The mayor was so upset that this could happen in his town, he promised to buy a brand new identical bike. It took him three months to raise the money from the citizens of the town and a further two months to ship it in from the United States. My friend had a great time while he waited.'

'Have you heard about the Japanese guy carrying his bike?' Evan asked. We nodded, but until now we had thought it was a myth. 'I met him near Cordoba. He had his bike slung over his shoulders and I could not resist asking, "Why?" He told me he had cycled all the way down from Alaska, when he arrived in Mexico. There is a game the truck drivers play, which is to see how many cyclists they can force off the road. Having been pushed off the road some eight times, he decided enough was enough and he started to walk. He has been walking for some eighteen months now with his bike on his shoulders. He hopes to make it to Tierra del Fuego.'

Surely, only the Japanese could contemplate and achieve such a feat.

That night I was sitting quietly on the toilet, when Mike came storming into the bathroom.

'David has just come up with the most ridiculous suggestion. He wants to ride over the highest pass in South America, which only happens to be some five hundred miles out of our way.' As I sat there, I had to admit I was intrigued. Mike was always one for exaggeration, so realistically his estimate could be halved. The highest pass some 250 miles away was certainly worth considering. We now had another dilemma to test us as a team.

The sensitive issue of the pass was dropped for a couple of days. The road took us along the side of the River Calchaqui, a fertile green ribbon amongst the arid desert. Lining our path lay red chillies drying in the sun and humble mud villages huddled around white-washed churches. It was not long before we lost David. Thinking something had befallen him, Mike and I cycled back, only to find him sipping sweet white wine with a bunch of merry and singing locals. The wine was good, but the singing was terrible, especially as David by now was joining in. They took us on a weaving path to show us how *vino patero* was made. Grapes were poured into a big wooden vat, they then took their shoes off and started to march around with the juice squelching up between their toes. They asked us in, but it had been a hot and sweaty day on the road, so we declined in the interests of the wine. We need not have been so coy, for while we watched one of the guys blew his nose into the grapes. We could not leave until we had three water bottles full of the sweet wine.

Light-headed and with David still singing some totally incomprehensible Spanish song, we passed through the *Quebrada de las Flechas* (the Ravine of Arrows). The rocks here were remarkable. They were stacked up vertically and looked like painted dominoes on the verge of tumbling. The gap created by the road was the only break in the sequence. On the other side we cycled into the sun-drenched village of Angastaco. It was midday and deserted, and the only sign of life was a scruffy, dusty mongrel licking its paws in the shade of a mud-brick house. We felt we had walked on to a set for Noel Coward's song, 'Mad Dogs and Englishmen go out in the Midday Sun'. Two Indians appeared from under a pimento tree in the plaza. They were popping coca leaves and came over to offer us some. They taught us to nip the stalks off the green leaves and then to fold them to make a compact bunch. They showed us the trick of lacing the leaves with bicarbonate of soda, which helped to release the juices. Then they showed us how to place the 'plug' in the side of our mouths and move it around with our tongues.

'The leaves will give you energy and help you cope with the altitude,' they advised us. 'They are also a good stimulant for sex.'

For the time being they tasted bitter, sent my mouth numb and made my brain tingle.

That night we stopped at *Estancia El Carmen,* and we were put up in the porch of the estate church. We were shown inside and the pews, pulpit and altar were all made from the pock-marked wood of the carbon cactus. The sun woke us up early and we followed the river to the oasis of Molinos. Nearly all the houses were shrouded in white, apart from the twin-domed church built in 1720, which was dressed in a yellowish paste to preserve it. I wrote in my diary:

'What a beautiful and romantic place. It would be perfect for a honeymoon.' The coca leaves were starting to have an effect and with only Mike and David as company, I thought the sooner we got to Salta the better.

There was friction amongst us. The strain of four gruelling weeks on the road was taking its toll and now the dilemma of the pass hung around our necks like a millstone. At Seclantos, David reached breaking point.

'I cannot stand it anymore,' David told us. 'Everything I say is a subject of derision. I feel left out of decisions and you both seem to be constantly ganging up against me. I am not enjoying it any more and if things do not improve, I am honestly thinking of going it alone. It would be a great shame.'

I thought it would be more than a shame, it would be a disaster! I was surprised. I knew there had been some problems between us, but I regarded it as a temporary state brought on by both physical and mental exhaustion. I certainly had not thought for one minute it could lead to us splitting up.

DAY 191 CRISIS IN THE TEAM

'What D said has set me thinking. Looking back over the last few weeks, we have started to lose respect for each other and we have crawled into our own egocentric shells. D is right – if this goes any further it could be terminal and rip the heart out of the expedition. Splitting up would rank as the greatest failure in my life. Thank goodness D spoke when he did, because we still have a chance to save our team and the expedition.'

Mike was preoccupied with thoughts of the *Abra del Acay*, the highest pass in South America. No definite decision had been made, but he knew David and I had set our hearts on going over it.

'Look guys, I cannot explain it, but I have bad vibes about going over this pass,' Mike told us.

His diary at the time showed the true depth of this feeling.

DAY 192 MIKE'S DIARY

'Of this I have fears, but fears are to be overcome. However should things go horribly wrong, which who knows they may, it is better to have fought and lost than not to have fought at all. The words of Shakespeare spring to mind:

> *To be or not to be that is the question*
> *Whether it is nobler in the mind to suffer*
> *The slings and arrows of outrageous fortune*
> *Or take arms against a sea of troubles*
> *For in that sleep of death what dreams may come*
> *When we have shuffled off this mortal coil.*

All very dramatic I know, but this is a dramatic time. We are all not getting on well and we are attempting to do something extremely demanding, for what I believe to be the wrong reasons. So we can say at an illustrious dinner party, "We climbed over the highest pass in South America".

I honestly have major reservations about the altitude amongst other things, but it's there and it's to be overcome and I never was one to resist a challenge. Maybe it will bring our friendly troupe back together again. I certainly hope so!

I just hope our little guardian angel is watching over us all. I love life and I love the two people fortune and fate has put me on this adventure with.

Maybe the coca leaves will help us in our fortitude and enable us to fly over the pass. "With wings of celestial freedom, that will carry us to the balancing of the sun" (words from the Yes album Tomato*).*

I have just thought of home, whilst singing, "I wish I was at home at Christmas". I miss the comfort and security, and a hug here and there wouldn't go amiss. It has been a long time since I spoke to my parents. There is so much I have to share with them. It is strange to think after twenty-eight years, I know so little about my parents and I do hope I get the opportunity to find out and tell them how much I love them.'

All these thoughts were going on in the house of Oscar, the mayor of the town of Selantos. We were guests in his home and his hospitality of food, beds and friendship helped us to sort out the turmoil in our minds. He assured us the pass could be passed and he offered to carry any surplus luggage to Salta. We took him up on his offer and with lightened loads we set off for the final town of Cachi, where we would have to make the decision between the pass or Salta.

The Indian town of Cachi, which means 'salt' in the Inca language of *Quechua*, has a very old church made entirely out of cactus wood, one of the few materials available in the area. It was here that we went to the police station and asked about the pass.

'It is certainly possible, but you will need coca leaves, bicarbonate of soda, garlic and a tin of mentanol to combat *el soroche*. Do you know you will be reaching a height of 5,000 metres (16,500 feet)?' a young policeman told us.

Whatever happened to energy, stamina and a touch of madness, I thought. *El soroche* was altitude sickness, which starts to take affect at over 3,000 metres (9,900 feet). We had been warned the most notable effects were breathlessness, headaches, fitful sleep and flatulence.

'You must also carry many warm clothes for the wind and air can be so cold at the top. Whatever you do, do not spend the night up there because there is a big danger of hypothermia. A French cyclist tried about two years ago but he had to be brought down because of the *soroche* and the cold. The last reports were that there is a limited amount of snow up there and we know the road is clear because the Camel Trophy Land-Rover Rally went through there only a week ago. There were many nose bleeds amongst the drivers, but that was the only problem.'

We then went to the local '*gomeria*' (tyre specialists) to patch up our ailing tyres and also to weld some loose joints on our pannier racks. Pedro, the mechanic with dirt encrusted hands, long shaggy beard, hair in a ponytail and soiled jeans falling down over his hips, worked for three hours fixing the bikes and tyres. When we told him of our plans, he wished us 'good luck' and waved our money aside. The pass by all accounts was possible and the bikes were now prepared, but the crucial question remained: '*were we ready in ourselves?*' In the final discussions around the campfire, we declared we would only succeed if we all believed in what we were doing. This put Mike in an impossible position, for he knew David and I had set our hearts on the pass and his competitive spirit would not allow him to say 'No!' We were agreed and not even a night at the disco dancing to such classics as 'I have a Yellow Tractor' could take Mike's mind off the challenge ahead.

We planned to go over the pass in three stages in order to acclimatise: one day to La Poma (11,220 feet), the next to Casa Sherpa (13,860 feet) and then over the top (16,154 feet). A series of punctures conspired against us and we only made it to the tiny hamlet of El Rodeo. There was a tense football match taking place and Mike and I were asked to make up the numbers. However, one burst down the left wing left me breathless and legless in the thin air. After only a few minutes Mike and I were substituted and we joined a group of bowler hatted ladies cheering and screaming encouragement from the touchline.

We were put up at the local school in the dormitories vacated by the children at weekends. The school bell forced us out of bed early in the morning and from the dusty playground we watched the children descending from all directions. They were all in time for the flag raising ceremony at eight o'clock. As the flag rose, the valley resounded with the sound of the children singing the Argentine national anthem. Classes were suspended, while we showed them our bikes, recalled our experiences and gave a geography lesson on where we lived. Roberto, a wide-eyed seven year old, was confused.

'If you live on the other side of the world, why do the British own Los Malvinas?' Roberto, in the innocence of youth, had a point. The children were most fascinated, however, by our white sun block and they insisted on having their faces painted. We had to leave in the interests of their education.

We climbed out of the shade and lush green vegetation of the valley on to a black volcanic plain. It was hard to believe anybody could live up here, but huddled in the fold of the hills beside a small river lay the village of La Poma. Here the locals claim they only die of old age, on account of the very invigorating climate at over 11,000 feet. We found this hard to believe. The children at the village school, many with sore red cheeks, chapped lips and snot-encrusted noses, hardly looked pictures of health and the men on the streets walked around with watery eyes induced by alcohol and the jagged scars of many fights. The 'riding' doctor (horses rather than planes for medical emergencies) told us the life expectancy in the village was forty-seven years, so perhaps they did survive these ailments.

Christian Martinez, the doctor on horseback, was financed by the government to ride around these remote villages administering medical aid. He came to La Poma every two weeks. He advised us about *el soroche*.

'There is no telling who it will hit. I have known the fittest of people being seriously affected, while their fat and unhealthy companions have had no problems at all. Just take it slowly, which on those bikes seems to be your only option, and make sure you chew coca leaves and garlic and you will be all right. Inevitably, you will get headaches, experience increased flatulence, have problems sleeping and feel breathless, but if you ever, *ever*, start to feel a dull pain in the back of the neck just above the spine, come straight down. *Abra del Acay* is no place for heroes and do not expect to find any help up there.'

It seemed, for the next few days, we must resign ourselves to a rather unattractive state: cheeks bulging with coca leaves, the stench of garlic issuing from our pores and a constant barrage of farts. It was fortunate we had no families or friends around.

It was an emotional farewell to the people of La Poma. It seemed that the whole village turned out to wish us luck and to wave us on our way. The schoolchildren presented us with gifts of chocolate biscuits and apples and Beatriz Jesus Mamani, the headmistress, and several members of her staff burst into tears. It was all very moving. I cannot explain it, but I suddenly felt an overwhelming need to talk to my parents before we left. I thought, however, this was an impossible dream. The police had other ideas, for within minutes I was talking to my father over a radio. The exchange in Salta had made the link by holding a telephone handset close to their radio – the wonders of modern technology.

We climbed steadily on a diet of garlic and coca leaves, through the harsh mountainous landscape. Cacti, the odd goat and a man selling raffle tickets were the only signs of life. He came walking out of nowhere. He wore a red-checked shirt, torn brown trousers tied up with string, a floppy denim hat and a toothless crooked grin.

'Do you want to buy some raffle tickets?' he shouted.

'Well yes, but what are they in aid of?' Mike asked.

'It is so I can buy equipment to dig my gold mine. There is a very good prize, which from the state of your clothing, you would find most useful. It is my wife's sewing machine.'

His clothes were certainly not a good advertisement for the prize and we wondered if his wife had been consulted. We did, however, buy some tickets in admiration of his initiative. He was delighted;

'These are the first tickets I have sold this year (it was now May). You must leave an address, so I can let you know if you win.'

We thanked him, but requested if we won, he should give the sewing machine back to his wife. We wished him luck with his gold venture.

It was not until five o'clock that we arrived at the last house before the pass, *Casa Sherpa*. It was a small mud-bricked goatherd's cottage, which was the home of *Senor* and *Senora Sherpa* and their eleven children. They eked out an existence with the support of their three hundred goats, which gave them milk, cheese and meat. In a small outbuilding, they showed us a year's supply of flour and rice.

'We have everything we need and none of us ever go hungry,' *Senora Sherpa* told us.

'Don't you ever get lonely?' I asked.

'With all the children I never get a chance and after all we have each other,' she replied.

After the goats were herded into the corral from the mountains just before sunset, they asked us in for a goat *asado* (barbecue). The room was full of the smoke from the fire. There were many sounds and voices, but all we could see were misty shadows floating in and out of the flickering light. Delicious plates of meat and cups of *maté* were handed to us out of the gloom. Slowly we could make out pairs of eyes staring intently at us and a young voice asked us where we were from.

'Never heard of it, how close is it to Cachi?' came the reply. A thirty mile radius was the extent of their world and I felt quite envious of their life untouched by greed, jealousy, pretensions and crime.

They apologised that they could not put us up inside, because there was no space left on the dirt floor in the only other room. The family was worried we would freeze in the night, particularly as I was in exile from the tent owing to an uncontrollable bout of flatulence. I was warm enough in my sleeping bag, but I remember waking up in the middle of the night to see Senor Sherpa laying two goat skins on top of me. It was only in the morning we realised the extent of the cold. The river in which we had washed the previous evening was frozen over, and in collecting water from the well, Mike got his fingers stuck to the metal of the saucepan.

The family and goats came out to see us off. It was nine o'clock and we calculated we would be at the pass at about one o'clock; fifteen miles at a steady pace of under four miles an hour. No worries, we thought. Soon we came to realise why the road had been closed to cars for the last three years. Large boulders were strewn across our path and in places the river had broken its banks, forcing us to stop and gingerly guide our bikes through the torrents. It was at one of these points that *Woop-Woop* had an icy early morning bath. David swore in indignation at the thought of soggy clothes, but he did well to stop her disappearing down a waterfall. He could expect no help from either Mike or me because we were disabled by laughter at the thought of David having to return to the bottom of the valley to pick up his bike. Not only was the air getting thinner, but so was David's sense of humour.

We were not making the progress we had expected. Our straining legs and difficulties with breathing were forcing us to stop at regular intervals. Our spirits rose when we met a group of geologists prospecting for gold. They did not need to sell raffle tickets for they were financed by the Chilean Government. We asked them why they were in Argentina, and with a sly smile they said no one would ever catch them up here. They gave us white chocolate, orange juice and water to buy our silence and told us it was only another two hours to the top. It was now twelve-thirty. Our heightened morale did not last for long. Soon we could only push the bikes as our legs had turned to jelly and our lungs had started to burn through lack of oxygen. By the side of the road I wrote with a shaking hand.

DAY 196 ABRA DEL ACAY

'Maybe we are stark raving mad and perhaps Mike was right all along, but I just cannot face going back and giving up all that blood, sweat and tears, which has brought us up here.'

For all the gung-ho language, after a further two hours pushing and still with no sight of the pass, we faced a serious dilemma. It was three-thirty, we had only three hours of daylight left and we were at 15,000 feet; should we head down to a safe altitude and try again tomorrow or should we risk proceeding and hope we could cycle over the pass back to a safe height for sleeping? We decided on another thirty minutes and if there was no pass, then no go. We went through another succession of bends bearing false hopes and just when we were least expecting it, around a fairly innocuous looking corner, the landscape opened up to reveal the pass. We were surprised how far and how high it still was, but our hearts rose just to see it.

As we continued to climb I wrote the following snippets in my diary while I regained my breath.

'Oh where, oh where will this ever end? Can see the top but it seems to get no closer. Solely pushing now, but have to stop every fifty yards. The road is

bad, I am constantly losing my footing on the loose pebbles. The air is so thin, my head is throbbing like a madman. Mike tells us to think of the good things in life, and after scoring a century for Hampshire stroke by stroke, I start to count the guanacos in the valley. I get to ninety, when I find a guanaco foot on the road. Has to be a good omen; if a rabbit foot is, why not the foot of a guanaco? It goes in the pannier, side by side with the horse-shoe. D is struggling. Sit down to wait on what I think is soft grass, but it reveals itself as a cactus. Thanks a lot guanaco foot. Spines buried in my buttocks and poor D has to take them out. Not enough air for us to laugh.'

After what seemed like an eternity, we at last struggled to the summit at six o'clock, some five hours behind schedule. A battered sign announced 'Abra del Acay – 4,895m' (16,154 feet) and we took photos for posterity.

THE SUMMIT 6.05 P.M.

'Yes, it feels great but view is disappointing. Expected to be on top of the world but we remain surrounded by even higher mountains. Does not take away the sense of achievement and it would always be an experience only we could share. Elation and celebrations are muted though. It is terribly cold with a bitter wind blowing, but more importantly the sun has disappeared behind the mountains. Now only twenty minutes left of light. We must descend to a safe altitude. The descent and where we are going to stay worries me.'

It was a race against the setting sun. Safety lay 3,000 feet below and we had twenty minutes left of light. Thankfully, the road had improved and we could descend at speed. The problem was the chilling wind freezing our hands and feet. I experienced difficulty releasing the brakes and changing gear as I lost all feeling in my fingers. My feet, now numb, were like lead weights on the pedals. We were cold and exhausted, accordingly we were desperate to find some shelter rather than be exposed to the elements in our tent. The light was fading quickly and there was still no sign of human habitation. Then suddenly the rasping sound of a dog barking was carried on the wind and a herd of llamas, with red tassels in their ears, appeared on the horizon. Dogs circled around them and would occasionally nip a wayward one on the ankle to bring it in line with the rest of the herd. These llamas were coming in for the night, which meant a house must be close by. Soon a man appeared wheeling a stick and whistling shrilly to instruct the dogs. He was as surprised to see us as we were relieved to meet him.

He invited us back to his small cottage. Claudio's eighteen year old wife looked worried when she saw us and heard what we had just done. We must all have looked in quite a state, but Mike in particular was cause for concern, because he had turned ashen and started to shake uncontrollably. She took control.

'It is *la soroche*. You must get him to bed immediately and keep him warm. I will go and make a remedy my mother taught me.'

Mike was not getting any better and he was slipping in and out of bouts of delirium. Even in his sleeping bag and under a whole pile of llama skin, he was finding it difficult to expel the cold in his bones. David had to take the herbal remedy to his lips. We then forced him to eat some steamy corn beef hash. I will always remember the last words Mike said, before he was jolted into sleep;

'I hope I wake up and see another day.'

His hope and all our hopes were answered and he woke up feeling better, but still nauseous. It was bitterly cold outside and I could not help thinking that we probably would not have survived a night out in the open. We cooked up some porridge and shared it with Claudio and his young wife. They said they liked it but their faces told a different story. I wondered how long they would remember the three crazy *gringos*, who came to them in the night with *la soroche* and left after eating a funny, grey-looking substance. It was time to go down further to ease our throbbing heads.

The road soon joined the railway track of the *Tren a las Nubes* (Train to the Clouds). This audacious and remarkable project was built in stages between 1921 and 1948 and it stretched six hundred miles across the Andes between Salta and Antofagasta on the coast in Chile. In its quest to the clouds, it employs twenty-one tunnels, thirteen viaducts, thirty-one bridges, two loops and two zigzags. Unfortunately, the tenacity of the engineering was never rewarded, for by the time it was built developments in road and air transport had diluted its importance. It now remains a white elephant, used occasionally by tourist and freight trains.

The line, however, was to rediscover a sense of purpose and significance. For all the talk of the developments in roads, certainly the boulder-strewn and bridgeless track down the valley to Salta had been left in a timewarp. After tortuous progress downhill at an average speed of nine miles an hour and constant interruptions to seek the best way to cross the fast flowing river, we took to cycling between the rails of the train tracks. This was by far the best way to travel; no undulations, no traffic and no more getting our feet wet. There was even accommodation provided in the form of sleepy stations. We gave one station master the fright of his life when we accidentally set off an alarm, which was designed to be a warning of an approaching train. He came rushing out frantically pulling up his trousers and trying to wave a red and white flag at the same time. He was relieved rather than angry when he saw us, and laughing he said;

'I thought something was strange. The train is not due for another week!'

The railway and then eventually a paved road took us down to the provincial capital of Salta. We felt relieved and fulfilled. Mike no longer harboured any bad feelings, and on arriving at the outskirts of the city he said, 'I would not have missed that experience for the world'.

DAY 199 SALTA

'We were a team again. Adversity had brought us back together. Going over the pass had taught us we needed each other. Whether it was M rushing down the hill to help D push his bike, or D fixing my puncture when I did not feel up to it, or when I gave my chocolate ration to M. We knew now without each other we would be lost!

The pass had been a tremendous achievement. However, I could not forget the way D and I had bulldozed M into it, blinded by our own selfish reasons. We had ignored M.'s knees and his mental anxiety. I tried to imagine being in M.'s position. I felt guilty. How could I have lived with myself if something dreadful had happened up there? We had been lucky this time, but we could not count on being so fortunate next time.

Thankfully our thoughts were with cycling together into Bolivia and onwards to Lake Titicaca.'

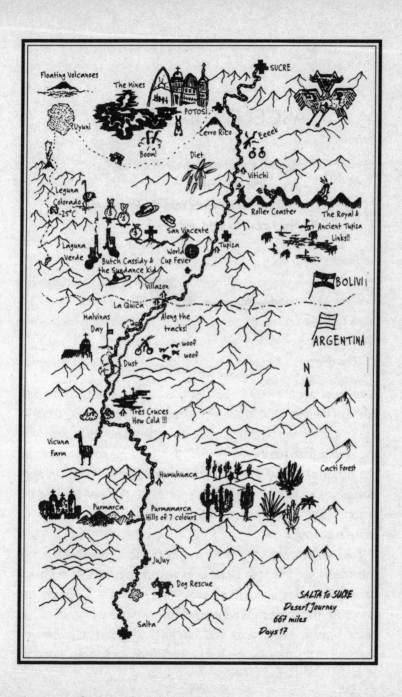

—16—
ASCENT TO BOLIVIA

'Does the road wind uphill all the way?
Yes, to the very end.
Will the day's journey take the whole long day?
From morn to night, my friend.'

CHRISTINA G.ROSSETTI 'Uphill'

Salta (population 294,000) lies encircled by mountains on the lush plains of the Lerma Valley. It was a place of strategic importance to the Incas for it was on their main route leading over the Andes. After the Spanish founded the city in 1582, they used this road to transport the riches of Latin America on the backs of Salta mules, through Bolivia and on to Lima in Peru. We were also destined to cycle this historic route 250 miles up on to the Andean altiplano and to the Bolivian border.

Salta has kept its past. It remains a city of colonial courtly charm. In the streets and the main plaza, colonnaded colonial-style buildings, ornate churches and carved wooden doorways suppress and dominate the modern urban architecture. While earthquakes had caused havoc in Mendoza and San Juan, Salta has stayed largely immune to this threat since 1692. There is no geological reason for this cessation, but rather that this date coincides with the arrival of two images: *Cristo del Milagro* and *Virgen del Milagro*. This holy lady and gentleman were dispatched from Spain in 1592 bound for the cathedral at Cordoba, but somehow by chance, or was it divine intervention, they ended up in Salta a hundred years later. They arrived at a time when the city was gripped by a terrifying series of earthquakes. At their wits end, the citizens paraded the images through the streets, and the earthquakes immediately ceased. The Cordoba bishops were so impressed that they agreed the images should stay in Salta as a tribute to the miracle. Since then the *Cristo* and the *Virgen* have been attracting up to 80,000 people each year for a two-week festival, when once again the images are paraded through the streets. We were told that extra priests from all over Argentina had to be drafted in to handle the demand for confessions.

The people of Salta are as seductive as the atmosphere. Before we left Britain, we had been warned the Argentines were arrogant, selfish and aloof. In our experience, this generalisation could not have been further from the truth. We had found them to be nothing but unpretentious, considerate and friendly. We were particularly moved by the interest and support they showed us when they heard we were raising money for the Leukaemia Research Fund. They would always want to know how much money we had raised, the details of the research and the chances of finding a cure. We also found a people who knew, cared and wanted to understand what was going on in the world around them. The citizens of Salta embodied all these qualities, but they took them to a level beyond all expectations.

The incidences of kindness and hospitality are too numerous to mention and one example will suffice to represent them all. My grandfather's ninetieth birthday was coming up and I felt upset and rather guilty that I would not be around to celebrate this great day with him. It was my hope that I could record a special message of congratulations on a video tape and send it to him. We had just completed an interview about the expedition on Canal 11, a national television station, when I mentioned to the producer, Alberto, my dilemma over my grandfather's birthday. He was sympathetic, but he was more intent on knowing one thing.

'Are you by any chance related to Clement Attlee, the Labour Prime Minister?' he asked.

'Yes,' I replied. 'He was my great second cousin.'

Alberto was overjoyed. 'He was truly a great man. I have nothing but respect for what he achieved in amongst the difficulties of peacetime Britain. It would be my honour to give you a video recorder and a cameraman for the morning. I will do it for Clement.'

I had often heard glowing accounts of my cousin, but what made this comment particularly special was that they came from a man who had never been to Britain before. I recorded the video in the main plaza of Salta under the statue of General San Martin, the Argentine conqueror of the Spanish. I also enlisted the help of a group of schoolchildren to sing *Feliz Cumpleanos* (Happy Birthday) to my grandfather. It was their singing that brought tears to my grandfather's eyes on the day of his birthday.

The overwhelming hospitality was not the only factor which kept us in Salta for some twelve days. Constantly preying on our mind was the thought of the gruelling uphill climb to the *altiplano*, the Andean plain lying at a height of 13,000 feet, and then onwards to Bolivia. We searched for a distraction and an excuse, and found it in arguably one of the natural wonders of the world, *las Cataratas del Iguazu* (the Waterfalls of Iguazu), some thirty-six hours away by bus. The statistics are impressive: 275 falls stretching over a frontage of 8,100 feet, cascading over a 200 foot precipice at a rate of 6,880 cubic feet a second. These dimensions only paint half the picture.

DAY 206 IGUAZU FALLS

'They are stunning, breathtaking and overwhelming. I am sitting in virgin rainforest, bright with orchids, begonias and serpentine festooning the branches. Myriads of painted butterflies are fluttering around my head and the forest is alive with the sounds and colours of toucans, parrots and cacique birds. The falls cascade and thunder before me. A high cloud of spray is thrown up, in which the sun creates flickering rainbows. To my surprise I watch swifts defying the power of the falls by darting in and out of the water. I listen to the soundtrack of the film The Mission *composed Ennio Morricone and get taken to another world. I had never dreamt anything could be so beautiful.'*

The thought of the altiplano brought us all back to earth. We really did not know what to expect in Bolivia, but amongst the people in Salta there seemed to be a consensus. It was poor and primitive. Salta thus offered the last opportunity to stock up on the luxuries of the modern world, or so the enterprising and persuasive shopkeepers told us.

At the bike shop they warned,

'In Bolivia, you will be lucky to find roads let alone bicycle tyres.' We bought three tyres.

At the opticians it was a similar story:

'Contact lenses in Bolivia, you must be joking! They have only just discovered glasses there.' I was forced to buy two bottles of lens solution at an extortionate price.

Even in the sober environs of the National Bank, the picture was not much better:

'I would advise you to get your money now. They will not know what a credit card is beyond a colourful piece of plastic. As for money, bartering for goods is still widespread, so perhaps you are better off taking two chickens!'

Was this really what it was like in Bolivia or were these the prejudiced views of people immersed in the delights and sophistication of the modern world? We decided to be cautious, and thus by the time we left Salta our bikes were very heavy indeed. What rotten timing we thought, when we considered the climbing ahead!

We opted for the winding subtropical route out of Salta called *La Cornisa* (lush vegetation). We passed through avenues of green trees and ferns, which exuded a heady fragrance and afforded a cool shade. The road was free of traffic and the only people we saw were three hippies waiting for a lift. They had been waiting for a long time, but they were not worried;

'It's cool, man. We have love, flowers and tranquillity. Peace go with you,' one of them chanted, acting out the perfect stereotype.

We stopped for lunch, and with relish and much salivating made ourselves marmite sandwiches. So far on the expedition this luxury had been denied us, but the arrival of a package in Salta from my parents had ended the abstinence. We were not alone in having lunch. While we were sitting there, we heard a rustling in the grass and there was a small snake swallowing a frog. I thought I would stick with marmite.

We spent the night in a fishing lodge on the shores of *Lago Cienaga*. It was an idyllic spot, but by no means tranquil because we were next door to a tree of argumentative white herons. They were still going at it in the morning when I awoke to a red-streaked sky of dawn and a light mist floating over the blue waters. Psychologically Sunday was always a bad day for us and today was no exception. It was a hangover of our working and partying days and we just could not kick the habit of feeling groggy and self-indulgent. We positively lingered over breakfast and it was not till after several false starts that we finally got going. Our progress did not last very long. We were crossing the man-made overflow to the lake, when we heard some distressed shouts and barking. We stopped and saw a couple pacing anxiously along the top of a concrete wall. From below came the sound of splashing and a succession of urgent barks. Alvero, their pet spaniel, had fallen in, but was finding it impossible to crawl up the smooth, steep-sided walls. Without help it was just a matter of time before Alvero drowned of exhaustion. We noticed a narrow ledge on the wall just above the waterline, on to which David and I lowered Mike. Alvero swam into his arms, and wide-eyed and shaking with fright we delivered him back to his relieved owners. If we had been travelling by any other mode of transport we would not have heard his plaintive howls.

We had a huge lunch to celebrate the saving of Alvero and we retired early in the shadow of the mountains we were destined to climb. At 14,000 feet, they were a formidable sight. The next day, it was hot and exhausting and we had to dig deep to keep going up the constant hill through Purmamarca, with its rock strata of the seven colours and on to the town of Humahuaca (9,000 feet). Here the friendly mayor put us up for the night in a Russian-style hotel, usually reserved for members of mining co-operatives. It was a soulless place, with wide, echoing corridors, darkened bar and restaurant, and noisy gurgling pipes. It gave me the creeps so I left Mike and David to seek alternative entertainment. In the street I bumped into the Argentine hippies we had passed just outside Salta and together we went out to eat. They had given us all nicknames.

'You are dead-ringers for the pop group "Police",' Charlie told me. 'You are the stocky, blond-haired guitarist, your friend with the long face was the drummer and the guy in the round sunglasses was Sting. Personally, I cannot stand the group. Give me Carlos Santana and Jimi Hendrix anytime. Do you know Jimi is still playing in the sky!'

When the conversation moved to the scourge of imperialism and the injustice of the Falklands War, I decided it was time for bed.

Surprise, surprise . . . it was uphill the next day. The paved road disappeared and we were taken into a barren landscape sucked dry by the harsh, sweltering sun. There was no escape from the heat and my body became bathed in sweat. Through my salt-encrusted eyes, I watched the only signs of life. Trucks and buses, throwing up huge plumes of dust, were twisting down the side of an imposing mountain. As each one passed another layer of dirt became caked on my sweaty skin. It was a great injustice because none of the buses seemed to have any people in them. To add to the fun David's pannier rack went again and Mike's knees started to play up. For my part I was feeling particularly lazy. I was very much a 'mood' cyclist; some days nothing could hold me back in my enthusiasm and I would race ahead at a delirious pace and on other days, which tended to be more frequent, I was not into it at all and I would crawl along. I could never find a happy medium, while Mike and David were much more consistent in their performances. Today was one of those days when I kept on asking, 'What am I doing here?' I think we were all asking that question, when after a roller-coaster ride of ups and downs along an appalling road, we arrived exhausted in the tiny altiplano outpost of Tres Cruces (11,000 feet). It has only one claim to fame, being the coldest place in Argentina when the sun goes down. No amount of singing or chest beating could relieve the numbing pain of a cold shower with the temperature at minus fifteen degrees centigrade outside. In hindsight I should have kept the layers of sweat-encrusted dirt; at least they would have provided a form of insulation.

On our way out of Tres Cruces the next day, our path was blocked by schoolchildren. We were forbidden to leave until we gave everyone a ride on our bikes, played football, took photographs, told them about Britain and thoroughly disrupted their morning classes. In the mêlée, I felt a tug on my sleeve. A young girl with rosy cheeks and large brown eyes was looking up at me.

'My name is Fatima,' she said. 'Please do not forget me.' Fatima, I remember you to this day.

Not for the first time, we left in the interests of education. The bleak landscape was alive with sweeping dust 'devils' whirling into the sky. At times we had to stop to let them pass, or quicken our pace to avoid them. From behind one 'devil' emerged an ancient lady and her dog. She was bent over a crooked stick and as we drew closer she raised her hand. We stopped and she turned her head upwards to reveal a face lined with the wrinkles of a life of hardship. She muttered incoherently, revealing a line of decayed teeth. We listened closely and eventually deciphered what she wanted.

'Please, can you tell me what day it is?' she asked.

'It is Thursday,' I replied.

'Thank you. And what month are we now in?'

'June. June 9th to be precise.'

'And what year is it?' she continued.

'1994.'

She looked pleased with the information. 'Good,' she said, 'I was right I *am* eighty today. I kept telling Salvador,' she pointed at the dog, 'but he would not believe me.' We wished her a happy birthday and gave her a bag of mandarins and a bar of chocolate.

We were soon to come to a milestone of the expedition, the end of *Ruta Cuarenta*. 180 days ago and 4,120 miles back in the far south, we had first taken this road through the deserts of Patagonia. Over the months, it had been both our tormentor and our guardian. It was the road of the hundred mile an hour winds, of the sandy culverts, and of the poisonous mutton. It was a bitter sweet moment to say goodbye to it for the final time. Our emotional state was extinguished by our arrival in the barrack-like mining town of Abra Pampa. It took a mere ten minutes riding around its dusty streets lined with sleeping drunks and dogs to sense the undercurrent of monotony and boredom and to discover we did not want to spend the night there. We decided to cycle on to Miraflores, the largest vicuna farm in Argentina.

Vicunas are smaller, rarer and more timid than their cameloid relatives; llamas, guanacos and alpacas. They have always been prized for their fine, soft wool, which is similar in touch and feel to cashmere. In the times of the Incas only the kings were permitted to wear this wool and today it remains just as exclusive owing to the rarity of the vicuna and the difficulties of domestication. We were told that during shearing a vicuna was likely to be so shocked, it would die of a heart attack. Thankfully our arrival seemed to have no adverse effect on the herds of vicunas and we were permitted to stay. We were soon befriended by Guadeloupe, the farm's pet guanaco, who had been taken in when she lost her mother in a road accident. She insisted on joining us for supper and it was then that she took a liking to my sleeping bag. It was for fear of a midnight foray from Guadeloupe that I ended up sleeping on a table.

In the early morning I was stirred into semi-consciousness. The table was swaying erratically on its legs and I thought I must jump off before it collapsed. I also remember that the heavy metal door was shaking and banging on its hinges. This unusual combination had such an effect on me, I promptly went back to sleep. When I awoke again, I was surprised still to be on the table and even more so to find it appeared to have regained its strength and was now solid below me. The door also now seemed to be immovable. I put it down as a dream until we were asked whether we had felt the earthquake. A table was obviously the place to be, for Mike and David lying on the floor had slept through it.

It was while we were riding back to the main highway through herds of llamas, that I had a baffling thought. It all revolved around asking a llama its name in Spanish. I stopped opposite a majestic brown and white fleeced animal and asked,

'Como se llama?' (What is your name?)

'Mi llama es llama,' came the puzzling reply.

No wonder they always had such a supercilious look. They must have thought humans were rather stupid.

This thought occupied my mind all the way to the village of Marques (11,500 feet). It was a poverty-stricken place and seemed to lie under a constant cloud of dust. The resident nurse told us that nearly all the villagers were suffering from serious throat and eye infections, which she was powerless to treat. She had been waiting for a consignment of medicine from Buenos Aires for some three months but nothing had arrived. She took us to a twenty month old child called Sophia. Her little face was screwed up in pain and her chest jumped with each deep rasping cough of tuberculosis.

'Have you got anything to relieve the pain?' she asked.

We gave her some painkillers from our medical kit, which seemed to be such a futile gesture. I have never felt so helpless!

After a night at the village police station, we awoke to what we thought would be our last morning in Argentina. I noticed the flag in the dusty plaza was at half mast, and I asked the policemen if someone famous had died.

'No, it is to remember the death of the numerous young soldiers who died in the war for Las Malvinas. Today is Las Malvinas Day,' he explained. I could not think of a better day to leave Argentina.

We took to the Salta to La Quiaca railway line to avoid the corrugations and traffic of the road. At times the track was littered with sleepers, so we rode down the embankment to follow the llama tracks across the altiplano. On several occasions we were mistaken for llamas by roaming dogs, who gave chase and attempted to shepherd us into a corral. There was nothing like the sight and sound of a baying pack to set my heart racing and to quicken our progress. In this way, the border town of La Quiaca soon came into view and thus on Las Malvinas Day, June 11, we left Argentina for Bolivia.

DAY 218 GOODBYE TO ARGENTINA

'We had been warned before leaving England, that the Falklands War could well be a contentious issue while travelling in Argentina. Certainly the War had been mentioned but not in a confrontational and malicious way. In general the Argentines we met held the mature view that it was a conflict between two governments and not between two peoples. They were, however, interested to hear a British opinion, for after all why did Britain feel so strongly about some islands which lay tens of thousands of miles away? They would listen but not necessarily agree with the claim revolving around a question of principle.

Neither did we find the arrogant, pretentious and highly-strung Argentines people had told us about. Perhaps they were all holed up in the capital, Buenos Aires, and we had missed them in the mad dash to the domestic airport. I doubted it, for in all the places we visited in Argentina, whether it was a city, town or village, we did not find the merest hint of these characteristics. In their place we discovered friendliness, generosity, dignity and a genuine interest in our mission. While the Chileans would simply say, "what are you doing?" and then "Ah, cycling for leukaemia, but don't you just love our country?" the Argentines would ask with interest "Ah, leukaemia, what type of treatments are doctors now looking to?" The Argentines had an impressive awareness of issues at both a national and a global level and were constantly looking to extend this knowledge.

Yes, we would miss Argentina and its people who had done so much to support us for no other reason than to be helpful.'

—17—
WORLD CUP FEVER

'This is one of the most important events in Bolivian history.'

A Bolivian commentator reporting when the German and Bolivian soccer
teams took to the field to open the World Cup of 1994 in the U.S.

A small, litter-strewn river separated the towns of La Quiaca in
Argentina and Villazón in Bolivia. A bridge of a mere forty yards
represented a dramatic change in culture. The relative sophistication
of Argentina was replaced by a mêlée of street stalls, clawing beggars,
ladies in voluminous petticoats and bowler hats, and men shouting
out the price of sacks of coca leaves. Prices had indeed dropped
dramatically. Using the *'Golphe'* bar index (toffee and wafer biscuits
coated in milk chocolate), prices were now a quarter of what they
were in Argentina. Four *Golphe* bars for the price of one, it was
beyond our wildest dreams!

It was, however, not easy to spend our new found wealth in
Villazón. We were searching for a place to stay when we spied a
faded sign announcing 'Hotel Altiplano.'

'Do you have a room for the night?' Mike asked.

'Yes, I have a room,' replied the lady behind the desk. She wore a
bowler hat tied with a red ribbon and, to my surprise, she had piercing
blue eyes. 'But I do not have any beds.'

This was not our only surprise – Villazón, it transpired, was a town of surprises. In the two days we spent there, we discovered bars devoid of alcohol, a disco where no music played, a cinema without films and restaurants with no food. After fifteen hours, we were getting hungry, so we decided to buy lunch at the market. Following directions from the locals, we found ourselves in a covered building lined with stalls and seething with people. We found no bread, mandarins or even a tin of sardines, but in their place bats spread-eagled across wire lines, curled up llama foetuses and, most bizarre for a landlocked country, dried starfish. Suddenly, we forgot about our hunger.

'What does this taste like?' I asked, fingering the outstretched body of a bat with prominent ears.

'It is not to be eaten,' the old stall holder laughed, 'but nail it over a front door and it will ward off the evil spirits. This llama foetus, for instance, should be buried in the foundations of a new home, to bring luck and prosperity. I think you should know you are in the Witches market. The food market is up the hill on the right.'

We left embarrassed and to the sound of laughter. Later we were to find that life in Bolivia was inextricably laced with pagan superstitions.

DAY 219 VILLAZON

'I did not like Villazón and thus my first impression of Bolivia was tainted. The town and its people were victims of location. Typical of many border towns, it had lost its identity and self respect. The town had sold its soul to the pursuit of the Argentine peso. Our clothes, looks and bicycles betrayed us as both non-Argentine and non-wealthy, so the reception we received was cold and unfriendly. Even when we ventured into the back streets untouched by commercialism and peso adulation, we were not warmly accepted. We sensed from the stares and the twitching curtains, an inherent timidity laced with suspicion. We looked for escapism at night, but found

that the cold and boredom forced everybody to bed by nine o'clock. Please let Villazon be an exception rather than a representation of the rest of Bolivia.'

We could not leave the town soon enough. We cycled into the *altiplano*, in search of friends and excitement. At nightfall, we found ourselves at the school in the village of Tambo. It was a collection of squat mud brick houses surrounding the white-washed school and church. The roofs were thatched with straw with the exception of the school, which sat proudly under a green corrugated iron roof. Chickens pecked for scraps on the dusty dirt streets and pigs fought for water laying in the muddy puddles. Under a cloud of swirling dust, a group of children were playing football with a stuffed sock. On seeing us they ran away screaming and laughing at the sight of three strange looking cyclists. A lady appeared in the shadow of a doorway and called out to invite us over for tea. In the darkness of the kitchen we recognised two of the children in the playground. The lady smiled;

'They came rushing in saying the white-lipped warriors had arrived,' she said. 'By the way, what is that white stuff on your lips and face. Is it tribal?'

It was now our turn to laugh. We had never thought sun-screen could make such an impression.

Her two children suddenly lost all their inhibitions and dragged us out onto the playground. Slowly other children appeared from the mud-bricked houses and we were soon surrounded and undergoing an inquisition: 'Where are you from?' 'Why have you got white lips?' 'Why are your legs so hairy?'

To answer the first question we blew up our inflatable globe. The children, however, were not interested in a geography lesson, but were more intent on using it as a replacement for the stuffed sock. It was only three days to go before Bolivia played Germany in the World Cup. The children insisted we pretended to be Germany and they proceeded to run circles around us. At 5 – 1 to Bolivia the game mercifully came to a premature end when the globe got a puncture.

The celebrations of the result went on well into the evening. There was much singing, dancing and sun-screen face painting. My lasting memory was of Oswaldo. At four years old he was displaying an acute sense of nationalism in his smart waistcoat in the red, yellow and green of the Bolivian flag over a white shirt with pleated sleeves. We painted his face in the image of a cat and on his head he wore a towering bowler hat over which he had slipped one of our Davy lamp style torches. He was whirling around in circles to create the effect of a disco for his sisters who were dancing energetically to the song, *'Yo tengo el tractor amarillo'* (I have a yellow tractor). The light at intervals caught the evidence of the last lesson, a grammar test featuring Quechen, the old Inca language. The children could have gone on all night, but we were exhausted from the cycling and football. Only after we had agreed to continue in the morning, did the children leave us to collapse under the classroom desks. I went to sleep relieved and happy. This was the true Bolivia and it was evident that Villazón was a victim of circumstances.

All thirty-seven pupils of the school arrived early the next morning. They wore immaculate white uniforms, which defied their life within their mud homes. Their feet and untreated sores did however reveal their poverty – few wore shoes and several children had seeping septic wounds on their legs and ears. Their thoughts were not on their Quechen grammar test and they were more intent on dragging us out of bed for another football match and dance session. Relief came at eight o'clock with the flag-raising ceremony and the singing of the national anthem. They then tucked into breakfast of a bread roll and a mug of milk, while we cooked up some porridge and finished off the last of the marmite. They were intrigued because they had never seen this lumpy pale paste or black stuff before. They all insisted on tasting them and without exception they grimaced in disgust. Many felt sorry for us and offered their bread roll and milk. Cordelia, Oswaldo's sister, spoke for them all when she said,

'You must be poorer than us, because you are forced to eat such food.'

Then in an act of compassion, she came over and kissed us on both cheeks.

Moved and overcome we cycled off, chased by waving, laughing children. We rode off the altiplano down a river valley lined with fields, animals and villages. Here agriculture and machines have yet to meet; horses pulled the wooden ploughs, the corn was threshed by hand and crops were cut down by the scythe. Administering all these physical and demanding activities were ladies in bowler hats and petticoats. There was not a man to be seen. We wondered where they were: could they be at home looking after the babies, preparing the food and doing the sewing? When we stopped for lunch we found out. It was one o'clock when we walked into a darkened bar. It was full of men drunk on *singali* (Bolivian white brandy) and it was obvious they had been there for some time.

In the evening we arrived at Tupiza, the town situated in the heart of Butch Cassidy and the Sundance Kid territory. According to local sources their end was very different from the Hollywood movie with Robert Redford and Paul Newman. On 4 November, 1908, the pair held up the payroll of the Aramayo mining company at Salo just to the north of Tupiza. Two days later they were discovered by only a four-man police patrol in the village of San Vincente and after a brief shoot-out they were killed. Cassidy and Sundance were buried in an unmarked grave in the village cemetery. An end devoid of the romance, glamour and the dramatic shoot-out depicted in the movie. Just four against two, policemen doing their job and a nailed wooden cross bearing no name. Despite this we were still interested in visiting the sight of their demise. I went to the captain of police to ask for directions. He informed me in no uncertain terms he could not help me.

I bumped into him again in the evening back at our hotel. He sat with a colleague surrounded by empty bottles of *singali*. He recognised me and invited me to grab a chair and join them. Captain Martinez was a fat, bull-like man with an aggressive chin and menacing eyes. His green police uniform was about two sizes too small and I thought one more movement would spell the end of the straining buttons and bulging seams. For the time being, he was getting drunk.

'So how is your pilgrimage to the grave of Cassidy and Sundance going?' Captain Martinez slurred.

'We now have directions, so we will be going up there in the next couple of days,' I replied.

'Bloody gringos,' he shouted. 'All you do is come here to pay homage to those two ruffians who stole our money and shot our people. They were nothing . . . *nothing* but common thieves.'

He then swayed to his feet and drew his pistol from his holster. He bent over to look me straight in the eye and while he twirled the pistol around his middle finger, he screamed,

'They were no heroes, just a pair of ruthless gringo cowards. Yes, *cowards* they were, constantly running and running. We are the heroes you are looking for, the brave and courageous police of Bolivia.' He stood up and pointed to the medals and badge on his puffed out chest. He then slowly raised his right arm and squeezed the trigger of the pistol. The shot went clean through the roof, leaving a harsh singing in my ears and the bitter smell of cordite. He seemed oblivious to the fragments of masonry falling into his hair and the dust floating down on to his jacket.

'I will not let you leave until I have shown you a grave of my own,' he continued in a snarling malicious voice. 'It is the grave of my grandfather. He was in the four-man band who killed those two gringo bastards.'

He put one of his fat fingers on my chest and commanded, 'Just so you have no ideas about leaving, I want your passport. I want . . .' his voice tailed off. I watched as his eyes glazed over and he collapsed head first onto the table. The room started to echo to the sound of his snoring.

His colleague, who had been sitting quietly in the corner, smiled. 'I apologise for the Captain. Do not worry, he is always like that when he has too much *singali*,' he said. He pointed to the ceiling and it was peppered with the pockmarks of previous shootings. 'Freddie, the manager, always puts us in this room because there are no beds upstairs. He would have forgotten all about it in the morning, so do not bother with your passport. By the way, the bit about his grandfather is absolute drivel.'

It was the day of the opening match of the World Cup, the match between Bolivia and Germany. The town of Tupiza was in a fit of excitement because it was Bolivia's first ever appearance in the tournament. I walked up to the main plaza. There was a parade of at least three hundred young children marching to the national anthem and a specially composed World Cup song. Their faces were daubed in the red, yellow and green of the Bolivian colours and they had clothes to match: red shirts, yellow belts and green skirts or trousers. At intervals, they blew the whistles around their necks in time with the music. Just to see the sheer joy in their faces and pride of their march was very moving.

I was sitting on a bench next to an old man. With just one look at his watery white eyes I could tell he was blind.

'Hello gringo, where are you from?' he whispered without turning his head.

'From England,' I replied.

'Oh good, you are not German. I hope you will be supporting Bolivia this afternoon. Do you know this is the proudest day of my life!'

'Do not worry I would dearly love to see Bolivia beat Germany. But please can you answer me one thing, how did you know I was a gringo?'

'You smell different,' he said.

We joined the people of Tupiza in watching the match. We were in a crowded room of some sixty people back at our hotel. When the Bolivian national anthem played and the camera panned over the faces of the players, everybody stood up and there was not a dry eye in the place. For sixty-six minutes, Bolivia valiantly held their own against the world champions. Then Rudi Voller raced through the offside trap and beat the Bolivian goalkeeper to his right, as he rushed off his line. Heads fell between knees and several men rose to shout abuse at the referee, claiming Voller was blatantly offside. Soon the room started to chant,

'Aranchana, Aranchana, Aranchana, Bring on Aranchana!'

It seemed the manager of the team over in the USA heard this small gathering, for within seconds the long flowing hair and the number 10 shirt of Aranchana, their leading scorer, was seen running on the pitch. Our crowd rose in rapturous applause. It could be said Aranchana had a memorable World Cup. After three minutes and fifty-six seconds on the field, he went in dangerously high on a German player and was sent off, condemning him to take no further part in the tournament. The room was stunned, but again the same men rose to hurl insults at the referee. The final score was 1 – 0 to Germany and the verdict was an honourable defeat.

On the streets one would have thought Bolivia had won. Cars paraded around, flying flags and hooting their horns. In the main plaza, there was a steel band playing. Young and old were dancing together in unbridled joy and in the middle twirling around in circles, with his smiling face held high, was my blind friend from the bench. Suddenly, by an unseen hand, I was dragged into the midst of the gyrating masses. It was similar to a Scottish reel, interlocking spins and arm arched tunnels. My partner was the dark and beautiful Sandra and somehow, while doing the conga, we arranged to meet for a game of tennis the next day.

Before the tennis, we had been invited to play golf by Mattho, an American working for the Peace Corps (US equivalent to the VSO), which sends graduates to share their skills with local communities in Third World countries. The course was intriguingly named the Tupiza Golf Links. I was confused by the title because I had always thought 'links' referred to a course by the sea. By no stretch of the imagination were we anywhere near the sea and furthermore I knew Bolivia was landlocked. I was soon to find this name was not far from the truth for there was a lot of sand. The sand, however, rather than being restricted to imposing dunes lining the fairways, was to be found on the 'greens,' or perhaps the 'browns' is a more appropriate term. The novelty did not stop there; small round llama stools were used to elevate the golf balls and the fairways were crowded with llamas and boys playing football. To add to the difficulties, both Mike and I were left-handed. There was only one set of golf clubs in the whole of Tupiza and they were, of course, right-handed. Mattho had enlisted the assistance of a local caddie in the shape of a seven year old girl. Could she help with club selection or read the putts over the ruts and bumps of the 'browns?' No, she had a pig trained to nose the ball closer to the hole. For the record, the pig's name was Seve!

Even with the help of Seve, the Tupiza Golf Links was not the place to lower one's handicap and the nine holes took some three hours. I was, therefore, just a bit late for my tennis match, but thankfully Sandra was still waiting in the plaza. When I saw her, two thoughts arrested my mind: she was very beautiful, and there was absolutely no way we would be playing tennis. She was wearing a short tailored black skirt, a laced white blouse and high-heeled velvet shoes. She informed me we were off to her uncle's birthday party. It was a family affair and even though I was hopelessly underdressed and a gringo, I was greeted with open arms. The party was awash with *singali* and a sweet birthday cake made from vegetables and chicken. It was a heady combination. I was soon being taught the Bolivian *cueca* dance to the accompaniment of Sandra's nephews on the *pututo* (pan pipes), the *huankare* (drums) and the *charango* (guitar). After a while I was asked to take the lead and I took them through a session of rock 'n' roll. The night ended, as far as this book is concerned, by reading the poems of Pablo Neruda to each other in both Spanish and English by the light of the moon.

I was very reluctant to leave Tupiza and Sandra the next day. Often our nomadic life had its advantages, but on this occasion I yearned to stay still. I was not at all enthused by the tough and long climb up on to the altiplano and I was sorely tempted to turn the bike round and freewheel back to Tupiza. After a three hour ascent we did eventually make the 1,600 feet back to the *altiplano*. We were exhausted as the effects of the World Cup celebrations took their toll, so we stopped early at a small country hospital. It was run by a friendly doctor and his wife. They took us in on the promise we would cook them dinner in return for sleeping on the floor. Instead of glass jars of medicines lining the walls, there were bundles of different curative herbs.

'The local people do not believe in anything else and thus we prescribe only herbs. Without belief and trust medicine is ineffective,' the doctor explained. 'The greatest problem out here is chagas disease. I would say that half of the people in the district have it and I am helpless to treat it because there is no known cure. Each year about fifteen of my patients die of heart failure brought on by the disease.'

'If there is no cure, is there any way to stop the spread of the disease?' I asked.

'It is difficult, the people need to come out of their traditional adobe housing, for it is their thatched or leaf roofs which are the breeding ground of the *vinchuca* beetle,' the doctor continued. 'This beetle, whose nickname is *'the assassin'*, feeds on blood and in doing so passes on the Chagas parasite. How can this happen when we and the government have no money? You must avoid sleeping in these houses, for it is then the beetle is most likely to strike. Scratch the bite and the poison works its way into the blood stream,' he warned.

The next day a strong, dust-laden wind was blowing across the plain. While the doctor was unable to go on his daily rounds, which entailed a fifteen mile walk to see all his patients, we headed off with bowed heads. Thankfully, the road soon dropped down into a river valley and in a tiny hamlet we found Mattho in a ditch. The Peace Corps were putting in a new water system and all the locals had turned out to do the digging and lay the piping under the supervision of Mattho.

'It is very important,' he explained, 'to get the villagers to do the work themselves. With work comes understanding and respect. I know of a Japanese development agency that did not enlist the help of the locals and used solely their own expertise. To this day the people there still draw their water from the well, because they do not trust or understand the new water system. It is sad how such well-intentioned funds can be wasted in this way!'

In his seven months in Bolivia, Mattho had picked up one of their characteristics. He informed us that the road was fairly level to Potosi, apart from a steep bit at the end to skirt around the *Cerro Rico* (Rich Hill). Mattho must have dreamt it, for we found a roller-coaster of a road, with extreme highs and lows. It was typical to struggle to the top of a pass and to be faced with a bittersweet view. Sweet because of the road plunging downwards, and bitter because of the sight of it snaking upwards to yet another pass. In one day we went over seven passes, which was the equivalent of climbing just over 10,000 feet or three times the height of Snowdon (3,800 feet). Where the hell was the famed altiplano, the high plain? We began to think it was a myth dreamed up by the locals to keep cyclists happy. We would have found it easier to cope with the truth.

It was on yet another downhill stretch that I heard three shrill blasts on a whistle. This was our distress signal. I called out to David who was a short distance ahead and we returned to find Mike in the middle of the road with his bike. Apart from a few cuts and bruises he was unhurt, but the damage to the bike looked serious. The front pannier rack had worked loose and fallen down onto the tyre. This had caused *Shadowfax* to stop suddenly, catapulting Mike over the handlebars. The forward momentum had mangled the rack and buckled the front wheel. While I threw up my hands in despair and tried a few strategic kicks, David was positively licking his lips in anticipation of solving the problem. I was delegated to make lunch while Mike and David went to work. It took three hours and nine sardine sandwiches to get *Shadowfax* back on the road again minus a front rack. The luggage was distributed evenly and we ventured tentatively on.

I was feeling absolutely exhausted as well as sick of sardines. There may be four shops in an altiplano village and you could bet your bottom peso they all only sold the same five foods: sacks of potatoes, canned tomatoes, bags of rice and pasta, and dusty tins of sardines. This had been our diet for breakfast, lunch and supper for the last three days. Tonight, however, we were in for a treat because in the last village behind the sardines, David had found a tin of tuna. The thought of it was the one thing keeping me going on a road which created the illusion of heading downhill when it was actually going up.

With the next village proving to be elusive, we stopped at a small farmstead. As luck would have it they had an empty hut, with two beds of layered ponchos. We settled down to the feast of tuna lightly laced with tomatoes sitting on a bed of rice. It looked beautiful and oh so appetising. *'Variety is the spice of life'* I thought as I took my first mouthful. It was a strange sensation because it tasted exactly like sardines. Perhaps our diet of the last few days had permanently damaged my taste buds. I crunched into a tell-tale backbone and then I knew that for some unknown reason several sardines had jumped into a tin of tuna. I looked closely at the open tin; yes it did say *ATUN* (tuna) in large bold letters, but in the small print above it read:

Sardines in the style of

ATUN

It just goes to show creative advertising was very much alive high up on the Bolivian altiplano.

Forty miles and a 6,000 feet climb lay between us and Potosi (13,431 feet), the highest city of its size in the world. We were not the only ones on the road. First we passed a train of some fifty llamas carrying blocks of salt mined from the salt lakes nearby. The salt was being taken to the city to exchange for provisions. Each llama had red and white tassels fluttering from their ears, to distinguish them from a rival train. Moving faster were convoys of trucks taking miners back home for the holiday weekend, which featured the crunch football match with South Korea. Everybody on the road was in a party mood and we received constant encouragement in the form of cheers, horn hooting and one lady even lifted her petticoats and raised her bowler hat. I remember just when I had reached my lowest ebb, a lorry driver stopped and handed down a bag of mandarins.

'Your need is greater than mine,' he said, before driving off.

They tasted delicious after the constant diet of sardines.

Even the mandarins could not help us with the ever thinning air. Breathing was difficult and progress was reduced to a snail's pace. We had to dig deep, because after all we dearly wanted to make it to Potosi by nightfall to see the South Korean match. The altitude was again effecting Mike badly: throbbing headache, slurring speech and loss of co-ordination. He even refused the sardine sandwiches at lunchtime. A taxi driver stopped to offer encouragement and gave us the welcome news, there was only one more hill. Over the next rise appeared the famous *Cerro Rico*, the mountain of immense mineral wealth. Directly below lay the twisting, narrow, cobbled streets of Potosi.

—18—
SILVER AND SALT

'Rich Potosi, treasure of the world, king of the mountains, envy of kings.'

CHARLES V Holy Roman Emperor, in 1556.

The city of Potosi was inadvertently founded by a llama herder, the Indian Huallpa. One evening in 1545, he was up on a hill tending his flock, when the weather suddenly closed in. The mist and rain brought poor visibility and made it too dangerous to return down the mountain to his village. He decided to brave the elements up on the hillside and wait until the next day in the hope that the weather would clear. It was intensely cold, so he lit a fire and huddled underneath a llama skin. As he sipped at his coca leaf tea, he noticed a curious phenomenon. From below the fire a silver stream had appeared, which started to meander down the hill. It was then he realised he was camped on a mountain of silver.

Unfortunately, he could not keep his find a secret from the Spanish. Under them, the *Cerro Rico* (Rich Hill) echoed with the sound of hammers and picks as a labyrinth of tunnels were chiselled out by local Indians and imported African slaves in an attempt to quench the

Spanish desire for silver. Huallpa's village grew to become the city of Potosi. In only twenty-eight years, it was the same size as London and bigger than Paris, Madrid or Rome. In 1650, the city had become the third largest city in the world behind Shanghai and Alexandria. Potosi was now a shadow of its former glory, but there were still vestiges of the past – La Casa de Moneda (the Mint), Las Cajas Reales (the Royal Treasury) and several great mansions hidden amongst the twisting streets.

In peoples' minds, Potosi still maintains its association with great wealth. Even today there is an expression in Spain, 'este es un Potosi' (it's a Potosi), which describes anything superlatively rich. Silver dominates the gossip of the locals. They whisper that the silver taken out of the Cerro Rico could build a bridge all the way from Potosi to Madrid and they believe there is still enough silver in there to build a bridge back again. But in the same breath they speak of the immense human cost.

'Eight million lives have been lost in the Hill. Do you know, the bones of all those men could build a bridge stretching much further than any bridge of silver,' an old-timer told us.

The Cerro Rico is still being worked today. We met, Freddie Manami, a miner, in a downtown bar and he agreed to show us around in return for a packet of cigarettes, a bag of coca leaves, five sticks of dynamite, fuses and detonators. This would be a tough request anywhere else in the world, but in Potosi this shopping list is equivalent to buying a pint of milk and a newspaper, except they would cost you more. Freddie's gift came to the princely sum of eighty pence.

Freddie led us up to the narrow entrance of just one of the many mines, which honeycomb the Cerro Rico. It was covered in blood. It was not the blood of the eight million people, but was from an unfortunate llama sacrificed to keep the spirits happy and thus ensure the mine's safety. Many miners were now sitting around taking a tea break from the chiselling, dynamiting and heaving down below. Without exception they smoked cigarettes, had bulging cheeks stuffed with coca leaves and were covered in dust. They were all members of a miner's co-operative, which owned and operated the mine. The profits were distributed according to experience and exposure to danger. Working at the face commanded the highest premium, followed by those who heaved the ore to the surface. The job of messenger through the maze of tunnels was at the bottom of the pay scale. If a seam was discovered, the miners at the face could earn up to £140 a week. Not bad when one considers the annual income per head in Bolivia is about £400.

We were issued with overalls, hard hats and crude ironware lamps which were operated by the reaction of carbon on water. Freddie led us down the low tight tunnel and it was as if we were stepping into a 'past' which was happening today. There were no machines, for reasons of cost and the intricate method required for extraction, so everything was still done by hand. We met 'carriers' struggling to carry the heavy sacks of ore up to the top. At the face, we met men and boys working with picks and hammers, searching for strategic places to place the sticks of dynamite, in the hope of revealing a seam of silver. It was here we met Julio. He looked young enough to be at school.

'How old are you?' I asked.

'Thirteen years old,' Julio replied.

'Do you enjoy it down here?'

'I have been here six months now and I love it,' he replied. 'It is what I have always wanted to do. I have followed my father and grandfather down the mine.'

I noticed his eyes were bright with excitement. It was sad to think that by the law of averages, Julio would be dead by the age of thirty-three, the life expectancy in the mines.

The mine was dangerous. There was a constant threat of rock falls as costs of excavation were kept to a minimum. The greatest killer was the repeated exposure to the dusty choking air. Floating around were fibres from the rocks which could cause pulmonary silicosis, i.e. terminal damage to the lungs. The miners did not look to conventional methods to improve their chances of survival, but instead they worshipped the *tio* (uncle), the pagan god of the mine. The *tio* was modelled out of clay in the form of the head and shoulders of an old man. He had green glass eyes, a moustache and beard made from human hair, a coronet of interlaced coca leaves and dramatic horns festooned with pink and white ribbons. In his lap had been placed a pile of coca leaves and a plastic bottle of alcohol, while in his mouth was half an extinguished cigarette. This apparently was not a good sign! For the *tio* to finish a cigarette was a sign of good luck and continued safety, but the cigarette going out in mid-smoke spelt impending danger.

DAY 274 DOWN THE MINES 3.00 P.M.

'I thought, what a load of suspicious rubbish! As if in answer a loud bang echoed down the tunnel bringing with it a cloud of swirling dust. Our lamps blew out and we were left choking in the darkness. Freddie could not suppress an edginess in his voice.

"They have started the afternoon's blasting," he shouted, "we had better get out of here quick. Keep your heads down and follow my light!"

Bent double, we felt our way along the damp walls, constantly slipping on the muddy floor. Another explosion went off and this time it was much closer. We could feel the force of the blast in the trembling walls, and particles of rock cascaded down on to our heads.

"We must move faster," Freddie screamed.

Panic had set in. In the darkness, I clawed at the floors and walls with my fingers in the mad dash to the top. My lungs were on the verge of bursting as I choked on the thick dust-laden air. I felt trapped and an overwhelming feeling of claustrophobia invaded my thoughts. I was convinced Freddie was lost in the labyrinth of tunnels – we were going down and the tunnel was becoming narrower.

Inadvertently I was still clutching the dynamite and the detonators. I had been warned to keep them separate because of the high chance of the detonators exploding, but now in the panic I had put them together to ensure one hand was free. I stumbled on a rock and dropped this potential bomb. They fell down a small hole and I could hear the sound of the bags bouncing off the stone walls before landing with a thud at the bottom. I held my breath waiting for the explosion, which would put us amongst the eight million people to lose their lives down the mine. It did not happen and the only sounds were Freddie's voice urging us to keep going as the end was now in sight. My heart lifted when I saw the tiny pinprick of light at the end of the tunnel.'

We emerged, blinking, out into the bright sunlight. Our clothes were in tatters and covered in mud. Our faces were blackened by the thick dust and our hands were encrusted with dirt. I vowed never to become a miner! My heart went out to all the African slaves who had been taken from the fresh air and the heat of the jungle, to these damp, cold and oppressive tunnels at over 14,500 feet above sea level. No wonder they had died in such great numbers. I thought of Julio and boys like him who knew no other life than to become a miner. For them, it was status, a mark of manhood and the only acceptable way to make a living. Who could blame them? I hoped they would buck the trend and live to a ripe old age as rich men.

While the mines have long been a vocation for the men of Potosi, the ladies of the city were lured into the many convents. A nun has for centuries been a calling of great kudos and status for a lady and her family. The most prestigious of all the convents in Potosi was *El Convento de Santa Teresa*. In its heyday in the seventeenth century, the convent was the home to some fifty nuns from aristocratic families and there was a strict waiting list based on wealth. The entrance was marked by a heavy oak door and once the would-be nun had stepped across this threshold, she knew she would never leave in life or in death. For the first five years contact with family was restricted to talking across a covered grill and then, after this probationary period, visual contact and the exchange of gifts was permitted but only through a heavily barred window. At no time was there any physical contact. The only person permitted to enter through the door was a doctor in medical emergencies, but in other circumstances the Pope alone had the authority to allow entry.

Conditions of entry were now more relaxed and I was permitted through the imposing wooden gates. The convent walls were lined with religious paintings designed to excite humility. Pictures of Christ nailed to the blood-splattered cross, pilgrims crawling on their knees, sinners burning in hell and bloody acts of forgiveness. There was one room devoted to the repentance of sins. It was full of the tools of flagellation and torture: whips, coarse hair vests, an iron choker for the neck, thumb screws and chastity belts sewn with metal hooks. In the dining room, at the head of the long wooden tables and benches, sat a human skull. It was to remind the nuns of their vulnerability to death while they ate. When death came they were buried in coffins under the convent chapel floor. Today, there are still five nuns living hidden within these walls.

As well as mines and convents, Potosi is also in striking distance of the largest salt lake in the world close to the town of Uyuni, and the isolated marvels of *Laguna Colorada* (Red Lake) and *Laguna Verde* (Green Lake). In the interests of time, we left the bikes and took a bus. On the way out of the city, we noticed the hillsides had been recently planted with trees. They were eucalyptus trees and were part of an international project to freshen and cleanse the air around the mines. We also crossed the main river flowing from the city. It was greeny yellow and a choking stench filled the bus. This was the river a Canadian development agency had come over to monitor. They had been shocked by the level of pollution and had ordered chemicals to be sent in from Canada to control the contamination. For four months now, this order had been sitting in customs in La Paz, because the authorities were concerned the chemicals could be used in the production of drugs. Tony, Sarah, Susan and Bob, members of the agency, had arrived in Potosi keen and motivated, but now after six months of fighting bureaucracy, they were disillusioned and bored. It all seemed such a waste of well-meaning and intelligent minds.

The town of Urunyi was bitterly cold and lay unprotected on the edge of the salt lake. There was one compensation. It was a very healthy place because no germs or diseases can fester amongst the salt and in the cold. We joined an international group of twelve to take two jeeps on the four day trek across the salt lake and on to the coloured lakes and the geysers. We started to cross the salt lake on the two foot hardened crust which covers the water, and it was like entering a blinding desert of white stretching as far as the eye could see. Dotted on the horizon were distant islands and volcanoes and because of a shimmering haze hovering above the lake they appeared to be suspended in space.

We stopped at an opencast salt mine. Here in heat and the blinding sun, one man dug up some four tonnes of salt in a day, while others chiselled out salt bricks from the encrusted floor. Any profits the mine made were swallowed up by the time and cost of transportation from such a distant location. Llamas were used to take the salt down to the towns in the valleys, but they can carry only the equivalent of fifty pence of salt per load, and the round trip usually took over a week. It did not make economic sense, so how then could they survive? One enterprising mining captain had literally put his salt into tourism and in so doing solved the problem of transportation. He was in the process of building the world's first hotel fashioned solely from salt bricks.

'People will come for the novelty of it all,' he explained. 'I will have no problems making a profit, because it is costing me nothing to build.'

I could not help but to be sceptical. 'What about water, electricity and sewage?' I asked. 'Oh and by the way, what happens if it rains?'

He dismissed these questions with the wave of his hand, 'I will deal with these problems when the hotel is built.'

We wished him luck and headed off across the salt. We were bound for *Isla Pescado* (the island of the fish). We discovered it was not named after the fish swimming around in the salt, but because of its shape. In fact more like a fish studded with cacti. We had lunch at a table and on chairs made of salt and then drove off for the distant shore.

As we clocked up a total of eighty miles on the salt lake I recalled a story from a fellow cyclist, Chris, who we had met in Mendoza. Chris had been here on a bicycle. He had followed the railway across the border from Chile into Bolivia and then on to this lake. It was heavy going because it was just after the rains and the salt was quite soft in places. This, however, was the least of his worries, for without sunglasses he was constantly dazzled by the glare off the white salt. He had to sleep the coldest night of his life on the salt and when he opened his eyes in the morning, he found he was blind. A day later

Chris was picked up by a Bolivian military patrol, who found him riding in circles across the salt. He was taken to hospital and it was not until two weeks later that he regained his sight. It had been a wise choice to opt for the jeep.

This was until some fifteen minutes later when we had a puncture. Not a problem, just put on the spare, and we could drive out of the middle of nowhere. That was assuming we had a spare - which we didn't! Juan, our driver, was not alarmed for triumphantly he produced a puncture repair kit. How he thought he was going to mend the slash in the tyre with that I did not know! We were destined, however, never to find out because the top had been left off the glue. Puncture kit apart, we found it quite amazing to be heading into one of the remotest areas of Bolivia without a spare tyre. Fortunately, our 'sister' jeep was behind, so we nicked a spare tyre off them. No sooner had this tyre taken the weight of our jeep, then it started to deflate with an alarming hiss. Now we really were stuck and there was nothing for it than to drink the four day supply of *singali*. Within an hour another jeep came along and our driver managed to persuade him to give up his spare tyre.

At nightfall we arrived in the remote village of San Juan. The *campesinos* (rural Indians) were coming to the end of a forty-eight hour fiesta in celebration of *La Luna*. The high spirited stage had passed many hours before and now it was a case of dogged determination to stay vertical and see the fiesta through. The streets, however, were lined with sleeping bodies who had given up the fight against the locally brewed grain alcohol. I took one sip and spontaneously felt my toes twitch and the tips of my fingers tingle. I was convinced any more would make me blind. As further bodies started to fall, the mayor of the village took to his trombone and started to lead a stomping march around the streets. One could sense his level of concentration; right foot forward, left foot forward and on and on. We tried to sleep on a floor vibrating to the sound of the trombone and the stamping of feet. In the morning, when I went out into the *campo* (countryside) for a call of nature, I found the mayor fast asleep in the dusty street cuddling his trombone.

In the late afternoon, after bouncing cheek-by-jowl along a dusty, rugged track for some seven hours, we arrived at the red algae-coloured waters of *Laguna Colorada*. The lake was at its best at sunset, for then the waters became a flaming red, offset by the arctic-white dunes of salt and gypsum around the shore. The lake was said to be the home of three different types of flamingo. I am no twitcher and to me they all looked alike with the same pink feathers and loping walk. Juan, our driver, advised me to take a closer look.

'The leg and bill colourations are the easiest way to distinguish the three breeds,' he explained. 'The rare James flamingos have dark, red brick legs and a small black tip on a bright yellow bill; the Chilean has brownish-blue legs with red knee joints and an almost white bill with a brown-black tip, while the Andean has bright yellow legs and black on the front half of its bill.' I think there must have been some in-breeding going on, because the only red knee joints I could see were on a pair of bright yellow legs.

We were staying at a *campamento*, which consisted of a collection of wooden huts on the shore of the lake. For Eustaquio Berna, the manager and his family, it was a remote and harsh existence. His children had to grow up quickly. We first met Jasmine, his twelve year old daughter, when we were crawling on our chests to get a closer look at the flamingos. She was singing while she skipped along in a long red coat and fawn bowler hat. She started to collect firewood around our prone bodies as if it was the most natural thing in the world to find *gringos* lying in the altiplano. The flamingos did not take the blindest bit of notice, so we thought it was safe to blow our cover. On standing up the birds immediately took fright and flew away.

'They are used to me,' Jasmine apologised.

'What are you doing out here?' Mike enquired, as we were a good mile from the huts.

'I am building and lighting fires to keep the foxes away from the sheep,' Jasmine replied.

It was also Jasmine who collected the firewood and laid the fire in our hut, to protect us from the temperature of minus twenty-five degrees centigrade during the night.

The next morning it was still bitterly cold when we headed off to *Laguna Verde*. At 16,700 feet we stopped at some bubbling and steaming geysers but they were frustratingly too hot for us to bathe our freezing limbs. Thankfully, a few miles down the sandy track were some hot pools by the side of a lake. It was truly wonderful lying in them sipping hot chocolate and staring dreamily over the frosted and bleak, but beautiful altiplano landscape. I dipped my head in the warm water, and it was a measure of the extreme temperature that, within sixty seconds, my hair had frozen into spiky icicles.

'You look like a punk rocker,' David observed.

The unwelcome thought of leaving this source of warmth was exacerbated by the three Belgian girls in our party. Sylvie, Genevieve and Isabelle had sneaked down and stolen our clothes, leaving us naked on the altiplano.

These girls had been the subject of great debate in our jeep. We were travelling with two couples: Dan and Diana from Canada and Franz and Gabi from Germany. They had been constantly egging us on as three single guys to do something about these girls.

'The very least you can do is offer to keep them warm during these cold nights,' Dan had suggested. Of course, we were too shy to do anything of the sort! But our eyes, however, did meet during the quest for our hidden clothes and then at the wind-lashed, frothy jade waters of *Laguna Verde*. By the time we returned to the *campamento* at *Laguna Colorada* there was much cause for speculation, especially when we all disappeared into the gypsum dunes to watch the sunset over the lake.

It was our last night, so a party was in order. We managed to buy some locally brewed alcohol that came in delicate plastic containers.

'Whatever you do, do not drink it neat. It has to be diluted by three times the quantity,' Eustaquio, the manager, had warned.

With our plastic container we went down to the hut of the Belgian girls. Conversation became more and more difficult as we grappled with the effects of the alcohol and the heady mixture of speaking French, Spanish and English. In their hut was a German guy, who was sick from the altitude and constantly having to get up to go outside. In order to give him space the girls asked if they could stay in our hut. Thus, we each returned with a companion, much to the surprise and amazement of Dan, Diana, Franz and Gabi. To this day, they do not know the real reason for the girls coming back. It was with great sadness that we had to leave them all and return to Potosi and our bikes. Diana wrote a touching comment in my diary: *'We had become tired of travelling, but you guys have refreshed us and given us a renewed vigour to continue.'*

We also had a renewed vigour for cycling, after some twelve days of abstinence. We left Potosi for the official capital of Bolivia, Sucre, which lay some hundred miles across the mountains. To our surprise we were on a paved road – it had been some four hundred miles since our last one! Only three per cent of the roads are paved in Bolivia, so it was some achievement to have found this one. The tarmac honeymoon did not last long, for after only thirty miles, we were back on the familiar dirt roads with the wind against us. We stopped at a poverty-stricken village for lunch and we had an audience of twenty children pressing their noses against the window of a roadside cafe while we ate potatoes floating in a tinned tomato sauce. We were cold and exhausted but our egos forced us to continue. A mere three miles later we collapsed by a tumble-down farm. It was managed by a small old man with bandaged feet and rotten teeth. He was kind enough to show us to a barn. We had fears of an approaching storm and the deadly *vinchuca* beetles in the roof, so we put up the tent inside the barn.

The small old man came to see us off the next day. He was fingering our equipment and asking us how much everything cost. We were finding it difficult to pack up around him. I felt sure I had put my watch just inside the tent, but to my surprise it was no longer there. I thought I might have packed it by mistake, but a thorough search among my bags and then Mike's and David's revealed nothing. In this time the old man was becoming increasingly agitated. I knew he had taken it, but did not want to embarrass him by a confrontation. We decided to make great play of all walking away to fetch some water. The old man gave a shout and there he was standing triumphantly with the watch in his hand, claiming he had found it under a rock.

DAY 284 BETRAYED TRUST 10.30 P.M.

'I could not blame him, for we had provided him with the temptation and the opportunity. The watch probably represented the amount of money he could make in four months of working. It did upset me, however, because this incident was the first of its kind on the expedition and it had happened in Bolivia, a country we had learnt to love a people we had grown to trust. In Bolivia, we had found nothing but kindness, generosity and respect. We had never been seen as a source of wealth or money, but were instead regarded even by the humblest of families as extremely poor because we were forced to ride around on bicycles. They would tell us:

"You are our guests. We feel sorry for you, for you have to travel by bike, while we can afford to take the bus."

It was a sobering experience to be exposed for the first time for what we were: rich gringos. I reassured myself that he probably had good reason. He might well have taken it to buy medicine to ease the pain for his wife, whose deep rasping cough of tuberculosis had kept us awake well into the night. I just wished he had asked us for help.'

As well as tending not to pave its roads, Bolivia builds them in the most unique places. We were on one such road; it ran down the floor of a river bed. It was the dry season, so the road was just about passable through the numerous fords across the river. David had an aversion to getting his feet wet and would always look for a dry crossing, thus earning him the nickname of 'Twinkle Toes'. In contrast, Mike and I rode across with gay abandon. There was a road crew shoring up a bank where the river had seeped across the road.

'What happens to this road in the wet season?' I asked.

'It drowns,' one of the workman laughed, 'it is often impassable for about three months.' This was not a small farm track we were talking about, it was the main road which linked two of the principal cities in Bolivia. He seemed to read my thoughts and explained,

'It is all a question of money and the lack of it!'

The river bed, however, was an absolute luxury in comparison to the sea of sand we encountered on the climb out of the valley.

The condition of the road slowed our progress somewhat. In normal circumstances we would have stopped at nightfall some thirty miles short of Sucre, but we had a special incentive. The Belgian girls were waiting for us there. To see them again was a small price to pay for being chased by baying hounds and dodging potholes in the darkness. Unfortunately, by the time we arrived we were not in a fit state to perform to their wishes. They did, however, stay for another day!

Sucre was indeed a romantic city, as its several nicknames suggest: The Athens of America, The City of Four Names, The Cradle of Liberty and The White City of the Americas. While it has lost its position as capital of Bolivia to La Paz, it has retained the Supreme Court and its courtly colonial charm. All new buildings in the centre have to be built by law in a colonial style and painted white. In amongst these, Sucre offers an array of cosmopolitan temptations which we had never dreamt we would find in Bolivia: French and Swiss restaurants, chocolate shops and bohemian coffee bars. It was all such a far cry from the tinned sardines and potatoes. It was in Sucre we took our first malaria tablets. The next day we would ride away from the cold of the altiplano, but also far from the warmth of Sylvie, Genevieve and Isabelle!

—19—
SOUND OF THE SAMBA

'I must learn Spanish one of these days
Only for that slow sweet name's sake!'

ROBERT BROWNING 'The Flower's Name'

From Sucre (9,210 feet) the road dropped three hundred miles into the depths of the jungle and the city of Santa Cruz. It promised to be days of freewheeling and shedding clothes. We were not disappointed. The road out of Sucre took us to the crest of a hill and then we rode down into a lush green valley alive with the sounds of birds and insects. Unfortunately, I was becoming like the infamous Stefan; I drowned out these songs of nature by listening to the enthusiastic Spanish commentary of the World Cup quarterfinal between Brazil and Holland. The hallmark of Latin American commentaries, the elongated 'Gooooooo . . . ll' echoed through the valley five times in a dramatic match.

What with stopping constantly to re-tune the radio and patching up a large gash in the bicycle tyre of a stranded *campesino* (country peasant), we fell short of the village of Illimamahuasi. It was thus that we found ourselves at a remote country hospital. I saw in my thirty-

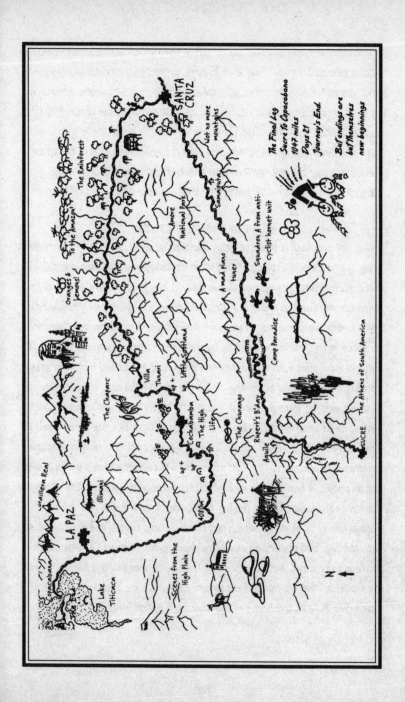

first birthday lying on the bare, rusty springs of a discarded bed. It was a present from Mike and David, who both ended up sleeping on the dusty floor. Any thoughts of an indulgent lie-in were destroyed by a cockerel who took up residence just outside the door. He had a sore throat, which made his crow resemble a spluttering machine gun. He was not on his own, for when David was in the midst of a call of nature, he got rammed in the buttocks by a hungry pig. The start of my birthday was certainly unusual and not short of laughter.

10/7 DAY 246 MY BIRTHDAY

'I was not amused! It had not been the plan at all to cycle on my birthday. Lying in a hot thermal spring sipping at an ice-cold pisco had been mentioned, but certainly not cycling. But this is Bolivia, the place where the best laid plans are destined to change. I surprised myself, I was not only enjoying it, I was loving every minute. I reminisced of birthdays gone by, but there was no place in the world I wanted to be more than here, riding with M and D along a road alive with the sights and sounds of bright red macaws, green parakeets and azure humming-birds. Word had got out that it was my birthday and we were greeted in villages by locals bearing glasses of chicha (fermented maize drink). It looks, smells and tastes like the water used to wash dirty socks. It was a case of closing my eyes and thinking of England. Whatever happened to the iced pisco! Even though the locals swore it was not alcoholic, it had quite a kick which sent me on a weaving path through the heat of the day. D was feeling weak and ill, but it was not the chicha. Serious bowel movements, which had started at the time of the confrontation with the pig, had continued and were draining his strength. D was not in a fit state to proceed, but he kept going. I knew he was doing it for me. It was my birthday and we needed a town to celebrate in. Thanks to D we did make it to Aquile, the home of the charango (small guitar).'

After ringing my parents and opening my presents, we planned to paint the town red. We lasted two drinks and a plate of beef and potatoes before collapsing into bed. It was, however, a birthday to remember.

The police in Aquile informed us of a short cut to Santa Cruz. The road was not on any maps as it had been recently built with money donated by the United States of America.

'It will save you days and days,' the police told us.

It seemed too good to be true. To start off it was. The road followed a beautiful river valley which breathed colour and life into the surrounding countryside. Our path was lined with *campesinos* tending their vineyards, crops of tomatoes and fields of sugar cane. We stopped to watch two horses turning a wheel to crush the sugar cane and we were beckoned over to sample the milky white extract and, to my horror, the cauldrons of black bubbling malt. Malt, which along with beetroot is on my all time hate list, had been the bane of my childhood. Now my earliest nightmares returned to haunt me as, not wishing to offend, I swallowed the sticky malt. It trickled into a stomach just recovering from a heavy dose of *chicha*. There were rumbles of protest. I ran behind a tree and was violently sick.

Shortly afterwards, with my stomach still churning, we turned a corner and saw two condors flying just above our heads. I could hear the rush of air as they passed and could see the outstretched fingers at the tips of their wings, the white of their collars and their beady intense eyes. Their movement spooked a colony of some fifty parakeets. They flew erratically ahead in a chorus of high-pitched alarm. The condors were indifferent and glided away on a spiralling thermal, leaving the parakeets breathless in a willow tree. In the excitement our hands trembled on the straps of our camera bags, thus delaying us until the moment had passed. There are times, this being one of them, when it is better not to dedicate an incident or a memory to film. Often a photograph can dilute the drama and excitement of a special occasion. The feelings, emotion and atmosphere are forgotten and replaced with a still image. To this day the sight and sound of the condors and parakeets remains alive and vivid in our minds.

Nearby, just below the road, we discovered a small, grassy plateau by the side of the river. The grass looked so soft and the river so cool, we felt compelled to stop. We pitched our tent and went for an invigorating swim to wash off the sweat and dust of a day's cycling. After a dinner of tuna and pasta, I settled into my sleeping bag under a canopy of stars. I looked up at the crescent moon and thought it would make the most perfect hammock. By candle light I became absorbed in the antics of Frodo Baggins in the *The Lord of the Rings*.

U.S. funded roads are great while the money lasts. Evidently funds had run out at the town of Saipina, where a perfectly serviceable road became a rutted and sandy nightmare. The powdery sand was about a foot thick and as well as burying the tyres, it hid all the holes and rocks. Conditions were made worse by the constant stream of trucks showering us in clouds of dust. We came to a deep ford through a river. The water rose well over our chains, which created a wet magnet for all the sand and grit on the other side. The grating sound soon became unbearable and we had to stop to clean the chains. We crossed this river seven times! The road then rose steeply to take us out of the valley. While we struggled to keep our legs moving forwards and to direct the bikes across the bumps, wasps swarmed around our heads. When you reached up to brush a wasp out of your hair or off your face, not only was there a good chance of being stung, but of losing control of the bike.

The only way out of these situations was to laugh. Thankfully today we had a one man stand-up comedy act in David. Not for the first time, he was having problems with his Spanish. We stopped exhausted by the side of a wooden hut. In the dusty courtyard was a long, tilted pole flying a white flag. A policeman in Aquile had told us such a sign meant the house sold *chicha*. A lady peered shyly from the shadows of the porch and David, ever the gregarious and friendly type, shouted,

'Good afternoon. Congratulations on the birth of your child.'

'*Que* (what),' she enquired with a puzzled look. Mike and I were just as confused.

'The birth of your child,' said David, undeterred. 'You have the white flag flying in your garden.'

The lady burst out into laughter; 'The flag means I sell *chicha* (the drink), not that I have had a *chica* (child).'

'That explains it then. I thought this area was going through a baby boom.' Quite often half the houses in a village would be selling *chicha*.

David's confidence in Spanish was not to be dented, for a few hours later at a roadside stall run by two delightful sisters, he announced;

'There are many pineapples on the road.'

'Where?' the sisters asked, anxious to add this tropical fruit to their stall.

'All over the place, they are forever sticking into my tyres.'

The Spanish for pineapples is *pinas*, while for thorns it is *espinas*. It was this display of linguistic comedy that helped us to forget the wasps and the condition of the road.

I do not know whether it was on account of David's Spanish, but we were soon to lose Mike. I think he wanted to be alone to get a firm grasp on his own sanity. Together we embarked on yet another short cut. One would have thought we would have learnt our lesson, but no, here we were again grabbing at straws. The man at the village store had been persuasive:

'You have two alternatives. Either you go the long way round of about fifteen miles or you take a short cut of five miles. They both lead you to the same place, the main road to Santa Cruz.'

We decided on the shorter route. It followed an oil pipeline. Unfortunately, oil can flow up and down gradients beyond the capabilities of a bicycle. David and I lost Mike when we went off in search of gentler slopes. We followed an overgrown track up the hill and I gambled my bottom dollar that this would take us on to the main road. As was usual when I was particularly convinced about something, the total opposite proved to be the case; the track ended in a dead end at a woodcutter's cottage. Instead of the demoralisation of retracing our tracks, we decided to cut across through the woods to the pipeline and Mike. We pushed *Arriba* and *Woop-Woop* one at a time up a narrow, twisting path until we eventually found ourselves back at the pipeline.

We looked up and down and Mike was nowhere to be seen. We shouted and blew our whistles, but heard nothing. David then demonstrated the practical side of his character with an ingenious idea. He picked up a stone and started to tap on the hollow cement pipeline. We both put our ears to the pipe and some twenty seconds later came a sequence of answering knocks. We knew it was Mike because they were to the tune of 'Tubular Bells' by Mike Oldfield. We were reunited at a truck stop cafe on the main road.

The cafe was run by Veronica. She had a jagged scar across her right cheek, which she had received from a broken *singali* bottle while trying to break up a fight between two truck drivers. She was very self-conscious of the scar and was constantly hiding it with her hand. Veronica had been forced to grow up quickly – she was only fourteen years old.

'I long to go to school, but I cannot leave my mother and my younger brother here alone. There are just the three of us. My father drove off in a truck five years ago and has yet to return. Will you please teach me English so one day I can travel to the United States of America?' she requested.

We were delighted to help, but we needed a place to stay the night.

'You cannot stay in the cafe,' Veronica replied. 'You will never get any sleep for the drivers are coming in and out all the time. Do not worry, I will ask my mother.'

She disappeared and five minutes later returned to say we could stay with her mother.

'How about a game of poker?' Veronica asked. 'We can play for money if you like.'

We arrogantly thought there was no way we could take the money of a fourteen year old girl, so we politely declined. It was a good decision, for if we had, we would have lost in all probability: our bikes, panniers and the clothes we stood up in. Veronica was a real professional; she juggled the cards from hand to hand and deftly flicked two cards to each of us. She looked at her cards with a blank expression and then took us on an audacious and ultimately successful bluff. So intense were the stares she gave me, I was convinced she could read my cards from my eyes. Before we submitted to a crushing defeat Veronica had learnt all the English words relating to poker. If she ever did get to America, the tables of Las Vegas should beware!

It was time for bed. We were shown to a darkened room. There were three beds and in the larger bed, two people were sleeping peacefully. It was Veronica's mother and brother. It was both touching and hard to believe that her mother had agreed to share her room with three complete strangers and that her younger brother had given up his bed for us.

'*Sueno con las angelicas* (dream with the angels),' Veronica wished us. 'I will try not to wake you when I finish work at four o'clock.' We felt so humble being tucked into bed by a fourteen year old girl.

The next day was my grandfather's ninetieth birthday. While I had sent him the video message from Salta, I was keen to talk to him on this milestone in his life. Veronica informed us that there was no telephone for forty-five miles which, given the five hour time difference meant we had better start riding if I was going to catch him before he went to bed. It was hot progress and lunch was spent in the shade of a spreading mandarin tree eating its fruits. This diet led to several unscheduled stops in the afternoon, but by four o'clock we had arrived in the Mairama, the town with a phone. A big iron gate with a rusty padlock barred the entrance to the telephone exchange.

'It has not been open for three weeks,' a passer-by informed me. 'The only other phone in the town is at the hospital.'

The doctor could not have been more understanding or astonished.

'Did you say ninety years old? That is an incredible age. I have never met or heard of anybody of that age. Do you mind if I stay in the room while you talk to him?' the doctor requested. In fact, he was not alone, for while I talked, nurses and patients crowded into the room. I overheard a nurse whisper in the ear of a latecomer:

'Please be quiet. He is speaking to a person who is ninety years old.'

In a country where the average life expectancy is fifty-three years, this is indeed a ripe old age.

We spent the night at a *hospedaje* run by Peter, the only piano tuner in Bolivia. Some fourteen years before, Peter and his wife had returned to their native country of Holland after a year's travelling. They quickly became disillusioned and lost direction in their life.

'I was a psychologist. I became fed up with 'people tuning', mainly dealing with hang-ups about sex and money. We realised there was more to life, so we sold everything and settled here in Samaipata,' Peter explained. 'Here I have learnt to tune pianos instead of people.'

I could understand why they had no regrets. It was a beautiful spot set in a lush green valley, benefiting from a tropical climate and cooling breezes blowing off the mountains. They had bought the ten acres of land for £600 and lived in a caravan for two years while they built their own house. They had then built up an organic garden, which with the milk from the cows and goats, allowed them to be self-sufficient in food. Up until now they had resisted the temptation of a television and a telephone, but there was a move afoot to install the latter in the interests of furthering their tuning and tourism business.

Witnessing the delights of escapism and self-sufficiency delayed our start until after midday. The plan for the day was to ride the seventy-five miles to Santa Cruz and just as we were setting off we met Torsten, an Austrian cyclist. He had come up from our destination that morning. He had heard about us.

'So you are the three English cyclists. Stefan was right about you being allergic to cycling in the mornings,' Torsten greeted us. We chatted about mutual friends; Carole and Dougie, the cyclists in Tierra del Fuego and Thomas and Petra, the Swiss bikers and it was not until two o'clock that we finally left Samaipata. A paved road took us speeding out of the mountains into the hot steamy jungle below. The air was alive with the vibrant sound of the samba and the hum of insects. Instead of the traditional bowler hats and voluminous petticoats of the altiplano, the people sauntered around in baseball caps and skimpy shorts and danced to the music of the steel drums rather than the pan pipes. Gone were the barren plains and the condors gliding overhead and now lush, green vegetation alive with the colours and sounds of parrots lined the road.

It was with a rising tide of excitement that we arrived in Santa Cruz de la Sierra at nightfall. Since the 1950s, Santa Cruz has undergone staggering growth. It has been transformed from a backwater cattle-producing town of 30,000 to become Bolivia's second city with over 80,000 people. While the commercial production of sugar cane, oil plants, cotton and citrus fruits have had a part to play, the cultivation of the coca leaf is the single most important factor in this phenomenal growth. Coca leaves are not only used for chewing by Indians, miners and cyclists on the altiplano, but they also go to make the white powder called cocaine. Coca thrives in the conditions around Santa Cruz where it is possible to harvest up to four crops a year, and it is no surprise that the area is the principal contributor to a total production which is believed to be worth $2 billion a year. As Bolivia is the poorest country in Latin America, it is a travesty that only a quarter of this figure returns to the country, while the rest is swallowed up by rich and unscrupulous exploiters.

Santa Cruz, as the centre of cocaine smuggling, appeared to have taken the lion's share of this quarter. The city exuded wealth around every corner. On our first night we were recommended to go to the district of Equipetrol. It centred around a tree-lined avenue alive with the flashing lights of numerous bars, restaurants and discos. Parading down the pavements were rich young things sporting the latest designer clothes and talking in American accents, while on the street sports cars and open-top jeeps cruised up and down checking out the scene. Occasionally, a black Mercedes with darkened windows swept past, which had the men reaching for their pockets and the girls leaning suggestively against the trees. With our tattered and empty money belts and our dusty clothes, we were out of our depth amongst this blatant pursuit of the 'American dream'. This was not Bolivia, just a secluded and disturbing island of wealth built principally on cocaine.

— 20 —
RETURN TO PAN-PIPES

'Surely, surely, slumber is more sweet than toil'

ALFRED, LORD TENNYSON 'The Lotus Eaters'

The time had come to cycle back to the *altiplano*. Ahead lay two hundred miles of jungle, two massive climbs totalling 24,750 feet, the city of Cochabamba and finally, some five hundred and fifty miles away, the capital city of La Paz. We decided to take the new road to Cochabamba, marked by a bold red line on our map. Red meant paved, according to the key at the bottom. About thirty miles out of Santa Cruz the route deteriorated to rutted, dried mud. Either we were on the wrong road or the map was lying. I stopped to ask a workman digging a ditch.

'Excuse me, where is the paved road?' I asked.

'What paved road?' came the ominous reply.

'The one to Cochabamba.'

'Oh, that is easy to answer. There isn't one. Well, not until you get within ninety-five kms (65 miles) of the city, so from here you have nearly three hundred kms (200 miles) of dirt road.' He noticed our look of dismay. 'It could be worse. Just think what it would be like if it was raining, the mud can get very sticky,' he said to reassure us.

In a way we wished it was raining to cool us down in the searing heat. There was nothing worse than being hot and sweaty on a busy dirt road, for the dust thrown up by the traffic clings to the skin and eyes. But while we were panting along feeling sorry for ourselves we did spare a thought for the *campesinos* marching along beside us. They were walking in protest to Cochabamba to demonstrate their resistance to the new laws initiated by the Americans to control and stop the production of coca leaves. In the 1980s, during a period of extreme economic depression and rising unemployment, many peasants turned to the cocaine trade in order to survive from day to day. Today, they still rely on the profits of coca to feed themselves and their families. Suddenly, the Americans had come along, and with the reluctant support of the Bolivian Government, decreed that cultivation had to be controlled. It was a heavy-handed and insensitive policy, which failed to consider or recommend viable alternatives to coca leaves. Pineapples had been mentioned in passing, but they could only yield one third of the profits made from the coca. They were thus marching to save their livelihood or, as one banner declared:

'COCA IS OUR LIFE'

One could almost imagine this slogan being echoed at a cocktail party in an apartment on 45th Street, New York.

On the road we came across many drug enforcement road blocks run by the American trained soldiers nicknamed 'Snow Leopards'. 'Snow' because cocaine in its final form is a white powder, and 'Leopards' to excite fear in the traffickers and farmers. On the bikes we were not seen as suspicious, for as one Snow Leopard observed:

'Who the hell would be crazy enough to traffic drugs by bicycle! What d'you think, Joe?'

This was another result of American training, because they had all been taught to call each other 'Joe'.

We spent three days riding through the jungle.

DAY 262 THE HEAT OF THE JUNGLE 11.30 P.M.

'It had been hot before, but not like this. The air is thick with humidity and jungle is steaming. Sweat is trickling down my arms making it difficult to write and causing the ink to run. The temperature is in the nineties but it feels hotter because the air is like a suffocating blanket. Our bodies cry out for water, but ours is a thirst which cannot be quenched. All I can think about is the coolness of the altiplano.'

We finally arrived in the village of Tunari, which nestles in the shadow of the mountains. We longed for the fresh breezes and the chilly nights of the hills. We ascended up along a twisting road encroached by lush vegetation on either side, and at the bottom of a particularly imposing hill we stopped for a lunch of oranges and papaya. David opened up the papaya with his Swiss Army knife and recoiled in horror.

'What on earth is the matter?' Mike asked.

Shiny black seeds lay nestling in the soft flesh. 'Look,' David said. 'A lizard has laid its eggs inside.'

Fortunately, Mike believed him so there was all the more papaya for David and me.

Just as the climb became more severe, the fruit (or was it the lizard eggs) got a hold on David's bowels and sent him rushing, armed with a few strands of *papel hygienco* (toilet paper), into the dense undergrowth. I had become accustomed to just how long David took on such a mission, so Mike and I decided to venture on. Soon

Mike too experienced a call of nature and I optimistically shouted back that I would meet him at the top. After about an hour of climbing I felt tired and lonely, and as it was nearing the sacred time of four o'clock I decided to brew up some tea in the shelter of a hut used by the road maintenance crew. A short time later Mike arrived but there was still no sign of David. It was then that it started to rain. David was legendary in both his aversion to getting his feet wet and to cycling in the rain, so we assumed he would be sheltering under a bush somewhere. We settled down for another cuppa. An hour later it had stopped raining but David was nowhere to be seen. What the hell had happened to him? We thought it might be his knee which had been troubling him recently or it could be his bike was damaged or then again he might have simply fallen asleep. The last alternative became a distinct possibility after a driver coming up the hill was adamant he had seen no cyclist.

'Perhaps he has been kidnapped,' Mike suggested.

We laughed at the thought of the kidnappers having to put up with David's Spanish.

There was only one thing for it – to head back down the hill to search for David. It was demoralising to undo all the hard work climbing and we received many stares of disbelief from the road crew.

'I thought you said you were heading for Cochabamba,' one of them commented.

'Well we are, but we have lost our friend,' I replied.

'I am sure three cyclists passed here.' He then conducted an animated discussion with his colleagues. 'We are all definite about seeing three cyclists. We reckon you are looking for the one with the white lips.'

That was definitely a reference to the copious amount of sun-screen make-up David applied to his lips each day. So where was he? Mike mirrored my thoughts when he said,

'If he has fallen asleep in the undergrowth, I will kill him!'

Another thought reluctantly drifted into my head. What if David had inadvertently passed us, while we were having tea by the hut. It did not bear thinking about, but we had to because it now seemed the only explanation. With a feeling of foreboding we stopped a truck coming down the mountain and asked the driver if he had seen a cyclist with white lips. To our surprise he was an Australian.

'Yeah sure, he'd be about at the top of the mountain by now. When you see him again, tell him he looks like a fair dinkum gay boy with that white lipstick,' he replied. At least now we had an incentive to see David again.

By this time it was seven o'clock, some three hours after the fateful tea-break, and the sun was starting to set. We stopped yet another truck and hitched a lift up the mountain. We found David nearing the top.

'I thought you buggers had left me,' David said.

'We thought you had fallen asleep, you plonker,' Mike and I declared. 'Oh, by the way, there is a truck driver back there who thinks you are gay.'

This was the exchange between a finely tuned expedition team, who had been together for some nine months now!

We spent the night at the grandly named Hotel Cochabamba; not only was it seventy-eight miles from the city, but there were no beds and we had to make do with flour sacks. After the debacle of the afternoon before, Mike and I had to get up extremely early to ride down to the infamous road maintenance hut and climb back up to the hotel, to ensure we kept our route intact. In contrast, David had a lie-in. Mike and I were annoyed and rather jealous to find him still sleeping like a baby after our gruelling fourteen mile climb. On leaving the hotel we were welcomed with the paved road at last and a sweeping downhill stretch, but this was the lull before the storm for there was still one more daunting mountainous ridge to cross.

DAY 265 ON THE CLIMB TO COCHABAMBA

'Up, up and up. The climb is relentless and endless. The weight of the panniers is a terrible millstone to bear. My legs are sapped of energy and my lungs are straining for air. If it was not for the kindness and support of the people, I would undoubtedly have given up.'

We collapsed exhausted in sight of yet another steep section. An old lady emerged out of a tiny wooden hut. She called us over and invited us to share her lunch of tea and bread dipped in goat's fat. Only one mile and thirty minutes later a car stopped and two young girls armed with pineapples stood in our path. We must have looked quite a sight, bathed in sweat and grime. I was right!

'Gosh, you all look pretty awful,' they said with a hint of an American accent. Then giggling they gave us three pineapples and drove off waving and hooting their horn. As we sat down to devour our gift, we each found a folded piece of paper hidden amongst the spines. It read, *'When you are in Cochabamba, please give us a ring. Love from, Marcela and Veronica xxxx.'*

At last we reached the top of the mountain range and on the other side lay Cochabamba over 3,000 feet below. The city nestled in a fertile green basin, surrounded by abundant crops of barley, wheat, alfalfa and orchards of citrus fruits. Cochabamba, with a population of over 40,000, had long held the title of Bolivia's second city, but it has recently lost that honour to Santa Cruz. The people of the city or *Cochabambinos* are proud of the luscious climate, which they believe ranks amongst the finest in the world. They tell you:

'*Las golondrinas nunca migran de Cochabamba*' (The swallows never migrate from Cochabamba). On the day we arrived it was cloudy and windy. We were far from impressed – a view which was shared by the local swallows who sat shivering on the swinging telephone lines. The maize crops touching either side of the road hinted at Cochabamba's other claim to fame. It is 'The City of *Chicha*'. There was even an advertising hoarding promoting the virtues of the foul tasting liquid. It proclaimed: '*I want chicha, I search for chicha, for chicha are my wanderings. Lady, give me a glass to satisfy my longing.*' I hoped there would be other drinks available in Cochabamba.

The climate, as well as allowing cholera, amoebic dysentery and swallows to thrive, brings fertility to the surrounding countryside and wealth to the people of the city. Marcela and Veronica were in the high echelons of society. There was much money floating around. They and their friends drove fast cars and open-top jeeps, talked with American accents they had picked up while studying there, and frequented exclusive bars and restaurants. We felt out of place in our functional and unimaginative clothes, but my main concern, which was echoed constantly by the customary bouncers on the doors, were my tattered training shoes. I had worn them almost every day of the expedition and it was now starting to show. David, of course, sailed through wearing his brown brogues.

We did not stay long in Cochabamba, which was just as well for our finances. La Paz was beckoning a mere two hundred and fifty miles away. This statistic hid an undulating climb to 14,800 feet. It made our route out of the jungle appear tame. We were not to be disappointed for we found ourselves struggling along mile upon mile of spiralling paved road. In these circumstances, the last thing we wanted to do was to leave the kitty money belt behind. I had the ignominy of achieving this feat. Unfortunately, I only realised at the top of a particularly gruelling climb. I left Mike and David and hitched a lift back down the mountain to the restaurant where we had eaten breakfast. I remembered leaving the kitty on a low mud wall while I packed my panniers. The kitty was no longer there. The sour waitress who had served us looked surprised to see me.

'Have you seen the money belt I left here?' I enquired.

'No . . . No . . . I have seen nothing,' she stammered. I sensed the edginess of guilt in her voice.

'Has anybody else been in here since we left?' I asked.

'Oh yes,' she said with more confidence, 'a truck load of men did pull in for cigarettes. When I think of it now, I did see one of them counting some American dollars.'

This little ruse did not work because we had no dollars in our money belt. She certainly knew where it was, but was not going to tell me. I went outside in frustration and a young boy sidled up and whispered;

'Mister, I will tell you where it is for a reward.'

But before I could agree, his father in a fierce voice had called him in. The villagers had closed ranks and I was banging my head against a wall of secrecy. I returned empty-handed and now it was David and Mike's turn to enter the fray. After a night of negotiations the money belt and our finances notebook was returned to us. This was far more important than any money.

It was a bitter pill to swallow, not for the money we lost, but it was the first animosity we had experienced on the entire expedition. The villagers, as well as being guarded and reserved, had at times been hostile towards us. One old man had said,

'Why should we give you back your money? You *gringos* came over here in the first place raping our land and stealing our riches. It is about time we got something in return!'

I was angry and upset by this attitude and it made me become disillusioned with the cycling at a time when I needed the most commitment. It just did not seem to matter anymore. I started to struggle a long way behind Mike and David and I even resorted to off-loading some of my luggage, something my pride had never allowed me to do before. It was an endless climb, and with there being no hint of the summit, I lost all will to drive my legs or *Arriba* any further. Thus, with my legs possessing all the rigidity of jelly, I was walking more than cycling. By the time I arrived in the next village, I was a physical and mental wreck!

While I dropped my bike to the ground, there was a tap on my shoulder. Standing behind me was a boy of around four years old, wearing a dirty blue 'Teenage Mutant Ninja' tee-shirt. He looked as though he was suffering from some disease, because his head was abnormally large and his hair was patchy in places. Grabbing my hand, he pulled me down to his level. He then gave me a kiss on either cheek and a short hug, before wishing me *'buena suerte'* (good luck) and marching off with the wave of his hand. It was such a comforting and spontaneous gesture that I burst into tears.

The boy gave me strength and renewed enthusiasm. I started to think positively: this was indeed the last mountain to climb before La Paz. We could see the summit when we stopped to watch a small altiplano village in the middle of a fiesta. It was a colourful and happy scene; everybody from the very young to the very old were dressed in bright traditional costumes and dancing to the music from the pan-pipes and *charangos*. Suddenly they saw us on the road and the music stopped. We thought we had better be going because we did not want to disturb and upset this merry gathering. The children, however, had other ideas for they came rushing across to block our path and to invite us to join in. It was wonderful to experience so much uninhibited joy, fun and laughter shared by all ages. There were sack races which involved the children and their grandparents, a competition to knock the Coke bottle off the wall, a tug-of-war match and prizes for the best dance partners. I was dragged into the dancing ring by an energetic and rhythmical old lady, who was at least sixty. She made me dizzy and we had a good laugh, but we ended up coming a valiant last with no votes. I gave the lady one of my tee-shirts to make up for not winning a prize.

They wanted us to stay and to sample some of their local brew, which they claimed to be the most potent in Bolivia. Alcohol and cycling up mountains to reach La Paz do not go together, so we reluctantly declined and were waved on our way. The fiesta had delayed us and when we did make it to the summit at 14,800 feet, the sun was low in the sky. It was not until one hour of descending at speed through the darkness that we found somewhere to stay. It was a remote restaurant frequented throughout the night by truck drivers, who had the most terrible taste in music. Any form of sleep was impossible.

La Paz was so close now; just a mere hundred and forty mile dash across the flat *altiplano*. The only things that could stop us were the fickle wind or an accident with the bikes. It was strange, but the nearer we got to the shores of Lake Titicaca, a mere short hop from La Paz, the more obsessed I became about something happening that would prevent one or all of us from finishing. I started to be more cautious and to take less risks. No longer did I race downhill, wait for that annoying squeak on the wheel to disappear, or overtake a lumbering truck. It was a time for self-restraint and thus it proved to be a steady and uneventful ride across the last stretch of altiplano. That was until we reached the outskirts of La Paz . . .

—21—
COPACABANA DREAMS

'Keep right on to the end of the road,
Where all you love you've been dreaming of
Will be there at the end of the road.'

SIR HARRY LAUDER 'The End of the Road'

We had suddenly left the barrenness of the *altiplano* for the junk yards, auto repair shops and bare concrete housing of the suburb of El Alto. The air became thick with the pungent smells of open sewers and the choking fumes from the belching traffic. The road, which seemed to have escaped attention from the time of the Incas, was littered with potholes and the rotting putrid carcasses of unfortunate dogs. As we swerved around these obstacles we were forced into the path of the baying cars and trucks. Paranoia set in. Every close shave made me think: 'No, not here! Only one hundred miles from Lake Titicaca.'

I stopped. My legs and hands were shaking. I watched some local Indian children splashing in a muddy puddle. Their clothes hung around them in tatters and their hair was lacquered with dirt. They were laughing; laughing in the face of poverty. The mother of one of the boys watched and smiled while she pounded her laundry in a stream choked with litter and sewage. Despite the laughter and smiles, we were shocked by the ugliness and scowl of what we assumed to be La Paz.

Then suddenly the capital appeared. It lay hidden in a crack in the *altiplano* – a gaping natural canyon stretching some three miles across from rim to rim.

DAY 272 ARRIVING IN LA PAZ 1.00 P.M.

'The ground literally fell away to reveal the most spectacular city I have ever seen. More dramatic than either Sydney or Hong Kong. Row upon row of shanty dwellings cascaded down the slopes, only coming to a halt when they reached the small concentration of modern high-rise buildings; banks, hotels and embassies, situated on the canyon floor. Twisting roads and paths swept downwards. Cars and people teemed like excited ants over a disturbed nest. In stark contrast, the triple peaks of Mount Illimani (21,130 feet) stood silent and serene. Each snowy peak glistened in the clear translucent air.'

I could now relate to the feelings expressed by Jean Manzon and Miguel-Angel Asturias in their book, *Bolivia – An Undiscovered Land*.

'Overwhelmed, speechless, stupefied, blinded by too much light, the traveller arriving for the first time in La Paz experiences a sensation of awakening, of coming from the vast desolate desert, as if out of a nightmare, into the Garden of Eden. The conquistadors were expert at choosing sites for towns, at smelling out the winds and tempests, at discovering good soil and fresh springs, at exorcising evil spirits. These were the men who came upon this crack in the plateau, this gentle gracious valley, where the sky is undergrowth beneath the arched branches of willows and carob trees. It is a land of marvels, half-way between the Lima of the viceroys, and the inexhaustible wealth of Potosi.

It is La Paz of Our Lady of Peace, La Paz of the peaceful sky, of the peaceful air, La Paz of Illimani lit by the snows.'

We dropped downwards and stopped outside Iglesia de San Francisco. Here the noise of the traffic was drowned by the plaintive shrill cries of the market-sellers. Lining the side streets were Aymara Indian ladies, all sitting proudly below bowler hats which seemed more in keeping with a London street rather than the city of La Paz. A city gent, however, would not be seen dead in a dark green or brown bowler hat tied up with a red ribbon, neither would he choose to braid his hair into long plaits joined by a tuft of black wool. Colourful voluminous skirts billowed up around their waists as they sat calling for buyers. I searched for reasons for this traditional attire – escape from the sun, keeping warm and protecting virtue – but I missed one very practical reason. I noticed a lady crouching in the middle of the narrow street. For several seconds I wondered what she was doing there until a trickle of urine emerged from under her layers of petticoats.

'Oranges', 'Potatoes', 'Llama foetus' and 'Toothpaste', the ladies cried. Yes, there was some for everybody. If you wanted fruit, flowers, vegetables, medicine and even a colourful plateful of herbs, seeds and assorted critter parts to ward off evil spirits, you would not be disappointed.

La Paz was founded in October 1548 by a Spaniard, Captain Alonzo de Mendoza, and was named *Cuidad de Nuestra Senora de La Paz* – The City of Our Lady of Peace. Ever since then it has been far from peaceful and has experienced a turbulent history. Spain controlled La Paz with a firm grip, during which time the city was often under siege from the rebellious Aymara Indians. Peace, however, did not come with independence in 1825, for since then 189 governments have flitted in and out of power, few staying long enough to leave any lasting effects. A track record which left Simon Bolivar, the Great Liberator, disenchanted and exasperated with his namesake republic.

'Hapless Bolivia has had four different leaders in less than two weeks! Only the kingdom of Hell could offer so appalling a picture discrediting humanity!' he was once heard to utter.

This governmental merry-go-round has earned Bolivia an entry into the *Guinness Book of Records* as the most politically unstable country in the world. Bolivian presidents and generals have gained the reputation as 'endangered species' owing to the abnormally high mortality rate. This was unfortunate for President Gualberto Villarroel, who was publicly hanged in La Paz by 'distraught' widows in 1946, but perhaps just retribution for the cruel and eccentric General Mariano Melgarejo (1865-1871). According to the Bolivian historian Tomas O'Connor d'Arlach, the General was a Francophile and a drunkard. He writes that after one particular drinking spree, the General sounded the alarm and had his army parade in the city square of La Paz. Everyone was surprised and mystified.

'Soldiers,' he slurred, 'the integrity of France is menaced by the Prussians. He who menaces France, menaces civilisation and liberty. I shall protect the French who are our best friends and whom I so love. You are going to swim the ocean with me. But take care to keep your powder dry!' The soldiers never did swim to Europe neither did the Prussians have to face the might of the Bolivian Army, for within hours it started to rain heavily and the General gradually sobered up. On account of a sore head, he aborted the mission.

We found however, a La Paz bathing in unprecedented peace. Since 1989, democracy had reigned free from the threat of military intervention. We had ten days until we were due on the shores of Lake Titicaca at 2.00 p.m. on August 16 – a date we had plucked out of the air some six months before. I would like to write that we spent these days promoting awareness of leukaemia and the expedition and preparing studiously for the final leg. The British Embassy and their Consul, Robin Shackleton did their best with the setting up of many media interviews. But in amongst rushing to and from the offices of Channel 7 and the *Bolivian Times*, we were distracted. Simon Heazell arrived to complete the team and witness the end, along with Miriam and Jono, David's mother and brother, Helen, Mike's sister and a friend of mine, John. They needed entertaining and we were only too willing to oblige. Amidst the parties, dancing and games of golf at the highest course in the world, I had a chance to reflect on Bolivia.

DAY 276 IN LA PAZ

'Of all the countries we have been to, Bolivia is my favourite. The poorest, highest and most undiscovered of all the Latin American republics. It is a country struggling to come to terms with the modern world but never quite making it. This is no failure but an attribute. Bolivia has kept its identity, and traditions, and has remained happy within itself. So many countries make the mistake of striving to be something they are not, which inevitably leads to damaged expectations and pervading disillusionment.

I will never forget the opening day of the World Cup Finals, when Bolivia played Germany. Men, women and children watched with heads held high and tears running down their cheeks. They had no expectations, they were just delighted to be there. In the face of defeat there was little disappointment and thus they embarked on an uninhibited celebration. In life, too, the majority of the people we have met have not harboured expectations. Poverty, disease and dying is such a way of life they are thankful for each day. For them the past has gone, the future has not yet come and the present is all they have.

I know I will never forget Bolivia. Chile and Argentina for all their charms were not so different in many respects from Europe. Bolivia, however, is an enigma. What can one say about a country where the women wear bowler hats, where coca leaves are a staple diet, where a navy is maintained without a sea and where dried llama foetuses are sold on the streets. A country that never fails to surprise, to conjure up the unexpected and to reduce the best laid plans to tatters.

I hope Bolivia will not change and will resist the encroachment of the modern world and continue operating beyond accepted norms. After all, the country has survived a greater threat in the past – colonisation by the Spanish. During this period the people had clung to their traditions and language so effectively that they are still practised in today's society. I have every faith Bolivia will remain the place I have grown to love.'

In La Paz we met many people and organisations attempting to change and develop Bolivia. They were all well-intentioned but for the most part misdirected. Take, for instance, the group of American graduates studying measures to control the spread of Chagas disease. After six months of research, a list of recommendations was presented to the government. The solution pivoted around the ability of persuading *campesinos* to move out of their traditional thatched mud homes into brick or concrete based structures where the beetles would find it difficult to breed. On paper it sounded simple, but who was going to pay for the new housing? Neither the *campesinos* nor the government could afford them. It would have been better to have spent the available money for the research directly on improving housing. Meanwhile up to 25% of Bolivia's population will continue to suffer and die from this incurable and fatal disease.

In the face of Chagas we felt humble while we talked of the dangers of leukaemia in front of television cameras in the Plaza Murillo, the main square in La Paz. It was the day of our departure to Copacabana and Lake Titicaca. We had not enjoyed the best of preparations, for the night before we had held a leaving party. Not wanting to disappoint our guests we had consumed copious amounts of tequila and had thus woken with throbbing heads. Hardly the best condition to face the flashing, whirring cameras and field the barrage of questions asked in Spanish. We were indeed delighted and surprised at the interest from the media as we neared our final destination. One television station had even laid on a cameraman to cover the entire length of our final leg. This worried us. We would have to forget about our hangovers and put on an impressive show of fitness and technique. No siesta, no stopping for tea and no grimaces going uphill; just nonchalant smiles. There was one last question,

'Do you have a message for the people of Bolivia?'

'Yes,' Mike replied. 'We would like to thank them from the bottom of our hearts. Their hospitality, kindness and support has been overwhelming. They should know that we would not be standing here today if it had not been for their help.'

We said goodbye to family and friends and embarked on the climb out of the canyon to the altiplano. The route to Copacabana was no lap of honour. We had to rise 3,000 feet just to get out of the city and then a twenty-five mile uphill stretch awaited us just beyond the Straits of Tiquina. It did not promise to be the easiest hundred miles. We started well, fuelled by adrenaline and driven by the need to impress our friends who were following in a minibus, and the cameraman from Channel 7, who was patiently covering our every move. After an hour our friends left for Lake Titicaca and we were left with the TV cameraman. Following the display of early pace, it was not long before our legs started to tire and our breathing came reduced to short gasps. It was a hot day and sweat was stinging my eyes. It seemed that Mike was also having problems seeing. He had started to weave around the road and I noticed his head kept jerking forwards. It happened as if in slow motion. Mike and *Shadowfax* left the road and rolled gently down a slope into a ditch. Not even the impact of falling off woke him up. It was then that the cameraman decided to leave us.

'I am sorry but this does not make compelling television,' he said apologetically and drove off. David and I breathed a huge sigh of relief and joined Mike in the ditch for a siesta.

We slept for two hours before being woken by a freshening wind. Why should the penultimate day be any different? The wind throughout the expedition had remained remarkably consistent. Whatever way we turned whether it was north, south, east or west, it would be in our faces. Stranger still was that other cyclists travelling in the opposite direction swore it was they who had to fight the wind. The wind, it seemed, was never a friend but a constant adversary and this fact had become firmly entrenched in cycling mythology. The wind on the evening of August 15 was no myth. We were reduced even more to a crawling pace and it was not long before we pulled into a hostel well short of our planned destination for the night and still over fifty miles short of Copacabana.

We had to get up extremely early to stand any chance of making it to the plaza by two o'clock. Thankfully the wind had died down. After five miles we rose over the crest of the hill and saw for the first time the sapphire-blue of Lake Titicaca. While the waters sparkled as if millions of gems were floating on the surface and the jagged snow-capped sierra glistened on the far side, it was easy to imagine that the lake was indeed the birthplace of the Sun. The Incas believed this was where the Sun first shone on the *Isla del Sol* (Island of the Sun) before illuminating the rest of the world. It was here the Sun placed its children with the mission to instruct and guide the barbarous people dwelling on earth and it was thus that the Inca race was born. In the Spanish times, there were legends of entire cities and immense treasure lying below the crystal waters. These cities and wealth remain undiscovered.

To us Lake Titicaca had as much significance as it did to the Incas. Our quest for 287 days now lay before us. But the expedition would not be over until we had bathed in the waters at Copacabana and sprinkled the sea taken from the shores of Tierra Del Fuego into the sacred waters. We arrived at the Straits of Tiquina and boarded a creaking wooden ferry which took us across to the Copacabana peninsular. The road now turned to dirt and started to twist upwards. The time was twelve-thirty and thirty miles still to go. It was then that we knew we would be late. Why break the habit of the expedition?

16/8 DAY 283 MIXED EMOTIONS 1.30 P.M.

'As we near our final destination, I am experiencing mixed emotions. I have bouts of sheer elation but they soon become tinged with feelings of sadness. Yes I am overjoyed we are on the verge of completing the expedition. Within minutes of fulfilling our dream and the belief of all those who had supported us. But there is sadness. It is now difficult to imagine a life away from Mike, David, Arriba and South America. I have loved the camaraderie, the laughs and the nomadic existence full of surprises and devoid of plans. It has been, however, a life divorced from reality and it is this that beckons on reaching the shores of Lake Titicaca. I am tempted to cycle on beyond Titicaca. But no, we have to finish, for after all, the expedition will only be truly complete once we have returned to England – back to our families, friends, sponsors and the Leukaemia Research Fund.'

As our wheels slowed on the steep dirt road, time sped by and it was not until three o'clock that we reached the crest of a formidable ridge. It was then that we knew we had been through the last climb. Four hundred feet below lay Copacabana, nestling between two hills on the shores of Lake Titicaca. Dominating the town were the pink twin towers of the cathedral, which was the home to *La Virgen Morena del Lago* (The Dark Virgin of the Lake). Since 1583, her dark wooden image had inspired innumerable miracles and as a result she had built up quite a following in Bolivia and Peru. On the first two days of February, pilgrims come and kiss the Virgin's tiny feet, before drinking from the sacred waters of the Sun God. We were, however, pilgrims of a different kind, nearing the end of a pilgrimage for ourselves and for people affected by leukaemia. We had not come for the Virgin or the Sun God, but to complete the South American Titicaca Expedition.

We started to weave slowly down to the town.

IN SIGHT OF THE FINISH 3.15 P.M.

'I had often dreamt of the end in Copacabana. In my dreams, I had fondly imagined streets lined with people cheering and waving flags. Strung across the entrance to the plaza was a large banner announcing our arrival and achievement. I fought back tears as family and friends rushed out to greet and congratulate us. Then there were the media hordes, fighting for an interview and an answer to the question, "How do you feel now that it is all over?"'

These dreams, however, were delusions of grandeur. As we cycled into the plaza at three-forty on August 16 we were met by no media hordes, no banners, no friends or family. In fact only one person had defied the siesta in Copacabana that day. Fate dictated that we were to share our moment of triumph with a wizened old man clutching a bottle of *singali*. He became worried when he saw our tears and came staggering over.

'Don't cry,' he said with concern. 'Here, this will help you forget your sadness.'

'These are tears of joy,' I replied. 'We just cycled from Tierra del Fuego.'

'Never heard of it. Is it beyond La Paz?'

'Yes, about 10,000 kms (6,130 miles) to the south,' I said.

'What did you cycle that for? You must be mad!' he grunted, before returning to his bench for a sleep.

It appeared that even now, there were still question marks surrounding our sanity.

Copacabana did eventually wake up and our friends and family emerged from the shadows. Apparently they had waited in the plaza until 3.00 p.m. when an arriving bus driver had informed them we would be at least another two hours. Now we could complete the final three hundred yards to the shores of Lake Titicaca with an audience. For the final yards, Simon Heazell rode side-saddle on the back of *Shadowfax*. It was thus that the complete team of the South American Titicaca Expedition cycled into the sacred waters of Titicaca. The trail was now over and not even the icy waters could numb our joy.

DAY 283 THE LAST ENTRY

'I am overcome with feelings of wild elation and happiness. Beyond this, though, will it change our lives forever? Who knows, only time would tell. What I do know, however, is that I will always have the memories and feel an immense gratitude to Mike, David and Simon. Together we have made it happen. Without doubt they were the greatest companions I could have ever hoped for. I pray that one day we will ride again.'

THE END

EPILOGUE

It is now five years on and there are several questions we would like to answer.

What have you been doing since the expedition?
Rupert: I wanted to write a book so that our experiences would never be forgotten. I knew I was not a natural or a reclusive writer, and thus I needed time and distractions. But how was I to finance it? I was offered a post at Port Regis Preparatory School near Shaftesbury, Dorset and managed to apportion my time between teaching History and writing. On Sunday, October 16, 1995, I met Julie Ahern, and on December 14, 1996 we were married. We are now settled in Wiltshire, with a baby daughter, India Daisy Rose, who we hope one day to take to Latin America.
Mike: Since returning from one dream I tried to pursue another – winning the British Golf Open as an amateur. Unfortunately my talent didn't live up to my ambition. I was offered an interesting position within IMG again. After four years back in the corporate life, there are still times when I long for a dusty road fading into the distance.
David: Crash, bang, realisation strikes – nine to five engineering had lost its appeal. I rejected repetitive routines for a looser bondage to the hands of the clock. I decided salvation lay in setting up and running a small business. I attended a business course with the aim of setting up a cycling touring company. In February '96, however, I turned to helping my younger brother develop Laser Quest war games in Indonesia and Hong Kong and I turned my hand to project management for a Hong Kong based company specialising in

telecommunications and security systems. Ultimately I was defeated by tight Government regulations and rising rental prices. Since returning, I have enjoyed pursuing these exciting opportunities and have learnt much from my experiences.

Do you still cycle?
Rupert: For the first six months, I got the shakes every time I saw *Arriba*, but now we are the best of friends. I taught mountain biking to the children at Port Regis but I was forced to give it up when they quickly passed me in terms of skill, stamina and courage. My image as a mighty Andean cyclist was shattered for good. I still find mending a puncture a problem.
Mike: Errrr no! *Shadowfax*, my trusty steed, still sleeps in a cellar with the puncture she caught at La Paz airport. The sites, sound and delights of London traffic do not have quite the same appeal as the peaceful *altiplano*. I'm determined to start up again.
David: Yes, but not with a passion. I can claim to have been on a cycling holiday in Ireland.

Has the expedition changed you? (We are always asked this at our lectures.)
Rupert: The expedition gave me the opportunity to discover what I wanted out of life and the courage to pursue it. Money lost its driving force and I have found a greater quality of life in benefiting others, living in the country and being married. I am more tolerant now (Jules finds this hard to believe). I suppose this is what ten months with David's smelly feet and Mike's taste of music does to you. There is not a day that goes past without my thinking of something associated with the expedition, and certainly I cannot imagine what life would have been like if we had not gone.
Mike: I am still stressed and overworked but I am now in a better state to deal with it. I find great solace in opening my box of delights

from the expedition. For me it's a great treasure chest of sights, sounds and songs. People are, I think, generally afraid of what they can lose rather than what they can gain by such ventures. I know that because I was like that. The journey, however, also gave me a profound understanding of what I do want and how to achieve it. I now also appreciate the time to think.

David: The expedition has confirmed my view that there is more to life than nine to fives. I was able to evaluate my life, so when we returned to England, I had the confidence to explore other opportunities. It also shifted my needs and has persuaded me to look for different kinds of fulfilment. One question still remains – what do I want from life?

Why did the expedition succeed?
Together we made a great team. The weakness of one was the strength of another. We did not take ourselves too seriously, possessing the ability to laugh at ourselves as well as each other. Three gave us democracy, which meant that decisions could be taken quickly and without anyone's feelings being hurt. Above all, we respected, trusted, tolerated and listened to each other.

EXPEDITION EQUIPMENT

Bicycle Equipment
Make: Madison Ridgeback 704 RS with Tange tubing
Wheels: Mavic M7 CD Rims (36 spoke)
Tyres: Specialized and Nimbus
Headset: Ritchey
Stem: Kalloy Uno
Brakes: Shimano Deore XT (front cantilever)
Gears: Shimano Deore XT (lever shifts)
Chain: Shimano narrow
Saddle: Madison Gel XCI
Pannier Racks: Blackburn Expedition
Panniers: Agu Sport Quorum
Waterbottle Cages: Blackburn
Pump: Blackburn
Speedometer: Sigma Sport
Lock: Buffo

Camping Equipment
Tents: Northface Bullfrog and Tadpole
Sleeping bags: Mountain Air (3 seasons)
Liner: Silk inner sheet
Sleeping mat: Karrimat (5 ft)
Stove: Whisperlite multi fuel
Cutlery: Knife, fork, spoon and wooden spoon
Crockery: Plastic plates and beakers
Pans: 2 aluminium pots and frying pans
Bag of Spices

Clothes (per person)
Hi-Tech trainers
Sandals
Sprayway Gortex jacket and trousers
Berghaus fleece
Wolfskin fleece trousers
Mountain Air down jacket
Rohan trousers

2 prs cycling shorts
4 prs boxer shorts
6 prs socks (4 cotton/2 wool)
Scarf
Balaclava
Berghaus thermal underwear
Trek cycling gloves
Mountain Air gloves
Berghaus Gortex socks
Oakley sunglasses
Trek cycling helmet
Smart cotton shirt and trousers
Bombay Sapphire cap

Medical Kit
Antibiotics
Dioralyte
Disprin
2 syringes
Scissors
Tweezers
Plasters
Knee and ankle stretch bandage
Conventional bandage
Steri-strips
Absorbent dressing
Cotton wool
Paracetamol
Multi vitamins
Vitamin C
Dental kit
Iodine solution
Puritabs
Malaria tablets
Anti-histamine
Worming tablets
Immodium
Homoeopathic medicines

Sunblock
Lipsyl

Photographic Equipment
Rollei 35 camera
Canon SureShot
Olympus (mju)
Canon EOS 5
Canon 24mm lense
Canon 35-110mm and 150-300mm zoom lenses
Canon flash
Fuji film (print/slide) 100/200 ASA
Kodak film (print/slide) 100/200 ASA

Miscellaneous Equipment
Karrimor rucksack (35 l)
Altimeter/Barometer
Compass
Sony short-wave radio
Sony tape recorder
Conventional whistle
Maps
Waterproof map case
Pages from guide books
Duracell batteries
Needle and thread
Diaries
Notebooks
Writing materials
Passport
Passport photos
Insurance documents
Embassy letters
Kipling money belts
Assorted plastic bags

Rubber bands
Parachute string
Bungies

Evostik glue
Candles
Miner's light
Travellers Cheques
Dollars
Credit cards
Photos of family
Spanish dictionary

Presents
Union Jack lighters
Postcards of London
Holograms
Magic Bands
Marbles
Biros
Pencils
Balloons
British coins and stamps
Keyrings

Luxuries
Jeans
Brogues
Fishing rod
Line, hooks, float, spinners
Chess set
Music tapes
Selected Poems of Pablo Neruda
Books of Gabriel Garcia Marquez
Books of Isabel Allende
The Lord of the Rings
St. Christopher
Horseshoe
Silver sixpence
Silver dollar

Other books you should read . . .

Running A Hotel On The Roof Of The World
Five Years In Tibet

Alec Le Sueur

The Holiday Inn, Lhasa, would have proved any hotel inspector's worst nightmare. An hilarious behind the scenes look at the running of an unheated, rat infested and highly confused hotel set against the breathtaking beauty of the Himalayas.

• Highly entertaining but also illuminating and informative

• No other foreigner has spent so long in Tibet since the days of Heinrich Harrer

• Le Sueur provides a fascinating insight into an intriguing country which so few foreigners have been permitted to visit.

Paperback £7.99

Two Feet, Four Paws
The Girl Who Walked Her Dog 4500 Miles

Spud Talbot-Ponsonby
Foreword by Ffyona Campbell

An inspiring travelogue about a feisty girl and a dog from a broken home who set off on a walk that is the equivalent distance of London to Calcutta. Spud walked her dog around the entire coastline of Britain, backed up by an ancient camper van called the *Spudtruck*, to raise funds for the charity Shelter. Share in the tears, sweat and champange and discover the true state of the island.

Paperback £7.99

Small Steps With Heavy Hooves
A Mother's Walk Back to Health in the Highlands

Spud Talbot-Ponsonby

Spud, author of the hugely successful book *Two Feet, Four Paws*, tells her tale of two remarkable journeys. Her travels along the drove roads of Scotland with a horse, dog and 16 month old son provide a time to reflect on an even harder journey — of single motherhood and a devastating diagnosis of cancer. The Highland walk gives Spud time to regain health and beautifully explore her true love of the natural world around. A remarkable book, moving and uplifting.

Paperback £6.99

Don't Lean Out of the Window!
The Inter-Rail Experience

Stewart Ferris and Paul Bassett

When the authors bought their Inter-Rail tickets, those magic passports to unlimited rail travel in Europe for a month, they had no idea that they would soon tear through more than a country a day, constantly escaping from a trail of bemused girls, angry policemen, angry campsite owners, angry nutters, more bemused girls, angry restaurateurs, and other assorted angry Europeans.

This book is an hilarious travelogue about three Inter-Railers who endure water cannons, arrests, undesirables and each other during a hot, sticky month that left most of the continent dazed, confused and smelling of 'Inter-Rail Feet'.

'A most entertaining read. Marvellous. Jolly well done.'
Stephen Fry

Paperback £6.99

For a full list of our travel titles please write to Summersdale Publishers, 46 West Street, Chichester, West Sussex, PO19 1RP